Anonymous

Atlantic Tales

Anonymous

Atlantic Tales

ISBN/EAN: 9783337343095

Printed in Europe, USA, Canada, Australia, Japan

Cover: Foto ©Andreas Hilbeck / pixelio.de

More available books at **www.hansebooks.com**

ATLANTIC TALES.

A COLLECTION OF STORIES

From the Atlantic Monthly.

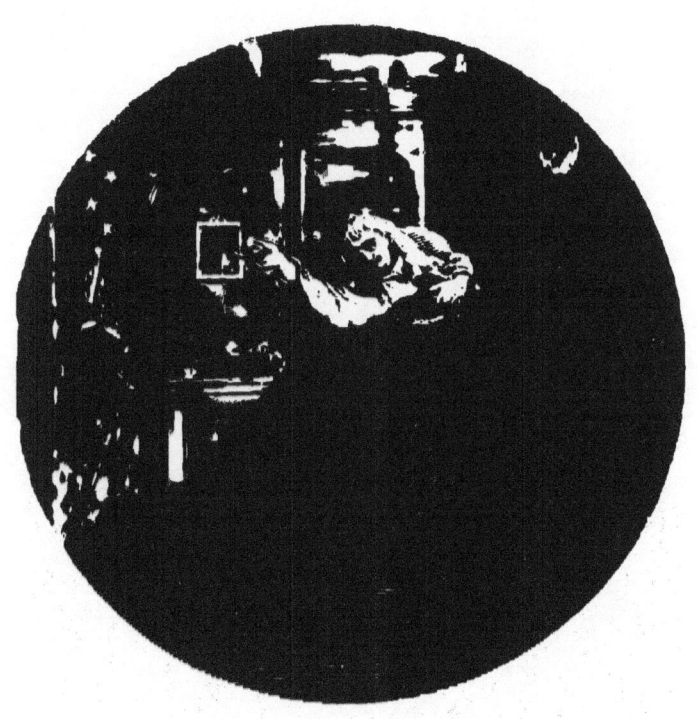

BOSTON:
TICKNOR AND FIELDS.
1867.

My Double; and how he undid
    me . . . .   *Edward Everett Hale*   1

The Diamond Lens . . . . .   *Fitz James O'Brien* .   21

Life in the Iron-Mills . . .   *Miss R. B. Harding*   50

The Pursuit of Knowledge un-
    der Difficulties . . . .   *Gail Hamilton* . . . 93

A Raft that no Man made . .   *Robert T. S. Lowell* . 147

Why Thomas was Discharged .   *George Arnold* . . 162

Victor and Jacqueline . . .   *Miss Caroline Chesebro* 180

Elkanah Brewster's Tempta-
    tion . . . .   *Charles Nordhoff* . 248

The Queen of the Red Chess-
    men . . . .   *Miss Lucretia P. Hale* 271

Miss Lucinda . . . .   *Miss Rose Terry* . . 299

The Denslow Palace . . . .   *J. D. Whelpley* . . 336

Friend Eli's Daughter . . .   *Bayard Taylor* . . 367

A Half-Life and Half a Life .   *Miss E. H. Appleton* 398

The Man without a Country .   *Edward Everett Hale* 448

MY DOUBLE;

AND HOW HE UNDID ME.

T is not often that I trouble you, my readers. I should not trouble you now, but for the importunities of my wife, who "feels to insist" that a duty to society is unfulfilled, till I have told why I had to have a double, and how he undid me. She is sure, she says, that intelligent persons cannot understand that pressure upon public servants which alone drives any man into the employment of a double. And while I fear she thinks, at the bottom of her heart, that my fortunes will never be remade, she has a faint hope, that, as another Rasselas, I may teach a lesson to future publics, from which they may profit, though we die. Owing to the behavior of my double, or, if you please, to that public pressure which compelled me to employ him, I have plenty of leisure to write this communication.

I am, or rather was, a minister, of the Sandemanian connection. I was settled in the active, wide-awake town of Naguadavick, on one of the finest water-powers in Maine. We used to call it a Western town in the heart of the civilization of New England. A charming place it was and is. A spirited, brave young parish had I ; and it seemed as if we might have all "the joy of eventful living" to our hearts' content.

Alas ! how little we knew on the day of my ordination,

and in those halcyon moments of our first housekeeping !
To be the confidential friend in a hundred families in the
town, — cutting the social trifle, as my friend Haliburton
says, "from the top of the whipped-syllabub to the bottom
of the sponge-cake, which is the foundation," — to keep
abreast of the thought of the age in one's study, and to do
one's best on Sunday to interweave that thought with the
active life of an active town, and to inspirit both and make
both infinite by glimpses of the Eternal Glory, seemed such
an exquisite forelook into one's life ! Enough to do, and all
so real and so grand ! If this vision could only have lasted.

The truth is, that this vision was not in itself a delusion,
nor, indeed, half bright enough. If one could only have
been left to do his own business, the vision would have accomplished itself and brought out new paraheliacal visions,
each as bright as the original. The misery was and is, as
we found out, I and Polly, before long, that, besides the
vision, and besides the usual human and finite failures in
life, (such as breaking the old pitcher that came over in the
"Mayflower," and putting into the fire the Alpenstock with
which her father climbed Mont Blanc,) — besides these, I
say, (imitating the style of Robinson Crusoe,) there were
pitchforked in on us a great rowen-heap of humbugs,
handed down from some unknown seed-time, in which we
were expected, and I chiefly, to fulfil certain public functions
before the community, of the character of those fulfilled by
the third row of supernumeraries who stand behind the
Sepoys in the spectacle of the "Cataract of the Ganges."
They were the duties, in a word, which one performs as
member of one or another social class or subdivision, wholly
distinct from what one does as A. by himself A.   What invisible power put these functions on me, it would be very
hard to tell.   But such power there was and is.   And I had
not been at work a year before I found I was living two
lives, one real and one merely functional, — for two sets of
people, one my parish, whom I loved, and the other a vague
public, for whom I did not care two straws.   All this was in

a vague notion, which everybody had and has, that this second life would eventually bring out some great results, unknown at present, to somebody somewhere.

Crazed by this duality of life, I first read Dr. Wigan on the "Duality of the Brain," hoping that I could train one side of my head to do these outside jobs, and the other to do my intimate and real duties. For Richard Greenough once told me, that, in studying for the statue of Franklin, he found that the left side of the great man's face was philosophic and reflective, and the right side funny and smiling. If you will go and look at the bronze statue, you will find he has repeated this observation there for posterity. The eastern profile is the portrait of the statesman Franklin, the western of Poor Richard. But Dr. Wigan does not go into these niceties of this subject, and I failed. It was then, that, on my wife's suggestion, I resolved to look out for a Double.

I was, at first, singularly successful. We happened to be recreating at Stafford Springs that summer. We rode out one day, for one of the relaxations of that watering-place, to the great Monson Poor-House. We were passing through one of the large halls, when my destiny was fulfilled! I saw my man!

He was not shaven. He had on no spectacles. He was dressed in a green baize roundabout and faded blue overalls, worn sadly at the knee. But I saw at once that he was of my height, five feet four and a half. He had black hair, worn off by his hat. So have and have not I. He stooped in walking. So do I. His hands were large, and mine. And — choicest gift of Fate in all — he had, not "a strawberry-mark on his left arm," but a cut from a juvenile brickbat over his right eye, slightly affecting the play of that eyebrow. Reader, so have I ! — My fate was sealed !

A word with Mr. Holley, one of the inspectors, settled the whole thing. It proved that this Dennis Shea was a harmless, amiable fellow, of the class known as shiftless, who had sealed his fate by marrying a dumb wife, who was at that moment ironing in the laundry. Before I left Stafford, I had hired both for five years. We had applied to Judge Pynchon, then the probate judge at Springfield, to change the name of Dennis Shea to Frederic Ingham. We had explained to the Judge, what was the precise truth, that an eccentric gentleman wished to adopt Dennis under this new name into his family. It never occurred to him that Dennis might be more than fourteen years old. And thus, to shorten this preface, when we returned one night to my parsonage at Naguadavick, there entered Mrs. Ingham, her new dumb laundress, myself, who am Mr. Frederic Ingham, and my double, who was Mr. Frederic Ingham by as good right as I.

Oh, the fun we had the next morning in shaving his beard to my pattern, cutting his hair to match mine, and teaching him how to wear and how to take off gold-bowed spectacles! Really, they were electro-plate and the glass was plain (for the poor fellow's eyes were excellent). Then in four successive afternoons I taught him four speeches. I had found these would be quite enough for the supernumerary-Sepoy line of life, and it was well for me they were. For though he was good-natured, he was very shiftless, and it was, as our national proverb says, "like pulling teeth" to teach him. But at the end of the next week he could say, with quite my easy and frisky air, —

1. "Very well, thank you. And you?" This for an answer to casual salutations.

2. "I am very glad you liked it."

3. "There has been so much said, and, on the whole, so well said, that I will not occupy the time."

4. "I agree, in general, with my friend the other side of the room."

At first I had a feeling that I was going to be at great cost for clothing him. But it proved, of course, at once, that, whenever he was out, I should be at home. And I went, during the bright period of his success, to so few of those awful pageants which require a black dress-coat and what the ungodly call, after Mr. Dickens, a white choker, that in the happy retreat of my own dressing-gowns and jackets my days went by as happily and cheaply as those of another Thalaba. And Polly declares there was never a year when the tailoring cost so little. He lived (Dennis, not Thalaba) in his wife's room over the kitchen. He had orders never to show himself at that window. When he appeared in the front of the house, I retired to my sanctissimum and my dressing-gown. In short, the Dutchman and his wife, in the old weather-box, had not less to do with each other than he and I. He made the furnace-fire and split the wood before daylight ; then he went to sleep again, and slept late ; then came for orders, with a red silk bandanna tied round his head, with his overalls on, and his dress-coat and spectacles off. If we happened to be interrupted, no one guessed that he was Frederic Ingham as well as I ; and, in the neighborhood, there grew up an impression that the minister's Irishman worked day-times in the factory-village at New Coventry. After I had given him his orders, I never saw him till the next day.

I launched him by sending him to a meeting of the Enlightenment Board. The Enlightenment Board consists of seventy-four members, of whom sixty-seven are necessary to form a quorum. One becomes a member under the regulations laid down in old Judge Dudley's will. I became one by being ordained pastor of a church in Naguadavick. You see you cannot help yourself, if you would. At this particular time we had had four successive meetings, averaging four hours each,—wholly occupied in whipping in a quorum. At the first only eleven men were present ; at the next, by force of three circulars, twenty-seven ; at the third, thanks to two days' canvassing by Auchmuty and myself, begging men to come, we had sixty. Half the others were in Europe. But without a quorum we could do nothing. All the rest of us waited grimly for our four hours, and adjourned without any action. At the fourth meeting we had flagged, and only got fifty-nine together. But on the first appearance of my double, — whom I sent on this fatal Monday to the fifth meeting, — he was the *sixty-seventh* man who entered the room. He was greeted with a storm of applause ! The poor fellow had missed his way, — read the street signs ill through his spectacles, (very ill, in fact, without them,) — and had not dared to inquire. He entered the room, — finding the president and secretary holding to their chairs two judges of the Supreme Court, who were also members *ex officio*, and were begging leave to go away. On his entrance all was changed. *Presto*, the by-laws were amended, and the Western property was given away. Nobody stopped to converse with him. He voted, as I had charged him to do, in every instance, with the minority. I won new laurels as a man of sense, though a little unpunctual, — and Dennis, *alias* Ingham, returned to the parsonage, astonished to see with how little wisdom the world is governed. He cut a few of my parishioners in the street ; but he had his glasses off, and I am known to be near-sighted. Eventually he recognized them more readily than I.

I "set him again" at the exhibition of the New Coventry Academy ; and here he undertook a "speaking part," — as, in my boyish, worldly days, I remember the bills used to say of Mlle. Céleste. We are all trustees of the New Coventry Academy ; and there has lately been " a good deal of feeling" because the Sandemanian trustees did not regularly attend the exhibitions. It has been intimated, indeed, that the Sandemanians are leaning towards Free-Will, and that we have, therefore, neglected these semiannual exhibitions, while there is no doubt that Auchmuty last year went to Commencement at Waterville. Now the head master at New Coventry is a real good fellow, who knows a Sanskrit root when he sees it, and often cracks etymologies with me, — so that, in strictness, I ought to go to their exhibitions. But think, reader, of sitting through three long July days in that Academy chapel, following the programme from

TUESDAY MORNING. *English Composition.* " SUNSHINE." Miss Jones.

round to

Trio on Three Pianos.   Duel from the Opera of " Midshipman
Easy."   *Marryatt.*

coming in at nine, Thursday evening ! Think of this, reader,
for men who know the world is trying to go backward, and
who would give their lives if they could help it on ! Well !
The double had succeeded so well at the Board, that I sent
him to the Academy. (Shade of Plato, pardon !) He arrived early on Tuesday, when, indeed, few but mothers and
clergymen are generally expected, and returned in the evening to us, covered with honors. He had dined at the right
hand of the chairman, and he spoke in high terms of the
repast. The chairman had expressed his interest in the
French conversation. " I am very glad you liked it," said
Dennis ; and the poor chairman, abashed, supposed the accent had been wrong. At the end of the day, the gentlemen
present had been called upon for speeches, — the Rev. Frederic Ingham first, as it happened ; upon which Dennis had
risen, and had said, " There has been so much said, and,
on the whole, so well said, that I will not occupy the time."
The girls were delighted, because Dr. Dabney, the year before, had given them at this occasion a scolding on impro-
priety of behavior at lyceum lectures. They all declared
Mr. Ingham was a love, — and *so* handsome ! (Dennis is
good-looking.) Three of them, with arms behind the others'
waists, followed him up to the wagon he rode home in ; and
a little girl with a blue sash had been sent to give him a
rosebud. After this *début* in speaking, he went to the exhibition for two days more, to the mutual satisfaction of all
concerned. Indeed, Polly reported that he had pronounced
the trustees' dinners of a higher grade than those of the parsonage. When the next term began, I found six of the
Academy girls had obtained permission to come across the
river and attend our church. But this arrangement did not
long continue.

After this he went to several Commencements for me, and

ate the dinners provided ; he sat through three of our Quarterly Conventions for me, — always voting judiciously, by the simple rule mentioned above, of siding with the minority. And I, meanwhile, who had before been losing caste among my friends, as holding myself aloof from the associations of "the Body," began to rise in everybody's favor. "Ingham's a good fellow, — always on hand"; "never talks much, — but does the right thing at the right time"; "is not as unpunctual as he used to be, — he comes early, and sits through to the end." "He has got over his old talkative habit, too. I spoke to a friend of his about it once ; and I think Ingham took it kindly," etc., etc.

This voting power of Dennis was particularly valuable at the quarterly meetings of the Proprietors of the Naguadavick Ferry. My wife inherited from her father some shares in that enterprise, which is not yet fully developed, though it doubtless will become a very valuable property. The law of Maine then forbade stockholders to appear by proxy at such meetings. Polly disliked to go, not being, in fact, a "hens'-rights hen," and transferred her stock to me. I, after going once, disliked it more than she. But Dennis went to the next meeting, and liked it very much. He said the arm-chairs were good, the collation good, and the free rides to stockholders pleasant. He was a little frightened when they first took him upon one of the ferry-boats, but after two or three quarterly meetings he became quite brave.

Thus far I never had any difficulty with him. Indeed, being of that type which is called shiftless, he was only too happy to be told daily what to do, and to be charged not to be forthputting or in any way original in his discharge of that duty. He learned, however, to discriminate between the lines of his life, and very much preferred these stockholders' meetings and trustees' dinners and Commencement collations to another set of occasions, from which he used to beg off most piteously. Our excellent brother, Dr. Fillmore, had taken a notion at this time that our Sandemanian churches needed more expression of mutual sympathy. He insisted upon it that we were remiss. He said, that, if the Bishop came to preach at Naguadavick, all the Episcopal clergy of the neighborhood were present ; if Dr. Pond came, all the Congregational clergymen turned out to hear him ; if Dr. Nichols, all the Unitarians ; and he thought we owed it to each other, that, whenever there was an occasional service at a Sandemanian church, the other brethren should all, if possible, attend. "It looked well," if nothing more. Now this really meant that I had not been to hear one of Dr. Fillmore's lectures on the Ethnology of Religion. He forgot that he did not hear one of my course on the "Sandemanianism of Anselm." But I felt badly when he said it ; and afterwards I always made Dennis go to hear all the brethren preach, when I was not preaching myself. This was what he took exceptions to, — the only thing, as I said, which he ever did except to. Now came the advantage of his long morning-nap, and of the green tea with which Polly supplied the kitchen. But he would plead, so humbly, to be let off, only from one or two ! I never excepted him, however. I knew the lectures were of value, and I thought it best he should be able to keep the connection.

Polly is more rash than I am, as the reader has observed in the outset of this memoir. She risked Dennis one night under the eyes of her own sex. Governor Gorges had always been very kind to us ; and when he gave his great annual party to the town, asked us. I confess I hated to go. I was deep in the new volume of Pfeiffer's "Mystics," which Haliburton had just sent me from Boston. "But how rude," said Polly, "not to return the Governor's civility and Mrs. Gorges's, when they will be sure to ask why you are away !" Still I demurred, and at last she, with the wit of Eve and of Semiramis conjoined, let me off by saying, that, if I would go in with her, and sustain the initial conversations with the Governor and the ladies staying there, she would risk Dennis for the rest of the evening. And

1*

that was just what we did. She took Dennis in training all
that afternoon, instructed him in fashionable conversation,
cautioned him against the temptations of the supper-table,
—and at nine in the evening he drove us all down in the
carryall. I made the grand star-*entrée* with Polly and the
pretty Walton girls, who were staying with us. We had put
Dennis into a great rough top-coat, without his glasses,—
and the girls never dreamed, in the darkness, of looking at
him. He sat in the carriage, at the door, while we entered.
I did the agreeable to Mrs. Gorges, was introduced to her
niece, Miss Fernanda, — I complimented Judge Jeffries on
his decision in the great case of D'Aulnay *vs.* Laconia Mining Co., — I stepped into the dressing-room for a moment,
— stepped out for another, — walked home, after a nod with
Dennis, and tying the horse to a pump ; — and while I
walked home, Mr. Frederic Ingham, my double, stepped in
through the library into the Gorges' grand saloon.

Oh ! Polly died of laughing as she told me of it at midnight ! And even here, where I have to teach my hands to
hew the beech for stakes to fence our cave, she dies of laughing as she recalls it, — and says that single occasion was
worth all we have paid for it. Gallant Eve that she is !
She joined Dennis at the library-door, and in an instant
presented him to Dr. Ochterlony, from Baltimore, who was
on a visit in town, and was talking with her as Dennis came
in. " Mr. Ingham would like to hear what you were telling
us about your success among the German population." And
Dennis bowed and said, in spite of a scowl from Polly, " I 'm
very glad you liked it." But Dr. Ochterlony did not observe, and plunged into the tide of explanation, — Dennis
listening like a prime-minister, and bowing like a mandarin,
—which is, I suppose, the same thing. Polly declared it
was just like Haliburton's Latin conversation with the Hun-
garian minister, of which he is very fond of telling. " *Quæne
sit historia Reformatiónis in Ungariá ?* " quoth Haliburton,
after some thought. And his *confrère* replied gallantly,
" *In seculo decimo tertio,*" etc., etc., etc. ; and from *decimo*

tertio * to the nineteenth century and a half lasted till the oysters came. So was it that before Dr. Ochterlony came to the "success," or near it, Governor Gorges came to Dennis and asked him to hand Mrs. Jeffries down to supper, a request which he heard with great joy.

Polly was skipping round the room, I guess, gay as a lark. Auchmuty came to her "in pity for poor Ingham," who was so bored by the stupid pundit, — and Auchmuty could not understand why I stood it so long. But when Dennis took Mrs. Jeffries down, Polly could not resist standing near them. He was a little flustered, till the sight of the eatables and drinkables gave him the same Mercian courage which it gave Diggory. A little excited then, he attempted one or two of his speeches to the Judge's lady. But little he knew how hard it was to get in even a *promptu* there edgewise. "Very well, I thank you," said he, after the eating elements were adjusted; "and you?" And then did not he have to hear about the mumps, and the measles, and arnica, and belladonna, and chamomile-flower, and dodecatheon, till she changed oysters for salad, — and then about the old practice and the new, and what her sister said, and what her sister's friend said, and what the physician to her sister's friend said, and then what was said by the brother of the sister of the physician of the friend of her sister, exactly as if it had been in Ollendorff? There was a moment's pause, as she declined Champagne. "I am very glad you liked it," said Dennis again, which he never should have said, but to one who complimented a sermon. "Oh! you are so sharp, Mr. Ingham! No! I never drink any wine at all, — except sometimes in summer a little currant spirits, — from our own currants, you know. My own mother, — that is, I call her my own mother, because, you know, I do not remember," etc., etc., etc.; till they came to the candied orange at the end of the feast, — when Dennis, rather confused, thought

---

* Which means, "In the thirteenth century," my dear little bell-and-coral reader. You have rightly guessed that the question means, "What is the history of the Reformation in Hungary?"

he must say something, and tried No. 4, — "I agree, in general, with my friend the other side of the room," — which he never should have said but at a public meeting. But Mrs. Jeffries, who never listens expecting to understand, caught him up instantly with, "Well, I'm sure my husband returns the compliment; he always agrees with you, — though we do worship with the Methodists; — but you know, Mr. Ingham," etc., etc., etc., till the move was made up-stairs; — and as Dennis led her through the hall, he was scarcely understood by any but Polly, as he said, "There has been so much said, and, on the whole, so well said, that I will not occupy the time."

His great resource the rest of the evening was, standing in the library, carrying on animated conversations with one and another in much the same way. Polly had initiated him in the mysteries of a discovery of mine, that it is not necessary to finish your sentences in a crowd, but by a sort of mumble, omitting sibilants and dentals. This, indeed, if your words fail you, answers even in public extempore speech, — but better where other talking is going on. Thus, — "We missed you at the Natural-History Society, Ingham." Ingham replies, — "I am very gligloglum, that is, that you were mmmmm." By gradually dropping the voice, the interlocutor is compelled to supply the answer. "Mrs. Ingham, I hope your friend Augusta is better." Augusta has not been ill. Polly cannot think of explaining, however, and answers, — "Thank you, Ma'am; she is very rearason wewahwewoh," in lower and lower tones. And Mrs. Throckmorton, who forgot the subject of which she spoke as soon as she asked the question, is quite satisfied. Dennis could see into the card-room, and came to Polly to ask if he might not go and play all-fours. But, of course, she sternly refused. At midnight they came home delighted. Polly, as I said, wild to tell me the story of victory; only both the pretty Walton girls said, — "Cousin Frederick, you did not come near me all the evening."

We always called him Dennis at home, for convenience,

though his real name was Frederic Ingham, as I have explained. When the election-day came round, however, I found that by some accident there was only one Frederic Ingham's name on the voting-list; and, as I was quite busy that day in writing some foreign letters to Halle, I thought I would forego my privilege of suffrage, and stay quietly at home, telling Dennis that he might use the record on the voting-list and vote. I gave him a ticket, which I told him he might use, if he liked to. That was that very sharp election in Maine which the readers of the "Atlantic" so well remember, and it had been intimated in public that the ministers would do well not to appear at the polls. Of course, after that, we had to appear by self or proxy. Still, Naguadavick was not then a city, and this standing in a double queue at town-meeting several hours to vote was a bore of the first water; and so, when I found that there was but one Frederic Ingham on the list, and that one of us must give up, I stayed at home and finished the letters, (which, indeed, procured for Fothergill his coveted appointment of Professor of Astronomy at Leavenworth,) and I gave Dennis, as we called him, the chance. Something in the matter gave a good deal of popularity to the Frederic Ingham name; and at the adjourned election, next week, Frederic Ingham was chosen to the legislature. Whether this was I or Dennis, I never really knew. My friends seemed to think it was I; but I felt, that, as Dennis had done the popular thing, he was entitled to the honor; so I sent him to Augusta when the time came, and he took the oaths. And a very valuable member he made. They appointed him on the Committee on Parishes; but I wrote a letter for him, resigning, on the ground that he took an interest in our claim to the stumpage in the minister's sixteenths of Gore A, next No. 7, in the 10th Range. He never made any speeches, and always voted with the minority, which was what he was sent to do. He made me and himself a great many good friends, some of whom I did not afterwards recognize as quickly as Dennis did my parishioners. On one or two occasions, when there was wood to saw at home, I kept him at home ; but I took those occasions to go to Augusta myself. Finding myself often in his vacant seat at these times, I watched the proceedings with a good deal of care ; and once was so much excited that I delivered my somewhat celebrated speech on the Central School-District question, a speech of which the " State of Maine " printed some extra copies. I believe there is no formal rule permitting strangers to speak ; but no one objected.

Dennis himself, as I said, never spoke at all. But our experience this session led me to think, that, if, by some such " general understanding " as the reports speak of in legislation daily, every member of Congress might leave a double to sit through those deadly sessions, and to answer to roll-calls and do the legitimate party-voting, which appears stereotyped in the regular list of Ashe, Bocock, Black, etc., we should gain decidedly in working-power. As things stand, the saddest state-prison I ever visit is that Representatives' Chamber in Washington. If a man leaves for an hour, twenty "correspondents" may be howling, "Where was Mr. Pendergrast when the Oregon bill passed ? " And if poor Pendergrast stays there ! Certainly, the worst use you can make of a man is to put him in prison !

I know, indeed, that public men of the highest rank have resorted to this expedient long ago. Dumas's novel of the " Iron Mask " turns on the brutal imprisonment of Louis the Fourteenth's double. There seems little doubt, in our own history, that it was the real General Pierce who shed tears when the delegate from Lawrence explained to him the sufferings of the people there, — and only General Pierce's double who had given the orders for the assault on that town, which was invaded the next day. My charming friend, George Withers, has, I am almost sure, a double, who preaches his afternoon sermons for him. This is the reason that the theology often varies so from that of the forenoon. But that double is almost as charming as the original. Some of the most well-defined men, who stand out most prominently on the background of history, are in this way stereoscopic men, who owe their distinct relief to the slight differences between the doubles. All this I know. My present suggestion is simply the great extension of the system, so that all public machine-work may be done by it.

But I see I loiter on my story, which is rushing to the plunge. Let me stop an instant more, however, to recall, were it only to myself, that charming year while all was yet well. After the double had become a matter of course, for nearly twelve months before he undid me, what a year it was ! Full of active life, full of happy love, of the hardest work, of the sweetest sleep, and the fulfilment of so many of the fresh aspirations and dreams of boyhood ! Dennis went to every school-committee meeting, and sat through all those late wranglings which used to keep me up till midnight and awake till morning. He attended all the lectures to which foreign exiles sent me tickets begging me to come for the love of Heaven and of Bohemia. He accepted and used all the tickets for charity concerts which were sent to me. He appeared everywhere where it was specially desirable that "our denomination," or "our party," or "our class," or "our family," or "our street," or "our town," or "our county," or " our State," should be fully represented. And I fell back to that charming life which in boyhood one dreams of, when he supposes he shall do his own duty and make his own sacrifices, without being tied up with those of other people. My rusty Sanskrit, Arabic, Hebrew, Greek, Latin, French, Italian, Spanish, German, and English began to take polish. Heavens ! how little I had done with them while I attended to my *public* duties ! My calls on my parishioners became the friendly, frequent, homelike sociabilities they were meant to be, instead of the hard work of a man goaded to desperation by the sight of his lists of arrears. And preaching ! what a luxury preaching was when I had on Sunday the whole result of an individual, personal week, from which to speak to a people whom all that week I had been meeting as hand-to-hand friend ! I never tired on

Sunday, and I was in condition to leave the sermon at home, if I chose, and preach it extempore, as all men should do always. Indeed, I wonder, when I think that a sensible people, like ours, — really more attached to their clergy than they were in the lost days, when the Mathers and Nortons were noblemen, — should choose to neutralize so much of their ministers' lives, and destroy so much of their early training, by this undefined passion for seeing them in public. It springs from our balancing of sects. If a spirited Episcopalian takes an interest in the almshouse, and is put on the Poor Board, every other denomination must have a minister there, lest the poorhouse be changed into St. Paul's Cathedral. If a Sandemanian is chosen president of the Young Men's Library, there must be a Methodist vice-president and a Baptist secretary. And if a Universalist Sunday-School Convention collects five hundred delegates, the next Congregationalist Sabbath-School Conference must be as large, "lest 'they' — whoever *they* may be — should think 'we' — whoever *we* may be — are going down."

Freed from these necessities, that happy year, I began to know my wife by sight. We saw each other sometimes. In those long mornings, when Dennis was in the study explaining to map-pedlers that I had eleven maps of Jerusalem already, and to school-book agents that I would see them hanged before I would be bribed to introduce their text-books into the schools, — she and I were at work together, as in those old dreamy days, — and in these of our log-cabin again. But all this could not last, — and at length poor Dennis, my double, overtasked in turn, undid me.

It was thus it happened. There is an excellent fellow, — once a minister, — I will call him Isaacs, — who deserves well of the world till he dies, and after, — because he once, in a real exigency, did the right thing, in the right way, at the right time, as no other man could do it. In the world's great football match, the ball by chance found him loitering on the outside of the field ; he closed with it, "camped" it, charged it home, — yes, right through the other side, — not disturbed, not frightened by his own success, — and breathless found himself a great man, — as the Great Delta rang applause. But he did not find himself a rich man; and the football has never come in his way again. From that moment to this moment he has been of no use, that one can see, at all. Still, for that great act we speak of Isaacs gratefully and remember him kindly; and he forges on, hoping to meet the football somewhere again. In that vague hope, he had arranged a "movement" for a general organization of the human family into Debating-Clubs, County Societies, State Unions, etc., etc., with a view of inducing all children to take hold of the handles of their knives and forks, instead of the metal. Children have bad habits in that way. The movement, of course, was absurd; but we all did our best to forward, not it, but him. It came time for the annual county-meeting on this subject to be held at Naguadavick. · Isaacs came round, good fellow! to arrange for it, — got the town-hall, got the Governor to preside, (the saint!—he ought to have triplet doubles provided him by law,) and then came to get me to speak. "No," I said, "I would not speak, if ten Governors presided. I do not believe in the enterprise. If I spoke, it should be to say children should take hold of the prongs of the forks and the blades of the knives. I would subscribe ten dollars, but I would not speak a mill." So poor Isaacs went his way, sadly, to coax Auchmuty to speak, and Delafield. I went out. Not long after, he came back, and told Polly that they had promised to speak, — the Governor would speak, — and he himself would close with the quarterly report, and some interesting anecdotes regarding Miss Biffin's way of handling her knife and Mr. Nellis's way of footing his fork. "Now if Mr. Ingham will only come and sit on the platform, he need not say one word; but it will show well in the paper, — it will show that the Sandemanians take as much interest in the movement as the Armenians or the Mesopotamians, and will be a great favor to me." Polly, good soul! was tempted, and she promised. She knew

B

Mrs. Isaacs was starving, and the babies, — she knew Dennis was at home, — and she promised ! Night came, and I returned. I heard her story. I was sorry. I doubted. But Polly had promised to beg me, and I dared all ! I told Dennis to hold his peace, under all circumstances, and sent him down.

It was not half an hour more before he returned, wild with excitement, — in a perfect Irish fury, — which it was long before I understood. But I knew at once that he had undone me !

What happened was this. The audience got together, attracted by Governor Gorges's name. There were a thousand people. Poor Gorges was late from Augusta. They became impatient. He came in direct from the train at last, really ignorant of the object of the meeting. He opened it in the fewest possible words, and said other gentlemen were present who would entertain them better than he. The audience were disappointed, but waited. The Governor, prompted by Isaacs, said, " The Honorable Mr. Delafield will address you." Delafield had forgotten the knives and forks, and was playing the Ruy Lopez opening at the chess-club. " The Rev. Mr. Auchmuty will address you." Auchmuty had promised to speak late, and was at the school-committee. " I see Dr. Stearns in the hall; perhaps he will say a word." Dr. Stearns said he had come to listen and not to speak. The Governor and Isaacs whispered. The Governor looked at Dennis, who was resplendent on the platform; but Isaacs, to give him his due, shook his head. But the look was enough. A miserable lad, ill-bred, who had once been in Boston, thought it would sound well to call for me, and peeped out, " Ingham !" A few more wretches cried, " Ingham ! Ingham !" Still Isaacs was firm; but the Governor, anxious, indeed, to revent a row, knew I would say something, and said, Our friend Mr. Ingham is always prepared, — and though we had not relied upon him, he will say a word, perhaps." Applause followed, which turned Dennis's head. He rose, fluttered, and tried No. 3 : "There has been so much said, and, on the whole, so well said, that I will not longer occupy the time ! " and sat down, looking for his hat ; for things seemed squally. But the people cried, "Go on ! go on !" and some applauded. Dennis, still confused, but flattered by the applause, to which neither he nor I are used, rose again, and this time tried No. 2 : "I am very glad you liked it !" in a sonorous, clear delivery. My best friends stared. All the people who did not know me personally yelled with delight at the aspect of the evening ; the Governor was beside himself, and poor Isaacs thought he was undone ! Alas, it was I ! A boy in the gallery cried in a loud tone, "It 's all an infernal humbug," just as Dennis, waving his hand, commanded silence, and tried No. 4 : "I agree, in general, with my friend the other side of the room." The poor Governor doubted his senses, and crossed to stop him, — not in time, however. The same gallery-boy shouted, "How 's your mother ? " — and Dennis, now completely lost, tried, as his last shot, No. 1, vainly : "Very well, thank you ; and you ? "

I think I must have been undone already. But Dennis, like another Lockhard, chose "to make sicker." The audience rose in a whirl of amazement, rage, and sorrow. Some other impertinence, aimed at Dennis, broke all restraint, and, in pure Irish, he delivered himself of an address to the gallery, inviting any person who wished to fight to come down and do so, — stating, that they were all dogs and cowards and the sons of dogs and cowards, — that he would take any five of them single-handed. "Shure, I have said all his Riverence and the Misthress bade me say," cried he, in defiance ; and, seizing the Governor's cane from his hand, brandished it, quarter-staff fashion, above his head. He was, indeed, got from the hall only with the greatest difficulty by the Governor, the City Marshal, who had been called in, and the Superintendent of my Sunday-School.

The universal impression, of course, was, that the Rev.

Frederic Ingham had lost all command of himself in some of those haunts of intoxication which for fifteen years I have been laboring to destroy. Till this moment, indeed, that is the impression in Naguadavick. This number of the "Atlantic" will relieve from it a hundred friends of mine who have been sadly wounded by that notion now for years ; — but I shall not be likely ever to show my head there again.

No ! My double has undone me.

We left town at seven the next morning. I came to No. 9, in the Third Range, and settled on the Minister's Lot. In the new towns in Maine, the first settled minister has a gift of a hundred acres of land. I am the first settled minister in No. 9. My wife and little Paulina are my parish. We raise corn enough to live on in summer. We kill bear's meat enough to carbonize it in winter. I work on steadily on my "Traces of Sandemanianism in the Sixth and Seventh Centuries," which I hope to publish next year. We are very happy, but the world thinks we are undone.

THE DIAMOND LENS.

I.

THE BENDING OF THE TWIG.

ROM a very early period of my life the entire bent of my inclinations had been towards microscopic investigations. When I was not more than ten years old, a distant relative of our family, hoping to astonish my inexperience, constructed a simple microscope for me, by drilling in a disk of copper a small hole, in which a drop of pure water was sustained by capillary attraction. This very primitive apparatus, magnifying some fifty diameters, presented, it is true, only indistinct and imperfect forms, but still sufficiently wonderful to work up my imagination to a preternatural state of excitement.

Seeing me so interested in this rude instrument, my cousin explained to me all that he knew about the principles of the microscope, related to me a few of the wonders which had been accomplished through its agency, and ended by promising to send me one regularly constructed, immediately on his return to the city. I counted the days, the hours, the minutes, that intervened between that promise and his departure.

Meantime I was not idle. Every transparent substance that bore the remotest semblance to a lens I eagerly seized upon and employed in vain attempts to realize that instrument, the theory of whose construction I as yet only vaguely comprehended. All panes of glass containing those oblate spheroidal knots familiarly known as "bull's eyes" were ruthlessly destroyed, in the hope of obtaining lenses of marvellous power. I even went so far as to extract the crystalline humor from the eyes of fishes and animals, and endeavored to press it into the microscopic service. I plead guilty to having stolen the glasses from my Aunt Agatha's spectacles, with a dim idea of grinding them into lenses of wondrous magnifying properties, — in which attempt it is scarcely necessary to say that I totally failed.

At last the promised instrument came. It was of that order known as Field's simple microscope, and had cost perhaps about fifteen dollars. As far as educational purposes went, a better apparatus could not have been selected. Accompanying it was a small treatise on the microscope, — its history, uses, and discoveries. I comprehended then for the first time the "Arabian Nights' Entertainments." The dull veil of ordinary existence that hung across the world seemed suddenly to roll away, and to lay bare a land of enchantments. I felt towards my companions as the seer might feel towards the ordinary masses of men. I held conversations with Nature in a tongue which they could not understand. I was in daily communication with living wonders, such as they never imagined in their wildest visions. I penetrated beyond the external portal of things, and roamed through the sanctuaries. Where they beheld only a drop of rain slowly rolling down the window-glass, I saw a universe of beings animated with all the passions common to physical life, and convulsing their minute sphere with struggles as fierce and protracted as those of men. In the common spots of mould, which my mother, good housekeeper that she was, fiercely scooped away from her jam pots, there abode for me, under the name of mildew, enchanted gardens, filled with dells and avenues of the densest foliage and most astonishing verdure, while from the fantastic boughs of these microscopic forests hung strange fruits glittering with green and silver and gold.

It was no scientific thirst that at this time filled my mind. It was the pure enjoyment of a poet to whom a world of wonders has been disclosed. I talked of my solitary pleasures to none. Alone with my microscope, I dimmed my sight, day after day and night after night poring over the marvels which it unfolded to me. I was like one who, having discovered the ancient Eden still existing in all its primitive glory, should resolve to enjoy it in solitude, and never betray to mortal the secret of its locality. The rod of my life was bent at this moment. I destined myself to be a microscopist.

Of course, like every novice, I fancied myself a discoverer. I was ignorant at the time of the thousands of acute intellects engaged in the same pursuit as myself, and with the advantages of instruments a thousand times more powerful than mine. The names of Leeuwenhoek, Williamson, Spencer, Ehrenberg, Schultz, Dujardin, Schact, and Schleiden were then entirely unknown to me, or if known, I was ignorant of their patient and wonderful researches. In every fresh specimen of Cryptogamia which I placed beneath my instrument, I believed that I discovered wonders of which the world was as yet ignorant. I remember well the thrill of delight and admiration that shot through me the first time that I discovered the common wheel-animalcule (*Rotifera vulgaris*) expanding and contracting its flexible spokes, and seemingly rotating through the water. Alas ! as I grew older, and obtained some works treating of my favorite study, I found that I was only on the threshold of a science to the investigation of which some of the greatest men of the age were devoting their lives and intellects.

As I grew up, my parents, who saw but little likelihood of anything practical resulting from the examination of bits of moss and drops of water through a brass tube and a piece of glass, were anxious that I should choose a profession. It was their desire that I should enter the counting-house of my uncle, Ethan Blake, a prosperous merchant, who carried on business in New York. This suggestion I decisively combated. I had no taste for trade ; I should only make a failure ; in short, I refused to become a merchant.

But it was necessary for me to select some pursuit. My parents were staid New England people, who insisted on the necessity of labor ; and therefore, although, thanks to the bequest of my poor Aunt Agatha, I should, on coming of age, inherit a small fortune sufficient to place me above want, it was decided, that, instead of waiting for this, I should act the nobler part, and employ the intervening years in rendering myself independent.

After much cogitation I complied with the wishes of my family, and selected a profession. I determined to study medicine at the New York Academy. This disposition of my future suited me. A removal from my relatives would enable me to dispose of my time as I pleased, without fear of detection. As long as I paid my Academy fees, I might shirk attending the lectures, if I chose ; and as I never had the remotest intention of standing an examination, there was no danger of my being "plucked." Besides, a metropolis was the place for me. There I could obtain excellent instruments, the newest publications, intimacy with men of pursuits kindred to my own, — in short, all things necessary to insure a profitable devotion of my life to my beloved science. I had an abundance of money, few desires that were not bounded by my illuminating mirror on one side and my object-glass on the other ; what, therefore, was to prevent my becoming an illustrious investigator of the veiled worlds ? It was with the most buoyant hopes that I left my New England home and established myself in New York.

II.

THE LONGING OF A MAN OF SCIENCE.

MY first step, of course, was to find suitable apartments. These I obtained, after a couple of days' search, in Fourth Avenue ; a very pretty second-floor unfurnished, containing sitting-room, bedroom, and a smaller apartment which I intended to fit up as a laboratory. I furnished my lodgings simply, but rather elegantly, and then devoted all my energies to the adornment of the temple of my worship. I visited Pike, the celebrated optician, and passed in review his splendid collection of microscopes, — Field's Compound, Higham's, Spencer's, Nachet's Binocular, (that founded on the principles of the stereoscope,) and at length fixed upon that form known as Spencer's Trunnion Microscope, as combining the greatest number of improvements with an almost perfect freedom from tremor. Along with this I purchased every possible accessory, — drawtubes, micrometers, a *camera-lucida*, lever-stage, achromatic condensers, white cloud illuminators, prisms, parabolic condensers, polarizing apparatus, forceps, aquatic boxes, fishing-tubes, with a host of other articles, all of which would have been useful in the hands of an experienced microscopist, but, as I afterwards discovered, were not of the slightest present value to me. It takes years of practice to know how to use a complicated microscope. The optician looked suspiciously at me as I made these wholesale purchases. He evidently was uncertain whether to set me down as some scientific celebrity or a madman. I think he inclined to the latter belief. I suppose I was mad. Every great genius is mad upon the subject in which he is greatest. The unsuccessful madman is disgraced, and called a lunatic.

Mad or not, I set myself to work with a zeal which few scientific students have ever equalled. I had everything to

learn relative to the delicate study upon which I had em-
barked, — a study involving the most earnest patience, the
most rigid analytic powers, the steadiest hand, the most untiring eye, the most refined and subtile manipulation.

For a long time half my apparatus lay inactively on the
shelves of my laboratory, which was now most amply furnished with every possible contrivance for facilitating my
investigations.   The fact was that I did not know how to
use some of my scientific accessories, — never having been
taught microscopics, — and those whose use I understood
theoretically were of little avail, until by practice I could
attain the necessary delicacy of handling.   Still, such was
the fury of my ambition, such the untiring perseverance of
my experiments, that, difficult of credit as it may be, in the
course of one year I became theoretically and practically an
accomplished microscopist.

During this period of my labors, in which I submitted
specimens of every substance that came under my observation to the action of my lenses, I became a discoverer, — in
a small way, it is true, for I was very young, but still a discoverer.   It was I who destroyed Ehrenberg's theory that
the *Volvox globator* was an animal, and proved that his
"monads" with stomachs and eyes were merely phases of
the formation of a vegetable cell, and were, when they
reached their mature state, incapable of the act of conjuga-
tion, or any true generative act, without which no organism
rising to any stage of life higher than vegetable can be said
to be complete.   It was I who resolved the singular problem of rotation in the cells and hairs of plants into ciliary
attraction, in spite of the assertions of Mr. Wenham and
others, that my explanation was the result of an optical
illusion.

But notwithstanding these discoveries, laboriously and
painfully made as they were, I felt horribly dissatisfied.   At
every step I found myself stopped by the imperfections of
my instruments.   Like all active microscopists, I gave my
imagination full play.   Indeed, it is a common complaint

against many such, that they supply the defects of their instruments with the creations of their brains. I imagined depths beyond depths in Nature which the limited power of my lenses prohibited me from exploring. I lay awake at night constructing imaginary microscopes of immeasurable power, with which I seemed to pierce through all the envelopes of matter down to its original atom. How I cursed those imperfect mediums which necessity through ignorance compelled me to use ! How I longed to discover the secret of some perfect lens whose magnifying power should be limited only by the resolvability of the object, and which at the same time should be free from spherical and chromatic aberrations, in short from all the obstacles over which the poor microscopist finds himself continually stumbling ! I felt convinced that the simple microscope, composed of a single lens of such vast yet perfect power, was possible of construction. To attempt to bring the compound microscope up to such a pitch would have been commencing at the wrong end ; this latter being simply a partially successful endeavor to remedy those very defects of the simple instrument, which, if conquered, would leave nothing to be desired.

It was in this mood of mind that I became a constructive microscopist. After another year passed in this new pursuit, experimenting on every imaginable substance, — glass, gems, flints, crystals, artificial crystals formed of the alloy of various vitreous materials, — in short, having constructed as many varieties of lenses as Argus had eyes, I found myself precisely where I started, with nothing gained save an extensive knowledge of glass-making. I was almost dead with despair. My parents were surprised at my apparent want of progress in my medical studies, (I had not attended one lecture since my arrival in the city,) and the expenses of my mad pursuit had been so great as to embarrass me very seriously.

I was in this frame of mind one day, experimenting in my laboratory on a small diamond, — that stone, from its

great refracting power, having always occupied my attention
more than any other, — when a young Frenchman, who
lived on the floor above me, and who was in the habit of occasionally visiting me, entered the room.

I think that Jules Simon was a Jew. He had many traits
of the Hebrew character : a love of jewelry, of dress, and of
good living. There was something mysterious about him.
He always had something to sell, and yet went into excellent society. When I say sell, I should perhaps have said
peddle ; for his operations were generally confined to the
disposal of single articles, — a picture, for instance, or a
rare carving in ivory, or a pair of duelling-pistols, or the
dress of a Mexican *caballero.* When I was first furnishing
my rooms, he paid me a visit, which ended in my purchasing an antique silver lamp, which he assured me was a Cel-
lini, — it was handsome enough even for that,—and some
other knickknacks for my sitting-room. Why Simon
should pursue this petty trade I never could imagine. He
apparently had plenty of money, and had the *entrée* of the
best houses in the city, — taking care, however, I suppose,
to drive no bargains within the enchanted circle of the
Upper Ten. I came at length to the conclusion that this
peddling was but a mask to cover some greater object, and
even went so far as to believe my young acquaintance to be
implicated in the slave-trade. That, however, was none of
my affair.

On the present occasion, Simon entered my room in a
state of considerable excitement.

"*Ah ! mon ami !*" he cried, before I could even offer
him the ordinary salutation, "it has occurred to me to be
the witness of the most astonishing things in the world. I
promenade myself to the house of Madame ——. How
does the little animal — *le renard* — name himself in the
Latin ?"

"Vulpes," I answered.

"Ah ! yes, — Vulpes. I promenade myself to the house
of Madame Vulpes."

" The spirit medium ? "

" Yes, the great medium. Great Heavens ! what a woman ! I write on a slip of paper many of questions concerning affairs the most secret, — affairs that conceal themselves in the abysses of my heart the most profound ; and behold ! by example ! what occurs ! This devil of a woman makes me replies the most truthful to all of them. She talks to me of things that I do not love to talk of to myself. What am I to think ? I am fixed to the earth ! "

" Am I to understand you, M. Simon, that this Mrs. Vulpes replied to questions secretly written by you, which questions related to events known only to yourself ? "

" Ah ! more than that, more than that," he answered, with an air of some alarm. " She related to me things — But," he added, after a pause, and suddenly changing his manner, " why occupy ourselves with these follies ? It was all the Biology, without doubt. It goes without saying that it has not my credence. But why are we here, *mon ami ?* It has occurred to me to discover the most beautiful thing as you can imagine, — a vase with green lizards on it, composed by the great Bernard Palissy. It is in my apartment ; let us mount. I go to show it to you."

I followed Simon mechanically ; but my thoughts were far from Palissy and his enamelled ware, although I, like him, was seeking in the dark after a great discovery. This casual mention of the spiritualist, Madame Vulpes, set me on a new track. What if this spiritualism should be really a great fact ? What if, through communication with subtiler organisms than my own, I could reach, at a single bound, the goal which perhaps a life of agonizing mental toil would never enable me to attain ?

While purchasing the Palissy vase from my friend Simon, I was mentally arranging a visit to Madame Vulpes.

III.

THE SPIRIT OF LEEUWENHOEK.

TWO evenings after this, thanks to an arrangement by letter and the promise of an ample fee, I found Madame Vulpes awaiting me at her residence alone. She was a coarse-featured woman, with a keen and rather cruel dark eye, and an exceedingly sensual expression about her mouth and under jaw. She received me in perfect silence, in an apartment on the ground floor, very sparely furnished. In the centre of the room, close to where Mrs. Vulpes sat, there was a common round mahogany table. If I had come for the purpose of sweeping her chimney, the woman could not have looked more indifferent to my appearance. There was no attempt to inspire the visitor with any awe. Everything bore a simple and practical aspect. This intercourse with the spiritual world was evidently as familiar an occupation with Mrs. Vulpes as eating her dinner or riding in an omnibus.

"You come for a communication, Mr. Linley?" said the medium, in a dry, business-like tone of voice.

"By appointment, — yes."

"What sort of communication do you want? — a written one?"

"Yes, — I wish for a written one."

"From any particular spirit?"

"Yes."

"Have you ever known this spirit on this earth?"

"Never. He died long before I was born. I wish merely to obtain from him some information which he ought to be able to give better than any other."

"Will you seat yourself at the table, Mr. Linley," said the medium, "and place your hands upon it?"

I obeyed, — Mrs. Vulpes being seated opposite me, with her hands also on the table. We remained thus for about a minute and a half, when a violent succession of raps came on the table, on the back of my chair, on the floor immediately under my feet, and even on the window-panes. Mrs. Vulpes smiled composedly.

"They are very strong to-night," she remarked. "You are fortunate." She then continued, "Will the spirits communicate with this gentleman?"

Vigorous affirmative.

"Will the particular spirit he desires to speak with communicate?"

A very confused rapping followed this question.

"I know what they mean," said Mrs. Vulpes, addressing herself to me; "they wish you to write down the name of the particular spirit that you desire to converse with. Is that so?" she added, speaking to her invisible guests.

That it was so was evident from the numerous affirmatory responses. While this was going on, I tore a slip from my pocket-book, and scribbled a name under the table.

"Will this spirit communicate in writing with this gentleman?" asked the medium once more.

After a moment's pause her hand seemed to be seized with a violent tremor, shaking so forcibly that the table vibrated. She said that a spirit had seized her hand and would write. I handed her some sheets of paper that were on the table, and a pencil. The latter she held loosely in her hand, which presently began to move over the paper with a singular and seemingly involuntary motion. After a few moments had elapsed she handed me the paper, on which I found written, in a large, uncultivated hand, the words, "He is not here, but has been sent for." A pause of a minute or so now ensued, during which Mrs. Vulpes remained perfectly silent, but the raps continued at regular intervals. When the short period I mention had elapsed, the hand of the medium was again seized with its convulsive tremor, and she wrote, under this strange influence, a few words on the paper, which she handed to me. They were as follows: —

" I am here.   Question me.

" LEEUWENHOEK."

I was astounded.   The name was identical with that I
had written beneath the table, and carefully kept concealed.
Neither was it at all probable that an uncultivated woman
like Mrs. Vulpes should know even the name of the great
father of microscopics.   It may have been Biology ; but this
theory was soon doomed to be destroyed.   I wrote on my
slip — still concealing it from Mrs. Vulpes — a series of questions, which, to avoid tediousness, I shall place with the
responses in the order in which they occurred.

I. — Can the microscope be brought to perfection ?

SPIRIT. — Yes.

I. — Am I destined to accomplish this great task ?

SPIRIT. — You are.

I. — I wish to know how to proceed to attain this end.
For the love which you bear to science, help me !

SPIRIT. — A diamond of one hundred and forty carats,
submitted to electro-magnetic currents for a long period, will
experience a rearrangement of its atoms *inter se*, and from
that stone you will form the universal lens.

I. — Will great discoveries result from the use of such a
lens ?

SPIRIT. — So great, that all that has gone before is as
nothing.

I. — But the refractive power of the diamond is so immense, that the image will be formed within the lens.   How
is that difficulty to be surmounted ?

SPIRIT. — Pierce the lens through its axis, and the difficulty is obviated.   The image will be formed in the pierced
space, which will itself serve as a tube to look through.
Now I am called.   Good night !

I cannot at all describe the effect that these extraordinary
communications had upon me.   I felt completely bewildered.   No biological theory could account for the *discovery*
of the lens.   The medium might, by means of biological
rapport with my mind, have gone so far as to read my ques-

tions, and reply to them coherently. But Bioiogy could not enable her to discover that magnetic currents would so alter the crystals of the diamond as to remedy its previous defects, and admit of its being polished into a perfect lens. Some such theory may have passed through my head, it is true ; but if so, I had forgotten it. In my excited condition of mind there was no course left but to become a convert, and it was in a state of the most painful nervous exaltation that I left the medium's house that evening. She accompanied me to the door, hoping that I was satisfied. The raps followed us as we went through the hall, sounding on the balusters, the flooring, and even the lintels of the door. I hastily expressed my satisfaction, and escaped hurriedly into the cool night air. I walked home with but one thought possessing me, — how to obtain a diamond of the immense size required. My entire means multipled a hundred times over would have been inadequate to its purchase. Besides, such stones are rare, and become historical. I could find such only in the regalia of Eastern or European monarchs.

IV.

THE EYE OF MORNING.

THERE was a light in Simon's room as I entered my house. A vague impulse urged me to visit him. As I opened the door of his sitting-room, unannounced, he was bending, with his back toward me, over a carcel lamp, apparently engaged in minutely examining some object which he held in his hands. As I entered, he started suddenly, thrust his hand into his breast pocket, and turned to me with a face crimson with confusion.

"What ! " I cried, "poring over the miniature of some fair lady ? Well, don't blush so much ; I won't ask to see it."

22 *

c

Simon laughed awkwardly enough, but made none of the negative protestations usual on such occasions. He asked me to take a seat.

"Simon," said I, "I have just come from Madame Vulpes."

This time Simon turned as white as a sheet, and seemed stupefied, as if a sudden electric shock had smitten him. He babbled some incoherent words, and went hastily to a small closet where he usually kept his liquors. Although astonished at his emotion, I was too preoccupied with my own idea to pay much attention to anything else.

"You say truly when you call Madame Vulpes a devil of a woman," I continued. "Simon, she told me wonderful things to-night, or rather was the means of telling me wonderful things. Ah! if I could only get a diamond that weighed one hundred and forty carats!"

Scarcely had the sigh with which I uttered this desire died upon my lips, when Simon, with the aspect of a wild beast, glared at me savagely, and rushing to the mantel-piece, where some foreign weapons hung on the wall, caught up a Malay creese, and brandished it furiously before him.

"No!" he cried in French, into which he always broke when excited. "No! you shall not have it! You are per-fidious! You have consulted with that demon, and desire my treasure! But I will die first! Me! I am brave! You cannot make me fear!"

All this, uttered in a loud voice trembling with excitement, astounded me. I saw at a glance that I had accidentally trodden upon the edges of Simon's secret, whatever it was. It was necessary to reassure him.

"My dear Simon," I said, "I am entirely at a loss to know what you mean. I went to Madame Vulpes to consult with her on a scientific problem, to the solution of which I discovered that a diamond of the size I just mentioned was necessary. You were never alluded to during the evening, nor, so far as I was concerned, even thought of. What can be the meaning of this outburst? If you happen to have a set of valuable diamonds in your possession, you need fear nothing from me. The diamond which I require you could not possess ; or if you did possess it, you would not be living here."

Something in my tone must' have completely reassured him ; for his expression immediately changed to a sort of constrained merriment, combined, however, with a certain suspicious attention to my movements. He laughed, and said that I must bear with him ; that he was at certain moments subject to a species of vertigo, which betrayed itself in incoherent speeches, and that the attacks passed off as rapidly as they came. He put his weapon aside while making this explanation, and endeavored, with some success, to assume a more cheerful air.

All this did not impose on me in the least. I was too much accustomed to analytical labors to be baffled by so flimsy a veil. I determined to probe the mystery to the bottom.

"Simon," I said, gayly, "let us forget all this over a bottle of Burgundy. I have a case of Lausseure's *Clos Vougeot* down-stairs, fragrant with the odors and ruddy with the sunlight of the Côte d'Or. Let us have up a couple of bottles. What say you?"

"With all my heart," answered Simon, smilingly.

I produced the wine, and we seated ourselves to drink. It was of a famous vintage, that of 1848, a year when war and wine throve together, — and its pure, but powerful juice seemed to impart renewed vitality to the system. By the time we had half finished the second bottle, Simon's head, which I knew was a weak one, had begun to yield, while I remained calm as ever, only that every draught seemed to send a flush of vigor through my limbs. Simon's utterance became more and more indistinct. He took to singing French *chansons* of a not very moral tendency. I rose suddenly from the table just at the conclusion of one of those incoherent verses, and, fixing my eyes on him with a quiet smile, said :

"Simon, I have deceived you. I learned your secret this evening. You may as well be frank with me. Mrs. Vulpes, or rather one of her spirits, told me all."

He started with horror. His intoxication seemed for the moment to fade away, and he made a movement towards the weapon that he had a short time before laid down. I stopped him with my hand.

"Monster!" he cried, passionately, "I am ruined! What shall I do? You shall never have it! I swear by my mother!"

"I don't want it," I said; "rest secure, but be frank with me. Tell me all about it."

The drunkenness began to return. He protested with maudlin earnestness that I was entirely mistaken,—that I was intoxicated; then asked me to swear eternal secrecy, and promised to disclose the mystery to me. I pledged myself, of course, to all. With an uneasy look in his eyes, and hands unsteady with drink and nervousness, he drew a small case from his breast and opened it. Heavens! How the mild lamp-light was shivered into a thousand prismatic arrows, as it fell upon a vast rose-diamond that glittered in the case! I was no judge of diamonds, but I saw at a glance that this was a gem of rare size and purity. I looked at Simon with wonder, and—must I confess it?—with envy. How could he have obtained this treasure? In reply to my questions, I could just gather from his drunken statements (of which, I fancy, half the incoherence was affected) that he had been superintending a gang of slaves engaged in diamond-washing in Brazil; that he had seen one of them secrete a diamond, but, instead of informing his employers, had quietly watched the negro until he saw him bury his treasure; that he had dug it up, and fled with it, but that as yet he was afraid to attempt to dispose of it publicly,—so valuable a gem being almost certain to attract too much attention to its owner's antecedents,—and he had not been able to discover any of those obscure channels by which such matters are conveyed away safely. He added, that, in accordance with Oriental practice, he had named his diamond by the fanciful title of " The Eye of Morning."

While Simon was relating this to me, I regarded the great diamond attentively. Never had I beheld anything so beautiful. All the glories of light, ever imagined or described, seemed to pulsate in its crystalline chambers. Its weight, as I learned from Simon, was exactly one hundred and forty carats. Here was an amazing coincidence. The hand of Destiny seemed in it. On the very evening when the spirit of Leeuwenhoek communicates to me the great secret of the microscope, the priceless means which he directs me to employ start up within my easy reach ! I determined, with the most perfect deliberation, to possess myself of Simon's diamond.

I sat opposite him while he nodded over his glass, and calmly revolved the whole affair. I did not for an instant contemplate so foolish an act as a common theft, which would of course be discovered, or at least necessitate flight and concealment, all of which must interfere with my scientific plans. There was but one step to be taken, — to kill Simon. After all, what was the life of a little peddling Jew, in comparison with the interests of science ? Human beings are taken every day from the condemned prisons to be experimented on by surgeons. This man, Simon, was by his own confession, a criminal, a robber, and I believed on my soul a murderer. He deserved death quite as much as any felon condemned by the laws ; why should I not, like government, contrive that his punishment should contribute to the progress of human knowledge ?

The means for accomplishing everything I desired lay within my reach. There stood upon the mantel-piece a bottle half full of French laudanum. Simon was so occupied with his diamond, which I had just restored to him, that it was an affair of no difficulty to drug his glass. In a quarter of an hour he was in a profound sleep.

I now opened his waistcoat, took the diamond from the inner pocket in which he had placed it, and removed him to the bed, on which I laid him so that his feet hung down over the edge. I had possessed myself of the Malay creese, which I held in my right hand, while with the other I discovered, as accurately as I could by pulsation, the exact locality of the heart. It was essential that all the aspects of his death should lead to the surmise of self-murder. I calculated the exact angle at which it was probable that the weapon, if levelled by Simon's own hand, would enter his breast; then with one powerful blow I thrust it up to the hilt in the very spot which I desired to penetrate. A convulsive thrill ran through Simon's limbs. I heard a smothered sound issue from his throat, precisely like the bursting of a large air-bubble, sent up by a diver, when it reaches the surface of the water; he turned half round on his side, and, as if to assist my plans more effectually, his right hand, moved by some mere spasmodic impulse, clasped the handle of the creese, which it remained holding with extraordinary muscular tenacity. Beyond this there was no apparent struggle. The laudanum, I presume, paralyzed the usual nervous action. He must have died instantaneously.

There was yet something to be done. To make it certain that all suspicion of the act should be diverted from any inhabitant of the house to Simon himself, it was necessary that the door should be found in the morning *locked on the inside.* How to do this, and afterwards escape myself? Not by the window; that was a physical impossibility. Besides, I was determined that the windows *also* should be found bolted. The solution was simple enough. I descended softly to my own room for a peculiar instrument which I had used for holding small slippery substances, such as minute spheres of glass, etc. This instrument was nothing more than a long, slender hand-vice, with a very powerful grip, and a considerable leverage, which last was accidentally owing to the shape of the handle. Nothing was simpler than, when the key was in the lock, to seize the end of its stem in this vice, through the keyhole, from the outside, and so lock the door. Previously, however, to doing this, I burned a number of papers on Simon's hearth. Suicides almost always burn papers before they destroy themselves. I also emptied some more laudanum into Simon's glass, — having first removed from it all traces of wine, — cleaned the other wine-glass, and brought the bottles away with me. If traces of two persons drinking had been found in the room, the question naturally would have arisen, Who was the second? Besides, the wine-bottles might have been identified as belonging to me. The laudanum I poured out to account for its presence in his stomach, in case of a *post-mortem* examination. The theory naturally would be, that he first intended to poison himself, but, after swallowing a little of the drug, was either disgusted with its taste, or changed his mind from other motives, and chose the dagger. These arrangements made, I walked out, leaving the gas burning, locked the door with my vice, and went to bed.

Simon's death was not discovered until nearly three in the afternoon. The servant, astonished at seeing the gas burning, — the light streaming on the dark landing from under the door, — peeped through the keyhole and saw Simon on the bed. She gave the alarm. The door was burst open, and the neighborhood was in a fever of excitement.

Every one in the house was arrested, myself included. There was an inquest; but no clew to his death, beyond that of suicide, could be obtained. Curiously enough, he had made several speeches to his friends, the preceding week, that seemed to point to self-destruction. One gentleman swore that Simon had said in his presence that " he was tired of life." His landlord affirmed that Simon, when paying him his last month's rent, remarked that " he would not pay him rent much longer." All the other evidence corresponded, — the door locked inside, the position of the corpse, the burnt papers. As I anticipated, no one knew of the possession of the diamond by Simon, so that no motive was suggested for his murder. The jury, after a prolonged examination, brought in the usual verdict, and the neighborhood once more settled down into its accustomed quiet.

V.

ANIMULA.

THE three months succeeding Simon's catastrophe I devoted night and day to my diamond lens. I had constructed a vast galvanic battery, composed of nearly two thousand pairs of plates, — a higher power I dared not use, lest the diamond should be calcined. By means of this enormous engine I was enabled to send a powerful current of electricity continually through my great diamond, which it seemed to me gained in lustre every day. At the expiration of a month I commenced the grinding and polishing of the lens, a work of intense toil and exquisite delicacy. The great density of the stone, and the care required to be taken with the curvatures of the surfaces of the lens, rendered the labor the severest and most harassing that I had yet undergone.

At last the eventful moment came ; the lens was completed. I stood trembling on the threshold of new worlds. I had the realization of Alexander's famous wish before me. The lens lay on the table, ready to be placed upon its platform. My hand fairly shook as I enveloped a drop of water with a thin coating of oil of turpentine, preparatory to its examination, — a process necessary in order to prevent the rapid evaporation of the water. I now placed the drop on a thin slip of glass under the lens, and throwing upon it, by the combined aid of a prism and a mirror, a powerful stream of light, I approached my eye to the minute hole drilled through the axis of the lens. For an instant I saw nothing save what seemed to be an illuminated chaos, a vast luminous abyss. A pure white light, cloudless and serene, and seemingly limitless as space itself, was my first impression. Gently, and with the greatest care, I depressed the lens a few hairs' breadths. The wondrous illumination still continued, but as the lens approached the object, a scene of indescribable beauty was unfolded to my view.

I seemed to gaze upon a vast space, the limits of which extended far beyond my vision. An atmosphere of magical luminousness permeated the entire field of view. I was amazed to see no trace of animalculous life. Not a living thing, apparently, inhabited that dazzling expanse. I comprehended instantly, that, by the wondrous power of my lens, I had penetrated beyond the grosser particles of aqueous matter, beyond the realms of Infusoria and Protozoa, down to the original gaseous globule, into whose luminous interior I was gazing, as into an almost boundless dome filled with a supernatural radiance.

It was, however, no brilliant void into which I looked. On every side I beheld beautiful inorganic forms, of unknown texture, and colored with the most enchanting hues. These forms presented the appearance of what might be called, for want of a more specific definition, foliated clouds of the highest rarity ; that is, they undulated and broke into vegetable formations, and were tinged with splendors compared with which the gilding of our autumn woodlands is as dross compared with gold. Far away into the illimitable distance stretched long avenues of these gaseous forests, dimly transparent, and painted with prismatic hues of unimaginable brilliancy. The pendent branches waved along the fluid glades until every vista seemed to break through half-lucent ranks of many-colored drooping silken pennons. What seemed to be either fruits or flowers, pied with a thousand hues lustrous and ever varying, bubbled from the crowns of this fairy foliage. No hills, no lakes, no rivers, no forms animate or inanimate were to be seen, save those vast auroral copses that floated serenely in the luminous stillness, with leaves and fruits and flowers gleaming with unknown fires, unrealizable by mere imagination.

How strange, I thought, that this sphere should be thus condemned to solitude! I had hoped, at least, to discover some new form of animal life, — perhaps of a lower class than any with which we are at present acquainted, — but still, some living organism. I find my newly discovered world, if I may so speak, a beautiful chromatic desert.

While I was speculating on the singular arrangements of the internal economy of Nature, with which she so frequently splinters into atoms our most compact theories, I thought I beheld a form moving slowly through the glades of one of the prismatic forests. I looked more attentively, and found that I was not mistaken. Words cannot depict the anxiety with which I awaited the nearer approach of this mysterious object. Was it merely some inanimate substance, held in suspense in the attenuated atmosphere of the globule? or was it an animal endowed with vitality and motion? It approached, flitting behind the gauzy, colored veils of cloud-foliage, for seconds dimly revealed, then vanishing. At last the violet pennons that trailed nearest to me vibrated; they were gently pushed aside, and the Form floated out into the broad light.

It was a female human shape. When I say "human," I mean it possessed the outlines of humanity, — but there the analogy ends. Its adorable beauty lifted it illimitable heights beyond the loveliest daughter of Adam.

I cannot, I dare not, attempt to inventory the charms of this divine revelation of perfect beauty. Those eyes of mystic violet, dewy and serene, evade my words. Her long lustrous hair following her glorious head in a golden wake, like the track sown in heaven by a falling star, seems to quench my most burning phrases with its splendors. If all the bees of Hybla nestled upon my lips, they would still sing but hoarsely the wondrous harmonies of outline that enclosed her form.

She swept out from between the rainbow-curtains of the

cloud-trees into the broad sea of light that lay beyond. Her
motions were those of some graceful Naiad, cleaving, by a
mere effort of her will, the clear, unruffled waters that fill
the chambers of the sea.   She floated forth with the serene
grace of a frail bubble ascending through the still atmosphere of. a June day.   The perfect roundness of her limbs
formed suave and enchanting curves.   It was like listening
to the most spiritual symphony of Beethoven the divine, to
watch the harmonious flow of lines.   This, indeed, was a
pleasure cheaply purchased at any price.   What cared I, if
I had waded to the portal of this wonder through another's
blood ?   I would have given my own to enjoy one such moment of intoxication and delight.

Breathless with gazing on this lovely wonder, and forgetful for an instant of everything save her presence, I withdrew my eye from the microscope eagerly, — alas ! As my
gaze fell on the thin slide that lay beneath my instrument,
the bright light from mirror and from prism sparkled on a
colorless drop of water ! There, in that tiny bead of dew,
this beautiful being was forever imprisoned. The planet
Neptune was not more distant from me than she. I hastened
once more to apply my eye to the microscope.

Animula (let me now call her by that dear name which I
subsequently bestowed on her) had changed her position.
She had again approached the wondrous forest, and was
gazing earnestly upwards.   Presently one of the trees — as
I must call them — unfolded a long ciliary process, with
which it seized one of the gleaming fruits that glittered on
its summit, and sweeping slowly down, held it within reach
of Animula.   The sylph took it in her delicate hand, and
began to eat.   My attention was so entirely absorbed by
her, that I could not apply myself to the task of determining
whether this singular plant was or was not instinct with
volition.

I watched her, as she made her repast, with the most profound attention.   The suppleness of her motions sent a thrill
of delight through my frame ; mv heart beat madly as she

turned her beautiful eyes in the direction of the spot in which I stood. What would I not have given to have had the power to precipitate myself into that luminous ocean, and float with her through those groves of purple and gold! While I was thus breathlessly following her every movement, she suddenly started, seemed to listen for a moment, and then cleaving the brilliant ether in which she was floating, like a flash of light, pierced through the opaline forest, and disappeared.

Instantly a series of the most singular sensations attacked me. It seemed as if I had suddenly gone blind. The luminous sphere was still before me, but my daylight had vanished. What caused this sudden disappearance? Had she a lover, or a husband? Yes, that was the solution! Some signal from a happy fellow-being had vibrated through the avenues of the forest, and she had obeyed the summons.

The agony of my sensations, as I arrived at this conclusion, startled me. I tried to reject the conviction that my reason forced upon me. I battled against the fatal conclusion, — but in vain. It was so. I had no escape from it. I loved an animalcule!

It is true, that, thanks to the marvellous power of my microscope, she appeared of human proportions. Instead of presenting the revolting aspect of the coarser creatures, that live and struggle and die, in the more easily resolvable portions of the water-drop, she was fair and delicate and of surpassing beauty. But of what account was all that? Every time that my eye was withdrawn from the instrument, it fell on a miserable drop of water, within which, I must be content to know, dwelt all that could make my life lovely.

Could she but see me once! Could I for one moment pierce the mystical walls that so inexorably rose to separate us, and whisper all that filled my soul, I might consent to be satisfied for the rest of my life with the knowledge of her remote sympathy. It would be something to have estab-'

lished even the faintest personal link to bind us together, — to know that at times, when roaming through those enchanted glades, she might think of the wonderful stranger, who had broken the monotony of her life with his presence, and left a gentle memory in her heart!

But it could not be. No invention, of which human intellect was capable, could break down the barriers that Nature had erected. I might feast my soul upon her wondrous beauty, yet she must always remain ignorant of the adoring eyes that day and night gazed upon her, and, even when closed, beheld her in dreams. With a bitter cry of anguish I fled from the room, and flinging myself on my bed, sobbed myself to sleep like a child.

VI.

THE SPILLING OF THE CUP.

I AROSE the next morning almost at daybreak, and rushed to my microscope. I trembled as I sought the luminous world in miniature that contained my all. Animula was there. I had left the gas-lamp, surrounded by its moderators, burning, when I went to bed the night before. I found the sylph bathing, as it were, with an expression of pleasure animating her features, in the brilliant light which surrounded her. She tossed her lustrous golden hair over her shoulders with innocent coquetry. She lay at full length in the transparent medium, in which she supported herself with ease, and gambolled with the enchanting grace that the Nymph Salmacis might have exhibited when she sought to conquer the modest Hermaphroditus. I tried an experiment to satisfy myself if her powers of reflection were developed. I lessened the lamp-light considerably. By the dim light that remained, I could see an expression of pain flit across her face. She looked upward suddenly, and her brows contracted. I flooded the stage of the microscope again with a full stream of light, and her whole expression changed. She sprang forward like some substance deprived of all weight. Her eyes sparkled, and her lips moved. Ah! if science had only the means of conducting and redupli-cating sounds, as it does the rays of light, what carols of happiness would then have entranced my ears! what jubi-lant hymns to Adonaïs would have thrilled the illumined air!

I now comprehended how it was that the Count de Gaba-lis peopled his mystic world with sylphs, — beautiful beings whose breath of life was lambent fire, and who sported for-ever in regions of purest ether and purest light. The Ro-sicrucian had anticipated the wonder that.I had practically realized.

How long this worship of my strange divinity went on thus I scarcely know. I lost all note of time. All day from early dawn, and far into the night, I was to be found peer-ing through that wonderful lens. I saw no one, went no-where, and scarce allowed myself sufficient time for my meals. My whole life was absorbed in contemplation as rapt as that of any of the Romish saints. Every hour that I gazed upon the divine form strengthened my passion, — a passion that was always overshadowed by the maddening conviction, that, although I could gaze on her at will, she never, never could behold me!

At length I grew so pale and emaciated, from want of rest, and continual brooding over my insane love and its cruel conditions, that I determined to make some effort to wean myself from it. "Come," I said, "this is at best but a fantasy. Your imagination has bestowed on Animula charms which in reality she does not possess. Seclusion from female society has produced this morbid condition of mind. Compare her with the beautiful women of your own world, and this false enchantment will vanish."

I looked over the newspapers by chance. There I be-held the advertisement of a celebrated *danseuse* who appeared nightly at Niblo's. The Signorina Caradolce had the reputation of being the most beautiful as well as the most graceful woman in the world. I instantly dressed and went to the theatre.

The curtain drew up. The usual semicircle of fairies in white muslin were standing on the right toe around the enamelled flower-bank, of green canvas, on which the belated prince was sleeping. Suddenly a flute is heard. The fairies start. The trees open, the fairies all stand on the left toe, and the queen enters. It was the Signorina. She bounded forward amid thunders of applause, and lighting on one foot remained poised in air. Heavens ! was this the great enchantress that had drawn monarchs at her chariot-wheels ? Those heavy muscular limbs, those thick ankles, those cavernous eyes, that stereotyped smile, those crudely painted cheeks ! Where were the vermeil blooms, the liquid expressive eyes, the harmonious limbs of Animula ?

The Signorina danced. What gross, discordant movements ! The play of her limbs was all false and artificial. Her bounds were painful athletic efforts ; her poses were angular and distressed the eye. I could bear it no longer ; with an exclamation of disgust that drew every eye upon me, I rose from my seat in the very middle of the Signorina's *pas-de-fascination*, and abruptly quitted the house.

I hastened home to feast my eyes once more on the lovely form of my sylph. I felt that henceforth to combat this passion would be impossible. I applied my eye to the lens. Animula was there, — but what could have happened ? Some terrible change seemed to have taken place during my absence. Some secret grief seemed to cloud the lovely features of her I gazed upon. Her face had grown thin and haggard ; her limbs trailed heavily ; the wondrous lustre of her golden hair had faded. She was ill ! — ill, and I could not assist her ! I believe at that moment I would have gladly forfeited all claims to my human birthright, if I could only have been dwarfed to the size of an animalcule, and permitted to console her from whom fate had forever divided me.

I racked my brain for the solution of this mystery. What was it that afflicted the sylph ? She seemed to suffer intense pain. Her features contracted, and she even writhed, as if with some internal agony. The wondrous forests appeared also to have lost half their beauty. Their hues were dim, and in some places 'faded away altogether. I watched Animula for hours with a breaking heart, and she seemed absolutely to wither away under my very eye. Suddenly I remembered that I had not looked at the water-drop for several days. In fact, I hated to see it ; for it reminded me of the natural barrier between Animula and myself. I hurriedly looked down on the stage of the microscope. The slide was still there, — but, great heavens ! the water-drop had vanished ! The awful truth burst upon me ; it had evaporated, until it had become so minute as to be invisible to the naked eye ; I had been gazing on its last atom, the one that contained Animula, — and she was dying !

I rushed again to the front of the lens, and looked through. Alas ! the last agony had seized her. The rainbow-hued forests had all melted away, and Animula lay struggling feebly in what seemed to be a spot of dim light. Ah ! the sight was horrible : the limbs once so round and lovely shrivelling up into nothings ; the eyes — those eyes that shone like heaven — being quenched into black dust ; the lustrous golden hair now lank and discolored. The last throe came. I beheld that final struggle of the blackening form — and I fainted.

When I awoke out of a trance of many hours, I found myself lying amid the wreck of my instrument, myself as shattered in mind and body as it. I crawled feebly to my bed, from which I did not rise for months.

They say now that I am mad ; but they are mistaken. I am poor, for I have neither the heart nor the will to work ; all my money is spent, and I live on charity. Young men's associations that love a joke invite me to lecture on Optics before them, for which they pay me, and laugh at me while I lecture. "Linley, the mad microscopist," is the name I go by. I suppose that I talk incoherently while I lecture. Who could talk sense when his brain is haunted by such ghastly memories, while ever and anon among the shapes of death I behold the radiant form of my lost Animula !

LIFE IN THE IRON–MILLS.

"Is this the end?
O Life, as futile, then, as frail!
What hope of answer or redress?"

 CLOUDY day: do you know what that is in a town of iron-works? The sky sank down before dawn, muddy, flat, immovable. The air is thick, clammy with the breath of crowded human beings. It stifles me. I open the window, and, looking out, can scarcely see through the rain the grocer's shop opposite, where a crowd of drunken Irishmen are puffing Lynchburg tobacco in their pipes. I can detect the scent through all the foul smells ranging loose in the air.

The idiosyncrasy of this town is smoke. It rolls sullenly in slow folds from the great chimneys of the iron-founderies, and settles down in black, slimy pools on the muddy streets. Smoke on the wharves, smoke on the dingy boats, on the yellow river, — clinging in a coating of greasy soot to the house-front, the two faded poplars, the faces of the passers-by. The long train of mules, dragging masses of pig-iron through the narrow street, have a foul vapor hanging to their reeking sides. Here, inside, is a little broken figure of an angel pointing upward from the mantel-shelf; but even its wings are covered with smoke, clotted and black. Smoke everywhere! A dirty canary chirps desolately in a cage beside me. Its dream of green fields and sunshine is a very old dream, — almost worn out, I think.

From the back-window I can see a narrow brick-yard sloping down to the river-side, strewed with rain-butts and tubs. The river, dull and tawny-colored, (*la belle rivière!*) drags itself sluggishly along, tired of the heavy weight of boats and coal-barges. What wonder? When I was a child, I used to fancy a look of weary, dumb appeal upon the face of the negro-like river slavishly bearing its burden day after day. Something of the same idle notion comes to me to-day, when from the street-window I look on the slow stream of human life creeping past, night and morning, to the great mills. Masses of men, with dull, besotted faces bent to the ground, sharpened here and there by pain or cunning; skin and muscle and flesh begrimed with smoke and ashes; stooping all night over boiling caldrons of metal, laired by day in dens of drunkenness and infamy; breathing from infancy to death an air saturated with fog and grease and soot, vileness for soul and body. What do you make of a case like that, amateur psychologist? You call it an altogether serious thing to be alive: to these men it is a drunken jest, a joke, — horrible to angels perhaps, to them commonplace enough. My fancy about the river was an idle one: it is no type of such a life. What if it be stagnant and slimy here? It knows that beyond there waits for it odorous sunlight, — quaint old gardens, dusky with soft, green foliage of apple-trees, and flushing crimson with roses, — air, and fields, and mountains. The future of the Welsh puddler passing just now is not so pleasant. To be stowed away, after his grimy work is done, in a hole in the muddy graveyard, and after that, — *not* air, nor green fields, nor curious roses.

Can you see how foggy the day is? As I stand here, idly tapping the window-pane, and looking out through the rain at the dirty back-yard and the coal-boats below, fragments of an old story float up before me, — a story of this house into which I happened to come to-day. You may think it a tiresome story enough, as foggy as the day, sharpened by no sudden flashes of pain or pleasure. I know: only the out-

line of a dull life, that long since, with thousands of dull
lives like its own, was vainly lived and lost : thousands of
them, — massed, vile, slimy lives, like those of the torpid
lizards in yonder stagnant water-butt. — Lost ? There is a
curious point for you to settle, my friend, who study psy-
chology in a lazy, *dilettante* way. Stop a moment. I am
going to be honest. This is what I want you to do. I
want you to hide your disgust, take no heed to your clean
clothes, and come right down with me, — here, into the
thickest of the fog and mud and foul effluvia. I want you
to hear this story. There is a secret down here, in this
nightmare fog, that has lain dumb for centuries : I want to
make it a real thing to you. You, Egoist, or Pantheist, or
Arminian, busy in making straight paths for your feet on
the hills, do not see it clearly, — this terrible question which
men here have gone mad and died trying to answer. I dare
not put this secret into words. I told you it was dumb.
These men, going by with drunken faces, and brains full of
unawakened power, do not ask it of Society or of God.
Their lives ask it ; their deaths ask it. There is no reply.
I will tell you plainly that I have a great hope ; and I bring
it to you to be tested. It is this : that this terrible dumb
question is its own reply ; that it is not the sentence of
death we think it, but, from the very extremity of its darkness, the most solemn prophecy which the world has known
of the Hope to come. I dare make my meaning no clearer,
but will only tell my story. It will, perhaps, seem to you as
foul and dark as this thick vapor about us, and as pregnant
with death ; but if your eyes are free as mine are to look
deeper, no perfume-tinted dawn will be so fair with promise
of the day that shall surely come.

My story is very simple, — only what I remember of the
life of one of these men, — a furnace-tender in one of Kirby
& John's rolling-mills, — Hugh Wolfe. You know the
mills ? They took the great order for the lower Virginia
railroads there last winter ; run usually with about a thousand men. I cannot tell why I choose the half-forgotten

story of this Wolfe more than that of myriads of these fur-
nace-hands. Perhaps because there is a secret, underlying
sympathy between that story and this day with its impure
fog and thwarted sunshine, — or perhaps simply for the
reason that this house is the one where the Wolfes lived.
There were the father and son, — both hands, as I said, in
one of Kirby & John's mills for making railroad-iron, — and
Deborah, their cousin, a picker in some of the cotton-mills.
The house was rented then to half a dozen families. The
Wolfes had two of the cellar-rooms. The old man, like
many of the puddlers and feeders of the mills, was Welsh,
— had spent half of his life in the Cornish tin-mines. You
may pick the Welsh emigrants, Cornish miners, out of the
throng passing the windows, any day. They are a trifle
more filthy ; their muscles are not so brawny ; they stoop
more. When they are drunk, they neither yell, nor shout,
nor stagger, but skulk along like beaten hounds. A pure,
unmixed blood, I fancy, shows itself in the slight angular
bodies and sharply-cut facial lines. It is nearly thirty years
since the Wolfes lived here. Their lives were like those of
their class : incessant labor, sleeping in kennel-like rooms,
eating rank pork and molasses, drinking — God and the dis-
tillers only know what ; with an occasional night in jail, to
atone for some drunken excess. Is that all of their lives ? —
of the portion given to them and these their duplicates
swarming the streets to-day ? — nothing beneath ? — all ?
So many a political reformer will tell you, — and many a
private reformer, too, who has gone among them with a
heart tender with Christ's charity, and come out outraged,
hardened.

One rainy night, about eleven o'clock, a crowd of half-
clothed women stopped outside of the cellar-door. They
were going home from the cotton-mill.

"Good-night, Deb," said one, a mulatto, steadying herself against the gas-post. She needed the post to steady
her. So did more than one of them.

"Dah 's a ball to Miss Potts' to-night. Ye 'd best come."

"Inteet, Deb, if hur 'll come, hur 'll hef fun," said a shrill Welsh voice in the crowd.

Two or three dirty hands were thrust out to catch the gown of the woman, who was groping for the latch of the door.

"No."

"No? Where's Kit Small, then?"

"Begorra! on the spools. Alleys behint, though we helped her, we dud. An wid ye! Let Deb alone! It's ondacent frettin' a quite body. Be the powers, an' we'll have a night of it! there'll be lashin's o' drink, — the Vargent be blessed and praised for't!"

They went on, the mulatto inclining for a moment to show fight, and drag the woman Wolfe off with them; but, being pacified, she staggered away.

Deborah groped her way into the cellar, and, after considerable stumbling, kindled a match, and lighted a tallow dip, that sent a yellow glimmer over the room. It was low, damp, — the earthen floor covered with a green, slimy moss, — a fetid air smothering the breath. Old Wolfe lay asleep on a heap of straw, wrapped in a torn horse-blanket. He was a pale, meek little man, with a white face and red rabbit-eyes. The woman Deborah was like him; only her face was even more ghastly, her lips bluer, her eyes more watery. She wore a faded cotton gown and a slouching bonnet. When she walked, one could see that she was deformed, almost a hunchback. She trod softly, so as not to waken him, and went through into the room beyond. There she found by the half-extinguished fire an iron saucepan filled with cold boiled potatoes, which she put upon a broken chair with a pint-cup of ale. Placing the old candlestick beside this dainty repast, she untied her bonnet, which hung limp and wet over her face, and prepared to eat her supper. It was the first food that had touched her lips since morning. There was enough of it, however: there is not always. She was hungry, — one could see that easily enough, — and not drunk, as most of her companions would have been found at this hour. She did not drink, this woman, — her face told that too, — nothing stronger than ale. Perhaps the weak, flaccid wretch had some stimulant in her pale life to keep her up, — some love or hope, it might be, or urgent need. When that stimulant was gone, she would take to whiskey. Man cannot live by work alone. While she was skinning the potatoes, and munching them, a noise behind her made her stop.

"Janey !" she called, lifting the candle and peering into the darkness. "Janey, are you there ?"

A heap of ragged coats was heaved up, and the face of a young girl emerged, staring sleepily at the woman.

"Deborah," she said, at last, "I 'm here the night."

"Yes, child. Hur 's welcome," she said, quietly eating on.

The girl's face was haggard and sickly ; her eyes were heavy with sleep and hunger : real Milesian eyes they were, dark, delicate blue, glooming out from black shadows with a pitiful fright.

"I was alone," she said, timidly.

"Where 's the father ?" asked Deborah, holding out a potato, which the girl greedily seized.

"He 's beyant, — wid Haley, — in the stone house." (Did you ever hear the word *jail* from an Irish mouth?) "I came here. Hugh told me never to stay me-lóne."

"Hugh ?"

"Yes."

A vexed frown crossed her face. The girl saw it, and added quickly, —

"I have not seen Hugh the day, Deb. The old man says his watch lasts till the mornin'."

The woman sprang up, and hastily began to arrange some bread and flitch in a tin pail, and to pour her own measure of ale into a bottle. Tying on her bonnet, she blew out the candle.

"Lay ye down, Janey dear," she said, gently, covering her with the old rags. "Hur can eat the potatoes, if hur 's hungry."

" Where are ye goin', Deb ?. The rain 's sharp."

" To the mill, with Hugh's supper."

" Let him bide till th' morn.   Sit ye down."

" No, no," — sharply pushing her off.   " The boy 'll starve."

She hurried from the cellar, while the child wearily coiled herself up for sleep.   The rain was falling heavily, as the woman, pail in hand, emerged from the mouth of the alley, and turned down the narrow street, that stretched out, long and black, miles before her.   Here and there a flicker of gas lighted an uncertain space of muddy footwalk and gut-ter ; the long rows of houses, except an occasional lager-bier shop, were closed ; now and then she met a band of mill-hands skulking to or from their work.

Not many even of the inhabitants of a manufacturing town know the vast machinery of system by which the bodies of workmen are governed, that goes on unceasingly from year to year.   The hands of each mill are divided into watches that relieve each other as regularly as the sentinels of an army.   By night and day the work goes on, the un-sleeping engines groan and shriek, the fiery pools of metal boil and surge.   Only for a day in the week, in half-courtesy to public censure, the fires are partially veiled ; but as soon as the clock strikes midnight, the great furnaces break forth with renewed fury, the clamor begins with fresh, breathless vigor, the engines sob and shriek like "gods in pain."

As Deborah hurried down through the heavy rain, the noise of these thousand engines sounded through the sleep and shadow of the city like far-off thunder.   The mill to which she was going lay on the river, a mile below the city-limits.   It was far, and she was weak, aching from standing twelve hours at the spools.   Yet it was her almost nightly walk to take this man his supper, though at every square she sat down to rest, and she knew she should receive small word of thanks.

Perhaps, if she had possessed an artist's eye, the pic-turesque oddity of the scene might have made her step stagger less, and the path seem shorter ; but to her the mills were only " summat deilish to look at by night."

The road leading to the mills had been quarried from the solid rock, which rose abrupt and bare on one side of the cinder-covered road, while the river, sluggish and black, crept past on the other. The mills for rolling iron are simply immense tent-like roofs, covering acres of ground, open on every side. Beneath these roofs Deborah looked in on a city of fires, that burned hot and fiercely in the night. Fire in every horrible form : pits of flame waving in the wind ; liquid metal-flames writhing in tortuous streams through the sand ; wide caldrons filled with boiling fire, over which bent ghastly wretches stirring the strange brewing ; and through all, crowds of half-clad men, looking like revengeful ghosts in the red light, hurried, throwing masses of glittering fire. It was like a street in Hell. Even Deborah muttered, as she crept through, " 'T looks like t' Devil's place ! " It did, — in more ways than one.

She found the man she was looking for, at last, heaping coal on a furnace. He had not time to eat his supper ; so she went behind the furnace, and waited. Only a few men were with him, and they noticed her only by a " Hyur comes t' hunchback, Wolfe."

Deborah was stupid with sleep ; her back pained her sharply ; and her teeth chattered with cold, with the rain that soaked her clothes and dripped from her at every step. She stood, however, patiently holding the pail, and waiting.

" Hout, woman ! ye look like a drowned cat. Come near to the fire," — said one of the men, approaching to scrape away the ashes.

She shook her head. Wolfe had forgotten her. He turned, hearing the man, and came closer.

. " I did no' think ; g' me my supper, woman."

She watched him eat with a painful eagerness. With a woman's quick instinct, she saw that he was not hungry, — was eating to please her. Her pale, watery eyes began to gather a strange light.

3*

"Is't good, Hugh ? T' ale was a bit sour, I feared."

" No, good enough." He hesitated a moment. " Ye 're tired, poor lass ! Bide here till I go. Lay down there on that heap of ash, and go to sleep."

He threw her an old coat for a pillow, and turned to his work. The heap was the refuse of the burnt iron, and was not a hard bed ; the half-smothered warmth, too, penetrated her limbs, dulling their pain and cold shiver.

Miserable enough she looked, lying there on the ashes like a limp, dirty rag, — yet not an unfitting figure to crown the scene of hopeless discomfort and veiled crime : more fitting, if one looked deeper into the heart of things, — at her thwarted woman's form, her colorless life, her waking stupor that smothered pain and hunger, — even more fit to be a type of her class. Deeper yet if one could look ; was there nothing worth reading in this wet, faded thing, half covered with ashes ? no story of a soul filled with groping, passionate love, heroic unselfishness, fierce jealousy ? of years of weary trying to please the one human being whom she loved, to gain one look of real heart-kindness from him ? If anything like this were hidden beneath the pale, bleared eyes, and dull, washed-out-looking face, no one had ever taken the trouble to read its faint signs : not the half-clothed furnace-tender, Wolfe, certainly. Yet he was kind to her : it was his nature to be kind, even to the very rats that swarmed in the cellar : kind to her in just the same way. She knew that. And it might be that very knowledge had given to her face its apathy and vacancy more than her low, torpid life. One sees that dead, vacant look steal sometimes over the rarest, finest of women's faces, — in the very midst, it may be, of their warmest summer's day ; and then one can guess at the secret of intolerable solitude that lies hid beneath the delicate laces and brilliant smile. There was no warmth, no brilliancy, no summer for this woman ; so the stupor and vacancy had time to gnaw into her face perpetually. She was young, too, though no one guessed it ; so the gnawing was the fiercer.

She lay quiet in the dark corner, listening, through the
monotonous din and uncertain glare of the works, to the
dull plash of the rain in the far distance, — shrinking back
whenever the man Wolfe happened to look towards her.
She knew, in spite of all his kindness, that there was that in
her face and form which made him loathe the sight of her.
She felt by instinct, although she could not comprehend it,
the finer nature of the man, which made him among his fel-
low-workmen something unique, set apart. She knew, that,
down under all the vileness and coarseness of his life, there
was a groping passion for whatever was beautiful and pure,
— that his soul sickened with disgust at her deformity, even
when his words were kindest. Through this dull consciousness, which never left her, came, like a sting, the recollection
of the dark blue eyes and lithe figure of the little Irish girl
she had left in the cellar. The recollection struck through
even her stupid intellect with a vivid glow of beauty and of
grace. Little Janey, timid, helpless, clinging to Hugh as
her only friend : that was the sharp thought, the bitter
thought, that drove into the glazed eyes a fierce light of pain.
You laugh at it ? Are pain and jealousy less savage realities
down here in this place I am taking you to than in your
own house or your own heart, — your heart, which they
clutch at sometimes ? The note is the same, I fancy, be the
octave high or low.

If you could go into this mill where Deborah lay, and
drag out from the hearts of these men the terrible tragedy
of their lives, taking it as a symptom of the disease of their
class, no ghost Horror would terrify you more. A reality
of soul-starvation, of living death, that meets you every day
under the besotted faces on the street — I can paint nothing of this, only give you the outside outlines of a night, a
crisis in the life of one man : whatever muddy depth of soul-
history lies beneath you can read according to the eyes God
has given you.

Wolfe, while Deborah watched him as a spaniel its master, bent over the furnace with his iron pole, unconscious of

her scrutiny, only stopping to receive orders. Physically, Nature had promised the man but little. He had already lost the strength and instinct vigor of a man, his muscles were thin, his nerves weak, his face (a meek, woman's face) haggard, yellow with consumption. In the mill he was known as one of the girl-men : " Molly Wolfe " was his *sobriquet.* He was never seen in the cockpit, did not own a terrier, drank but seldom ; when he did, desperately. He fought sometimes, but was always thrashed, pommelled to a jelly. The man was game enough, when his blood was up : but he was no favorite in the mill ; he had the taint of school-learning on him, — not to a dangerous extent, only a quarter or so in the free-school in fact, but enough to ruin him as a good hand in a fight.

For other reasons, too, he was not popular. Not one of themselves, they felt that, though outwardly as filthy and ash-covered ; silent, with foreign thoughts and longings breaking out through his quietness in innumerable curious ways : this one, for instance. In the neighboring furnace-buildings lay great heaps of the refuse from the ore after the pig-metal is run. *Korl* we call it here : a light, porous substance, of a delicate, waxen, flesh-colored tinge. Out of the blocks of this korl, Wolfe, in his off-hours from the furnace, had a habit of chipping and moulding figures, — hideous, fantastic enough, but sometimes strangely beautiful : even the mill-men saw that, while they jeered at him. It was a curious fancy in the man, almost a passion. The few hours for rest he spent hewing and hacking with his blunt knife, never speaking, until his watch came again, — working at one figure for months, and, when it was finished, breaking it to pieces perhaps, in a fit of disappointment. A morbid, gloomy man, untaught, unled, left to feed his soul in grossness and crime, and hard, grinding labor.

I want you to come down and look at this Wolfe, standing there among the lowest of his kind, and see him just as he is, that you may judge him justly when you hear the story of this night. I want you to look back, as he does

every day, at his birth in vice, his starved infancy ; to remember the heavy years he has groped through as boy and
man, — the slow, heavy years of constant, hot work. So
long ago he began, that he thinks sometimes he has worked
there for ages. There is no hope that it will ever end.
Think that God put into this man's soul a fierce thirst for
beauty, — to know it, to create it ; to *be* — something, he
knows not what, — other than he is. There are moments
when a passing cloud, the sun glinting on the purple this-
tles, a kindly smile, a child's face, will rouse him to a passion
of pain, — when his nature starts up with a mad cry of rage
against God, man, whoever it is that has forced this vile,
slimy life upon him. With all this groping, this mad desire,
a great blind intellect stumbling through wrong, a loving
poet's heart, the man was by habit only a coarse, vulgar laborer, familiar with sights and words you would blush to
name. Be just : when I tell you about this night, see him
as he is. Be just, — not like man's law, which seizes on one
isolated fact, but like God's judging angel, whose clear, sad
eye saw all the countless cankering days of this man's life,
all the countless nights, when, sick with starving, his soul
fainted in him, before it judged him for this night, the saddest
of all.

I called this night the crisis of his life. If it was, it stole
on him unawares. These great turning-days of life cast no
shadow before, slip by unconsciously. Only a trifle, a little
turn of the rudder, and the ship goes to heaven or hell.

Wolfe, while Deborah watched him, dug into the furnace
of melting iron with his pole, dully thinking only how many
rails the lump would yield. It was late, — nearly Sunday
morning ; another hour, and the heavy work would be done,
— only the furnaces to replenish and cover for the next day.
The workmen were growing more noisy, shouting, as they
had to do, to be heard over the deep clamor of the mills.
Suddenly they grew less boisterous, — at the far end, entirely silent. Something unusual had happened. After a
moment, the silence came nearer ; the men stopped their

jeers and drunken choruses. Deborah, stupidly lifting up her head, saw the cause of the quiet. A group of five or six men were slowly approaching, stopping to examine each furnace as they came. Visitors often came to see the mills after night : except by growing less noisy, the men took no notice of them. The furnace where Wolfe worked was near the bounds of the works ; they halted there hot and tired : a walk over one of these great founderies is no trifling task. The woman, drawing out of sight, turned over to sleep. Wolfe, seeing them stop, suddenly roused from his indifferent stupor, and watched them keenly. He knew some of them : the overseer, Clarke, — a son of Kirby, one of the mill-owners, — and a Doctor May, one of the town-physicians. The other two were strangers. Wolfe came closer. He seized eagerly every chance that brought him into contact with this mysterious class that shone down on him perpetually with the glamour of another order of being. What made the difference between them ? That was the mystery of his life. He had a vague notion that perhaps to-night he could find it out. One of the strangers sat down on a pile of bricks, and beckoned young Kirby to his side.

"This *is* hot, with a vengeance. A match, please ?" — lighting his cigar. "But the walk is worth the trouble. If it were not that you must have heard it so often, Kirby, I would tell you that your works look like Dante's Inferno."

Kirby laughed.

"Yes. Yonder is Farinata himself in the burning tomb," — pointing to some figure in the shimmering shadows.

"Judging from some of the faces of your men," said the other, "they bid fair to try the reality of Dante's vision, some day."

Young Kirby looked curiously around, as if seeing the faces of his hands for the first time.

"They're bad enough, that's true. A desperate set, I fancy. Eh, Clarke ?"

The overseer did not hear him. He was talking of net profits just then, — giving, in fact, a schedule of the annual

business of the firm to a sharp peering little Yankee, who
jotted down notes on a paper laid on the crown of his hat :
a reporter for one of the city papers, getting up a series of
reviews of the leading manufactories. The other gentlemen
had accompanied them merely for amusement. They were
silent until the notes were finished, drying their feet at the
furnaces, and sheltering their faces from the intolerable heat.
At last the overseer concluded with —

"I believe that is a pretty fair estimate, Captain."

"Here, some of you men.!" said Kirby, "bring up those
boards. We may as well sit down, gentlemen, until the
rain is over. It cannot last much longer at this rate."

"Pig-metal," — mumbled the reporter, — "um ! — coal facilities, — um ! — hands employed, twelve hundred, — bitu-
men, — um ! — all right, I believe, Mr. Clarke ; — sinking-
fund, — what did you say was your sinking-fund ?"

"Twelve hundred hands ?" said the stranger, the young
man who. had first spoken. "Do you control their votes,
Kirby ?"

"Control ? No." The young man smiled complacently.
"But my father brought seven hundred votes to the polls
for his candidate last November. No force-work, you understand, — only a speech or two, a hint to form themselves
into a society, and a bit of red and blue bunting to make
them a flag. The Invincible Roughs, — I believe that is
their name. I forget the motto : 'Our country's hope,' I
think."

There was a laugh. The young man talking to Kirby
sat with an amused light in his cool gray eye, surveying
critically the half-clothed figures of the puddlers, and the
slow swing of their brawny muscles. He was a stranger in
the city, — spending a couple of months in the borders of a
Slave State, to study the institutions of the South, — a
brother-in-law of Kirby's, — Mitchell. He was an amateur
gymnast, — hence his anatomical eye ; a patron, in a *blasé*
way, of the prize-ring ; a man who sucked the essence out
of a science or philosophy in an indifferent, gentlemanly

way; who took Kant, Novalis, Humboldt, for what they were worth in his own scales; accepting all, despising nothing, in heaven, earth, or hell, but one-idead men; with a temper yielding and brilliant as summer water, until his Self was touched, when it was ice, though brilliant still. Such men are not rare in the States.

As he knocked the ashes from his cigar, Wolfe caught with a quick pleasure the contour of the white hand, the blood-glow of a red ring he wore. His voice, too, and that of Kirby's, touched him like music, — low, even, with chording cadences. About this man Mitchell hung the impalpable atmosphere belonging to the thoroughbred gentleman. Wolfe, scraping away the ashes beside him, was conscious of it, did obeisance to it with his artist sense, unconscious that he did so.

The rain did not cease. Clarke and the reporter left the mills; the others, comfortably seated near the furnace, lingered, smoking and talking in a desultory way. Greek would not have been more unintelligible to the furnace-tenders, whose presence they soon forgot entirely. Kirby drew out a newspaper from his pocket and read aloud some article, which they discussed eagerly. At every sentence, Wolfe listened more and more like a dumb, hopeless animal, with a duller, more stolid look creeping over his face, glancing now and then at Mitchell, marking acutely every smallest sign of refinement, then back to himself, seeing as in a mirror his filthy body, his more stained soul.

Never! He had no words for such a thought, but he knew now, in all the sharpness of the bitter certainty, that between them there was a great gulf never to be passed. Never!

The bell of the mills rang for midnight. Sunday morning had dawned. Whatever hidden message lay in the tolling bells floated past these men unknown. Yet it was there. Veiled in the solemn music ushering the risen Saviour was a key-note to solve the darkest secrets of a world gone wrong, — even this social riddle which the brain of the grimy puddler grappled with madly to-night.

The men began to withdraw the metal from the caldrons. The mills were deserted on Sundays, except by the hands who fed the fires, and those who had no lodgings and slept usually on the ash-heaps. The three strangers sat still during the next hour, watching the men cover the furnaces, laughing now and then at some jest of Kirby's.

"Do you know," said Mitchell, "I like this view of the works better than when the glare was fiercest? These heavy shadows and the amphitheatre of smothered fires are ghostly, unreal. One could fancy these red smouldering lights to be the half-shut eyes of wild beasts, and the spectral figures their victims in the den."

Kirby laughed. "You are fanciful. Come, let us get out of the den. The spectral figures, as you call them, are a little too real for me to fancy a close proximity in the darkness, — unarmed, too."

The others rose, buttoning their overcoats, and lighting cigars.

"Raining still," said Doctor May, "and hard. Where did we leave the coach, Mitchell?"

"At the other side of the works. — Kirby, what 's that?"

Mitchell started back, half-frightened, as, suddenly turning a corner, the white figure of a woman faced him in the darkness, — a woman, white, of giant proportions, crouching on the ground, her arms flung out in some wild gesture of warning.

"Stop! Make that fire burn there!" cried Kirby, stopping short.

The flame burst out, flashing the gaunt figure into bold relief.

Mitchell drew a long breath.

"I thought it was alive," he said, going up curiously.

The others followed.

"Not marble, eh?" asked Kirby, touching it.

One of the lower overseers stopped.

"Korl, Sir."

"Who did it?"

E

"Can't say. Some of the hands; chipped it out in off-hours."

"Chipped to some purpose, I should say. What a flesh-tint the stuff has! Do you see, Mitchell?"

"I see."

He had stepped aside where the light fell boldest on the figure, looking at it in silence. There was not one line of beauty or grace in it: a nude woman's form, muscular, grown coarse with labor, the powerful limbs instinct with some one poignant longing. One idea: there it was in the tense, rigid muscles, the clutching hands, the wild, eager face, like that of a starving wolf's. Kirby and Dr. May walked around it, critical, curious. Mitchell stood aloof, silent. The figure touched him strangely.

"Not badly done," said Doctor May. "Where did the fellow learn that sweep of the muscles in the arm and hand? Look at them! They are groping, — do you see? — clutching: the peculiar action of a man dying of thirst."

"They have ample facilities for studying anatomy," sneered Kirby, glancing at the half-naked figures.

"Look," continued the Doctor, "at this bony wrist, and the strained sinews of the instep! A working-woman, — the very type of her class."

"God forbid!" muttered Mitchell.

"Why?" demanded May. "What does the fellow intend by the figure? I cannot catch the meaning."

"Ask him," said the other, dryly. "There he stands," — pointing to Wolfe, who stood with a group of men, leaning on his ash-rake.

The Doctor beckoned him with the affable smile which kind-hearted men put on, when talking to these people.

"Mr. Mitchell has picked you out as the man who did this, — I'm sure I don't know why. But what did you mean by it?"

"She be hungry."

Wolfe's eyes answered Mitchell, not the Doctor.

"Oh-h! But what a mistake you have made, my fine

fellow ! You have given no sign of starvation to the body. It is strong, — terribly strong. It has the mad, half-despairing gesture of drowning."

Wolfe stammered, glanced appealingly at Mitchell, who saw the soul of the thing, he knew. But the cool, probing eyes were turned on himself now, — mocking, cruel, relentless.

" Not hungry for meat," the furnace-tender said at last.

" What then ? Whiskey ? " jeered Kirby, with a coarse laugh.

Wolfe was silent a moment, thinking.

" I dunno," he said, with a bewildered look. " It mebbe. Summat to make her live, I think, — like you. Whiskey ull do it, in a way."

The young man laughed again. Mitchell flashed a look of disgust somewhere, — not at Wolfe.

" May," he broke out impatiently, " are you blind ? Look at that woman's face ! It asks questions of God, and says, ' I have a right to know.' Good God, how hungry it is ! "

They looked a moment ; then May turned to the mill-owner : —

" Have you many such hands as this ? What are you going to do with them ? Keep them at puddling iron ? "

Kirby shrugged his shoulders. Mitchell's look had irritated him.

" *Ce n'est pas mon affaire.* I have no fancy for nursing infant geniuses. I suppose there are some stray gleams of mind and soul among these wretches. The Lord will take care of his own ; or else they can work out their own salvation. I have heard you call our American system a ladder which any man can scale. Do you doubt it ? Or perhaps you want to banish all social ladders, and put us all on a flat table-land, — eh, May ? "

The Doctor looked vexed, puzzled. Some terrible problem lay hid in this woman's face, and troubled these men. Kirby waited for an answer, and, receiving none, went on, warming with his subject.

"I tell you, there's something wrong that no talk of 'Liberté' or 'Egalité' will do away. If I had the making of men, these men who do the lowest part of the world's work should be machines, — nothing more, — hands. It would be kindness. God help them! What are taste, reason, to creatures who must live such lives as that?" He pointed to Deborah, sleeping on the ash-heap. "So many nerves to sting them to pain. What if God had put your brain, with all its agony of touch, into your fingers, and bid you work and strike with that?"

"You think you could govern the world better?" laughed the Doctor.

"I do not think at all."

"That is true philosophy. Drift with the stream, because you cannot dive deep enough to find bottom, eh?"

"Exactly," rejoined Kirby. "I do not think. I wash my hands of all social problems, — slavery, caste, white or black. My duty to my operatives has a narrow limit, — the pay-hour on Saturday night. Outside of that, if they cut korl, or cut each other's throats, (the more popular amusement of the two,) I am not responsible."

The Doctor sighed, — a good honest sigh, from the depths of his stomach.

"God help us! Who is responsible?"

"Not I, I tell you," said Kirby, testily. "What has the man who pays them money to do with their souls' concerns, more than the grocer or butcher who takes it?"

"And yet," said Mitchell's cynical voice, "look at her! How hungry she is!"

Kirby tapped his boot with his cane. No one spoke. Only the dumb face of the rough image looking into their faces with the awful question, "What shall we do to be saved?" Only Wolfe's face, with its heavy weight of brain, its weak, uncertain mouth, its desperate eyes, out of which looked the soul of his class, — only Wolfe's face turned towards Kirby's. Mitchell laughed, — a cool, musical laugh.

"Money has spoken!" he said, seating himself lightly on

a stone with the air of an amused spectator at a play. "Are you answered?"— turning to Wolfe his clear, magnetic face.

Bright and deep and cold as Arctic air, the soul of the man lay tranquil beneath. He looked at the furnace-tender as he had looked at a rare mosaic in the morning ; only the man was the more amusing study of the two.

"Are you answered? Why, May, look at him ! '*De pro-fundis clamavi.*' Or, to quote in English, 'Hungry and thirsty, his soul faints in him.' And so Money sends back its answer into the depths through you, Kirby ! Very clear the answer, too !— I think I remember reading the same words somewhere : — washing your hands in Eau de Cologne, and saying, 'I am innocent of the blood of this man. See ye to it !'"

Kirby flushed angrily.

"You quote Scripture freely."

"Do I not quote correctly? I think I remember another line, which may amend my meaning : 'Inasmuch as ye did it unto one of the least of these, ye did it unto me.' Deist? Bless you, man, I was raised on the milk of the Word. Now, Doctor, the pocket of the world having uttered its voice, what has the heart to say ? You are a philanthropist, in a small way, — *n'est ce pas?* Here, boy, this gentleman can show you how to cut korl better, — or your destiny. Go on, May !"

"I think a mocking devil possesses you to-night," rejoined the Doctor, seriously.

He went to Wolfe and put his hand kindly on his arm. Something of a vague idea possessed the Doctor's brain that much good was to be done here by a friendly word or two : a latent genius to be warmed into life by a waited-for sunbeam. Here it was : he had brought it. So he went on complacently : —

"Do you know, boy, you have it in you to be a great sculptor, a great man?— do you understand?" (talking down to the capacity of his hearer : it is a way people have with children, and men like Wolfe,) — "to live a better, stronger life than I, or Mr. Kirby here? A man may make himself anything he chooses. God has given you stronger powers than many men, — me, for instance."

May stopped, heated, glowing with his own magnanimity. And it was magnanimous. The puddler had drunk in every word, looking through the Doctor's flurry, and generous heat, and self-approval, into his will, with those slow, absorbing eyes of his.

"Make yourself what you will. It is your right."

"I know," quietly. "Will you help me?"

Mitchell laughed again. The Doctor turned now, in a passion, —

"You know, Mitchell, I have not the means. You know, if I had, it is in my heart to take this boy and educate him for —"

"The glory of God, and the glory of John May."

May did not speak for a moment; then, controlled, he said, —

"Why should one be raised, when myriads are left? — I have not the money, boy," to Wolfe, shortly.

"Money?" He said it over slowly, as one repeats the guessed answer to a riddle, doubtfully. "That is it? Money?"

"Yes, money, — that is it," said Mitchell, rising, and drawing his furred coat about him. "You 've found the cure for all the world's diseases. — Come, May, find your good-humor, and come home. This damp wind chills my very bones. Come and preach your Saint-Simonian doctrines to-morrow to Kirby's hands. Let them have a clear idea of the rights of the soul, and I 'll venture next week they 'll strike for higher wages. That will be the end of it."

"Will you send the coach-driver to this side of the mills?" asked Kirby, turning to Wolfe.

He spoke kindly: it was his habit to do so. Deborah, seeing the puddler go, crept after him. The three men waited outside. Doctor May walked up and down, chafed. Suddenly he stopped.

"Go back, Mitchell! You say the pocket and the heart of the world speak without meaning to these people. What has its head to say? Taste, culture, refinement? Go!"

Mitchell was leaning against a brick wall. He turned his head indolently, and looked into the mills. There hung about the place a thick, unclean odor. The slightest motion of his hand marked that he perceived it, and his insufferable disgust. That was all. May said nothing, only quickened his angry tramp.

"Besides," added Mitchell, giving a corollary to his answer, "it would be of no use. I am not one of them."

"You do not mean"—said May, facing him.

"Yes, I mean just that. Reform is born of need, not pity. No vital movement of the people's has worked down, for good or evil; fermented, instead, carried up the heaving, cloggy mass. Think back through history, and you will know it. What will this lowest deep — thieves, Magdalens, negroes — do with the light filtered through ponderous Church creeds, Baconian theories, Goethe schemes? Some day, out of their bitter need will be thrown up their own light-bringer, — their Jean Paul, their Cromwell, their Messiah."

"Bah!" was the Doctor's inward criticism. However, in practice, he adopted the theory; for, when, night and morning, afterwards, he prayed that power might be given these degraded souls to rise, he glowed at heart, recognizing an accomplished duty.

Wolfe and the woman had stood in the shadow of the works as the coach drove off. The Doctor had held out his hand in a frank, generous way, telling him to "take care of himself, and to remember it was his right to rise." Mitchell had simply touched his hat, as to an equal, with a quiet look of thorough recognition. Kirby had thrown Deborah some money, which she found, and clutched eagerly enough. They were gone now, all of them. The man sat down on the cinder-road, looking up into the murky sky.

"'T be late, Hugh. Wunnot hur come?"

He shook his head doggedly, and the woman crouched out of his sight against the wall. Do you remember rare moments when a sudden light flashed over yourself, your world, God? when you stood on a mountain-peak, seeing your life as it might have been, as it is? one quick instant, when custom lost its force and every-day usage? when your friend, wife, brother, stood in a new light? your soul was bared, and the grave, — a foretaste of the nakedness of the Judgment-Day? So it came before him, his life, that night. The slow tides of pain he had borne gathered themselves up and surged against his soul. His squalid daily life, the brutal coarseness eating into his brain, as the ashes into his skin: before, these things had been a dull aching into his consciousness; to-night, they were reality. He griped the filthy red shirt that clung, stiff with soot, about him, and tore it savagely from his arm. The flesh beneath was muddy with grease and ashes, — and the heart beneath that ! And the soul? God knows.

Then flashed before his vivid poetic sense the man who had left him, — the pure face, the delicate, sinewy limbs, in harmony with all he knew of beauty or truth. In his cloudy fancy he had pictured a Something like this. He had found it in this Mitchell, even when he idly scoffed at his pain: a Man all-knowing, all-seeing, crowned by Nature, reigning, — the keen glance of his eye falling like a sceptre on other men. And yet his instinct taught him that he too — He ! He looked at himself with sudden loathing, sick, wrung his hands with a cry, and then was silent. With all the phantoms of his heated, ignorant fancy, Wolfe had not been vague in his ambitions. They were practical, slowly built up before him out of his knowledge of what he could do. Through years he had day by day made this hope a real thing to himself, — a clear, projected figure of himself, as he might become.

Able to speak, to know what was best, to raise these men and women working at his side up with him: sometimes he forgot this defined hope in the frantic anguish to escape, —

only to escape, — out of the wet, the pain, the ashes, somewhere, anywhere, — only for one moment of free air on a hillside, to lie down and let his sick soul throb itself out in the sunshine. But to-night he panted for life. The savage strength of his nature was roused ; his cry was fierce to God for justice.

"Look at me !" he said to Deborah, with a low, 'bitter laugh, striking his puny chest savagely. "What am I worth, Deb ? Is it my fault that I am no better ? My fault ? My fault ?"

He stopped, stung with a sudden remorse, seeing her hunchback shape writhing with sobs. For Deborah was crying thankless tears, according to the fashion of women.

"God forgi' me, woman ! Things go harder wi' you nor me. It's a worse share."

He got up and helped her to rise ; and they went doggedly down the muddy street, side by side.

"It's all wrong," he muttered, slowly, — "all wrong ! I dunnot understan'. But it 'll end some day."

"Come home, Hugh !" she said, coaxingly ; for he had stopped, looking around bewildered.

"Home, — and back to the mill !" He went on saying this over to himself, as if he would mutter down every pain in this dull despair.

She followed him through the fog, her blue lips chattering with cold. They reached the cellar at last. Old Wolfe had been drinking since she went out, and had crept nearer the door. The girl Janey slept heavily in the corner. He went up to her, touching softly the worn white arm with his fingers. Some bitterer thought stung him, as he stood there. He wiped the drops from his forehead, and went into the room beyond, livid, trembling. A hope, trifling, perhaps, but very dear, had died just then out of the poor puddler's life, as he looked at the sleeping, innocent girl, — some plan for the future, in which she had borne a part. He gave it up that moment, then and forever. Only a trifle, perhaps, to us : his face grew a shade paler, — that was all. But,

4

somehow, the man's soul, as God and the angels looked
down on it, never was the same afterwards.

Deborah followed him into the inner room. She carried
a candle, which she placed on the floor, closing the door
after her. She had seen the look on his face, as he turned
away ; her own grew deadly. Yet, as she came up to him,
her eyes glowed. He was seated on an old chest, quiet,
holding his face in his hands.

"Hugh ! " she said, softly.

He did not speak.

"Hugh, did hur hear what the man said, — him with the
clear voice ? Did hur hear ? Money, money, — that it wud
do all ? "

He pushed her away, — gently, but he was worn out ; her
rasping tone fretted him.

" Hugh ! "

The candle flared a pale yellow light over the cobwebbed
brick walls, and the woman standing there. He looked at
her. She was young, in deadly earnest ; her faded eyes,
and wet, ragged figure caught from their frantic eagerness a
power akin to beauty.

"Hugh, it is true ! Money ull do it ! Oh, Hugh, boy,
listen till me ! He said it true ! It is money ! "

" I know. Go back ! I do not want you here."

" Hugh, it is t' last time. I 'll never worrit hur again."

There were tears in her voice now, but she choked them
back.

" Hear till me only to-night ! If one of t' witch people
wud come, them we heard of t' home, and gif hur all hur
wants, what then ? Say, Hugh ! "

" What do you mean ? "

" I mean money."

Her whisper shrilled through his brain.

" If one of t' witch dwarfs wud come from t' lane moors
to-night, and gif hur money, to go out, — *out*, I say, — out,
lad, where t' sun shines, and t' heath grows, and t' ladies
walk in silken gownds, and God stays all t' time, — where t'

man lives that talked to us to-night, — Hugh knows, — Hugh could walk there like a king!"

He thought the woman mad, tried to check her, but she went on, fierce in her eager haste.

"If *I* were t' witch dwarf, if I had t' money, wud hur thank me? Wud hur take me out o' this place wid hur and Janey? I wud not come into the gran' house hur wud build, to vex hur wid t' hunch, — only at night, when t' shadows were dark, stand far off to see hur."

"Poor Deb! poor Deb!" he said, soothingly.

"It is here," she said, suddenly jerking into his hand a small roll. "I took it! I did it! I shall be hanged! I shall be burnt in hell, if anybody knows I took it! Me, me! not hur! Out of his pocket, as he leaned against t' bricks. Hur knows?"

She thrust it into his hand, and then, her errand done, began to gather chips together to make a fire, choking down hysteric sobs.

"Has it come to this?"

That was all he said. The Welsh Wolfe blood was honest. The roll was a small green pocket-book containing one or two gold pieces, and a check for an incredible amount, as it seemed to the poor puddler. He laid it down, hiding his face again in his hands.

"Hugh, don't be angry wud me! It's only poor Deb, — hur knows?"

He took the long skinny fingers kindly in his.

"Angry? God help me, no! Let me sleep. I am tired."

He threw himself heavily down on the wooden bench, stunned with pain and weariness. She brought some old rags to cover him.

It was late on Sunday evening before he awoke. I tell God's truth, when I say he had then no thought of keeping this money. Deborah had hid it in his pocket. He found it there. She watched him eagerly, as he took it out.

"I must gif it to him," he said, reading her face.

"Hur knows," she said with a bitter sigh of disappointment.   "But it is hur right to keep it."

His right !   The word struck him.   Doctor May had used
the same.   He washed himself, and went out to find this
man Mitchell.   His right !   Why did this chance word
cling to him so obstinately ?   Do you hear the fierce devils
whisper in his ear, as he went slowly down the darkening
street ?

The evening came on, slow and calm.   He seated himself at the end of an alley leading into one of the larger
streets.   His brain was clear to-night, keen, intent, master-
ing.   It would not start back, cowardly, from any hellish
temptation, but meet it face to face.   Therefore the great
temptation of his life came to him veiled by no sophistry,
but bold, defiant, owning its own vile name, trusting to one
bold blow for victory.

He did not deceive himself.   Theft !   That was it.   At
first the word sickened him ; then he grappled with it.
Sitting there on a broken cart-wheel, the fading day, the
noisy groups, the church-bells' tolling passed before him
like a panorama, while the sharp struggle went on within.
This money !   He took it out, and looked at it.   If he gave
it back, what then ?   He was going to be cool about it.

People going by to church saw only a sickly mill-boy
watching them quietly at the alley's mouth.   They did not
know that he was mad, or they would not have gone by so
quietly : mad with hunger ; stretching out his hands to the
world, that had given so much to them, for leave to live
the life God meant him to live.   His soul within him was
smothering to death ; he wanted so much, thought so much,
and *knew* — nothing.   There was nothing of which he was
certain, except the mill and things there.   Of God and
heaven he had heard so little, that they were to him what
fairy-land is to a child : something real, but not here ; very
far off.   His brain, greedy, dwarfed, full of thwarted energy
and unused powers, questioned these men and women going
by, coldly, bitterly, that night.   Was it not his right to live

as they, — a pure life, a good, true-hearted life, full of beauty and kind words ? He only wanted to know how to use the strength within him. His heart warmed, as he thought of it. He suffered himself to think of it longer. If he took the money?

Then he saw himself as he might be, strong, helpful, kindly. The night crept on, as this one image slowly evolved itself from the crowd of other thoughts and stood triumphant. He looked at it. As he might be ! What wonder, if it blinded him to delirium, — the madness that underlies all revolution, all progress, and all fall ?

You laugh at the shallow temptation ? You see the error underlying its argument so clearly, — that to him a true life was one of full development rather than self-restraint ? that he was deaf to the higher tone in a cry of voluntary suffering for truth's sake than in the fullest flow of spontaneous harmony ? I do not plead his cause. I only want to show you the mote in my brother's eye : then you can see clearly to take it out.

The money, — there it lay on his knee, a little blotted slip of paper, nothing in itself ; used to raise him out of the pit ; something straight from God's hand. A thief ! Well, what was it to be a thief ? He met the question at last face to face, wiping the clammy drops of sweat from his forehead. God made this money — the fresh air, too — for his children's use. He never made the difference between poor and rich. The Something who looked down on him that moment through the cool gray sky had a kindly face, he knew, — loved his children alike. Oh, he knew that !

There were times when the soft floods of color in the crimson and purple flames, or the clear depth of amber in the water below the bridge, had somehow given him a glimpse of another world than this, — of an infinite depth of beauty and of quiet somewhere, — somewhere, — a depth of quiet and rest and love. Looking up now, it became strangely real. The sun had sunk quite below the hills, but his last rays struck upward, touching the zenith. The fog had risen, and the town and river were steeped in its thick, gray damp ; but overhead, the sun-touched smoke-clouds opened like a cleft ocean, — shifting, rolling seas of crimson mist, waves of billowy silver veined with blood-scarlet, inner depths unfathomable of glancing light. Wolfe's artist-eye grew drunk with color. The gates of that other world ! Fading, flashing before him now ! What, in that world of Beauty, Content, and Right, were the petty laws, the mine and thine, of mill-owners and mill-hands ?

A consciousness of power stirred within him. He stood up. A man, — he thought, stretching out his hands, — free to work, to live, to love ! Free ! His right ! He folded the scrap of paper in his hand. As his nervous fingers took it in, limp and blotted, so his soul took in the mean temptation, lapped it in fancied rights, in dreams of improved existences, drifting and endless as the cloud-seas of color. Clutching it, as if the tightness of his hold would strengthen his sense of possession, he went aimlessly down the street. It was his watch at the mill. He need not go, need never go again, thank God ! — shaking off the thought with unspeakable loathing.

Shall I go over the history of the hours of that night ? how the man wandered from one to another of his old haunts, with a half-consciousness of bidding them farewell, —lanes and alleys and back-yards where the mill-hands lodged, — noting, with a new eagerness, the filth and drunkenness, the pig-pens, the ash-heaps covered with potatoskins, the bloated, pimpled women at the doors, — with a new disgust, a new sense of sudden triumph, and, under all, a new, vague dread, unknown before, smothered down, kept under, but still there ? It left him but once during the night, when, for the second time in his life, he entered a church. It was a sombre Gothic pile, where the stained light lost itself in far-retreating arches ; built to meet the requirements and sympathies of a far other class than Wolfe's. Yet it touched, moved him uncontrollably. The distances, the shadows, the still, marble figures, the mass of silent, kneeling worshippers, the mysterious music, thrilled, lifted his soul with a wonderful pain. Wolfe forgot himself, forgot the new life he was going to live, the mean terror gnawing underneath. The voice of the speaker strengthened the charm ; it was clear, feeling, full, strong. An old man, who had lived much, suffered much ; whose brain was keenly alive, dominant ; whose heart was summer-warm with charity. He taught it to-night. He held up Humanity in its grand total ; showed the great world-cancer to his people. Who could show it better ? He was a Christian reformer ; he had studied the age thoroughly ; his outlook at man had been free, world-wide, over all time. His faith stood sublime upon the Rock of Ages ; his fiery zeal guided vast schemes by which the Gospel was to be preached to all nations. How did he preach it to-night ? In burning, light-laden words he painted Jesus, the incarnate Life, Love, the universal Man : words that became reality in the lives of these people, — that lived again in beautiful words and actions, trifling, but heroic. Sin, as he defined it, was a real foe to them ; their trials, temptations, were his. His words passed far over the furnace-tender's grasp, toned to suit another class of culture ; they sounded in his ears a very pleasant song in an unknown tongue. He meant to cure this world-cancer with a steady eye that had never glared with hunger, and a hand that neither poverty nor strychnine-whiskey had taught to shake. In this morbid, distorted heart of the Welsh puddler he had failed.

Eighteen centuries ago, the Master of this man tried reform in the streets of a city as crowded and vile as this, and did not fail. His disciple, showing Him to-night to cultured hearers, showing the clearness of the God-power acting through Him, shrank back from one coarse fact ; that in birth and habit the man Christ was thrown up from the lowest of the people : his flesh, their flesh ; their blood, his blood ; tempted like them, to brutalize day by day ; to lie, to steal : the actual slime and want of their hourly life, and the wine-press he trod alone.

Yet, is there no meaning in this perpetually covered truth ? If the son of the carpenter had stood in the church that night, as he stood with the fishermen and harlots by the sea of Galilee, before His Father and their Father, despised and rejected of men, without a place to lay His head, wounded for their iniquities, bruised for their transgressions, would not that hungry mill-boy at least, in the back seat, have "known the man"? That Jesus did not stand there.

Wolfe rose at last, and turned from the church down the street. He looked up ; the night had come on foggy, damp ; the golden mists had vanished, and the sky lay dull and ash-colored. He wandered again aimlessly down the street, idly wondering what had become of the cloud-sea of crimson and scarlet. The trial-day of this man's life was over, and he had lost the victory. What followed was mere drifting circumstance, — a quicker walking over the path, — that was all. Do you want to hear the end of it ? You wish me to make a tragic story out of it ? Why, in the police-reports of the morning paper you can find a dozen such tragedies ; hints of shipwrecks unlike any that ever befell on the high seas ; hints that here a power was lost to heaven, — that there a soul went down where no tide can ebb or flow. Commonplace enough the hints are, — jocose sometimes, done up in rhyme.

Doctor May, a month after the night I have told you of, was reading to his wife at breakfast from this fourth column of the morning-paper : an unusual thing, — these police-reports not being, in general, choice reading for ladies ; but it was only one item he read.

"Oh, my dear ! You remember that man I told you of, that we saw at Kirby's mill ?—that was arrested for robbing Mitchell? Here he is ; just listen : — 'Circuit Court. Judge Day. Hugh Wolfe, operative in Kirby & John's Loudon Mills. Charge, grand larceny. Sentence, nineteen years hard labor in penitentiary.' — Scoundrel ! Serves him right ! After all our kindness that night ! Picking Mitchell's pocket at the very time !"

His wife said something about the ingratitude of that kind of people, and then they began to talk of something else.

Nineteen years! How easy that was to read! What a simple word for Judge Day to utter! Nineteen years! Half a lifetime!

Hugh Wolfe sat on the window-ledge of his cell, looking out. His ankles were ironed. Not usual in such cases; but he had made two desperate efforts to escape. "Well," as Haley, the jailer, said, "small blame to him! Nineteen years' imprisonment was not a pleasant thing to look forward to." Haley was very good-natured about it, though Wolfe had fought him savagely.

"When he was first caught," the jailer said afterwards, in telling the story, "before the trial, the fellow was cut down at once, — laid there on that pallet like a dead man, with his hands over his eyes. Never saw a man so cut down in my life. Time of the trial, too, came the queerest dodge of any customer I ever had. Would choose no lawyer. Judge gave him one, of course. Gibson it was. He tried to prove the fellow crazy; but it would n't go. Thing was plain as daylight: check found on him. 'T was a hard sentence, — all the law allows; but it was for 'xample's sake. These mill-hands are gettin' onbearable. When the sentence was read, he just looked up, and said the money was his by rights, and that all the world had gone wrong. That night, after the trial, a gentleman came to see him here, name of Mitchell, — him as he stole from. Talked to him for an hour. Thought he came for curiosity, like. After he was gone, thought Wolfe was remarkable quiet, and went into his cell. Found him very low; bed all bloody. Doctor said he had been bleeding at the lungs. He was as weak as a cat; yet, if ye 'll b'lieve me, he tried to get a-past me and get out. I just carried him like a baby, and threw him on the pallet. Three days after, he tried it again: that time reached the wall. Lord help you! he fought like a tiger, — giv' some terrible blows. Fightin' for life, you see;

4 *   F

for he can't live long, shut up in the stone crib down yonder.   Got a death-cough now.   'T took two of us to bring
him down that day ; so I just put the irons on his feet.
There he sits, in there.   Goin' to-morrow, with a batch
more of 'em.   That woman, hunchback, tried with him, —
you remember ? — she 's only got three years.   'Complice.
But *she 's* a woman, you know.   He 's been quiet ever since
I put on irons : giv' up, I suppose.   Looks white, sick-
lookin'.   It acts different on 'em, bein' sentenced.   Most of
'em gets reckless, devilish-like.   Some prays awful, and
sings them vile songs of the mills, all in a breath.   That
woman, now, she 's desper't'.   Been beggin' to see Hugh,
as she calls him, for three days.   I 'm a-goin' to let her in.
She don't go with him.   Here she is in this next cell.   I 'm
a-goin' now to let her in."

He let her in.   Wolfe did not see her.   She crept into a
corner of the cell, and stood watching him.   He was scratch-
ing the iron bars of the window with a piece of tin which he
had picked up, with an idle, uncertain, vacant stare, just as
a child or idiot would do.

" Tryin' to get out, old boy ?" laughed Haley.   " Them
irons will need a crowbar beside your tin, before you can
open 'em."

Wolfe laughed, too, in a senseless way.

" I think I 'll get out," he said.

" I believe his brain 's touched," said Haley, when he
came out.

The puddler scraped away with the tin for half an hour.
Still Deborah did not speak.   At last she ventured nearer,
and touched his arm.

" Blood ?" she said, looking at some spots on his coat
with a shudder.

He looked up at her.   " Why, Deb !" he said, smiling, —
such a bright, boyish smile, that it went to poor Deborah's
heart directly, and she sobbed and cried out loud.

" Oh, Hugh, lad ! Hugh ! dunnot look at me, when it wur
my fault !   To think I brought hur to it !   And I loved hur
so !   Oh, lad, I dud !"

The confession, even in this wretch, came with the woman's blush through the sharp cry.

He did not seem to hear her, — scraping away diligently at the bars with the bit of tin.

Was he going mad? She peered closely into his face. Something she saw there made her draw suddenly back, — something which Haley had not seen, that lay beneath the pinched, vacant look it had caught since the trial, or the curious gray shadow that rested on it. That gray shadow, — yes, she knew what that meant. She had often seen it creeping over women's faces for months, who died at last of slow hunger or consumption. That meant death, distant, lingering: but this — Whatever it was the woman saw, or thought she saw, used as she was to crime and misery, seemed to make her sick with a new horror. Forgetting her fear of him, she caught his shoulders, and looked keenly, steadily, into his eyes.

"Hugh!" she cried, in a desperate whisper, — "oh, boy, not that! for God's sake, not *that!*"

The vacant laugh went off his face, and he answered her in a muttered word or two that drove her away. Yet the words were kindly enough. Sitting there on his pallet, she cried silently a hopeless sort of tears, but did not speak again. The man looked up furtively at her now and then. Whatever his own trouble was, her distress vexed him with a momentary sting.

It was market-day. The narrow window of the jail looked down directly on the carts and wagons drawn up in a long line, where they had unloaded. He could see, too, and hear distinctly the clink of money as it changed hands, the busy crowd of whites and blacks shoving, pushing one another, and the chaffering and swearing at the stalls. Somehow, the sound, more than anything else had done, wakened him up, — made the whole real to him. He was done with the world and the business of it. He let the tin fall, and looked out, pressing his face close to the rusty bars. How they crowded and pushed! And he, — he should

never walk that pavement again ! There came Neff San-
ders, one of the feeders at the mill, with a basket on his
arm.   Sure enough, Neff was married the other week.   He
whistled, hoping he would look up ; but he did not.   He
wondered if Neff remembered he was there, — if any of the
boys thought of him up there, and thought that he never
was to go down that old cinder-road again.   Never again !
He had not quite understood it before ; but now he did.
Not for days or years, but never ! — that was it.

How clear the light fell on that stall in front of the market ! and how like a picture it was, the dark-green heaps of
corn, and the crimson beets, and golden melons !   There
was another with game : how the light flickered on that
pheasant's breast, with the purplish blood dripping over the
brown feathers !   He could see the red shining of the drops,
it was so near.   In one minute he could be down there.   It
was just a step.   So easy, as it seemed, so natural to go !
Yet it could never be — not in all the thousands of years to
come — that he should put his foot on that street again !
He thought of himself with a sorrowful pity, as of some one
else.   There was a dog down in the market, walking after
his master with such a stately, grave look ! — only a dog,
yet he could go backwards and forwards just as he pleased :
he had good luck !   Why, the very vilest cur, yelping there
in the gutter, had not lived his life, had been free to act out
whatever thought God had put into his brain ; while he —
No, he would not think of that !   He tried to put the thought
away, and to listen to a dispute between a countryman and
a woman about some meat ; but it would come back.   He,
what had he done to bear this ?

Then came the sudden picture of what might have been,
and now.   He knew what it was to be in the penitentiary,
— how it went with men there.   He knew how in these long
years he should slowly die, but not until soul and body had
become corrupt and rotten, — how, when he came out, if he
lived to come, even the lowest of the mill-hands would jeer
him, — how his hands would be weak, and his brain sense-

less and stupid. He believed he was almost that now. He put his hand to his head, with a puzzled, weary look. It ached, his head, with thinking. He tried to quiet himself. It was only right, perhaps ; he had done wrong. But was there right or wrong for such as he ? What was right? And who had ever taught him ? He thrust the whole matter away. A dark, cold quiet crept through his brain. It was all wrong ; but let it be ! It was nothing to him more than the others. Let it be !

The door grated, as Haley opened it.

"Come, my woman ! Must lock up for t' night. Come, stir yerself ! "

She went up and took Hugh's hand.

"Good-night, Deb," he said, carelessly.

She had not hoped he would say more ; but the tired pain on her mouth just then was bitterer than death. She took his passive hand and kissed it.

"Hur 'll never see Deb again ! " she ventured, her lips growing colder and more bloodless.

What did she say that for ? Did he not know it ? Yet he would not be impatient with poor old Deb. She had trouble of her own, as well as he.

"No, never again," he said, trying to be cheerful.

She stood just a moment, looking at him. Do you laugh at her, standing there, with her hunchback, her rags, her bleared, withered face, and the great despised love tugging at her heart ?

"Come you ! " called Haley, impatiently.

She did not move.

"Hugh ! " she whispered.

It was to be her last word. What was it ?

"Hugh, boy, not THAT ! "

He did not answer. She wrung her hands, trying to be silent, looking in his face in an agony of entreaty. He smiled again, kindly.

"It is best, Deb. I cannot bear to be hurted any more."

"Hur knows," she said, humbly.

"Tell my father good-by ; and — and kiss little Janey." ¹
She nodded, saying nothing, looked in his face again, and
went out of the door. As she went, she staggered.

"Drinkin' to-day ?" broke out Haley, pushing her before
him. "Where the Devil did you get it ? Here, in with
ye !" and he shoved her into her cell, next to Wolfe's, and
shut the door.

Along the wall of her cell there was a crack low down by
the floor, through which she could see the light from
Wolfe's. She had discovered it days before. She hurried
in now, and, kneeling down by it, listened, hoping to hear
some sound. Nothing but the rasping of the tin on the
bars. He was at his old amusement again. Something in
the noise jarred on her ear, for she shivered as she heard it.
Hugh rasped away at the bars. A dull old bit of tin, not
fit to cut korl with.

He looked out of the window again. People were leaving
the market now. A tall mulatto girl, following her mistress,
her basket on her head, crossed the street just below, and
looked up. She was laughing ; but, when she caught sight
of the haggard face peering out through the bars, suddenly
grew grave, and hurried by. A free, firm step, a clear-cut
olive face, with a scarlet turban tied on one side, dark,
shining eyes, and on the head the basket poised, filled with
fruit and flowers, under which the scarlet turban and bright
eyes looked out half-shadowed. The picture caught his eye.
It was good to see a face like that. He would try to-morrow, and cut one like it. *To-morrow !* He threw down the
tin, trembling, and covered his face with his hands. When
he looked up again, the daylight was gone.

Deborah, crouching near by on the other side of the
wall, heard no noise. He sat on the side of the low pallet,
thinking. Whatever was the mystery which the woman had
seen on his face, it came out now slowly, in the dark there,
and became fixed, — a something never seen on his face before. The evening was darkening fast. The market had
been over for an hour ; the rumbling of the carts over the

pavement grew more infrequent : he listened to each, as it passed, because he thought it was to be for the last time. For the same reason, it was, I suppose, that he strained his eyes to catch a glimpse of each passer-by, wondering who they were, what kind of homes they were going to, if they had children, — listening eagerly to every chance word in the street, as if — (God be merciful to the man ! what strange fancy was this ?) — as if he never should hear human voices again.

It was quite dark at last. The street was a lonely one. The last passenger, he thought, was gone. No, — there was a quick step : Joe Hill, lighting the lamps. Joe was a good old chap ; never passed a fellow without some joke or other. He remembered once seeing the place where he lived with his wife. " Granny Hill " the boys called her. Bedridden she was ; but so kind as Joe was to her ! kept the room so clean ! — and the old woman, when he was there, was laughing at " some of t' lad's foolishness." The step was far down the street ; but he could see him place the ladder, run up, and light the gas. A longing seized him to be spoken to once more.

" Joe ! " he called out of the grating. " Good-by, Joe ! "

The old man stopped a moment, listening uncertainly ; then hurried on. The prisoner thrust his hand out of the window, and called again, louder ; but Joe was too far down the street. It was a little thing ; but it hurt him, — this disappointment.

" Good-by, Joe ! " he called, sorrowfully enough.

" Be quiet ! " said one of the jailers, passing the door, striking on it with his club.

Oh, that was the last, was it ?

There was an inexpressible bitterness on his face, as he lay down on the bed, taking the bit of tin, which he had rasped to a tolerable degree of sharpness, in his hand, — to play with, it may be. He bared his arms, looking intently at their corded veins and sinews. Deborah, listening in the next cell, heard a slight clicking sound, often repeated. She shut her lips tightly, that she might not scream ; the cold drops of sweat broke over her, in her dumb agony.

"Hur knows best," she muttered at last, fiercely clutching the boards where she lay.

If she could have seen Wolfe, there was nothing about him to frighten her. He lay quite still, his arms out-stretched, looking at the pearly stream of moonlight coming `into the window. I think in that one hour that came then he lived back over all the years that had gone before. I think that all the low, vile life, all his wrongs, all his starved hopes, came then, and stung him with a farewell poison that made him sick unto death. He made neither moan nor cry, only turned his worn face now and then to the pure light, that seemed so far off, as one that said, "How long, O Lord ? how long ? "

The hour was over at last. The moon, passing over her nightly path, slowly came nearer, and threw the light across his bed on his feet. He watched it steadily, as it crept up, inch by inch, slowly. It seemed to him to carry with it a great silence. He had been so hot and tired there always in the mills ! The years had been so fierce and cruel ! There was coming now quiet and coolness and sleep. His tense limbs relaxed, and settled in a calm languor. The blood ran fainter and slow from his heart. He did not think now with a savage anger of what might be and was not ; he was conscious only of deep stillness creeping over him. At first he saw a sea of faces : the mill-men, — women he had known, drunken and bloated, — Janey's timid and pitiful, — poor old Debs : then they floated together like a mist, and faded away, leaving only the clear, pearly moon-light.

Whether, as the pure light crept up the stretched-out figure, it brought with it calm and peace, who shall say ? His dumb soul was alone with God in judgment. A Voice may have spoken for it from far-off Calvary, "Father, for-give them, for they know not what they do ! " Who dare say ? Fainter and fainter the heart rose and fell, slower and slower the moon floated from behind a cloud, until, when at last its full tide of white splendor swept over the cell, it seemed to wrap and fold into a deeper stillness the dead figure that never should move again. Silence deeper than the Night ! Nothing that moved, save the black, nauseous stream of blood dripping slowly from the pallet to the floor !

There was outcry and crowd enough in the cell the next day. The coroner and his jury, the local editors, Kirby himself, and boys with their hands thrust knowingly into their pockets and heads on one side, jammed into the corners. Coming and going all day. Only one woman. She came late, and outstayed them all. A Quaker, or Friend, as they call themselves. I think this woman was known by that name in heaven. A homely body, coarsely dressed in gray and white. Deborah (for Haley had let her in) took notice of her. She watched them all — sitting on the end of the pallet, holding his head in her arms — with the ferocity of a watch-dog, if any of them touched the body. There was no meekness, no sorrow, in her face ; the stuff out of which murderers are made, instead. All the time Haley and the woman were laying straight the limbs and cleaning the cell, Deborah sat still, keenly watching the Quaker's face. Of all the crowd there that day, this woman alone had not spoken to her, — only once or twice had put some cordial to her lips. After they all were gone, the woman, in the same still, gentle way, brought a vase of wood-leaves and berries, and placed it by the pallet, then opened the narrow window. The fresh air blew in, and swept the woody fragrance over the dead face. Deborah looked up with a quick wonder.

"Did hur know my boy wud like it ? Did hur know Hugh ?"

"I know Hugh now."

The white fingers passed in a slow, pitiful way over the dead, worn face. There was a heavy shadow in the quiet eyes.

" Did hur know where they'll bury Hugh ? " said Deborah in a shrill tone, catching her arm.

This had been the question hanging on her lips all day.

" In t' town-yard ? Under t' mud and ash ? T' lad 'll smother, woman ! He wur born on t' lane moor, where t' air is frick and strong. Take hur out, for God's sake, take hur out where t' air blows ! "

The Quaker hesitated, but only for a moment. She put her strong arm around Deborah and led her to the window.

" Thee sees the hills, friend, over the river ? Thee sees how the light lies warm there, and the winds of God blow all the day ? I live there, — where the blue smoke is, by the trees. Look at me." She turned Deborah's face to her own, clear and earnest. " Thee will believe me ? I will take Hugh and bury him there to-morrow."

Deborah did not doubt her. As the evening wore on, she leaned against the iron bars, looking at the hills that rose far off, through the thick sodden clouds, like a bright, unattainable calm. As she looked, a shadow of their solemn repose fell on her face : its fierce discontent faded into a pitiful, humble quiet. Slow, solemn tears gathered in her eyes : the poor weak eyes turned so hopelessly to the place where Hugh was to rest, the grave heights looking higher and brighter and more solemn than ever before. The Quaker watched her keenly. She came to her at last, and touched her arm.

" When thee comes back," she said, in a low, sorrowful tone, like one who speaks from a strong heart deeply moved with remorse or pity, " thee shall begin thy life again, — there on the hills. I came too late ; but not for thee, — by God's help, it may be."

Not too late. Three years after, the Quaker began her work. I end my story here. At evening-time it was light. There is no need to tire you with the long years of sunshine, and fresh air, and slow, patient Christ-love, needed to make healthy and hopeful this impure body and soul. There is a homely pine house, on one of these hills, whose windows overlook broad, wooded slopes and clover-crimsoned meadows, — niched into the very place where the light is warmest, the air freest. It is the Friends'. meeting-house. Once a week they sit there, in their grave, earnest way, waiting for the Spirit of Love to speak, opening their simple hearts to receive His words. There is a woman, old, deformed, who takes a humble place among them: waiting like them: in her gray dress, her worn face, pure and meek, turned now and then to the sky. A woman much loved by these silent, restful people; more silent than they, more humble, more loving. Waiting: with her eyes turned to hills higher and purer than these on which she lives, — dim and far off now, but to be reached some day. There may be in her heart some latent hope to meet there the love denied her here, — that she shall find him whom she lost, and that then she will not be all-unworthy. Who blames her? Something is lost in the passage of every soul from one eternity to the other, — something pure and beautiful, which might have been and was not: a hope, a talent, a love, over which the soul mourns, like Esau deprived of his birthright. What blame to the meek Quaker, if she took her lost hope to make the hills of heaven more fair?

Nothing remains to tell that the poor Welsh puddler once lived, but this figure of the mill-woman cut in korl. I have it here in a corner of my library. I keep it hid behind a curtain, — it is such a rough, ungainly thing. Yet there are about it touches, grand sweeps of outline, that show a master's hand. Sometimes, — to-night, for instance, — the curtain is accidentally drawn back, and I see a bare arm stretched out imploringly in the darkness, and an eager, wolfish face watching mine: a wan, woful face, through which the spirit of the dead korl-cutter looks out, with its thwarted life, its mighty hunger, its unfinished work. Its pale, vague lips seem to tremble with a terrible question. "Is this the End?" — they say, — "nothing beyond? — no more?" Why, you tell me you have seen that look in the eyes of dumb brutes, — horses dying under the lash. I know.

The deep of the night is passing while I write. The gas-light wakens from the shadows here and there the objects which lie scattered through the room : only faintly, though ; for they belong to the open sunlight. As I glance at them, they each recall some task or pleasure of the coming day. A half-moulded child's head ; Aphrodite ; a bough of forest-leaves ; music ; work ; homely fragments, in which lie the secrets of all eternal truth and beauty. Prophetic all ! Only this dumb, woful face seems to belong to and end with the night. I turn to look at it. Has the power of its desperate need commanded the darkness away ? While the room is yet steeped in heavy shadow, a cool, gray light suddenly touches its head like a blessing hand, and its groping arm points through the broken cloud to the far East, where, in the flickering, nebulous crimson, God has set the promise of the Dawn.

THE PURSUIT OF KNOWLEDGE UNDER
DIFFICULTIES;

AND WHAT CAME OF IT.

" **M**R. GEER ! "

Mr. Geer was unquestionably asleep.

This certainly did not indicate a sufficiently warm appreciation of Mrs. Geer's social charms ; but the enormity of the offence will be greatly modified by a brief review of the attending circumstances. If you will but consider that the crackling of burning wood in a huge Franklin stove is strongly soporific in its tendencies, — that the cushion of a capacious arm-chair, constructed and adjusted as if with a single eye to a delicious doze, nay, to a long succession of dozes, is a powerful temptation to a sleepy soul, — that the regular, and, it must be confessed, somewhat monotonous *click, click, click* of Mrs. Geer's knitting-needles only served to measure, without disturbing the silence, — and, lastly, that they had been husband and wife for thirty years, — you will not cease to wonder that Mr. Geer

> " was glorious,
> O'er all the ills of life victorious."

To most men, an interruption at such a time would have been particularly annoying ; but when Mrs. Geer spoke in that way, Mr. Geer, asleep or awake, always made a point of hearing ; so he roused himself, and turned his round, honest face and placid blue eyes on the partner of his bosom, who went on, —

"Mr. Geer, our Ivy will be seventeen, come fall."

"Possible?" replied Mr. Geer. "Who'd 'a' thunk it?"

Mr. Geer, as you may infer, was eminently a free-thinker, or rather, a free-actor, in respect of irregular verbs. In fact, he tyrannized over all parts of speech : wrested nouns and verbs from their original shape, till you could hardly recognize their distorted faces ; and committed that next worst sin to murdering one's mother, namely, — murdering one's mother-tongue, with an *abandon* that was absolutely fascinating. Having delivered his opinion thus sententiously, he at once subsided, closed his placid eyes, and retired into his inner world of — thought, perhaps.

"*Mr. Geer !*"

This time he fairly jumped from his seat, and cast about him scared, blinking eyes.

"Mr. Geer, how can you sleep away your precious time so ?"

"Sleep? I — I — am sure, I was never wider awake in my life."

"Well, then, tell me what I said."

"Said? Eh, — eh, — something about Ivy, was n't it ?"

And Mr. Geer nervously twitched up the skirts of his coat, and replaced his awry cushion, and began to think that perhaps, after all, he had been asleep. But Mrs. Geer was too much interested in the subject of her own cogitations to pursue her victory further ; so she answered, —

"Yes, and what *is* a-going to become of her ?"

"Lud, lud ! What's the matter ?" asked Mr. Geer, wildly.

"Matter? Why, she 'll be seventeen, come fall, and does n't know a thing."

"O Lud ! that all? That a'n't nothin'."

And Mr. Geer settled comfortably down into his armchair once more. He felt decidedly relieved. Visions of small-pox, cholera, and throat-distemper, the worst evils that he could think of and dread for his darling, had been conjured up by his wife's words; and when he found the real state of the case, a great burden, which had suddenly fallen on his heart, was as suddenly lifted.

"But I tell you it *is* something," continued Mrs. Geer, energetically. "Ivy is 'most a woman, and has never been ten miles from home in her life, and to no school but our little district — "

"And she's as pairk a gal," interrupted Mr. Geer, "as any you'll find in all the ten miles round, be the other who she will."

"She's well enough in her way," replied Mrs. Geer, in all the humility of motherly pride; "and so much the more reason why she should n't be let go so. There's Mr. Dingham sending his great logy girls to Miss Porter's seminary. (I wonder if he expects they'll ever turn out anything?) And here's our Ivy, bright as a button, and you full well able to maintain her like a lady, and have done nothing but turn her out to grass all her life, till she's fairly run wild. I declare it's a shame. She ought to be sent to school to-morrow."

"Nonsense, Sally! nonsense! I a'n't a-goin' to have no such doin's. Sha'n't go off to school. What's the use havin' her, if she can't stay at home with us? Let Mr. Dingham send his gals to Chiny, if he wants to. All the book-larnin' in the world won't make 'em equal to our Ivy with only her own head. I don't want her to go to gettin' up high-falutin' notions. She's all gold now. She don't need no improvin'. Sha'n't budge an inch. Sha'n't stir a step."

"But do consider, Mr. Geer, the child has got to leave us some time. We can't have her always."

"Why can't we?" exclaimed Mr. Geer, almost fiercely.

"Sure enough! Why can't we? There a'n't nobody besides you and me, I suppose, that thinks she's pairk. What's John Herricks and Dan Norris hangin' round for all the time?"

"And they may hang round till the cows come home ! Nary hair of Ivy's head shall they touch, — nary one of 'em !"

Just at this juncture of affairs, the damsel in question bounded into the room.

"Come here, Ivy," said the old man ; "your mother's been a-slanderin' you ; says you don't know nothin'."

Ivy knelt before him, rested her arms on his knees, and turned upon him a pair of palpably roguish eyes.

"Father, it *is* an awful slander. I do know a sight."

"Lud, child, yes ! I knew you did. No more you don't want to marry John Herricks, do you ?"

"O Daddy Geer ! O — h — h !"

"Nor Dan Norris ? nor none of 'em ? "

"Never a one, father."

"Nor don't you ever think of gettin' married and slavin' yourself out for nobody. I 'm plenty well able to take care of you, as long as I live. You 'll never live so happy as you do at home ; and you 'll break my heart to go away, Ivy."

"I 'll never go, papa." (She pronounced it with the accent on the first syllable.) "Indeed, I never will. I 'll never be married, as long as I live."

"No more you sha'n't, good child, good child !"

And again Farmer Geer betook himself to the depths of his arm-chair, with the complacent consciousness of having faithfully discharged his parental duties. "She should not go to school. She would not be married. She had said she would not, and of course she would not."

"Of course I shall not," mused Ivy, as she lay in her white bed. "What could put it into poor papa's head ? Marry John Herricks, with his everlasting smirk, and his diddling walk, and take care of all the Herricks' sisters and mothers and aunts, and the Herricks' cows and horses and pigs — and — hens — and — and — "

But Ivy had kept her thoughts on her marriage longer than ever before in her life ; and ere she had finished the inventory of John Herricks's personal property and real estate, the blue eyes were closed in the sweet, sound sleep of youth and health.

Mrs. Geer, in her estimate of her daughter's attainments, was partly right and partly wrong. Ivy had never been "finished" at Mrs. Porter's seminary, and was consequently in a highly unfinished condition. "Small Latin and less Greek" jostled each other in her head. German and French, Italian and Spanish, were strange tongues to Ivy. She could not dance, nor play, nor draw, nor paint, nor work little dogs on footstools.

What, then, could she do ?

Imprimis, she could climb a tree like a squirrel. *Secundo*, she could walk across the great beam in the barn like a year-old kitten. In the pursuit of hens' eggs she knew no obstacles ; from scaffold to scaffold, from haymow to haymow, she leaped defiant. She pulled out the hay from under the very noses of the astonished cows, to see if, perchance, some inexperienced pullet might there have deposited her golden treasure. With all four-footed beasts she was on the best of terms. The matronly and lazy old sheep she unceremoniously hustled aside, to administer consolation and caresses to the timid, quaking lamb in the corner behind. Without saddle or bridle she could

> " Ride a black horse
> To Banbury Cross."

(N. B. — I don't say she actually did. I only say she could ; and under sufficiently strong provocation, I have no doubt she would.) She knew where the purple violets and the white innocence first flecked the spring turf, and where the ground-sparrows hid their mottled eggs. All the little waddling, downy goslings, the feeble chickens, and faint-hearted, desponding turkeys, that broke the shell too soon, and shivered miserably because the spring sun was not high enough in the morning to warm them, she fed with pap, and cherished in cotton-wool, and nursed and watched with eager, happy eyes. O blessed Ivy Geer ! True Sister of Charity !

5   G

Thrice blessed stepmother of a brood whose name was Legion !

From the conjugal and filial conversation which I have faithfully reported, a casual observer, particularly if young and inexperienced, might infer that the question of Miss Ivy's education was definitively settled, and that she was henceforth to remain under the paternal roof. I should, myself, have fallen into the same error, had not a long and intimate acquaintance with the female sex generated and cherished a profound and mournful conviction of the truth of the maxim, that appearances are deceitful. E. g., a woman has set her heart on something, and is refused. She pouts and sulks : that is clouds, and will soon blow over. She scolds, storms, and raves (I speak in a figure ; I mean she does something as much like that as a tender, delicate, angelic woman can) : that is thunder, and only clears the air. She betakes herself to tears, sobs, and embroidered cambric : that is a shower, and everything will be greener and fresher after it. You may go your ways, — one to his farm, another to his merchandise ; the world will not wind up its affairs just yet. But, put the case, she goes on the even tenor of her way unmoved :

> " Beware ! beware !
> Trust her not ; she is fooling thee."

Thus Mrs. Geer, who was a thorough tactician. Like Napoleon, she was never more elated than after a defeat. Before consulting her husband at all, she had contemplated the subject in all its bearings, and had deliberately decided that Ivy was to go to school. The consent of the senior partner of the firm was a secondary matter, which time and judicious management would infallibly secure. Consequently, notwithstanding the unpropitious result of their first colloquy, she the next day commenced preparations for Ivy's departure, as unhesitatingly, as calmly, as assiduously, as if the day of that departure had been fixed.

Mrs. Geer was right. She knew she was, all the time.

She had a sublime faith in herself. She felt in her soul the divine afflatus, and pressed forward gloriously to her goal. Mr. Geer had as much firmness, not to say obstinacy, as falls to the lot of most men ; but Mrs. Geer had more ; and as Launce Outram, hard beset, so pathetically moaned, " A woman in the very house has such deused opportunities ! " so Farmer Geer grumbled, and squirmed, and remonstrated, and — yielded.

. Mrs. Geer.was *not* right. She had reckoned without her host. Her affairs were gliding down the very Appian Way of prosperity in a chariot-and-four, with footmen and out-riders, when, presto ! they turned a sharp and unexpected corner, and over went the whole establishment into a mirier mire than ever bespattered Dr. Slop.

To speak without a parable. When her expected Hegira was announced to Miss Mary Ives Geer, that young lady, to the ill-concealed vexation of her mother, and the not-at-tempted-to-be-concealed exultation of her father, expressed decided disapprobation of the whole scheme. As she was the chief *dramatis persona*, the very Hamlet of the play, this unlooked-for decision somewhat interfered with Mrs. Geer's plans. All the eloquence of that estimable woman was brought to bear on this one point ; but this one point was invincible. Expostulation and entreaty were alike vain. Neither ambition nor pleasure could hold out any allure-ments to Ivy. Maternal authority was at length hinted at, only hinted at, and the spoiled child declared that she had not had her own will and way for sixteen years to give up quietly in her seventeenth. One last resort, one forlorn hope, — one expedient, which had never failed to overcome her childish stubbornness : " Would she grieve her parents so much as to oppose this their darling wish ? " And Ivy burst into tears, and begged to know if she should show her love to her father and mother by going away from them. This drove the nail into her old father's heart, and then the little vixen clenched it by throwing herself into his arms, and sobbing, " O, papa ! would you turn your Ivy out of doors and break her heart ? "

Flimsiest of fallacies ! Shallowest of sophists ! But she was the only and beloved child of his old age ; so the fallacy passed unchallenged ; the strong arms closed around the naughty girl ; and the soothing voice murmured, — " There, there, Ivy ! don't cry, child ! Lud ! lud ! you sha'n't be bothered ; no more you sha'n't, lovey ! " and the *status quo* was restored.

> " It is not in the sea nor in the strife
>   We feel benumbed and wish to be no more,
>   But in the after silence on the shore,
>   When all is lost, except a little life,"

said one who had breasted the stormiest sea and plunged into the fiercest strife. Ivy, who had never read Byron, and therefore could not be suspected of any Byronical affectations, felt it, when, having gained her point, she sat down alone in her own room. When her single self had been pitted against superior numbers, age, experience, and parental authority, all her heroism was roused, and she was adequate to the emergency ; but her end gained, the excitement gone, the sense of disobedience alone remaining, and she was thoroughly uncomfortable, nay, miserable.

"Mamma is right ; I know I am a little goose," sobbed she. (The words were mental, intangible, unspoken ; the sobs physical, palpable, decided.) " I never did know anything, and I never shall, — and I don't care if I don't. I don't see any good in knowing so much. We don't have a great while to stay in the world any way, and I don't see why we can't be let alone and have a good time while we are here, and when we get to heaven we can take a fresh start. O, dear ! I never shall go to heaven, if I am so bad and vex mamma. But then papa did n't care. But then he would have liked me to go to school. But there, I won't ! I won't ! I *will not !* I 'll study at home. O, dear ! I wish papa was a great man, and knew everything, and could teach me. Well, he is just as happy, and just as rich, and everybody likes him just as well, as if he knew the whole world full ; and why can't I do so, too ? Rebecca Dingham,

indeed! Mercy! I hope I never shall be like her; I
would rather not know my A B C! What *shall* I do?
There's Mr. Brownslow might teach me; he knows enough.
But, dear me! he is as busy as he can be, all day long;
and Squire Merrill goes out of town every day; and there's
Dr. Mix, to be sure, but he smells so strong of paregoric,
and I don't believe he knows much, either; and there's nobody else in town that knows any more than anybody else;
and there's nothing for it but I must go to school, if I am
ever to know anything." (A renewal of sobs, uninterrupted
for several minutes.) "There's Mr. Clerron!" (A sudden
cessation.) "I suppose he knows more than the whole
town tumbled into one; and writes books, and —— mercy!
there's no end to his knowledge; and he's rich, and does
everything he likes, all day long. O, if I only *did* know
him! I would ask him straight off to teach me. I should
be scared to death. I've a great mind to ask him, as it is.
I can tell him who I am. He never will know any other
way, for he is n't acquainted with anybody. They say he is
as proud as Lucifer. If he were ten times prouder, I would
rather ask him than go to school. He might just as well
do something as not. I am sure, if God had made me him,
and him me, I should be glad to help him. I'll go straight
to him the first thing to-morrow morning."

Once seeing a possible way out of her difficulties, her sorrow vanished. Not quite so gayly as usual, it is true, did
she sing about the house that night; for she was summon-
ing all her powers to prepare an introductory speech to
Felix Clerron, Esq., a gentleman and a scholar. Her elo-
cutionary attempts were not quite satisfactory to herself, but
she was not to be daunted; and when morning came, she
took heart of grace, slung her broad-brimmed hat over her
arm, and began her march "over the hills and far away," in
search of her — fate.

"And did her mother really let her roam away, alone, on
such an errand, to a perfect stranger?"

"Humanly speaking," nothing was more unlikely than

that Mrs. Geer, a prudent, modest, and sensible woman, should give her consent to such an — to use the mildest term — unusual undertaking. Nor did she. The fact is, her consent was not asked. She knew nothing whatever of the plan.

"Worse and worse! Did the wilful girl go off without leave? without even informing her parents?"

I am sorry to say she did. In writing a story of real life, one cannot take that liberty with facts which is quite proper, not to say indispensable, in history, science, and *belles-lettres* generally. Duty compels me to adhere closely to the truth; and for whatever of obloquy may be heaped upon me, or upon my Ivy, I shall find consolation in the words of the illustrious Harrison; or perhaps it was the illustrious Taylor; I am not quite sure, however, that it was not the illustrious Washington : — "Do right, and let the consequences take care of themselves." I am therefore obliged to say, that Ivy's departure in pursuit of knowledge was entirely unknown to her respected and beloved parents. But you must remember that she was an only child, and a spoiled child, — spoiled as only stern New England Puritan parents, somewhat advanced in years, can spoil their children. I do not defend Ivy. On the contrary, notwithstanding my regard for her, I hand her over to the reprobation of an enlightened community; and I hereby entreat all young persons into whose hands this memoir may fall to take warning by the fate of poor Ivy, and never enter upon any important undertaking, until they have, to say the least, consulted those who are their natural guides, their warmest friends, and their most experienced counsellors.

While I have been writing this, Ivy Geer, light of heart, fleet of foot, and firm of will, has passed over hillside, through wood-path, and across meadow-land, and drawn near the domains of Felix Clerron, Esq. Light of heart perhaps I scarcely ought to say. Certainly, that enterprising organ had never before beat so furious a tattoo in Ivy's breast, as when she stood, hat in hand, on the steps of the somewhat stately dwelling. To do her justice, she had intended to do the penance of wearing her hat when she should have reached her destination ; but in her excitement she quite forgot it. So, as I said, she stood on the doorstep, as a royal maiden stood three hundred years before (not in the same place), with the " wind blowing her fair hair about her beautiful cheeks."

There had come to Ivy from the great, gay world a vague rumor, that, instead of knocking at a door, like a Christian, with your own good knuckles, for such case made and provided, modern fashion had introduced " the ringing and the dinging of the bells." This vague rumor found a local habitation, when Mr. Clerron came down upon the village and established himself, his men and women and horses and cattle ; but as Ivy stood on his doorstep, looking upward, downward, sidewise, with earnest, peering gaze, no bell, and no sign of bell, was visible ; nothing unusual, save a little door-knob at the right hand side of the door, — a thing which could not be accounted for. After long and serious deliberation, she came to the conclusion that the bell must be inside, and that the knob was a screw attached to it. So she tried to twist it, first one way, then the other ; but twist it would not. In despair she betook herself to her fingers and knocked. Nobody came. Twist again. No use. Knock again. Ditto. Then she went down to the gravelled path, selected one of the largest pebbles, took up her station before the door, and began to pound away. In a moment, a gentleman in dressing-gown and smoking-cap, with a cigar between his fingers, came round the corner. Seeing her, he threw away his cigar, lifted his velvet cap, bowed, and, with a gentle " allow me," stepped to the door, pulled the bell, and again passed out of sight. Ivy was not so confused at being detected in her assault and battery on the door of a respectable, peaceable, private gentleman, as not to make the silent reflection, " Pulled the knob, instead of twisting it. How easy it is to do a thing, if you only know how ! "

The summons was soon answered by a black gnome, and Ivy was ushered into a large room, which, to her dazzled, sun-weary eyes, seemed delightfully fresh and green-looking. Two minutes more of waiting, — then a step in the hall, a gently opening door, and Ivy felt rather than saw herself in the presence of the formidable Mr. Clerron. A single glance showed her that he was the person who had rung the bell for her, though the gay dressing-gown had been exchanged for a soberer suit. Mr. Clerron bowed. Ivy, hardly knowing what she did, faltered forth, "I am Ivy Geer." A half-curious, half-sarcastic smile glimmered behind the heavy beard, and gleamed beneath the heavy eyebrows, as he answered, "I am happy to make your acquaintance"; but another glance at the trembling form, the frightened, pale face, and quivering lips, changed the smile into one that was very good-natured, and even kind ; and he added, playfully, —

"I am Felix Clerron, very much at your service."

"You write books and are a very learned man," pursued Ivy, hurriedly, never lifting her eyes from the floor, and never ceasing to twirl her hat-strings.

There was no possibility of supposing her guilty of committing a little diplomatic flattery in conveying this succinct bit of information. She made the assertion with the air of one who has a disagreeable piece of business on hand, and is determined to go through with it as soon as possible. He bowed and smiled again ; quite unnecessarily, — since, as I have before remarked, Ivy's eyes were steadfastly fixed on the carpet. A slight pause for breath and she pitched ahead again.

"I am very ignorant, and I am growing old. I am almost seventeen. I don't know anything to speak of. Mamma wishes me to go to school. Papa did not, but now he does. I won't go. I would rather be stupid all my life long than leave home. But mamma is vexed, and I want to please her, and I thought, — Mr. Brownslow is so busy, and you, — if you have nothing to do, — and know so much, — I thought "——

She stopped short, utterly unable to proceed. Wonderfully different did this affair seem from the one she had planned the preceding evening. It is so much easier to fight the battle of life in our own chimney-corner, by the ruddy and genial firelight, than in broad day on the world's great battle-field !

Mr. Clerron, seeing Ivy's confusion, kindly came to her aid. " And you thought my superfluous time and wisdom might be transferred to you, thus making a more equal division of property ? "

" If you would be so good, — I, — yes, Sir."

" May I inquire how you propose to effect such an exchange ? "

He really did not intend to be anything but kind, but the whole matter presented itself to him in a very ludicrous light ; and in endeavoring to preserve proper gravity, he became severe. Ivy, all-unused to the world, still had a secret feeling that he was laughing at her. Tears, that would not be repressed, glistened in her downcast eyes, gathered on the long lashes, dropped silently to the floor. He saw that she was entirely a child, ignorant, artless, and sincere. His better feelings were roused, and he exclaimed, with real earnestness, —

" My dear young lady, I should rejoice to serve you in any way, I beg you to believe."

His words only hastened the catastrophe which seems to be always impending over the weaker sex. Ivy sobbed outright, — a perfect tempest. Felix Clerron looked on with a bachelor's dismay. " What in thunder ? Confound the girl ! " were his first reflections ; but her utter abandonment to sorrow melted his heart again, — not a very susceptible heart either ; but men, especially bachelors, are so — *green !* (the word is found in Cowper.)

He sat down by her side, stroked the hair from her burning forehead, as if she had been six instead of sixteen, and again and again assured her of his willingness to assist her.

5 *

" I must go home," whispered Ivy, as soon as she could command, or rather coax her voice.

His hospitality was shocked.

" Indeed you must not, till we have at least had a consultation. Tell me how much you know. What have you studied ? "

" O, nothing, Sir. I am very stupid."

" Ah ! we must begin with the Alphabet, then. Blocks or a primer ? "

Ivy smiled through her tears.

" Not quite so bad as that, Sir."

" You do know your letters ? Perhaps you can even count, and spell your name ; maybe write it. Pray, enlighten me."

Ivy grew calm as he became playful.

" I can cipher pretty well. I have been through Greenleaf's Large."

" House or meadow ? And the exact dimensions, if you please."

" Sir ? "

" I understood you to say you had traversed Greenleaf's Large. You did not designate what."

He was laughing at her now, indeed, but it was open and genial, and she joined.

" My Arithmetic, of course. I supposed everybody knew that. Everybody calls it so."

" Time is short. Yes. Do you like Arithmetic ? "

" Pretty well, some parts of it. Fractions and Partial Payments. But I can't bear Duodecimals, Position, and such things."

" Positions *are* occasionally embarrassing. And Grammar ? "

" I think it 's horrid. It 's all ' indicative mood, common noun, third person, singular number, and agrees with John.' "

" *Bravissima !* A comprehensive sketch ! A bird's-eye view, as one may say, — and not entertaining, certainly. What other branches have you pursued ? Drawing, for instance ? "

" O, no, Sir ! "

" Nor Music ? "

" No, Sir."

" Good ! excellent ! An overruling Providence has saved you and your friends from many a pitfall. Shall we proceed to History ? Be so good as to inform me who discovered America."

" I believe Columbus has the credit of it," replied Ivy, demurely.

" Non-committal, I see. Case goes strongly in his favor, but you reserve your judgment till further evidence."

" I think he was a wise and good and enterprising man."

" But are rather sceptical about that San Salvador story. A wise course. Never decide till both sides have been fairly presented. ' He that judgeth a matter before he heareth it, it is folly and shame unto him,' said thé wise man. Occasionally his after-judgment is equally discreditable. That is a thousand times worse. Exit Clio. Enter — well ! — Geographia. My young friend, what celebrated city has the honor of concentrating the laws, learning, and literature of Massachusetts, to wit, namely, is its capital ? "

" Boston, Sir."

" Your Geography has evidently been attended to. You have learned the basis fact. You have discovered the pivot on which the world turns. You have dug down to the antediluvian, ante-pyrean granite, — the primitive, unfused stratum of society. The force of learning can no farther go. Armed with that fact, you may march fearlessly forth to do battle with the world, the flesh, and — the — ahem — the King of Beasts ! Do you think you should like me for a teacher ? "

" I can't tell, Sir. I did not like you as anything awhile ago."

" But you like me better now ? You think I improve on acquaintance ? You detect signs of a moral reformation ? "

" No, Sir, I don't like you now. I only don't dislike you so much as I did."

" Spoken like a major-general, or, better still, like a brave little Yankee girl, as you are. I am an enthusiastic admirer of truth. I foresee we shall get on famously. I was rather premature in sounding the state of your affections, it must be confessed, — but we shall be rare friends by and by. On the whole, you are not particularly fond of books?"

" I like some books well enough, but not studying-books," said Ivy, with a sigh, "and I don't see any good in them. If it was n't for mamma, I never would open one, — never ! I would just as soon be a dunce as not ; I don't see anything very horrid in it."

" How should you, to be sure ? There is a distinction, however, which you must immediately learn to make. The dunce subjective is a very inoffensive animal, contented, happy, and harmless ; and, as you justly remark, inspires no horror, but rather an amiable and genial self-complacency. The dunce objective, on the contrary, is of an entirely different species. He is a bore of the first magnitude, — a poisoned arrow, that not only pierces, but inflames, — a dull knife, that not only cuts, but tears, — a cowardly little cur, that snaps occasionally, but snarls unceasingly ; whom, which, and that, it becomes the duty of all good citizens to sweep from the face of the earth."

" What is the difference between them ? How shall one know which is which ?"

" The dunce subjective is the dunce from his own point of view, — the dunce with his eyes turned inward, — confining his duncehood to the bosom of his family. The dunce objective is the dunce butting against his neighbor's study-door, — intruding, obtruding, protruding his insipid folly and still more insipid wisdom at all times and seasons. He is a creature utterly devoid of shame. He is like Milton's angels, in one respect at least : you may thrust him through and through with the two-edged sword of your satire, and at the end he shall be as intact and integral as at the beginning. Am I sufficiently obvious ?" He was talking, however, quite as much to himself as to Ivy, and with a bitterness evidently born of suffering.

" It is very obvious that I am both, according to your definition."

" It is very obvious that you are neither, but a sensible young girl, — with no great quantity of the manufactured article, perhaps, but plenty of raw material, capable of being wrought into fabric of the finest quality."

" Do you really think I can learn ? " asked Ivy, with a bright blush of pleasure.

" Can learn ? "

" As much as if I went to school ? "

" My dear miss, as the forest oak, ' cabined, cribbed, confined ' with multitudes of its fellows, grows stunted, scrubby, and dwarfed, but brought into the open fields alone, stretches out its arms to the blue heavens and its roots to the kindly earth, — so, in a word, shall you, under my fostering care, flourish like a green bay-tree, only not quite so high and mightily as I am flourishing now ; — that is, if I am to have the honor."

" Yes, Sir, I mean — I meant — I was thinking as if you were teaching me — I mean were going to teach me."

" Which I also mean, if your parents continue to wish it."

" O, they won't care ! "

" Won't care ? "

" No, Sir, they will be glad, I think. Papa, at least, will be glad to have me stay at home."

" Did not they direct you to come to me to-day ? "

Ivy blushed deeply, and replied, in a low voice, " No, Sir ; I knew mamma would not let me come, if I asked her."

" And to prevent any sudden temptation to disobedience, and a consequent forfeiture of your peace of mind, you took time by the forelock and came on your own responsibility ? "

" Yes, Sir."

" Very ingenious, upon my word ! But, my dear Miss Geer, I must confess I have not this happy feminine knack of keeping out of the way of temptation. I should prefer to consult your friends, even at the risk of losing the pleasure of your society."

" O, yes, Sir ! I don't care, now it is all settled."

And so, over hillside, along wood-path, and through
meadow-land, with light heart and smiling eyes, tripped Ivy
back again. To Mrs. Geer shelling peas in the shady
porch, and to Mr. Geer fanning himself with his straw hat
on the steps beside her, Ivy recounted the story of her adventures. Mrs. Geer was thunderstruck at Ivy's temerity ;
Mr. Geer was lost in admiration of her pluck. Mrs. Geer
termed it a wild-goose chase ; Mr. Geer declared Ivy to be
as smart as a steel trap. Mrs. Geer vetoed the whole plan ;
Mr. Geer did n't know. But when at sunset Mr. Clerron
rode over, and admired Mr. Geer's orchard, and praised the
points of his Durhams, and begged a root of Mrs. Geer's
scarlet verbena, and assured them he should be very glad to
refresh his own early studies, and also to form an acquaintance with the family, — he knew very few in the village, —
and if Mrs. Geer would drive over when Ivy came to recite,
— or perhaps they would rather he should come to their
house. O, no ! Mrs. Geer could not think of that. Just
as they pleased. Mrs. Simm, the housekeeper, would be
very glad to meet Mrs. Geer. By the way, Mrs. Simm was
a thrifty and sensible woman, and he was sure they would
be pleased with each other. When, in short, all this and
much more had been said, it was decided that Ivy should be
regularly installed pupil of Mr. Felix Clerron.

" *Eureka !* " cries the professional novel-reader, that far-
sighted and keen-scented hound that snuffs a *dénouement*
afar off ; and anon there rises before his eyes the vision of
poor little Stella drinking in love and learning, especially
love, from the divine eyes of the anything but divine Swift,
— of Shirley, the lioness, the pantheress, the leopardess, the
beautiful, fierce creature, sitting, tamed, quiet, meek, by the
side of Louis Moore, her tutor and master, — and of all the
legends of all the ages wherein Beauty has sat at the feet of
Wisdom, and Love has crept in unawares, and spoiled the
lesson while as yet half-unlearnt ; — so he cries, " She is
going the way of all heroines. The man and the girl, —

they will fall in love, marry, and live happily all the rest of their days."

Of course they will. Is there any reason why they should not? If any man can show just cause why they may not lawfully be joined together, let him now speak, or else hereafter forever hold his peace.

I repeat it, of course they will. You surely cannot suppose I should, in cold blood, sit down to write a story in which nobody was to fall in love or be in love! Scoff as you may, love is the one vital principle in all romance. Not only does your cheek flush and your eye sparkle, till heart, brain, and soul are all on fire, over the burning words of some Brontean Pythoness, but when you open the last thrilling work of Maggie Marigold, and are immediately submerged "in a weak, washy, everlasting flood" of insipidity, and heart-rending sorrow, you do not shut the book with a jerk. Why not? Because in the dismal distance you dimly descry two figures swimming, floating, struggling towards each other, and a languid curiosity detains you till you have ascertained, that, after infinite distress, Adolphus and Miranda have made

"One of the very best matches,
Both well mated for life :
She's got a fool for a husband,
He's got a fool for his wife."

Sir, scoff as you may, love is the one sunbeam of poetry that gilds with a softened splendor the hard, bare outline of many a prosaic life. "Work, work, work, from weary chime to chime"; tramp behind the plough, hammer on the lapstone, beat the anvil, drive the plane, from morn till dewy eve ; but when the dewy eve comes, ah ! Hesperus gleams soft and golden over the far-off pine-trees, but

"The star that lightens your bosom most,
And gives to your weary feet their speed,
Abides in a cottage beyond the mead."

It is useless to assert that the subject is worn threadbare.

Threadbare it may be to you, enervated and *blasé* man of pleasure, worn and hardened man of the world ; but it is not for you I write. The fountain which leaps up fresh and living in every new life can never be exhausted till the springs of all life are dry. Tell me, O lover, gazing into those tender eyes uplifted to yours, twining the silken rings around your bronzed finger, — does it abate one jot or tittle of your happiness to know that eyes just as tender, curls just as silken, have stirred the hearts of men for a thousand years ?

Love, then, is a *sine qua non* in stories ; and if love, why not marriage ? What pleasure can a humane and benevolent man find in separating two individuals whose chief, perhaps whose sole happiness, consists in being together ? For certain inscrutable reasons, Divine Benevolence permits evil to exist in the world. All who have a taste for misery can find it there in exhaustless quantities. Johns are every day falling in love with Katys, but marrying Isabels, and Isabels the same, *mutatis mutandis*. We submit to it because there is no alternative ; and we believe that good shall finally be wrought and wrested from evil. But let us not in mere wantonness introduce into our novel-world the work of our own hand, an abridged edition, a daguerrotype copy of the world without, of which we know so little and so much. I always do and always shall read the last page of a novel first ; and if I perceive there any indications that matters are not coming out " shipshape," my reading invariably terminates with the last page.

For the rest, please to remember that I am not writing about a princess of the blood, nor of the days of the bold barons, but only the life of a quiet little girl in a quiet little town in the eastern part of Massachusetts ; and so far as my experience and observation go, men and women in the eastern part of Massachusetts are not given to thrilling adventures, hairbreadth escapes, wonderful concatenations of circumstances, and blood and thunder generally, — but pursue the even tenor of their way, and of their love, with a sober and delightful equanimity. If you want a plot, go to the " Children of the Abbey," " Consuelo," and myriads of that kin, and help yourself. As for me, I must confess I hate plots. I see no pleasure in stumbling blindfolded through a story, unable to see a yard ahead, fancying every turn to be the last, and the road to go straight on to a glorious goal, — and, lo ! we are in a more hopeless labyrinth than ever. I have a sense of restraint. I want to breathe freely, and cannot. I want to have leisure to observe the style, the development of character, the author's tone of thought, and not be galloped through on the back of a breathless desire to know " how they are coming out."

But, my dear plot-loving friend, be easy. I will not leave you in the lurch. I am not going to marry my man and woman out of hand. An obstacle, of which I suppose you have never heard, — an obstacle entirely new, fresh, and unhackneyed, will arise ; so, I pray you, let patience have her perfect work.

Wonderful was the new world opened to Ivy Geer. It was as if a corse, cold, inert, lifeless, had suddenly sprung up, warm, invigorated, informed with a spirit which led her own spell-bound. Grammar, — Grammar, which had been a synonyme for all that was dry, irksome, useless, — a beating of the wind, the crackling of thorns under a pot, — Grammar even assumed for her a charm, a wonder, a glory. She saw how the great and wise had shrined in fitting words their purity, and wisdom, and sorrow, and suffering, and penitence ; and how, as this generation passed away, and another came forth which knew not God, the golden casket became dim, and the memory of its priceless gem faded away ; but how, at the touch of a mighty wand, the obedient lid flew back, and the long-hidden thought " sprang full-statured in an hour." She saw how love and beauty and freedom lay floating vaguely and aimlessly in a million minds till the poet came and crystallized them into clear-cut, prismatic words, tinged for each with the color of his own fancy, and wrought into a perfect mosaic, not for an age,

H

but for all time. Led by a strong hand, she trod with awe down the dim aisles of the Past, and saw how the soul of man, bound in its prison-house, had ever struggled to voice itself in words. Roaming in the dense forest with the stern and bloody Druid, — bounding over the waves with the fierce pirates who supplanted them, and in whose blue eyes and beneath whose fair locks gleamed indeed the ferocity of the savage, but lurked also, though unseen and unknown, the tender chivalry of the English gentleman, — gazing admiringly on the barbaric splendor of the cloth-of-gold, whereon trod regally, to the sound of harp and viol, the beauty and bravery of the old Norman nobility, she delighted to see how the mother-tongue, our dear mother-tongue, had laid all the nations under contribution to enrich her treasury, — gathering from one its strength, from another its stateliness, from a third its harmony, till the harsh, crude, rugged dialect of a barbarous horde became worthy to embody, as it does, the love, the wisdom, and the faith of half a world.

So Grammar taught Ivy to reverence language.

History, in the light of a guiding mind, ceased to be a bare record of slaughter and crime. Before her eyes filed, in a statelier pageant than they knew, the long procession of "simple great ones gone forever and ever by," and the countless lesser ones whose names are quenched in the darkness of a night that shall know no dawn. She saw the "great world spin forever down the ringing grooves of change"; but amid all the change, the confusion, the chaos, she saw the finger of God ever pointing, and heard the sublime monotone of the Divine voice ever saying to the children of men, "This is the way, walk ye in it." And Ivy thought she saw, and rejoiced in the thought, that, even when this warning was unheeded, — when on the brow of the mournful Earth "Ichabod, Ichabod," was forever engraven, — when the First Man with his own hand put from him the cup of innocence, and went forth from the happy garden, sin-stained and fallen, the whole head sick, and the whole heart faint, — even then she saw within him the Divine spark, the leaven of life, which had power to vitalize and vivify what Crime had smitten with death. Though sea and land teemed with strange perils, though night and day pursued him with mysterious terrors, though the now unfriendly elements combined to check his career, still, with unswerving purpose, undaunted courage, she saw him march constantly forward. Spirits of evil could not drive from his heart the prescience of greatness ; and his soul dwelt calmly under the foreshadow of a mighty future.

And as Ivy looked, she saw how the children of men became a great nation, and possessed the land far and wide. They delved into the bosom of the pleased earth, and brought forth the piled-up treasures of uncounted cycles. They unfolded the book of the skies, and sought to read the records thereon. They plunged into the unknown and terrible ocean, and decked their own brows with the gems they plucked from hers. And when conquered Nature had laid her hoards at their feet, their restless longings would not be satisfied. Brave young spirits, with the dew of their youth fresh upon them, set out in quest of a land beyond their ken. Over the mountains, across the seas, through the forests, there came to the ear of the dreaming girl the measured tramp of marching men, the softer footfalls of loving women, the pattering of the feet of little children. Many a day and many a night she saw them wander on towards the setting sun, till the Unseen Hand led them to a fair and fruitful country that opened its bounteous arms in welcome. Broad rivers, green fields, laughing valleys wooed them to plant their household gods, — and the foundations of Europe were laid. Here were sown the seeds of those heroic virtues which have since leaped into luxuriant life, — seeds of that irresistible power which fastened its grasp on Nature, and forced her to unfold the secret of her creation, — seeds of that far-reaching wisdom which in the light of the unveiled past has read the story of the unseen future.

And still under Ivy's eye they grouped themselves

Some gathered on the pleasant hills of the sunny South, and the beauty of earth and sea and sky passed into their souls forever. They caught the evanescent gleam, the passing shadow, and on unseemly canvas limned it for all time in forms of unuttered and unutterable loveliness. They shaped into glowing life the phantoms of grace that were always flitting before their enchanted eyes, and poured into inanimate marble their rapt and passionate souls. They struck the lyre to wild and stirring songs whose tremulous echoes still linger along the corridors of Time. Some sought the ice-bound North, and grappled with dangers by field and flood. They hunted the wild dragon to his mountain-fastnesses, and fought him at bay, and never quailed. Death, in its most fearful forms, they met with grim delight, and chanted the glories of the Valhalla waiting for heroes who should forever quaff the "foaming, pure, and shining mead" from skulls of foes in battle slain. Some crossed the sea, and on

> "that pale, that white-faced shore,
> Whose foot spurns back the ocean's swelling tide,"

they reared a sinewy and stalwart race, "whose morning drum-beat encircles the world."

And History taught Ivy to reverence man.

But there was one respect in which Ivy was both pupil and teacher. Never a word of Botany had fallen upon her ears; but through all the unconscious bliss of infancy, childhood, and girlhood, for sixteen happy years, she had lived among the flowers, and she knew their dear faces and their wild-wood names. She loved them with an almost human love. They were to her companions and friends. She knew their likings and dislikings, their joys and sorrows, — who among them chose the darkest nooks of the old woods, and who bloomed only to the brightest sunlight, — who sent their roots deep down among the mosses by the brook, and who smiled only on the southern hillside. Around each she wove a web of beautiful individuality, and more than one had received from her a new christening. It is true, that, when she came to study from a book, she made wry faces over the long, barbarous, Latin names which completely disguised her favorites, and in her heart deemed a great many of the definitions quite superfluous; but she had strong faith in her teacher, and when the technical was laid aside for the real, then, indeed, "her foot was on her native heath, and her name was MacGregor." A wild and merry chase she led her grave instructor. Morning, noon, or night, she was always ready. Under the blue sky, breathing the pure air, treading the green turf familiar from her infancy, she could not be otherwise than happy; but when was superadded to this the companionship of a mind vigorous, cultivated, and refined, she enjoyed it with a keen and intense delight. Nowhere else did her soul so entirely unfold to the genial light of this new sun which had suddenly mounted above her horizon. Nowhere else did the freshness and fulness and splendor of life dilate her whole being with a fine ecstasy.

And what was the end of all this? Just what you would have supposed. She had led a life of simple, unbounded love and trust, — a buoyant, elastic gladness, — a dream of sunshine. No gray cloud had ever lowered in her sky, no thunderbolt smitten her joys, no winter rain chilled her warmth. Only the white fleeciness of morning mist had flitted sometimes over her summer-sky, deepening the blue. Little cooling drops had fluttered down through the leafiness, only to span her with a rainbow in the glory of the setting sun. But the time had come. From the deep fountains of her heart the stone was to be rolled away. The secret chord was to be smitten by a master-hand, — a chord which, once stirred, may never cease to quiver.

At first Ivy worshipped very far off. Her friend was to her the embodiment of all knowledge and goodness and greatness. She marvelled to see him so at home in what was to her so strange. Every word that fell from his lips was an oracle. She secretly contrasted him with all the men she had ever met, to the utter discomfiture of the latter. Washington, the Apostle Paul, and Peter Parley were the only men of the past or present whom she considered at all worthy to be compared with him ; and in fact, if these three men and Felix Clerron had all stood before her, and offered each a different opinion on any given subject, I have scarcely a doubt as to whose would have commended itself to her as combining the soundest practical wisdom and the highest Christian benevolence.

So the summer passed on, and her shyness wore off, — and their intimacy became less and less that of teacher and pupil, and more and more that of friend and friend. With the sudden awakening of her intellectual nature, there woke also another power, of whose existence she had never dreamed. It was natural, that, in ranging the fields of thought so lately opened to her, she should often revert to him whose hand had unbarred the gates ; she was therefore not startled that the image of Felix Clerron was with her when she sat down and when she rose up, when she went out and when she came in. She ceased, indeed, to think *of* him. She thought *him.* She lived him. Her soul fed on his life. And so — and so — by a pleasant and flowery path, there came into Ivy's heart the old, old pain.

Now the thing was on this wise : —

One morning, when she went to recite, she did not find Mr. Clerron in the library, where he usually awaited her. After spending a few moments in looking over her lessons, she rose and was about to pass to the door to ring, when Mrs. Simm looked in, and, seeing Ivy, informed her that Mr. Clerron was in the garden, and desired her to come out. Ivy immediately followed Mrs. Simm into the garden. On the south side of the house was a piazza two stories high. Along the pillars which supported it a trellis-work had been constructed, reaching several feet above the roof of the piazza. About this climbed a vigorous grape-vine, which not only completely screened nearly the whole front of the piazza, but, reaching the top of the trellis, shot across, by

the aid of a few pieces of fine wire, and overran a part of
the roof of the house. Thus the roof of the piazza was the
floor of a beautiful apartment, whose walls and ceiling were
broad, rustling, green leaves, among which drooped now
innumerable heavy clusters of rich purple grapes.

From behind this leafy wall a well-known voice cried,
"All hail, my twining vine!" Ivy turned and looked up,
with the uncertain, inquiring smile we often wear when conscious that, though unseeing, we are not unseen; and presently two hands parted the leaves far enough for a very
sunshiny smile to gleam down on the upturned face.

"O, I wish I could come up there!" cried Ivy, clasping
her hands with childish eagerness.

"The wish is father to the deed."

"May I?"

"Be sure you may."

"But how shall I get in?"

"Are you afraid to come up the ladder?"

"No, I don't mean that; but how shall I get in where
you are, after I am up?"

"O, never fear! I'll draw you in safely enough."

"Lorful heart! Miss Ivy, what are you going to do?"
cried Mrs. Simm, in terror.

Ivy was already on the third round of the ladder, but she
stopped and answered, hesitatingly, —

"He said I might."

"He said you might, yes," continued Mrs. Simm, — talking *to* Ivy, but *at* Mr. Clerron, with whom she hardly dared
to remonstrate in a more direct way. "And if he said you
might throw yourself down Vineyard Cliff, it don't follow
that you are bound to do it. He goes into all sorts of hap-
hazard scrapes himself, but you can't follow him."

"But it looks so nice up there," pleaded Ivy, "and I have
been twice as high at home. I don't mind it at all."

"If your father chooses to let you run the risk of your
life, it's none of my lookout, but I a'n't going to have you
breaking your neck right under my nose. If you want to

get up there, I 'll show you the way in the house, and you can step right out of the window. Just wait till I 've told Ellen about the dinner."

As Mrs. Simm disappeared, Mr. Clerron said softly to Ivy, "Come!"—and in a moment Ivy bounded up the ladder and through an opening in the vine, and stood by his side.

"I 'm ready now, Miss Ivy," said Mrs. Simm, reappearing. "Miss Ivy! Where is the child?"

A merry laugh greeted her.

"O, you good-for-nothing!" cried the good-natured old housekeeper, "you 'll never die in your bed."

"Not for a good while, I hope," answered Mr. Clerron.

Then he made Ivy sit down by him, and took from the great basket the finest cluster of grapes.

"Is that reward enough for coming?"

"Coming into so beautiful a place as this is like what you read yesterday about poetry to Coleridge, 'its own exceeding great reward.'"

"And you don't want the grapes?"

"I don't know that I have any intrinsic objection to them as a free gift. It was only the principle that I opposed."

"Very well, we will go shares, then. You may have half for the free gift, and I will have half for the principle. Little tendril, you look as fresh as the morning."

"Don't I always?"

"I should say there was a *little* more dew than usual. Stand up and let me survey you, if perchance I may discover the cause."

Ivy rose, made a profound courtesy, and then turned slowly around, after the manner of the revolving fashion-figures in a milliner's window.

"I don't know," continued Mr. Clerron, when Ivy, after a couple of revolutions, resumed her seat. "You seem to be the same. I think it must be the frock."

"I don't wear a frock. I don't think it would improve my style of beauty if I did. Papa wears one sometimes."

" And what kind of a frock, pray, does ' papa ' wear ? "

" O, a horrid blue thing. Comes about down ·to his knees. Made of some kind of woollen stuff. Horrid ! "

" And what name do you give to that white thing with blue sprays in it ? "

" This ? "

" Yes."

" This is a dress."

" No. This, and your collar, and hat, and shoes, and sash are your dress. This is a frock."

Ivy shook her head doubtfully.

" You know a great deal, I know."

" So you informed me once before."

" O, don't mention that ! " said Ivy, blushing, and quickly added, " Do you know I have discovered the reason why you like me this morning ? "

" And every morning."

" Sir ? "

" Go on. What is the reason ? "

" It is because I clear-starched and ironed it myself with· my owny-dony hands ; and that, you know, is the reason it looks nicer than usual."

" Ah me ! I wish I wore dresses."

" You can, if you choose, I suppose. There is no one to hinder you."

" Simpleton ! that is not what you were intended to say. You should have asked the cause of so singular a wish, and then I had a pretty little speech all ready for you, — a verit· able compliment."

" It is well I did not ask, then. Mamma does not approve of compliments, and perhaps it would have made me vain."

" Incorrigible ! Why did you not ask me what the speech was, and thus give me an opportunity to relieve myself. Why, a body might die of a plethora of flattery, if he had nobody but you to discharge it against."

" He must take care, then, that the supply does not exceed the demand."

6

"Political economy, upon my word ! What shall we have next ?"

"Domestic, I suppose you would like. Men generally, indeed, prefer it to the other, I am told."

"Ah, Ivy, Ivy ! little you know about men, my child !"

He leaned back in his seat and was silent for some minutes. Ivy did not care to interrupt his thinking. Presently he said, —

"Ivy, how old are you ?"

"I shall be seventeen the last day of this month."

A short pause.

"And then eighteen."

"And then nineteen."

"And then twenty. In three years you will be twenty."

"Horrid old, is n't it ?"

He turned his head, and looked down upon her with what Ivy thought a curious kind of smile, but only said, —

"You must not say 'horrid' so much."

By and by Ivy grew rather tired of sitting silent and watching the rustle of the leaves, which hid every other prospect ; she turned a little so that she could look at him. He sat with folded arms, looking straight ahead ; and she thought his face wore a troubled expression. She felt as if she would like very much to smooth out the wrinkles in his forehead and run her fingers through his hair, as she sometimes did for her father. She had a great mind to ask him if she should ; then she reflected that it might make him nervous. Then she wondered if he had forgotten her lessons, and how long they were to sit there. Determined, at length, to have a change of some kind, she said, softly, —

"Mr. Clerron !"

He roused himself suddenly, and stood up.

"I thought, perhaps, you had a headache."

"No, Ivy. But this is not climbing the hill of science, is it ?"

"Not so much as it is climbing the piazza."

"Suppose we take a vacation to-day, and investigate the state of the atmosphere ?"

"Yes, sir, I am ready."

Ivy did not fully understand the nature of his proposition; but if he had proposed to "put a girdle round the
earth in forty minutes," she would have said and acted,
"Yes, sir, I am ready," just the same.

He took up the basket of grapes which he had gathered,
and led the way through the window, down-stairs. Ivy
waited for him at the hall-door, while he carried the grapes
to Mrs. Simm; then he joined her again and proposed to
walk through the woods a little while, before Ivy went
home.

"You must know, my docile pupil, that I am going to the
city to-morrow, on business, to be gone a week or two. So,
as you must perforce take a vacation then, why, we may as
well begin to vacate to-day, and enjoy it."

"I am sorry you are going away."

"You are? That is almost enough to pay me for going.
Why are you sorry?"

"Because I shall not see you for a week; and I have become so used to you, that somehow I don't seem to know
what to do with a day without you; and then the cars may
run off the track and kill you or hurt you, or you may get
the small-pox, or a great many things may happen."

"And suppose some of these terrible things should happen, — the last, for instance, — what would you do?"

"I? I should advise you to send for the doctor at once."
Mr. Clerron laughed.

"So you would not come and nurse me, and take care of
me, and get me well again?"

"No, because I should then be in danger of taking it
myself and giving it to papa and mamma; besides, they
would not let me, I am quite sure."

"So you love your papa and mamma better than — "

He stopped abruptly. Ivy finished for him.

"Better than words can tell. Papa particularly. Mamma, somehow, seems strong of herself, and does n't depend
upon me; but papa, — O, you don't know how he is to me!

I think, if I should die, he would die of grief. I have, I cannot help having, a kind of pity for him, he loves me so."

"Do you always pity people, when they love you very much ?"

" O no ! of course not. Besides, nobody loves me enough to be pitied, except papa. — Is n't it pleasant here ? How very green it is ! It looks just like summer. O Mr. Clerron, did you see the clouds this morning ?"

"There were none when I arose."

"Why, yes, sir, there was a great heap of them at sunrise."

"I am not prepared to contradict you."

"Perhaps you were not up at sunrise."

"I have an impression to that effect."

He smiled so comically, that Ivy could not help saying, though she was half afraid he might not be pleased, —

"I wonder whether you are an early riser."

"Yes, my dear, I consider myself tolerably early. I believe I have been up every morning but one, this week, by nine o'clock."

Ivy was horror-struck. Her country ideas of "early to bed and early to rise" received a great shock, as her looks plainly showed. He laughed gayly at her amazed face.

"You don't seem to appreciate me, Miss Geer."

"'Nine o'clock' !" repeated Ivy, slowly, — "'every morning but one'! and it is Tuesday to-day."

"Yes, but you know yesterday was a dark, cloudy day, and excellent for sleeping."

"But, Mr. Clerron, then you are not more than fairly up when I come. And when do you write ?"

"Always in the evening."   .

"But the evenings are so short, — or have been."

"Mine are not particularly so. From six to three is about long enough for one sitting."

"I should think so. And you must be so tired !"

"Not so tired as you think. You, now, rising at five or six, and running round all day, become so tired that you have to go to bed by nine ; of course you have no time for reflection and meditation. I, on the contrary, take life easily, — write in the night, when everything is still and quiet, — take my sleep when all the noise of the world's waking-up is going on, — and after creation is fairly settled for the day, I rise leisurely, breakfast leisurely, take a smoke leisurely, and leisurely wait the coming of my little pupil."

" Mr. Clerron ! "

" Well ! "

" May I tell you another thing I don't like in you ? a bad habit ? "

" As many as you please, provided you won't require me to reform."

" What is the use of telling it, then ? "

" But it may be a relief to you. You will have the satisfaction arising from doing your duty. We shall exchange opinions, and perhaps come to a better understanding. Go on."

" Well, sir, I wish you did not smoke so much."

" I don't smoke very much, little Ivy."

" I wish you would not at all. Mamma thinks it is very injurious, and wrong, even. And papa says cigars are bad things."

" Some of them are outrageous. But, my dear, granting your father and mother and yourself to be right, don't you see I am doing more to extirpate the evil than you, with all your principle ? I exterminate, destroy, and ruin them at the rate of three a day ; while you, I venture to say, never lifted a finger or lighted a spark against them."

" Now, sir, that is only a way of slipping round the question. And I really wish you did not. Before I knew you, I thought it was almost as bad to smoke as it was to steal. I know, however, now, that it cannot be ; still — "

" Feminine logic."

" I have not studied Logic yet ; still, as I was going to say, sir, I don't like to think of you as being in a kind of subjection to anything."

" Ivy, seriously, I am not in subjection to a cigar. I often don't smoke for months together. To prove it, I promise you I won't smoke for the next two months."

" O, I am so glad ! O, I am so much obliged to you ! And you are not in the least vexed that I spoke to you about it ? "

" Not in the least."

" I was afraid you would be. And one thing more, sir, I have been afraid of, the last few days. You know when I first knew you, or before I knew you, I supposed you did nothing but walk round and enjoy yourself all day. But now I know you do work very hard ; and I have feared that you could not well spare two hours every day for me, — particularly in the morning, which are almost always considered the best. But if you like to write in the evening, you would just as soon I would come in the morning ? "

" Certainly."

" But if two hours are too much, I hope you won't, at any time, hesitate to tell me. I have no claim on a moment, — only — "

" My dear Ivy Geer, pupil and friend, be so good as to understand, henceforth, that you cannot possibly come into my house at any time when you are not wanted ; nor stay any longer than I want you ; nor say anything that will not please me ; — well, I am not quite sure about that ; — but, at least, remember that I am always glad to see you, and teach you, and have you with me ; and that I can never hope to do you as much good as you do me every day of your blessed life."

" O Mr. Clerron ! " exclaimed Ivy, with a great gush of gratitude and happiness ; " do I, can I, do *you* any good ? "

" You do and can, my tendril ! You supply an element that was wanting in my life. You make every day beautiful to me. The flutter of your robes among these trees brings sunshine into my heart. Every morning I walk in my garden as soon as I am, as you say, fairly up, till I see you turn into the lane ; and every day I watch you till you disappear. You are fresh and truthful and natural, and you give me new life. And now, my dear little trembling benefactor, because we are nearly through the woods, I can go no farther with you; and because I am going away tomorrow, not to see you again for a week, and because I hope you will be a little lonesome while I am gone, why, I think I must let you — kiss me!"

Ivy had been looking intently into his face, with an expression, at first, of the most beaming, tearful delight, then gradually changing into waiting wonder; but when his sentence finally closed, she stood still, scarcely able to comprehend. He placed his hands on her temples, and, smiling involuntarily at her blushes and embarrassment, half in sport and half in tenderness, bent her head a little back, touched brow, cheeks, and lips, whispered softly, "Go now! God bless you for ever and ever, my darling!" and, turning walked hastily down the winding path. As for Ivy, she went home in a dream, blind and stunned with a great joy.

The week of Mr. Clerron's absence passed away more quickly than Ivy had supposed it would. The reason for this may be found in the fact that her thoughts were very busily occupied. She was more silent than usual, so much so that her father one day said to her, — "Ivy, I have n't heard you sing this long while, and seems to me you don't talk either. What 's the matter?"

"Do I look as if anything was the matter?" and the face she turned upon him was so radiant, that even the father's heart was satisfied.

Very quietly happy was Ivy to think she was of service to Mr. Clerron, that she could give him pleasure, — though she could in no wise understand how it was. She went over every event since her acquaintance with him; she felt how much he had done for her, and how much he had been to her; but she sought in vain to discover how she had been of any use to him. She only knew that she was the most ignorant and insignificant girl in the whole world, and that he was the best and greatest man. As this was very nearly the same conclusion at which she had arrived at an early period of their acquaintance, it cannot be said that her week of reflection was productive of any very valuable results.

The day before Mr. Clerron's expected return, Ivy sat down to prepare her lessons, and for the first time remembered that she had left her books in Mr. Clerron's library. She was not sorry to have so good an excuse for visiting the familiar room, though its usual occupant was not there to welcome her. Very quietly and joyfully happy, she trod slowly along the path through the woods where she last walked with Mr. Clerron. She was, indeed, at a loss to know why she was so calm. Always before, a sudden influx of joy testified itself by very active demonstrations. She was quite sure that she had never in her life been so happy as now; yet she never had felt less disposed to leap and dance and sing. The non-solution of the problem, however, did not ruffle her serenity. She was content to accept the facts, and await patiently the theory.

Arriving at the house, she went, as usual, into the library without ringing, — but, not finding the books, proceeded in search of Mrs. Simm. That notable lady was sitting behind a huge pile of clean clothes, sorting and mending to her heart's content. She looked up over her spectacles at Ivy's bright "good morning," and invited her to come in. Ivy declined, and begged to know if Mrs. Simm had seen her books. To be sure she had, like the good housekeeper that she was. "You 'll find them in the book-case, second shelf; but, Miss Ivy, I wish you would come in, for I 've had something on my mind that I 've felt to tell you this long while."

Ivy came in, took the seat opposite Mrs. Simm, and waited for her to speak; but Mrs. Simm seemed to be in no hurry to speak. She dropped her glasses; Ivy picked them up and handed them to her. She muttered something about the destructive habits of men, especially in regard to buttons; and presently, as if determined to come to the subject at once, abruptly exclaimed, —

"Miss Ivy, you're a real good girl, I know, and as innocent as a lamb. That's why I'm going to talk to you as I do. I know, if you were my child, I should want somebody to do the same by you."

Ivy could only stare in blank astonishment. After a moment's pause, Mrs. Simm continued, —

"I've seen how things have been going on for some time; but my mouth was shut, though my eyes were open. I didn't know but maybe I'd better speak to your mother about it; but then, thinks I to myself, she'll think it is a great deal worse than it is, and then, like enough, there'll be a rumpus. So I concluded, on the whole, I'd just tell you what I thought; and I know you are a sensible girl and will take it all right. Now you must promise me not to get mad."

"No," gasped Ivy.

"I like you a sight. It's no flattery, but the truth, to say I think you're as pretty-behaved a girl as you'll find in a thousand. And all the time you've been here, I never have known you to do a thing you hadn't ought to. And Mr. Clerron thinks so too, and there's the trouble. You see, dear, he's a man, and men go on their ways and like women, and talk to them, and sort of bewitch them, not meaning to do them any hurt, — and enjoy their company of an evening, and go about their own business in the morning, and never think of it again; but women stay at home, and brood over it, and think there's something in it, and build a fine air-castle, — and when they find it's all smoke, they mope and pine and take on. Now that's what I don't want you to do. Perhaps you'd think I'd better have spoken with Mr. Clerron; but it wouldn't signify the head of a pin. He'd either put on the Clerron look and scare you to death and not say a word, or else he'd hold it up in such a ridiculous way as to make you think it was ridiculous yourself. And I thought I'd put you on your guard a little, so as you needn't fall in love with him. You'll like him, of course. He likes you; but a young

6 * I

girl like you might make a mistake, if she was ever so modest and sweet, — and nobody could be modester or sweeter than you, — and think a man loved you to marry you, when he only pets and plays with you. Not that Mr. Clerron means to do anything wrong. He'd be perfectly miserable himself, if he thought he'd led you on. There ain't a more honorable man every way in the whole country. Now, Miss Ivy, it's all for your good I say this. I don't find fault with you, not a bit. It's only to save you trouble in store that I warn you to look where you stand, and see that you don't lose your heart before you know it. It's an awful thing for a woman, Miss Ivy, to get a notion after a man who hasn't got a notion after her. Men go out and work and delve and drive, and forget; but there ain't much in darning stockings and making pillow-cases to take a woman's thought off her troubles, and sometimes they get sp'iled for life."

Ivy had remained speechless from amazement; but when Mrs. Simm had finished, she said, with a sudden accession of womanly dignity that surprised the good housekeeper, —

"Mrs. Simm, I cannot conceive why you should speak in this way to me. If you suppose I am not quite able to take care of myself, I assure you you are very much mistaken."

"Lorful heart! Now, Miss Ivy, you promised you wouldn't be mad."

"And I have kept my promise. I am not mad."

"No, but you answer up short like, and that isn't what I thought of you, Ivy Geer."

Mrs. Simm looked so disappointed that Ivy took a lower tone, and at any rate she would have had to do it soon; for her fortitude gave way, and she burst into a flood of tears. She was not, by any means, a heroine, and could not put on the impenetrable mask of a woman of the world.

"Now, dear, don't be so distressful, dear, don't!" said Mrs. Simm, soothingly. "I can't bear to see you."

"I am sure I never thought of such a thing as falling in

love with Mr. Clerron or anybody else," sobbed Ivy, "and I don't know what should make you think so."

"Dear heart, I don't think so. I only told you, so you need n't."

"Why, I should as soon think of marrying the angel Gabriel!"

"O, don't talk so, dear; he's no more than man, after all; but still, you know, he's no fit match for you. To say nothing of his being older, and all that, I don't think it's the right place for you. Your father and mother are very nice folks; I am sure nobody could ask for better neighbors, and their good word is in everybody's mouth; and they've brought you up well, I am sure; but, my dear, you know it's nothing against you nor them that you ain't used to splendor, and you would n't take to it natural like. You'd get tired of that way of life, and want to go back to the old fashions, and you'd most likely have to leave your father and mother; for it's noways probable Mr. Clerron will stay here always; and when he goes back to the city, think what a dreary life you'd have betwixt his two proud sisters, on the one hand, — to be sure, there's no reason why they should be; their gran'ther was a tailor, and their grandma was his apprentice, and he got rich, and gave all his children learning; and Mr. Felix's father, he was a lawyer, and he got rich by speculation, and so the two girls always had on their high-heeled boots; but Mr. Clerron, he always laughs at them, and brings up "the grand-paternal shop," as he calls it, and provokes them terribly, I know. Well, that's neither here nor there; but, as I was saying, here you'll have them on the one side, and all the fine ladies on the other, and a great house and servants, and parties to see to, and, lorful heart! Miss Ivy, you'd die in three years; and if you know when you're well off, you'll stay at home, and marry and settle down near the old folks. Believe me, my dear, it's a bad thing both for the man and the woman, when she marries above her."

"Mrs. Simm," said Ivy, rising, "will you promise me one thing?"

"Certainly, child, if I can."

"Will you promise me never again to mention this thing to me, or allude to it in the most distant manner?"

"Miss Ivy, now,"—began Mrs. Simm, deprecatingly.

"Because," interrupted Ivy, speaking very thick and fast, "you cannot imagine how disagreeable it is to me. It makes me feel ashamed to think of what you have said, and that you could have thought it even. I suppose—indeed, I know—that you did it because you thought you ought; but you may be certain that I am in no danger from Mr. Clerron, nor is there the slightest probability that his fortune, or honor, or reputation, or sisters will ever be disturbed by me. I am very much obliged to you for your good intentions, and I wish you good morning."

"Don't, now, Miss Ivy, go so—"

But Miss Ivy was gone, and Mrs. Simm could only withdraw to her pile of clothes, and console herself by stitching and darning with renewed vigor. She felt rather uneasy about the result of her morning's work, though she had really done it from a conscientious sense of duty.

"Welladay," she sighed, at last, "she'd better be a little cut up and huffy now, than to walk into a ditch blindfolded; and I wash my hands of whatever may happen after this. I 've had my say and done my part."

Alas, Ivy Geer! The Indian summer day was just as calm and beautiful,—the far-off mountains wore their veil of mist just as aerially,—the brook rippled over the stones with just as soft a melody; but what "discord on the music" had fallen! what "darkness on the glory"! A miserable, dull, dead weight was the heart which throbbed so lightly but an hour before. Wearily, drearily, she dragged herself home. It was nearly sunset when she arrived, and she told her mother she was tired and had the headache, which was true,—though, if she had said heartache, it would have been truer. Her mother immediately did what ninety-nine mothers out of a hundred would do in similar circumstances, — made her swallow a cup of strong tea, and sent her to bed. Alas, alas that there are sorrows which the strongest tea cannot assuage!

When the last echo of her mother's footstep died on the stairs, and Ivy was alone in the darkness, the tide of bitterness and desolation swept unchecked over her soul, and she wept tears more passionate and desponding than her life had ever before known, — tears of shame and indignation and grief. It was true that the thought which Mrs. Simm had suggested had never crossed her mind before ; yet it is no less true, that, all-unconsciously, she had been weaving a golden web, whose threads, though too fine and delicate even for herself to perceive, were yet strong enough to entangle her life in their meshes. A secret chamber, far removed from the noise and din of the world, — a chamber whose soft and rose-tinted light threw its radiance over her whole future, and within whose quiet recesses she loved to sit alone and dream away the hours, — had been rudely · entered, and thrown violently open to the light of day, and Ivy saw with dismay how its pictures had become ghastly and its sacredness was defiled. With bitter, though needless and useless self-reproach, she saw how she had suffered herself to be fascinated. Sorrowfully, she felt that Mrs. Simm's words were true, and a great gulf lay between her and him. She pictured him moving easily and gracefully and naturally among scenes which to her inexperienced eye. were grand and stately; and then, with a sharp pain, she felt how constrained and awkward and entirely unfit for such a life was she. Then her thoughts reverted to her parents, — their unchanging love, their happiness depending on her, their solicitude and watchfulness, — and she felt as if ingratitude were added to her other sins, that she could have so attached herself to any other. And again came back the bitter, burning agony of shame that she had done the very thing that Mrs. Simm too late had warned her not to do ; she had been carried away by the kindness and tenderness of her friend, and, unasked, had laid the wealth of her heart at his feet. So the night flushed into morning; and the sun rose upon a pale face and a trembling form, — but not upon a faint heart; for Ivy, kneeling by the couch where her morning and evening prayer had gone up since lisping infancy, — kneeling no longer a child, but a woman, matured through love, matured, alas! through suffering, prayed for strength and comfort; prayed that her parents' love might be rendered back into their own bosoms a hundred-fold; prayed that her friend's kindness to her might not be an occasion of sin against God, and that she might be enabled to walk with a steady step in the path that lay before her. And she arose strengthened and comforted.

All the morning she lay quiet and silent on the lounge in the little sitting-room. Her mother, busied with household matters, only looked in upon her occasionally, and, as the eyes were always closed, did not speak, thinking her asleep. Ivy was not asleep. Ten thousand little sprites flitted swiftly through the chambers of her brain, humming, singing, weeping, but always busy, busy. Then softly came another tread, and she knew her dear old father had drawn a chair close to her, and was looking into her face. Tears came into her eyes, her lip involuntarily quivered, and then she felt the pressure of his — his! — surely that was not her father's kiss! She started up. No, no! that was not her father's face bending over her, — not her father's eyes smiling into hers; but, woe for Ivy! her soul thrilled with a deeper bliss, her heart leaped with a swifter bound, and for a moment all the experience and suffering and resolutions of the last night were as if they had never been. Only for a moment, and then with a strong effort she remembered the impassable gulf.

"A pretty welcome home you have given me!" said Mr. Clerron, lightly.

He saw that something was weighing on her spirits, but did not wish to distress her by seeming to notice it.

"I wait in my library, I walk in my garden, expecting every moment will bring you, — and lo! here you are lying, doing nothing but look pale and pretty as hard as you can."

Ivy smiled, but did not consider it prudent to speak.

"I found your books, however, and have brought them to you. You thought you would escape a lesson finely, did you not? But you see I have outwitted you."

"Yes, — I went for the books yesterday," said Ivy, "but I got talking with Mrs. Simm and forgot them."

"Ah!" he replied, looking somewhat surprised. "I did not know Mrs. Simm could be so entertaining. She must have exerted herself. Pray, now, if it would not be impertinent, what subject was it that drove everything else from your mind? The best way of preserving apples, I dare swear, or the superiority of pickled grapes to pickled cucumbers."

"No," said Ivy, with the ghost of another smile, — "we talked upon various subjects; but not those. How do you do, Mr. Clerron? Have you had a pleasant visit to the city?"

"Very well, I thank you, Miss Geer; and I have not had a remarkably pleasant visit, I am obliged to you. Have I the pleasure of seeing you quite well, Miss Geer, — quite fresh and buoyant?"

The lightness of tone which he had assumed had precisely the opposite effect intended.

> "Ye banks and braes o' bonny Doon,
>   How can ye bloom sae fresh and fair?
> How can ye chant, ye little birds,
> And I sae weary fu' o' care?"

is the wail of stricken humanity everywhere. And Ivy thought of Mr. Clerron, rich, learned, elegant, happy, on the current of whose life she only floated a pleasant ripple, — and of herself, poor, plain, ignorant, to whom he was the life of life, the all in all. I would not have you suppose this passed through her mind precisely as I have written it. By no means. The ideas rather trooped through in a pellmell sort of way; but. they got through just as effectually. Now, if Ivy had been content to let her muscles remain perfectly still, her face might have given no sign of the confusion within; but, with a foolish presumption, she undertook to smile, and so quite lost control of the little rebels, who immediately twisted themselves into a sob. Her whole frame convulsed with weeping and trying not to weep, he forced her gently back on the pillow, and, bending low, whispered softly, —

"Ivy what is it?"

"O, don't ask me! — please, don't! Please, go away!" murmured the poor child.

"I will, my dear, in a minute; but you.must think I should be a little anxious. I leave you as gay as a bird, and healthy and rosy, — and when I come back, I find you white and sad and ill. I am sure something weighs on your mind. I assure you, my little Ivy, and you must believe, that I am your true friend, — and if you would confide in me, perhaps I could bring you comfort. It would at least relieve you to let me help you bear the burden."

The burden being of such a nature, it is not at all probable that Ivy would have assented to his proposition; but the welcome entrance of her mother prevented the necessity of replying.

"O, you're awake! Well, I told Mr. Clerron he might come in, though I thought you wouldn't be. Slept well this morning, didn't you, deary, to make up for last night?"

"No, mamma, I haven't been asleep."

"Crying, my dear? Well, now, that's a pretty good one! Nervous she is, Mr. Clerron, always nervous, when the least thing ails her; and she didn't sleep a wink last night, which is a bad thing for the nerves, — and Ivy generally sleeps like a top. She walked over to your house yesterday, and when she got home she was entirely beat out, — looked as if she had been sick a week. I don't know why it was, for the walk couldn't have hurt her. She's always dancing round at home. I don't think she's been exactly well for four or five days. Her father and I both thought she'd been more quiet like than usual."

The sudden pang that shot across Ivy's face was not unobserved by Mr. Clerron. A thought came into his mind. He had risen at Mrs. Geer's entrance, and he now expressed his regret for Ivy's illness, and hoped that she would soon be well, and able to resume her studies ; and, with a few words of interest and inquiry to Mrs. Geer, took his leave.

"I wonder if Mrs. Simm *has* been making mischief!" thought he, as he stalked home rather more energetically than was his custom.

That unfortunate lady was in her sitting-room, starching muslins, when Mr. Clerron entered. She had surmised that he was gone to the farm, and had looked for his return with a shadow of dread. She saw by his face that something was wrong.

"Mrs. Simm," he began, somewhat abruptly, but not disrespectfully, "may I beg your pardon for inquiring what Ivy Geer talked to you about, yesterday?"

"O, good Lord! she ha'n't told you, has she?" cried Mrs. Simm, — her fear of God, for once, yielding to her greater fear of man. The embroidered collar, which she had been vigorously beating, dropped to the floor, and she gazed at him with such terror and dismay in every lineament, that he could not help being amused. He picked up the collar, which, in her perturbation, she had not noticed, and said, —

"No, she has told me nothing; but I find her excited and ill, and I have reason to believe it is connected with her visit here yesterday. If it is anything relating to me, and which I have a right to know, you would do me a great favor by enlightening me on the subject."

Mrs. Simm had not a particle of that knowledge in which Young America is so great a proficient, namely, the "knowing how to get out of a scrape." She was, besides, alarmed at the effect of her words on Ivy, supposing nothing less than that the girl was in the last stages of a swift consumption; so she sat down, and, rubbing her starchy hands together, with many a deprecatory "you know," and apologetic "I am sure I thought I was acting for the best," gave, considering her agitation, a tolerably accurate account of the whole interview. Her interlocutor saw plainly that she had acted from a sincere conscientiousness, and not from a meddlesome, mischievous interference; so he only thanked her for her kind interest, and suggested that he had now arrived at an age when it would, perhaps, be well for him to conduct matters, particularly of so delicate a nature, solely according to his own judgment. He was sorry to have given her any trouble.

"Scissors cuts only what comes between 'em," soliloquized Mrs. Simm, when the door closed behind him. "If ever I meddle with a courting-business again, my name ain't Martha Simm. No, they may go to Halifax, whoever they be, 'fore ever I 'll lift a finger."

It is a great pity that the world generally has not been brought to make the same wise resolution.

One, two, three, four days passed away, and still Ivy pondered the question so often wrung from man in his bewildered gropings, "What shall I do?" Every day brought her teacher and friend to comfort, amuse, and strengthen. Every morning she resolved to be on her guard, to remember the impassable gulf. Every evening she felt the silken cords drawing tighter and tighter around her soul, and binding her closer and closer to him. She thought she might die, and the thought gave her a sudden joy. Death would solve the problem at once. If only a few weeks or months lay before her, she could quietly rest on him, and give herself up to him and wait in heaven for all rough places to be made plain. But Ivy did not die. Youth and nursing and herb-tea were too strong for her, and the color came back to her cheek and the languor went out from her blue eyes. She saw nothing to be done but to resume her old routine. It would be difficult to say whether she was more glad or sorry at seeming to see this necessity. She knew her danger, and it was very fascinating. She did not look into the far-off future; she only prayed to be kept from day to day. Perhaps her course was wise; perhaps not. But she had to rely on her own judgment alone; and her judgment was founded on inexperience, which is not a trustworthy basis.

A new difficulty arose. Ivy found that she could not resume her old habits. To be sure, she learned her lessons just as perfectly at home as she had ever done. Just as punctual to the appointed hour, she went to recite them; but no sooner had her foot crossed Mr. Clerron's threshold than her spirit seemed to die within her. She remembered neither words nor ideas. Day after day, she attempted to go through her recitation as usual, and, day after day, she hesitated, stammered, and utterly failed. His gentle assistance only increased her embarrassment. This she was too proud to endure; and, one day, after an unsuccessful effort, she closed the book with a quick, impatient gesture, and exclaimed, —

"Mr. Clerron, I shall not recite any more!"

The agitated flush which had suffused her face gave way to paleness. He saw that she was under strong excitement, and quietly replied, —

"Very well, you need not, if you are tired. You are not quite well yet, and must not try to do too much. We will commence here to-morrow."

"No, sir, — I shall not recite any more at all."

"Till to-morrow."

"Never any more!"

There was a moment's pause.

"You must not lose patience, my dear. In a few days you will recite as well as ever. A fine notion, forsooth, because you have been ill, and forgotten a little, to give up studying! And what is to become of my laurels, pray, — all the glory I am to get by your proficiency?"

"I shall study at home just the same, but I shall not recite."

"Why not?"

His look became serious.

"Because I cannot. I do not think it best, — and — and I will not."

Another pause.

"Ivy, do you not like your teacher?"

"No, sir. *I hate you!*"

The words seemed to flash from her lips. She sprang up and stood erect before him, her eyes on fire, and every nerve quivering with intense excitement. He was shocked and startled. It was a new phase of her character, — a new revelation. He, too, arose, and walked to the window. If Ivy could have seen the workings of his face, there would have been a revelation to her also. But she was too highly excited to notice anything. He came back to her and spoke in a low voice, —

"Ivy, this is too much. This I did not expect."

He laid his hand upon her head as he had often done before. She shook it off passionately.

"Yes, I hate you. I hate you, because —"

"Because I wanted you to love me?"

"No, sir; because I do love you, and you bring me only wretchedness. I have never been happy since the miserable day I first saw you."

"Then, Ivy, I have utterly failed in what it has been my constant endeavor to do."

"No, sir, you have succeeded in what you endeavored to do. You have taught me. You have given me knowledge and thought, and showed me the source of knowledge. But I had better have been the ignorant girl you found me. You have taken from me what I can never find again. I have made a bitter exchange. I was ignorant and stupid, I know, — but I was happy and contented; and now I am wretched and miserable and wicked. You have come between me and my home and my father and mother, — between me and all the bliss of my past and all my hope for the future."

"And thus, Ivy, have you come between me and my past and my future; — yet not thus. You shut out from my heart all the sorrow and vexation and strife that have clouded my life, and fill it with your own dear presence. You come between me and my future, because, in looking forward, I see only you. I should have known better. There is a gulf between us; but if I could make you happy — "

"I don't want you to make me happy. I know there is a gulf between us. I saw it while you were gone. I measured it and fathomed it. I shall not leap across. Stay you on your side quietly; I shall stay as quietly on mine."

"It is too late for that, Ivy, — too late now. But you are not to blame, my child. Little sunbeam that you are, I will not cloud you. Go shine upon other lives as you have shone upon mine! light up other hearths as you have mine! and I will bless you forever, though mine — "

He turned away with an expression on his face that Ivy could not read. Her passion was gone. She hesitated a moment, then went to his side and laid her hand softly on his arm. There was a strange moistened gleam in his eyes as he turned them upon her.

"Mr. Clerron, I do not understand you."

"My dear, you never can understand me."

"I know it," said Ivy, with her old humility; "but, at least, I might understand whether I have vexed you."

"You have not vexed me."

"I spoke proudly and rudely to you. I was angry, and so unhappy. I shall always be so; I shall never be happy again; but I want you to be, and you do not look as if you were."

If Ivy had not been a little fool, she would not have spoken so; but she was, so she did.

"I beg your pardon, little tendril. I was so occupied

with my own preconceived ideas that I forgot to sympathize with you. Tell me why or how I have made you unhappy. But I know; you need not. I assure you, however, that you are entirely wrong. It was a prudish and whimsical notion of my good old housekeeper's. You are never to think of it again. *I* never attributed such a thought or feeling to you."

" Did you suppose that was all that made me unhappy?"

" Can there be anything else?"

" I am glad you think so. Perhaps I should not have been unhappy but for that, at least not so soon ; but that alone could never have made me so."

Little fool again ! She was like a chicken thrusting its head into a corner and thinking itself out of danger because it cannot see the danger. She had no notion that she was giving him the least clew to the truth, but considered herself speaking with more than Delphic prudence. She rather liked to coast along the shores of her trouble and see how near she could approach without running aground ; but she struck before she knew it.

Mr. Clerron's face suddenly changed. He took both her hands, and drew her towards him.

"Ivy, perhaps I have been misunderstanding you. I will at least find out the truth. Ivy, do you know that I love you, that I have loved you almost from the first, that I would gladly here and now take you to my heart and keep you here forever?"

" I do not know it," faltered Ivy, half beside herself.

" Know it now, then ! I am older than you, and I seem to myself so far removed from you that I have feared to ask you to trust your happiness to my keeping, lest I should lose you entirely ; but sometimes you say or do something which gives me hope. My experience has been very different from yours. I am not worthy to clasp your purity and loveliness. Still I would do it if— Tell me, Ivy, does it give you pain or pleasure?"

Ivy took his hands, as he had before held hers, gazed steadily into his eyes, and said, —

" Mr. Clerron, are you in earnest ? Do you love me ? "

" I am, Ivy. I do love you."

" How do you love me ? "

" I love you with all the strength and power that God has given me."

" You do not simply pity me ? You have not, because you heard from Mrs. Simm, or suspected, yourself, that I was weak enough to mistake your kindness and nobleness, — you have not in pity resolved to sacrifice your happiness to mine ? "

" No, Ivy, — nothing of the kind. I pity only myself. I reverence you. I think — I have hoped that you loved me as a teacher and friend. I dared not believe you could ever do more; now something within tells me that you can. Can you, Ivy ? If the love and tenderness and devotion of my whole life can make you happy, happiness shall not fail to be yours."

Ivy's gaze never for a moment drooped under his, earnest and piercing though it was.

" Now I am happy," she said, slowly and distinctly. " Now I am blessed. I can never ask anything more."

" But I ask something more," he replied, bending forward eagerly. " I ask much more. I want your love. Shall I have it? And I want you."

" My love ? " She blushed slightly, but spoke without hesitation. " Have I not given it, — long, long before you asked it, before you even cared for my friendship ? Not love only, but life, my very whole being, centred in you, does now, and will always. Is it right to say this ? — But I am not ashamed. I shall always be proud to have loved you, though only to lose you, — and to be loved by you is glory enough for all my future."

One moment Ivy rested in the arms that clasped her; but as he whispered, " Thus you answer the second question ? You give me yourself too ? " she hastily freed herself.

" Never ! "

" Ivy ! "

"Never!" more firmly than before.

"What does this mean?" he said, sternly. "Are you trifling?"

There was such a frown on his brow as Ivy had never seen. She quailed before it.

"Do not be angry! Alas! I am not trifling. Life itself is not worth so much as your love. But the impassable gulf is between us just the same."

"What is it? Who put it there?"

"God put it there. Mrs. Simm showed it to me."

"Mrs. Simm be —! A prating gossip! Ivy, I told you you were never to mention that again, — never to think of it; and you must obey me."

"I will try to obey you in that."

"And very soon you shall promise to obey me in all things. But I will not be hard with you. The yoke shall rest very lightly, — so lightly you shall not feel it. You will not do as much, I dare say. You will make me acknowledge your power every day, dear little vixen! Ivy, why do you draw back? Why do you not come to me?"

"I cannot come to you, Mr. Clerron, any more. I must go home now, and stay at home."

"When your home is here, Ivy, stay at home. For the present, don't go. Wait a little."

"You do not understand me. You will not understand me," said Ivy, bursting into tears. "I *must* leave you. Don't make the way so difficult."

"I will make it so difficult that you cannot walk in it. Why do you wish to leave me? Have you not said that you loved me?"

"It is because I love you that I go. I am not fit for you. I was not made for you. I can never make you happy. I cannot go among your friends, your sisters. I am ignorant. You would be ashamed of me, and then you would not love me; you could not; and I should lose the thing I most value. No, Mr. Clerron, — I would rather keep your love in my own heart and my own home."

" Ivy, can you be happy without me ? "

" I shall not be without you. My heart is full of lifelong joyful memories. You need not regret me. Yes, I shall be happy. I shall work with mind and hands. I shall not pine away in a mean and feeble life. I shall be strong, and cheerful, and active, and helpful ; and I think I shall not cease to love you in heaven."

" But there is, maybe, a long road for us to travel before we reach heaven, and I want you to help me along. Ivy, I am not so spiritual as you. I cannot live on memory, I want you before me all the time. I want to see you and talk with you every day. Why do you speak of such things ? Is it the soul or its surroundings that you value? Do *you* respect or care for wealth and station ? Do *you* consider a woman your superior because she wears a finer dress than you ? "

" I ? No, sir ! No, indeed ! you very well know. But the world does, and you move in the world ; and I do not want the world to pity you because you have an uncouth, ignorant wife. *I* don't want to be despised by those who are above me only in station."

" Little aristocrat, you are prouder than I. Will you sacrifice your happiness and mine to your pride ? "

" Proud perhaps I am, but it is not all pride. I think you are noble, but I think also you could not help losing patience when you found that I could not accommodate myself to the station to which you had raised me. Then you would not respect me. I am, indeed, too proud to wish to lose that ; and losing your respect, as I said before, I should not long keep your love."

" But you will accommodate yourself to any station. My dear, you are young, and know so little about this world, which is such a bugbear to you. Why, there is very little that will be greatly unlike this. At first you might be a little bewildered, but I shall be by you all the time, and you shall feel and fear nothing, and gradually you will learn what little you need to know ; and most of all, you

J

will be yourself the best and the loveliest of women. Dear Ivy, I would not part with your sweet, unconscious simplicity for all the accomplishments and acquired elegancies of the finest lady in the world." (What men always say.) "You are not ignorant of anything you ought to know, and your ignorance of the world is an additional charm to one who knows so much of its wickedness as I. But we will not talk of it. There is no need. This shall be our home, and here the world will not trouble us."

"And I cannot give up my dear father and mother. You and your friends — "

"They are my friends, valued and dear to me, and dearer still they shall be as the parents of my dear little wife — "

"I was going to say — "

"But you shall not say it. I utterly forbid you ever to mention it again. You are mine, all my own. Your friends are my friends, your honor my honor, your happiness my happiness henceforth; and what God joins together let not man or woman put asunder."

"Ah!" whispered Ivy, faintly; for she was yielding, and just beginning to receive the sense of great and unexpected bliss, "but if you should be wrong, — if you should ever repent of this, it is not your happiness alone, but mine, too, that will be destroyed."

"Ivy, am I a mere school-boy to swear eternal fidelity for a week? Have I not been tossing hither and thither on the world's tide ever since you lay in your cradle, and do I not know my position and my power and my habits and my love? And knowing all this, do I not know that this dear head " — etc., etc., etc., etc.

But I said I was not going to marry my man and woman, did I not? Nor have I. To be sure, you may have detected premonitory symptoms, but I said nothing about that. I only promised not to marry them, and I have not married them.

And that is the end of my story.

A RAFT THAT NO MAN MADE.

AM a soldier: but my tale, this time, is not of war.

The man of whom the Muse talked to the blind bard of old had grown wise in wayfaring. He had seen such men and cities as the sun shines on, and the great wonders of land and sea; and he had visited the farther countries, whose indwellers, having been once at home in the green fields and under the sky and roofs of the cheery earth, were now gone forth and forward into a dim and shadowed land, from which they found no backward path to these old haunts, and their old loves : —

'Ήέρι καὶ νεφέλῃ κεκαλυμμένοι· οὐδέ ποτ' αὐτοὺς
'Ηέλιος φαέθων καταδέρκεται ἀκτίνεσσιν.

Od. XI.

At the Charter-House I learned the story of the King of Ithaca, and read it for something better than a task; and since, though I have never seen so many cities as the much-wandering man, nor grown so wise, yet have heard and seen and remembered, for myself, words and things from crowded streets and fairs and shows and wave-washed quays and murmurous market-places, in many lands; and for his Κιμμερίων ἀνδρῶν δῆμος, — his people wrapt in cloud and vapor, whom "no glad sun finds with his beams," — have been borne along a perilous path through thick mists, among the crashing ice of the Upper Atlantic, as well as sweltered upon a Southern sea, and have learned something of men and something of God.

I was in Newfoundland, a lieutenant of Royal Engineers, in Major Gore's time, and went about a good deal among the people, in surveying for Government. One of my old friends there was Skipper Benjie Westham of Brigus, a shortish, stout, bald man, with a cheerful, honest face and a kind voice ; and he, mending a caplin-seine one day, told me this story, which I will try to tell after him.

We were upon the high ground, beyond where the church stands now, and Prudence, the fisherman's daughter, and Ralph Barrows, her husband, were with Skipper Benjie when he began ; and I had an hour by the watch to spend. The neighborhood, all about, was still ; the only men who were in sight were so far off that we heard nothing from them ; no wind was stirring near us, and a slow sail could be seen outside. Everything was right for listening and telling.

" I can tell 'ee what I sid * myself, sir," said Skipper Benjie. " It is n' like a story that 's put down in books : it 's on'y like what we planters † tells of a winter's night or sech ; but it 's *feelun*, mubbe, an' 'ee won't expect much off a man as could n' never read, — not so much as Bible or Prayer-Book, even."

Skipper Benjie looked just like what he was thought : a true-hearted, healthy man, a good fisherman, and a good seaman. There was no need of any one's saying it. So I only waited till he went on speaking.

"'T was one time I goed to th' Ice, sir. I never goed but once, an' 't was a'most the first v'yage ever was, ef 't was n' the *very* first ; an' 't was the last for me, an' worse agen for the rest-part o' that crew, that never goed no more ! 'T was tarrible sad douns wi' they ! "

This preface was accompanied by some preliminary handling of the caplin-seine, also, to find out the broken places and get them about him. Ralph and Prudence deftly helped him. Then, making his story wait, after this opening, he took one hole to begin at in mending, chose

---

* Saw. † Fishermen.

his seat, and drew the seine up to his knee. At the same time I got nearer to the fellowship of the family by persuading the planter (who yielded with a pleasant smile) to let me try my hand at the netting. Prudence quietly took to herself a share of the work, and Ralph alone was unbusied.

"They calls th' Ice a wicked place, — Sundays an' weekin days all alike ; an' to my seemun it 's a cruel, bloody place, jes' so well, — but not all thinks alike, surely. — Rafe, lad, mubbe 'ee 'd ruther go down cove-ways, an' overhaul the punt a bit."

Ralph, who perhaps had stood waiting for the very dismissal that he now got, assented and left us three. Prudence, to be sure, looked after him as if she would a good deal rather go with him than stay ; but she stayed, nevertheless, and worked at the seine. I interpreted to myself Skipper Benjie's sending away of one of his hearers by supposing that his son-in-law had often heard his tales ; but the planter explained himself : —

"'Ee sees, sir, I knocked off goun to th' Ice becase 't was sech a tarrible cruel place, to my seemun. They swiles * be so knowun like, — as knowun as a dog, in a manner, an' lovun to their own, like Christens, a'most, more than bastes ; an' they 'm got red blood, for all they lives most-partly in water ; an' then I found 'em so friendly, when I was wantun friends badly. But I s'pose the swile-fishery 's needful ; an' I knows, in course, that even Christens' blood 's got to be taken sometimes, when it 's bad blood, an' I would n' be childish about they things ; on'y, — ef it 's me, — when I can live by fishun, I don' want to go an' club an' shoot an' cut an' slash among poor harmless things that 'ould never harm man or 'oman, an' 'ould cry great tears down for pity-sake, an got a sound like a Christen ; I 'ould n' like to go a-swilun for gain, — not after beun among 'em, way I was, anyways."

This apology made it plain that Skipper Benjie was large-

* Seals.

hearted enough, or indulgent enough, not to seek to strain others, even his own family, up to his own way in everything; and it might easily be thought that the young fisherman had different feelings about sealing from those that the planter's story was meant to bring out. All being ready, he began his tale again : —

"I shipped wi' Skipper Isra'l Gooden, from Carbonear : the schooner was the Baccaloue, wi' forty men, all told. 'T was of a Sunday morn'n 'e 'ould sail, twel'th day o' March, wi' another schooner in company, — the Sparrow. There was a many of us was n' too good, but we thowt wrong of 'e's takun the Lord's Day to 'e'sself. — Wull, sir, afore I comed 'ome, I was in a great desert country, an' floated on sea wi' a monstrous great raft that no man never made, creakun an' crashun an' groanun an' tumblun an' wastun an' goun to pieces, an' no man on her but me, an' full o' livun things, — dreadful !

"About a five hours out, 't was, we first sid the blink,* an' comed up wi' th' Ice about off Cape Bonavis'. We fell in wi' it south, an worked up nothe along : but we did n' see swiles for two or three days yet ; on'y we was workun along ; pokun the cakes of ice away, an' haulun through wi' main strength sometimes, holdun on wi' bights o' ropes out o' the bow ; an' more times, agen, in clear water : sometimes mist all round us, 'ee could n' see the ship's len'th, sca'ce ; an' more times snow, jes' so thick ; an' then a gale o' wind, mubbe, would a'most blow all the spars out of her, seemunly.

"We kep' sight o' th' other schooner, most-partly ; an' when we did n' keep it, we 'd get it agen. So one night 't was a beautiful moonlight night : I think I never sid a moon so bright as that moon was ; an' such lovely sights a body 'ould n' think could be ! Little islands, an' bigger, agen, there was, on every hand, shinun so bright, wi' great, awful-lookun shadows ! an' then the sea all black, between ! They did look so beautiful as ef a body could go an' bide

* A dull glare on the horizon, from the immense masses of ice.

on em, in a manner; an' the sky was jes' so blue, an' the
stars all shinun out, an' the moon all so bright! I never
looked upon the like. An' so I stood in the bows; an' I
don't know ef I thowt o' God first, but I was thinkun o' my
girl that I was troth-plight wi' then, an' a many things,
when all of a sudden we comed upon the hardest ice we'd
a-had; an' into it; an' then, wi' pokun an' haulun, workun
along. An' there was a cry goed up,—like the cry of a
babby, 't was, an' I thowt mubbe 't was a somethun had
got upon one o' they islands; but I said, agen, 'How could
it?' an' one John Harris said 'e thowt 't was a bird. Then
another man (Moffis 'e's name was) started off wi' what
they calls a gaff, ('t is somethun like a short boat-hook,)
over the bows, an' run; an' we sid un strike, an' strike,
an' we hard it go wump! wump! an' the cry goun up
so tarrible feelun, seemed as ef 'e was murderun some poor
wild Inden child 'e'd a-found, (on'y mubbe 'e would n' do
so bad as that: but there 've a-been tarrible bloody, cruel
work wi' Indens in my time,) an' then 'e comed back wi'
a white-coat * over 'e's shoulder; an' the poor thing was n'
dead, but cried an' soughed like any poor little babby."

The young wife was very restless at this point, and, though
she did not look up, I saw her tears. The stout fisherman
smoothed out the net a little upon his knee, and drew it
in closer, and heaved a great sigh: he did not look at his
hearers.

"When 'e throwed it down, it walloped, an' cried, an'
soughed,—an' its poor eyes blinded wi' blood! ('Ee sees,
sir," said the planter, by way of excusing his tenderness,
"they swiles were friends to I, after.) Dear, O dear! I
could n' stand it; for 'e *might* ha' killed un; an' so 'e goes
for a quart o' rum, for fetchun first swile, an' I went an'
put the poor thing out o' pain. I did n' want to look at
they beautiful islands no more, somehow. Bumby it comed
on thick, an' then snow.

"Nex' day swiles bawlun † every way, poor things! (I

---

* A young seal.   † Technical word for the crying of the seals.

knowed their voice, now,) but 't was blowun a gale o' wind,
an' we under bare poles, an' snow comun agen, so fast as
ever it could come : but out the men 'ould go, all mad like,
an' my watch goed, an' so I mus' go. (I did n' think what
I was goun to !) The skipper never said no ; but to keep
near the schooner, an' fetch in first we could, close by ; an'
keep near the schooner.

"So we got abroad, an' the men that was wi' me jes
began to knock right an' left : 't was heartless to see an'
hear it. They laved two old uns an' a young whelp to me,
as they runned by. The mother did cry like a Christen,
in a manner, an' the big tears 'ould run down, an' they 'ould
both be so brave for the poor whelp that 'ould cuddle up
an' cry ; an' the mother looked this way an' that way, wi'
big, pooty, black eyes, to see what was the manun of it,
when they 'd never doned any harm in God's world that 'E
made, an' would n', even ef you killed 'em : on'y the poor
mother baste ketched my gaff, that I was goun to strike
wi', betwixt her teeth, an' 1 could n' get it away. 'T was n'
like fishun ! (I was weak hearted like : I s'pose 't was wi'
what was comun that I did n' know.) Then comed a hail,
all of a sudden, from the schooner ; (we had n' been gone
mor n' a five minutes, ef 't was so much, — no, not mor 'n
a three :) but I was glad to hear it come then, however :
an' so every man ran, one afore t' other. There the schooner was, tearun through all, an' we runnun for dear life. I
falled among the slob,* and got out agen. 'T was another
man pushun agen me doned it. I could n' 'elp myself from
goun in, an' when I got out I was astarn of all, an' there
was the schooner carryun on, right through to clear water !
So, hold of a bight o' line, or anything ! an' they swung
up in over bows an' sides ! an' swash ! she struck the
water, an' was out o' sight in a minute an' the snow drivun
as ef 't would bury her, an' a man laved behind on a pan
of ice, an' the great black say two fathom ahead, an' the
storm-wind blowun 'im into it ! "

* Broken ice, between large cakes, or against the shore.

The planter stopped speaking. We had all gone along so with the story, that the stout seafarer, as he wrought the whole scene up about us, seemed instinctively to lean back and brace his feet against the ground, and clutch his net. The young woman looked up, this time; and the cold snow-blast seemed to howl through that still summer's noon, and the terrific ice-fields and hills to be crashing against the solid earth that we sat upon, and all things round changed to the far-off stormy ocean and boundless frozen wastes.

The planter began to speak again : —

" So I falled right down upon th' ice, sayun, ' Lard, help me ! Lard, help me ! ' an' crawlun away, wi' the snow in my face, (I was afeard, a'most, to stand,) ' Lard, help me ! Lard, help me ! '

" 'T was n' all hard ice, but many places lolly ; * an' once I goed right down wi' my hand-wristès an' my armès in cold water, part-ways to the bottom o' th' ocean ; and a'most head-first into un, as I 'd a-been in wi' my legs afore : but, thanks be to God ! 'E helped me out of un, but colder an' wetter agen.

" In course I wanted to folly the schooner ; so I runned up along, a little ways from the edge, an' then I runned down along ; but 't was all great black ocean outside, an' she gone miles an' miles away ; an' by two hours' time, even ef she 'd come to, itself, an' all clear weather, I could n' never see her ; an' ef she could come back, she could n' never find me, more 'n I could find any one o' the flakes o' snow. The schooner was gone, an' I was laved out o' the world !

" Bumby, when I got on the big field agen, I stood up on my feet, an' I sid that was my ship ! She had n' e'er a sail, an' she had n' e'er a spar, an' she had n' e'er a compass, an' she had n' e'er a helm, an' she had n' no hold, an' she had n' no cabin. I could n' sail her, nor I could n' steer her, nor I could n' anchor her, nor bring her to, but she

* Snow in water, not yet frozen, but looking like the white ice.

would go, wind or calm, an' she'd never come to port, but out in th' ocean she'd go to pieces! I sid 't was so, an' I must take it, an' do my best wi' it. 'T was jest a great, white, frozen raft, driftun bodily away, wi' storm blowun over, an' current runnun under, an' snow comun down so thick, an' a poor Christen laved all alone wi' it. 'T would drift as long as anything was of it, an' 't was n' likely there'd be any life in the poor man by time th' ice goed to naw-thun; an' the swiles 'ould swim back agen up to the Nothe!

"I was th' only one, seemunly, to be cast out alive, an' wi' the dearest maid in the world (so I thought) waitun for me. I s'pose 'ee might ha' knowed somethun better, sir; but I was n' larned, an' I ran so fast as ever I could up the way I thowt home was, an' I groaned, an' groaned, an' shook my handès, an' then I thowt, 'Mubbe I may be goun wrong way.' So I groaned to the Lard to stop the snow. Then I on'y ran this way an' that way, an' groaned for snow to knock off.* I knowed we was driftun mubbe a twenty leagues a day, and anyways I wanted to be doun what I could, keepun up over th' Ice so well as I could, Noofoundland-ways, an' I might come to somethun, — to a schooner or somethun; anyways I'd get up so near as I could. So I looked for a lee. I s'pose 'ee'd ha' knowed better what to do, sir," said the planter, here again appealing to me, and showing by his question that he understood me, in spite of my pea-jacket.

I had been so carried along with his story that I had felt as if I were the man on the Ice myself, and assured him that, though I could get along pretty well on land, *and could even do something at netting*, I should have been very awkward in his place.

"Wull, sir, I looked for a lee. ('T would n' ha' been so cold, to say cold, ef it had n' a-blowed so tarrible hard.) First step, I stumbled upon somethun in the snow, seemed soft, like a body! Then I comed all together, hopun an' fearun an' all together. Down I goed upon my knees to

* To stop.

un, an' I smoothed away the snow, all tremblun, an' there was a moan, as ef 't was a-livun.

"'O Lard!' I said, 'who's this? Be this one of our men?'

"But how could it? So I scraped the snow away, but 't was easy to see 't was smaller than a man. There was n' no man on that dreadful place but me! Wull, sir, 't was a poor swile, wi' blood runnun all under; an' I got my cuffs * an' sleeves all red wi' it. It looked like a fellow-creatur's blood, a'most, an' I was a lost man, left to die away out there in th' Ice, an' I said, 'Poor thing! poor thing!' an' I did n' mind about the wind, or th' ice, or the schooner goun away from me afore a gale (I *would n'* mind about 'em), an' a poor lost Christen may show a good turn to a hurt thing, ef 't was on'y a baste. So I smoothed away the snow wi' my cuffs, an' I sid 't was a poor thing wi' her whelp close by her, an' her tongue out, as ef she'd a-died fondlun an' lickun it; an' a great puddle o' blood, — it looked tarrible heartless, when I was so nigh to death, an' was n' hungry. An' then I feeled a stick, an' I thowt, 'It may be a help to me,' an' so I pulled un, an' it would n' come, an' I found she was lyun on it so I hauled agen, an', when it comed, 't was my gaff the poor baste had got away from me, an' got it under her, an' she was a-lyun on it. Some o' the men, when they was runnun for dear life, must ha' struck 'em, out o' madness like, an' laved 'em to die where they was. 'T was the whelp was n' quite dead. 'Ee 'll think 't was foolish, sir, but it seemed as though they was somethun to me, an' I 'd a-lost the last friendly thing there was.

" I found a big hummock an' sheltered under it, standun on my feet, wi' nawthun to do but think, an' think, an' pray to God; an' so I doned. I could n' help feelun to God then, surely. Nawthun to do, an' no place to go, tull snow cleared away; but jes' drift wi' the great Ice down from the Nothe, away down over the say, a sixty mile a day, mubbe. I was n' a good Christen, an' I could n' help

* Mittens.

a-thinkun o' home an' she I was troth-plight wi', an' I doubled over myself an' groaned, — I could n' help it: but bumby it comed into me to say my prayers, an' it seemed as thof she was askun me to pray, (an' she *was* good, sir, al'ays,) an' I seemed all opened, somehow, an' I knowed how to pray."

While the words were coming tenderly from the weather-beaten fisherman, I could not help being moved, and glanced over toward the daughter's seat; but she was gone, and, turning round, I saw her going quietly, almost stealthily, and very quickly, *toward the cove.*

The father gave no heed to her leaving, but went on with his tale : —

" Then the wind began to fall down, an' the snow knocked off altogether, an' the sun comed out; an' I sid th' Ice, field-ice an' icebargs, an' every one of 'em flashun up as ef they 'd kendled up a bonfire, but no sign of a schooner! no sign of a schooner! nor no sign o' man's douns, but on'y ice, every way, high an' low, an' some places black water, in-among; an' on'y the poor swiles bawlun all over, an' I standun amongst 'em.

"While I was lookun out, I sid a great icebarg (they calls 'em) a quarter of a mile away, or thereabouts, standun up, — one end a twenty fathom out o' water, an' about a forty fathom across, wi' hills like, an' houses, — an' then, jest as ef 'e was alive an' had tooked a notion in 'e'sself, seemunly, all of a sudden 'e rared up, an' turned over an' over, wi' a tarrible thunderun noise, an' comed right on, breakun everything an' throwun up great seas : 't was fright-some for a lone body away out among 'em! I stood an' looked at un, but then agen I thowt I may jes' so well be goun to thick ice an' over Noofoundland-ways a piece, so well as I could. So I said my bit of a prayer, an' told Un I could n' help myself; an' I made my confession how bad I 'd been, an' I was sorry, an' ef 'E 'd be so pitiful an' for-give me; an' ef I mus' loss my life, ef 'E 'd be so good as make me a good Christen first, — an' make *they* happy, in course.

" So then I started ; an' first I goed to where my gaff
was, by the mother-swile an' her whelp. There was swiles
every two or three yards a'most, old uns an' young uns, all
round, everywhere ; an' I feeled shamed in a manner : but
I got my gaff, an' cleaned un, an' then, in God's name, I
took the big swile, that was dead by its dead whelp, an'
hauled it away, where the t' other poor things could n' si'
me, an' I sculped * it, an' took the pelt ; — for I thowt I 'd
wear un, now the poor dead thing did n' want to make oose
of un no more, — an' partly because 't was sech a lovun
thing. An' so I set out, walkun this way, for a spurt, an'
then t' other way, keepun up mostly a Nor-norwest, so well
as I could : sometimes away round th' open, an' more times
round a lump of ice, an' more times, agen, off from one an'
on to another, every minute. I did n' feel hungry, for I
drinked fresh water off th' ice. No schooner ! no schooner !

" Bumby the sun was goun down : 't was slow work
feelun my way along, an' I did n' want to look about : but
then agen I thowt God 'ad made it to be sid ; an' so I
come to, an' turned all round, an' looked ; an' surely it
seemed like another world, some way, 't was so beautiful, —
yellow, an' different sorts o' red, like the sky itself in a
manner, an' flashun like glass. So then it comed night :
an' I thowt I should n' go to bed, an' I may forget my
prayers, an' so I 'd, mubbe, best say 'em right away ; an'
so I doned : ' Lighten our darkness,' and others we was
oosed to say : an' it comed into my mind the Lard said to
Saint Peter, ' Why did n' 'ee have faith ? ' when there was
nawthun on the water for un to go on ; an' I had ice under
foot, — 't was but frozen water, but 't was frozen, — an' I
thanked Un.

" I could n' help thinkun o' Brigus an' them I 'd laved
in it, an' then I prayed for 'em ; an' I could n' help cryun,
a'most : but then I give over agen, an' would n' think, ef I
could help it ; on'y tryun to say an odd psalm, all through
singun-psalms an' other, for I knowed a many of 'em by

* Skinned.

singun wi' Patience, on'y now I cared more about 'em : I said that one, —

> ' Sech as in ships an' brickle barks
>   Into the seas descend,
> Their merchantun, through fearful floods,
>   To compass an' to end :
> They men are force-put to behold
>   The Lard's works, what they be ;
> An' in the dreadful deep the same
>   Most marvellous they see.'

An' I said a many more, (I can't be accountable how many I said,) an' same uns many times over : for I would keep on ; an' 'ould sometimes sing 'em very loud in my poor way.

"A poor baste (a silver fox 'e was) comed an' looked at me ; an' when I turned round, he walked away a piece, an' then 'e comed back, an' looked.

"So I found a high piece, wi' a wall of ice atop for shelter, ef it comed on to blow ; an' so I stood, an' said, an' sung. I knowed well I was on'y driftun away.

"It was tarrible lonely in the night, when night comed : it 's no use ! 'T was tarrible lonely : but I 'ould n' think, ef I could help it ; an' I prayed a bit, an' kep' up my psalms, an' varses out o' the Bible, I 'd a-larned. I had n' a-prayed for sleep, but for wakun all night, an' there I was standun.

"The moon was out agen, so bright ; an' all the hills of ice shinun up to her ; an' stars twinklun, so busy, all over ; an' No'ther' Lights goun up wi' a faint blaze, seemunly, from th' ice, an' meetun up aloft ; an' sometimes a great groanun, an' more times tarrible loud shriekun ! There was great white fields, an' great white hills, like countries, comun down to be destroyed ; an' some great bargs a-goun faster, an' tearun through, breakun others to pieces ; an' the groanun an' screechun, — ef all the dead that ever was, wi' their white clothès — But no ! " said the stout fisherman, recalling himself from gazing, as he seemed to be, on the far-off ghastly scene, in memory.

"No! — an' thank 'E's marcy, I'm sittun by my own room. 'E took me off: but 't was a dreadful sight, — it's no use, — ef a body'd let 'e'sself think! I sid a great black bear, an' hard un growl; an' 't was feelun, like, to hear un so bold an' so stout, among all they dreadful things, an' bumby the time 'ould come when 'e could n' save 'e'sself, do what 'e woul'.

"An' more times 't was all still: on'y swiles bawlun, all over. Ef it had n' a-been for they poor swiles, how could I stan' it? Many's the one I'd a-ketched, day-time, an' talked to un, an' patted un on the head, as ef they'd a-been dogs by the door, like; an' they'd oose to shut their eyes, an' draw their poor foolish faces together. It seemed neighbor-like to have some live thing.

"So I kep' awake, sayun an' singun, an' it was n' very cold; an' so — first thing I knowed, I started, an there I was lyun in a heap; an' I must have been asleep, an' did n' know how 't was, nor how long I'd a-been so: an' some sort o' baste started away, an' 'e must have waked me up; I could n' rightly see what 't was, wi' sleepiness: an' then I hard a sound, sounded like breakers; an' that waked me fairly. 'T was like a lee-shore; an' 't was a comfort to think o' land, ef 't was on'y to be wrecked on itself; but I did n' go, an' I stood an' listened to un; an' now an' agen I'd walk a piece, back an' forth, an' back an' forth; an' so I passed a many, many longsome hours, seemunly, tull night goed down tarrible slowly, an' it comed up day o' t' other side: an' there was n' no land; nawthun but great mountains meltun an' breakun up, an' fields wastun away. I sid 't was a rollun barg made the noise like breakers, throwun up great seas o' both sides of un; no sight nor sign o' shore, nor ship, but dazun white, — enough to blind a body, — an' I knowed 't was all floatun away, over the say. Then I said my prayers, an' tooked a drink o' water, an' set out agen for Nor-norwest: 't was all I could do. Sometimes snow, an' more times fair agen; but no sign o' man's things, an' no sign o' land, on'y white ice an' black

water; an' ef a schooner was n' into un a'ready, 't was n'
likely they woul', for we was gettun furder an' furder away.
Tired I was wi' goun, though I had n' walked more n' a
twenty or thirty mile, mubbe, an' it all comun down so fast
as I could go up, an' faster, an' never stoppun! 'T was a
tarrible long journey up over the driftun ice, at sea! So,
then I went on a high bit to wait tull all was done : I thowt
't would be last to melt, an' mubbe, I thowt, 'e may capsize
wi' me, when I did n' know (for I don't say I was stout-
hearted) : an' I prayed Un to take care o' them I loved;
an' the tears comed. Then I felt somethun tryun to turn
me round like, an' it seemed as ef *she* was doun it, somehow, an' she seemed to be very nigh, somehow, an' I did n'
look.

"After a bit, I got up to look out where most swiles was,
for company, while I was livun : an' the first look struck
me a'most like a bullet ! There I sid a sail ! *'T was* a
sail, an' 't was like heaven openun, an' God settun her down
there. About three mile away she was, to nothe'ard, in th'
Ice.

"I could ha' sid, at first look, what schooner 't was; but
I did n' want to look hard at her. I kep' my peace, a spurt,
an' then I runned an' bawled out. ' Glory be to God ! ' an'
then I stopped an' made proper thanks to Un. An' there
she was, same as ef I 'd a-walked off from her an hour
ago ! It felt so long as ef I 'd been livun years, an' they
would n' know me, sca'ce. Somehow I did n' think I could
come up wi' her.

"I started, in the name o' God, wi' all my might, an'
went, an' went, — 't was a five mile, wi' goun round, — an'
got her, thank God ! 'T was n' the Baccaloue, (I sid that
long before,) 't was t' other schooner, the Sparrow, repairun
damages they 'd got day before. So that kep' 'em there,
an' I 'd a-been took from one an' brought to t' other.

"I could n' do a hand's turn tull we got into the Bay
agen, — I was so clear beat out. The Sparrow kep' her
men, an' fotch home about thirty-eight hundred swiles, an'

a poor man off th' Ice : but they, poor fellows, that I went
out wi' never comed no more ; an' I never went agen.

"I kep' the skin o' the poor baste, sir : that's 'e on my
cap."

When the planter had fairly finished his tale, it was a
little while before I could teach my eyes to see the things
about me in their places. The slow-going sail, outside, I
at first saw as the schooner that brought away the lost man
from the Ice ; the green of the earth would not, at first,
show itself through the white with which the fancy covered
it ; and at first I could not quite feel that the ground was
fast under my feet. I even mistook one of my own men
(the sight of whom was to warn me that I was wanted
elsewhere) for one of the crew of the schooner Sparrow of
a generation ago.

I got the tale and its scene gathered away, presently,
inside my mind, and shook myself into a present associa-
tion with surrounding things, and took my leave. I went
away the more gratified that I had a chance of lifting my
cap to a matron, dark-haired and comely, (who, I was sure,
at a glance, had once been the maiden of Benjie Westham's "troth-plight,") and receiving a handsome courtesy
in return

K

WHY THOMAS WAS DISCHARGED.

RANT Beach is a long promontory of rock and sand, jutting out at an acute angle from a barren portion of the coast. Its farthest extremity is marked by a pile of many-colored, wave-washed bowlders ; its junction with the mainland is the site of the Brant House, a watering-place of excellent repute.

The attractions of this spot are not numerous. There is surf-bathing all along the outer side of the beach, and good swimming on the inner. The fishing is fair ; and in still weather, yachting is rather a favorite amusement. Further than this, there is little to be said, save that the hotel is conducted upon liberal principles, and the society generally select.

But to the lover of Nature, — and who has the courage to avow himself aught else ? — the sea-shore can never be monotonous. The swirl and sweep of ever-shifting waters, — the flying mist of foam breaking away into a gray and ghostly distance down the beach, — the eternal drone of ocean, mingling itself with one's talk by day and with the light dance-music in the parlors by night, — all these are active sources of a passive pleasure. And to lie at length upon the tawny sand, watching, through half-closed eyes, the heaving waves, that mount against a dark-blue sky wherein great silvery masses of cloud float idly on, whiter than the sunlit sails that fade and grow and fade along the horizon, while some fair damsel sits close by, reading ancient ballads of a simple metre, or older legends of love and romance, — tell me, my eater of the fashionable lotos, is not this a diversion well worth your having?

There is an air of easy sociality among the guests at the Brant House, a disposition on the part of all to contribute to the general amusement, that makes a summer sojourn on the beach far more agreeable than in certain larger, more frequented watering-places, where one is always in danger of discovering that the gentlemanly person with whom he has been fraternizing is a faro-dealer, or that the lady who has half fascinated him is Anonyma herself. Still, some consider the Brant rather slow, and many good folk were a trifle surprised when Mr. Edwin Salisbury and Mr. Charles Burnham arrived by the late stage from Wika-hasset Station, with trunks enough for two first-class belles, and a most unexceptional man-servant in gray livery, in charge of two beautiful setter-dogs.

These gentlemen seemed to have imagined that they were about visiting some backwoods wilderness, some savage tract of country, "remote, unfriended, melancholy, slow"; for they brought almost everything with them that men of elegant leisure could require, as if the hotel were but four walls and a roof, which they must furnish with their own chattels. I am sure it took Thomas, the man-servant, a whole day to unpack the awnings, the bootjacks, the game-bags, the cigar-boxes, the guns, the camp-stools, the liquor-cases, the bathing-suits, and other paraphernalia that these pleasure-seekers brought. It must be owned, however, that their room, a large one in the Bachelor's Quarter, facing the sea, wore a very comfortable, sportsmanlike look, when all was arranged.

Thus surrounded, the young men betook themselves to the deliberate pursuit of idle pleasures. They arose at nine and went down to the shore, invariably returning at ten with one unfortunate snipe, which was preserved on ice, with much ceremony, till wanted. At this rate, it took them a week to shoot a breakfast; but to see them sally forth, splendid in velveteen and corduroy, with top-boots and

a complete harness of green cord and patent-leather straps,
you would have imagined that all game-birds were about to
become extinct in that region.   Their dogs, even, recognized this great-cry-and-little-wool condition of things, and
bounded off joyously at the start, but came home crest-
fallen, with an air of canine humiliation that would have
aroused Mr. Mayhew's tenderest sympathies.

After breakfasting, usually in their room, the friends enjoyed a long and contemplative smoke upon the wide
piazza in front of their windows, listlessly regarding the
ever-varied marine view that lay before them in flashing breadth and beauty.   Their next labor was to array
themselves in wonderful morning-costumes of very shaggy
English cloth, shiny flasks and field-glasses about their
shoulders, and loiter down the beach, to the point and back,
making much unnecessary effort over the walk, — a brief
mile, — which they spoke of with importance, as their "constitutional."   This killed time till bathing-hour, and then
came another smoke on the piazza, and another toilet, for
dinner.   After dinner, a siesta: in the room, when the
weather was fresh; when otherwise, in hammocks, hung
from the rafters of the piazza.   When they had been domi-
ciled a few days, they found it expedient to send home for
what they were pleased to term their "crabs" and "traps,"
and excited the envy of less fortunate guests by driving up
and down the beach at a racing gait to dissipate the languor of the after-dinner sleep.

This was their regular routine for the day, — varied, occasionally, when the tide served, by a fishing-trip down the
narrow bay inside the point.   For such emergencies, they
provided themselves with a sail-boat and skipper, hired for
the whole season, and arrayed themselves in a highly
nautical rig.   The results were, large quantities of sardines
and pale sherry consumed by the young men, and a reasonable number of sea-bass and black-fish caught by their
skipper.

There were no regular "hops" at the Brant House, but

dancing in a quiet way every evening, to a flute, violin, and violoncello, played by some of the waiters. For a time, Burnham and Salisbury did not mingle much in these festivities, but loitered about the halls and piazzas, very elegantly dressed and barbered, (Thomas was an unrivalled *coiffeur*,) and apparently somewhat *ennuyé.*

That two well-made, full-grown, intelligent, and healthy young men should lead such a life as this for an entire summer might surprise one of a more active temperament. The aimlessness and vacancy of an existence devoted to no earthly purpose save one's own comfort must soon weary any man who knows what is the meaning of real, earnest life, — life with a battle to be fought and a victory to be won. But these elegant young gentlemen comprehended nothing of all that: they had been born with golden spoons in their mouths, and educated only to swallow the delicately insipid lotos-honey that flows inexhaustibly from such shining spoons. Clothes, complexions, polish of manner, and the avoidance of any sort of shock, were the simple objects of their solicitude.

I do not know that I have any serious quarrel with such fellows, after all. They have some strong virtues. They are always clean; and your rough diamond, though manly and courageous as Cœur-de-Lion, is not apt to be scrupulously nice in his habits. Affability is another virtue. The Salisbury and Burnham kind of man bears malice toward no one, and is disagreeable only when assailed by some hammer-and-tongs utilitarian. All he asks is to be permitted to idle away his pleasant life unmolested. Lastly, he is extremely ornamental. We all like to see pretty things; and I am sure that Charley Burnham, in his fresh white duck suit, with his fine, thoroughbred face — gentle as a girl's — shaded by a snowy Panama, his blonde moustache carefully pointed, his golden hair clustering in the most picturesque possible waves, his little red neck-ribbon — the only bit of color in his dress — tied in a studiously careless knot, and his pure, untainted gloves of pearl-gray or lavender, was, if I may be allowed the expression, just as pretty as a picture. And Ned Salisbury was not less " a joy forever," according to the dictum of the late Mr. Keats. He was darker than Burnham, with very black hair, and a moustache worn in the manner the French call *triste*, which became him, and increased the air of pensive melancholy that distinguished his dark eyes, thoughtful attitudes, and slender figure. Not that he was in the least degree pensive or melancholy, or that he had cause to be; quite the contrary; but it was his style, and he did it well.

These two butterflies sat, one afternoon, upon the piazza, smoking very large cigars, lost, apparently, in profoundest meditation. Burnham, with his graceful head resting upon one delicate hand, his clear blue eyes full of a pleasant light, and his face warmed by a calm unconscious smile, might have been revolving some splended scheme of universal philanthropy. The only utterance, however, forced from him by the sublime thoughts that permeated his soul, was the emission of a white rolling volume of fragrant smoke, accompanied by two words :

" Doocèd hot ! "

Salisbury did not reply. He sat, leaning back, with his fingers interlaced behind his head, and his shadowy eyes downcast, as in sad remembrance of some long-lost love. So might a poet have looked, while steeped in mournfully rapturous day-dreams of remembered passion and severance. So might Tennyson's hero have mused, when he sang, —

> " O, that 't were possible,
>   After long grief and pain,
>   To find the arms of my true love
>   Round me once again ! "

But the poetic lips opened not to such numbers. Salisbury gazed, long and earnestly, and finally gave vent to his emotions, indicating, with the amber tip of his cigar-tube, the setter that slept in the sunshine at his feet.

" Shocking place, this, for dogs ! " — I regret to say he

pronounced it "dawgs."—"Why, Carlo is as fat—as fat as—as a—"

His mind was unequal to a simile, even, and he terminated the sentence in a murmur.

More silence; more smoke; more profound meditation. Directly, Charley Burnham looked around with some show of vitality.

"There comes the stage," said he.

The driver's bugle rang merrily among the drifted sand-hills that lay warm and glowing in the orange light of the setting sun. The young men leaned forward over the piazza-rail, and scrutinized the occupants of the vehicle, as it appeared.

"Old gentleman and lady, aw, and two children," said Ned Salisbury; "I hoped there would be some nice girls."

This, in a voice of ineffable tenderness and poetry, but with that odd, tired little drawl, so epidemic in some of our universities.

"Look there, by Jove!" cried Charley, with a real interest at last; "now that's what I call the regular thing!"

The "regular thing" was a low, four-wheeled pony-chaise of basket-work, drawn by two jolly little fat ponies, black and shiny as vulcanite, which jogged rapidly in, just far enough behind the stage to avoid its dust.

This vehicle was driven by a young lady of decided beauty, with a spice of Amazonian spirit. She was rather slender and very straight, with a jaunty little hat and feather perched coquettishly above her dark-brown hair, which was arranged in one heavy mass and confined in a silken net. Her complexion was clear, without brilliancy; her eyes blue as the ocean horizon, and spanned by sharp, characteristic brows; her mouth small and decisive; and her whole cast of features indicative of quick talent and independence.

Upon the seat beside her sat another damsel, leaning indolently back in the corner of the carriage. This one was a little fairer than the first, having one of those beauti-

ful English complexions of mingled rose and snow, and a
dash of gold-dust in her hair, where the sun touched it.
Her eyes, however, were dark hazel, and full of fire, shaded
and intensified by their long, sweeping lashes. Her mouth
was a rose-bud, and her chin and throat faultless in the
delicious curve of their lines. In a word, she was somewhat of the Venus-di-Milo type: her companion was more
of a Diana. Both were neatly habited in plain travelling-
dresses and cloaks of black and white plaid, and both
seemed utterly unconscious of the battery of eyes and eye-
glasses that enfiladed them from the whole length of the
piazza, as they passed.

"Who are they?" asked Salisbury; "I don't know
them."

"Nor I," said Burnham; "but they look like people to
know. They must be somebody."

Half an hour later, the hotel-office was besieged by a
score of young men, all anxious for a peep at the last
names upon the register. It is needless to say that our
friends were not in the crowd. Ned Salisbury was no more
the man to exhibit curiosity than Charley Burnham was
the man to join in a scramble for anything under the sun.
They had educated their emotions clear down, out of sight,
and piled upon them a mountain of well-bred inertia.

But, somehow or other, these fellows who take no trouble
are always the first to gain the end. A special Providence
seems to aid the poor, helpless creatures. So, while the
crowd still pressed at the office-desk, Jerry Swayne, the
head clerk, happened to pass directly by the piazza where
the inert ones sat, and, raising a comical eye, saluted them.

"Heavy arrivals to-night. See the turn-out?"

"Y-e-s," murmured Ned.

"Old Chapman and family. His daughter drove the
pony-phaëton, with her friend, a Miss Thurston. Regular
nobby ones. Chapman's the steamship-man, you know.
Worth thousands of millions! I'd like to be connected
with his family — by marriage, say!" — and Jerry went off,

rubbing his cropped head, and smiling all over, as was his wont.

"I know who they are now," said Charley. "Met a cousin of theirs, Joe Faulkner, abroad, two years ago. Doocèd fine fellow. Army."

The manly art of wagoning is not pursued very vigorously at Brant Beach. The roads are too heavy back from the water, and the drive is confined to a narrow strip of wet sand along the shore; so carriages are few, and the pony-chaise became a distinguished element at once. Salisbury and Burnham whirled past it in their light trotting-wagons at a furious pace, and looked hard at the two young ladies in passing, but without eliciting even the smallest glance from them in return.

"Confounded *distingué*-looking girls, and all that," owned Ned; "but, aw, fearfully unconscious of a fellow!"

This condition of matters continued until the young men were actually driven to acknowledge to each other that they should not mind knowing the occupants of the pony-carriage. It was a great concession, and was rewarded duly. A bright, handsome boy of seventeen, Miss Thurston's brother, came to pass a few days at the seaside, and fraternized with everybody, but was especially delighted with Ned Salisbury, who took him out sailing and shooting, and, I am afraid, gave him cigars stealthily, when out of range of Miss Thurston's fine eyes. The result was, that the first time the lad walked on the beach with the two girls, and met the young men, introductions of an enthusiastic nature were instantly sprung upon them. An attempt at conversation followed.

"How do you like Brant Beach?" asked Ned.

"O, it is a pretty place," said Miss Chapman, "but not lively enough."

"Well, Burnham and I find it pleasant; aw, we have lots of fun."

"Indeed! Why, what do you do?"

"O, I don't know. Everything."

"Is the shooting good? I saw you with your guns, yesterday."

"Well, there is n't a great deal of game. There is some fishing, but we have n't caught much."

"How do you kill time, then?"

Salisbury looked puzzled.

"Aw — it is a first-rate air, you know. The table is good, and you can sleep like a top. And then, you see, I like to smoke around, and do nothing, on the sea-shore. It is real jolly to lie on the sand, aw, with all sorts of little bugs running over you, and listen to the water swashing about ! "

"Let 's try it !" cried vivacious Miss Chapman; and down she sat on the sand. The others followed her example, and in five minutes they were picking up pretty pebbles and chatting away as sociably as could be. The rumble of the warning gong surprised them.

At dinner, Burnham and Salisbury took seats opposite the ladies, and were honored with an introduction to papa and mamma, a very dignified, heavy, rosy, old-school couple, who ate a good deal, and said very little. That evening, when flute and viol wooed the lotos-eaters to agitate the light fantastic toe, these young gentlemen found themselves in dancing humor, and revolved themselves into a grievous condition of glow and wilt, in various mystic and intoxicating measures with their new-made friends.

On retiring, somewhat after midnight, Miss Thurston paused, while "doing her hair," and addressed Miss Chapman.

"Did you observe, Hattie, how very handsome those gentlemen are? Mr. Burnham looks like a prince of the *sang azur*, and Mr. Salisbury like his poet-laureate."

"Yes, dear," responded Hattie; "I have been considering those flowers of the field and lilies of the valley."

"Ned," said Charley, at about the same time, "we won't find anything nicer here, this season, I think."

"They 're pretty well worth while," replied Ned; "and I 'm rather pleased with them."

"Which do you like best?"

"O, bother! I have n't thought of *that* yet."

The next day the young men delayed their "constitutional" until the ladies were ready to walk, and the four strolled off together, mamma and the children following in the pony-chaise. At the rocks on the end of the point, Ned got his feet very wet, fishing up specimens of sea-weed for the damsels; and Charley exerted himself super-humanly in assisting them to a ledge which they considered favorable for sketching purposes.

In the afternoon a sail was arranged, and they took dinner on board the boat, with any amount of hilarity and a good deal of discomfort. In the evening, more dancing, and vigorous attentions to both the young ladies, but without a shadow of partiality being shown by either of the four.

This was very nearly the history of many days. It does not take long to get acquainted with people who are willing, especially at a watering-place; and in the course of a few weeks, these young folks were, to all intents and purposes, old friends, — calling each other by their given names, and conducting themselves with an easy familiarity quite charming to behold. Their amusements were mostly in common now. The light wagons were made to hold two each, instead of one, and the matinal snipe escaped death, and was happy over his early worm.

One day, however, Laura Thurston had a headache, and Hattie Chapman stayed at home to take care of her; so Burnham and Salisbury had to amuse themselves alone. They took their boat, and idled about the water, inside the point, dozing under an awning, smoking, gaping, and wishing that headaches were out of fashion, while the taciturn and tarry skipper instructed the dignified and urbane Thomas in the science of trolling for blue-fish.

At length Ned tossed his cigar-end overboard, and braced himself for an effort.

"I say, Charley," said he, "this sort of thing can't go on forever, you know. I 've been thinking, lately."

"Phenomenon!" replied Charley; "and what have you been thinking about?"

"Those girls. We've got to choose."

"Why? Is n't it well enough as it is?"

"Yes,—so far. But I think, aw, that we don't quite do them justice. They're *grands partis*, you see. I hate to see clever girls wasting themselves on society, waiting and waiting,—and we fellows swimming about just like fish round a hook that is n't baited properly."

Charley raised himself upon his elbow.

"You don't mean to tell me, Ned, that you have matrimonial intentions?"

"O, no! Still, why not? We've all got to come to it, some day, I suppose."

"Not yet, though. It is a sacrifice we can escape for some years yet."

"Yes,—of course,—some years; but we may begin to look about us a bit. I'm, aw, I'm six-and-twenty, you know."

"And I'm very near that. I suppose a fellow can't put off the yoke too long. After thirty, chances are n't so good. I don't know, by Jove! but what we ought to begin thinking of it."

"But it *is* a sacrifice. Society must lose a fellow, though, one time or another. And I don't believe we will ever do better than we can now."

"Hardly, I suspect."

"And we're keeping other fellows away, maybe. It is a shame!"

Thomas ran his line in rapidly, with nothing on the hook.

"Capt'n Hull," he said, gravely, "I had the biggest kind of a fish then, I'm sure; but d'rectly I went to pull him in, sir, he took and let go."

"Yaäs," muttered the taciturn skipper, "the biggest fish allers falls back inter the warter."

"I've been thinking a little about this matter, too," said Charley, after a pause, "and I had about concluded we ought to pair off. But I 'll be confounded, if I know which I like best! They 're both nice girls."

"There is n't much choice," Ned replied. "If they were as different, now, as you and me, I 'd take the blonde, of course; aw, and you 'd take the brunette. But Hattie Chapman's eyes are blue, and her hair is n't black, you know; so you can't call her dark, exactly."

"No more than Laura is exactly light. Her hair is brown, more than golden, and her eyes are hazel. Has n't she a lovely complexion, though? By Jove!"

"Better than Hattie's. Yet I don't know but Hattie's features are a little the best."

"They are. Now, honest, Ned, which do you prefer? Say either; I 'll take the one you don't want. I have n't any choice."

"Neither have I."

"How will we settle?"

"Aw — throw for it?"

"Yes. Is n't there a backgammon-board forward, in that locker, Thomas?"

The board was found, and the dice produced.

"The highest takes which?"

"Say, Laura Thurston."

"Very good; throw."

"You first."

"No. Go on."

Charley threw, with about the same amount of excite- ment he might have exhibited in a turkey-raffle.

"Five-three," said he. "Now for your luck."

"Six-four! Laura 's mine. Satisfied?"

"Perfectly, — if you are. If not, I don't mind exchang- ing."

"O, no. I 'm satisfied."

Both reclined upon the deck once more, with a sigh of relief, and a long silence followed.

"I say," began Charley, after a time, "it is a comfort to have these little matters arranged without any trouble, eh?"

"Y-e-s."

"Do you know, I think I'll marry mine?"

"I will, if you will."

"Done! it is a bargain."

This "little matter" being arranged, a change gradually took place in the relations of the four. Ned Salisbury began to invite Laura Thurston out driving and in bathing somewhat oftener than before, and Hattie Chapman somewhat less often; while Charley Burnham followed suit with the last-named young lady. As the line of demarcation became fixed, the damsels recognized it, and accepted with gracious readiness the cavaliers that Fate, through the agency of a chance-falling pair of dice, had allotted to them.

The other guests of the house remarked the new position of affairs, and passed whispers about, to the effect that the girls had at last succeeded in getting their fish on hooks instead of in a net. No suitors could have been more devoted than our friends. It seemed as if each now bestowed upon the chosen one all the attentions he had hitherto given to both; and whether they went boating, sketching, or strolling upon the sands, they were the very picture of a *partie carrée* of lovers.

Naturally enough, as the young men became more in earnest, with the reticence common to my sex, they spoke less freely and frequently on the subject. Once, however, after an unusually pleasant afternoon, Salisbury ventured a few words.

"I say, we're a couple of lucky dogs! Who'd have thought, now, aw, that our summer was going to turn out so well? I'm sure I didn't. How do you get along, Charley, boy?"

"Deliciously. Smooth sailing enough! Was n't it a good idea, though, to pair off? I'm just as happy as a bee in clover. You seem to prosper, too, heh?"

"Could n't ask anything different. Nothing but devotion, and all that. I'm delighted. I say, when are you going to pop?"

" O, I don't know. It is only a matter of form. Sooner the better, I suppose, and have it over."

" I was thinking of next week. What do you say to a quiet picnic down on the rocks, and a walk afterward? We can separate, you know, and do the thing up systematically."

" All right. I will, if you will."

" That's another bargain. I notice there is n't much doubt about the result, though."

" Hardly ! "

A close observer might have seen that the gentlemen increased their attentions a little from that time. The objects of their devotion perceived it, and smiled more and more graciously upon them.

The day set for the picnic arrived duly, and was radiant. It pains me to confess that my heroes were a trifle nervous. Their apparel was more gorgeous and wonderful than ever, and Thomas, who was anxious to be off, courting Miss Chapman's lady's-maid, found his masters dreadfully exacting in the matter of hair-dressing. At length, however, the toilet was over, and " Solomon in all his glory " would have been vastly astonished at finding himself " arrayed as one of these."

The boat lay at the pier, receiving large quantities of supplies for the trip, stowed by Thomas, under the supervision of the grim and tarry skipper. When all was ready, the young men gingerly escorted their fair companions aboard, the lines were cast off, and the boat glided gently down the bay, leaving Thomas free to fly to the smart presence of Susan Jane, and to draw glowing pictures for her of a neat little porter-house in the city, wherein they should hold supreme sway, be happy with each other, and let rooms up-stairs for single gentlemen.

The brisk land-breeze, the swelling sail, the fluttering of the gay little flag at the gaff, the musical rippling of water under the counter, and the spirited motion of the boat, combined with the bland air and pleasant sunshine to inspire the party with much vivacity. They had not been many minutes afloat before the guitar-case was opened, and the girls' voices — Laura's soprano and Hattie's contralto — rang melodiously over the waves, mingled with feeble attempts at bass accompaniment from their gorgeous guardians.

Before these vocal exercises wearied, the skipper hauled down his jib, let go his anchor, and brought the craft to, just off the rocks ; and bringing the yawl along-side, unceremoniously plumped the girls down into it, without giving their cavaliers a chance for the least display of agile courtliness. Rowing ashore, this same tarry person left them huddled upon the beach with their hopes, their hampers, their emotions, and their baskets, and returned to the vessel to do a little private fishing on his own account till wanted.

The maidens gave vent to their high spirits by chasing each other among the rocks, gathering shells and sea-weed for the construction of those ephemeral little ornaments — fair, but frail — in which the sex delights, singing, laughing, quoting poetry, attitudinizing upon the peaks and ledges of the fine old bowlders, — mossy and weedy and green with the wash of a thousand storms, worn into strange shapes, and stained with the multitudinous dyes of mineral oxidization, — and, in brief, behaved themselves with all the charming *abandon* that so well becomes young girls, set free, by the *entourage* of a holiday ramble, from the buckram and clear-starch of social etiquette.

Meanwhile Ned and Charley smoked the pensive cigar of preparation in a sheltered corner, and gazed out seaward, dreaming and seeing nothing.

Erelong the breeze and the romp gave the young ladies not only a splendid color and sparkling eyes, but excellent appetites also. The baskets and hampers were speedily unpacked, the table-cloth laid on a broad, flat stone, so used by generations of Brant-House picnickers, and the party fell to. Laura's beautiful hair, a little disordered, swept her blooming cheek, and cast a pearly shadow upon her neck. Her bright eyes glanced archly out from under her half-raised veil, and there was something inexpressibly *naïve* in the freedom with which she ate, taking a bird's wing in her little fingers, and boldly attacking it with teeth as white and even as can be imagined. Notwithstanding all the mawkish nonsense that has been put forth by sentimentalists concerning feminine eating, I hold that it is one of the nicest things in the world to see a pretty woman enjoying the creature comforts ; and Byron himself, had he been one of this picnic party, would have been unable to resist the admiration that filled the souls of Burnham and Salisbury. Hattie Chapman stormed a fortress of boned turkey with a gusto equal to that of Laura, and made highly successful raids upon certain outlying salads and jellies. The young men were not in a very ravenous condition ; they were, as I have said, a little nervous, and bent their energies principally to admiring the ladies and coquetting with pickled oysters.

When the repast was over, with much accompanying chat and laughter, Ned glanced significantly at Charley, and proposed to Laura that they should walk up the beach to a place where, he said, there were "some pretty rocks and things, you know." She consented, and they marched off. Hattie also arose, and took her parasol, as if to follow, but Charley remained seated, tracing mysterious diagrams upon the table-cloth with his fork, and looking sublimely unconscious.

"Sha'n't we walk, too?" Hattie asked.

"O, why, the fact is," said he, hesitantly, "I — I sprained my ankle, getting out of that confounded boat ; so I don't feel much like exercise just now."

The young girl's face expressed concern.

"That is too bad ! Why did n't you tell us of it before ? Is it painful? I 'm so sorry !"

"N-no, — it does n't hurt much. I dare say it will be

8 * L

all right in a minute. And then — I 'd just as soon stay here — with you — as to walk anywhere."

This, very tenderly, with a little sigh.

Hattie sat down again, and began to talk to this factitious cripple, in the pleasant, purring way some damsels have, about the joys of the sea-shore, — the happy summer that was, alas! drawing to a close, — her own enjoyment of life, — and kindred topics, — till Charley saw an excellent opportunity to interrupt with some aspirations of his own, which, he averred, must be realized before his life could be considered a satisfactory success.

If you have ever been placed in analogous circumstances, you know, of course, just about the sort of thing that was being said by the two gentlemen at nearly the same moment: Ned, loitering slowly along the sands with Laura on his arm, — and Charley, stretched in indolent picturesqueness upon the rocks, with Hattie sitting beside him. If you do not know from experience, ask any candid friend who has been through the form and ceremony of an orthodox proposal.

When the pedestrians returned, the two couples looked very hard at each other. All were smiling and complacent, but devoid of any strange or unusual expression. Indeed, the countenance is subject to such severe education in good society, that one almost always looks smiling and complacent. Demonstration is not fashionable; and a man must preserve the same demeanor over the loss of a wife or a glove-button, over the gift of a heart's whole devotion or a bundle of cigars. Under all these visitations, the complacent smile is in favor, as the neatest, most serviceable, and convenient form of non-committalism.

The sun was approaching the blue range of misty hills that bounded the mainland swamps by this time; so the skipper was signalled, the dinner paraphernalia gathered up, and the party were soon *en route* for home once more. When the young ladies were safely in, Ned and Charley met in their room, and each caught the other looking at him stealthily. Both smiled.

" Did I give you time, Charley ? " asked Ned ; " we came back rather soon."

" O, yes, — plenty of time."

" Did you — aw, did you pop ? "

" Y-es. Did you ? "

" Well — yes."

" And you were — "

" Rejected, by Jove ! "

" So was I ! "

The day following this disastrous picnic, the baggage of Mr. Edwin Salisbury and Mr. Charles Burnham was sent to the depot at Wikahasset Station, and they presented themselves at the hotel-office with a request for their bill. As Jerry Swayne deposited their key upon its hook, he drew forth a small tri-cornered billet from the pigeon-hole beneath, and presented it.

" Left for you, this morning, gentlemen."

It was directed to both, and Charley read it over Ned's shoulder. It ran thus : —

" DEAR BOYS, — The next time you divert yourselves by throwing dice for two young ladies, we pray you not to do so in the presence of a valet who is upon terms of intimacy with the maid of one of them.

"With many sincere thanks for the amusement you have given us, — often when you least suspected it, — we bid you a lasting adieu, and remain, with the best wishes,

HATTIE CHAPMAN.
LAURA THURSTON."

" Brant House, Wednesday.

" It is all the fault of that, aw, that confounded Thomas ! " said Ned.

So Thomas was discharged.

VICTOR AND JACQUELINE.

I.

JACQUELINE GABRIE and Elsie Méril could not occupy one room, and remain, either of them, indifferent to so much as might be manifested of the other's inmost life. They could not emigrate together, peasants from Domrémy, — Jacqueline so strong, Elsie so fair; — could not labor in the same harvest-fields, children of old neighbors, without each being concerned in the welfare and affected by the circumstances of the other.

It was near ten o'clock, one evening, when Elsie Méril ran up the common stairway, and entered the room in the fourth story where she and Jacqueline lodged.

Victor Le Roy, student from Picardy, occupied the room next theirs, and was startled from his slumber by the voices of the girls. Elsie was fresh from the theatre, from the first play she had ever witnessed; she came home excited and delighted, ready to repeat and recite, as long as Jacqueline would listen.

And here was Jacqueline.

Early in the evening Elsie had sought her friend with a good deal of anxiety. A fellow-lodger and field-laborer had invited her to see the play, — and Jacqueline was far down the street, nursing old Antonine Duprè. To seek her, thus occupied, on such an errand, Elsie had the good taste and the selfishness to refrain from doing.

Therefore, after a little deliberation, she had gone to

the theatre, and there forgot her hard day-labor in the wonders of the stage, — forgot Jacqueline, and Antonine, and every care and duty. It was hard for her, when all was ended, to come back to compunction and explanation, yet to this she had come back.

Neither of the girls was thinking of the student, their neighbor ; but he was not only wakened by their voices, he amused himself by comparing them and their utterances with his preconceived notions of the girls. They might not have recognized him in the street, though they had often passed him on the stairs ; but he certainly could have · distinguished the pretty face of Elsie, or the strange face of Jacqueline, wherever he might meet them.

Elsie ran on with her story, not careful to inquire into the mood of Jacqueline, — suspicious of that mood, no doubt, — but at last, made breathless by her haste and agitation, she paused, looked anxiously at Jacqueline, and finally said, —

" You think I ought not to have gone ? "

" O, no, — it gave you pleasure."

A pause followed. It was broken at length by Elsie, exclaiming, in a voice changed from its former speaking, —

" Jacqueline Gabrie, you are homesick ! horribly homesick, Jacqueline ! "

" You do not ask for Antonine : yet you know I went to spend the day with her," said Jacqueline, very gravely.

" How is Antonine Duprè ? " asked Elsie.

" She is dead. I have told you a good many times that she must die. Now she is dead."

" Dead ? " repeated Elsie.

" You care as much as if a candle had gone out," said Jacqueline.

" She was as much to me as I to her," was the quick answer. " She never liked me. She did not like my mother before me. When you told her my name, the day we saw her first, I knew what she thought. So let that go. If I could have done her good, though, I would, Jacqueline."

" She has everything she needs, — a great deal more than we have. She is very happy, Elsie."

" Am not I ? Are not you, in spite of your dreadful look ? Your look is more terrible than the lady's in the play, just before she killed herself. Is that because Antonine is so well off ? "

" I wish that I could be where she is," sighed Jacqueline.

" You ? You are tired, Jacqueline. You look ill. You will not be fit for to-morrow. Come to bed. It is late."

As Jacqueline made no reply to this suggestion, Elsie began to reflect upon her words, and to consider wherefore and to whom she had spoken. Not quite satisfied with herself could she have been, for at length she said in quite another manner, —

" You always said, till now, you wished that you might live a hundred years. But it was not because you were afraid to die, you said so, Jacqueline."

" I don't know," was the answer, — sadly spoken. " Don't remind me of things I have said. I seem to have lost myself."

The voice and the words were effectual, if they were intended as an appeal to Elsie. Fain would she now exclude the stage and the play from her thoughts, — fain think and feel with Jacqueline, as it had long been her habit to do.

Jacqueline, however, was not eager to speak. And Elsie must draw yet nearer to her, and make her nearness felt, ere she could hope to receive the thought of her friend. By and by these words were uttered, solemn, slow, and dirge-like : —

" Antonine died just after sundown. I was alone with her. She did not think that she would die so soon. I did not. In the morning, John Leclerc came in to inquire how she spent the night. He prayed with her. And a hymn, — he read a hymn that she seemed to know, for all day she was humming it over. I can say some of the lines."

" Say them, Jacqueline," said the softened voice of Elsie.

Slowly, and as one recalls that of which he is uncertain, Jacqueline repeated what I copy more entire : —

"In the midst of life, behold,
　Death hath girt us round !
Whom for help, then, shall we pray ?
Where shall grace be found ?
　In thee, O Lord, alone !
We rue the evil we have done,
That thy wrath on us hath drawn.
　　Holy Lord and God !
　　Strong and holy God !
　Merciful and holy Saviour !
　'　Eternal God !
Sink us not beneath
Bitter pains of endless death !
　　Kyrie, eleison !"

" Then he went away," she continued. " But he did not think it was the last time he should speak to Antonine. In the afternoon I thought I saw a change, and I wanted to go for somebody. But she said, 'Stay with me. I want nothing.' So I sat by her bed. At last she said, 'Come, Lord Jesus ! come quickly !' and she started up in her bed, as if she saw him coming. And as if he were coming nearer, she smiled. That was the last, — without a struggle, or as much as a groan."

" No priest there ? " asked Elsie.

" No. When I spoke to her about it, she said her priest was Jesus Christ the Righteous, — and there was no other, — the High-Priest. She gave me her Bible. See how it has been used ! 'Search the Scriptures,' she said. She told me I was able to learn the truth. 'I loved your mother,' she said ; 'that is the reason I am so anxious you should know. It is by my spirit, said the Lord. Ask for that spirit,' she said. 'He is more willing to give than earthly parents are to give good gifts to their children.' She said these things, Elsie. If they are true, they must be better worth believing than all the riches of the world are worth the having."

The interest manifested by the student in this conversation had been on the increase since Jacqueline began to speak of Antonine Duprè. It was not, at this point of the conversation, waning.

"Your mother would not have agreed with Antonine," said Elsie, as if there were weight in the argument; for such a girl as Jacqueline could not speak earnestly in the hearing of a girl like Elsie without result, and the result was at this time resistance.

"She believed what she was taught in Domrémy," answered Jacqueline. "She believed in Absolution, Extreme Unction, in the need of another priest than Jesus Christ, — a representative they call it." She spoke slowly, as if interrogating each point of her speech.

"I believe as they believed before us," answered Elsie, coldly.

"We have learned many things since we came to Meaux," answered Jacqueline, with a patient gentleness, that indicated the perplexity and doubt with which the generous spirit was departing from the old dominion. She was indeed departing, with that reverence for the past which is not incompatible with the highest hope for the future. "Our Joan came from Domrémy, where she must crown the king," she continued. "We have much to learn."

"She lost her life," said Elsie, with vehemence.

"Yes, she did lose her life," Jacquelin quietly acquiesced.

"If she had known what must happen, would she have come?"

"Yes, she would have come."

"How late it is!" said Elsie, as if in sleep were certain rest from these vexatious thoughts.

Victor Le Roy was by this time lost in his own reflections. These girls had supplied an all-sufficient theme; whether they slept or wakened was no affair of his. He had somewhat to argue for himself about extreme unction, priestly intervention, confession, absolution, — something to say to himself about Leclerc, and the departed Antonine.

Late into the night he sat thinking of the marvel of Domrémy and of Antonine Duprè, of Picardy and of Meaux, of priests and of the High-Priest. Brave and aspiring, Victor Le Roy could not think of these things, involved in the names of things above specified, as more calculating, prudent spirits might have done. It was his business, as a student, to ascertain what powers were working in the world. All true characters, of past time or present, must be weighed and measured by him. Result was what he aimed at.

Jacqueline's words had not given him new thoughts, but unawares they did summon him to his appointed labor. He looked to find the truth. He must stand to do his work. He must haste to make his choice. Enthusiastic, chivalrous, and strong, he was seeking the divine right, night and day ; and to ascertain that, as it seemed, he had come from Picardy to Meaux.

Elsie Méril went to bed, as she had invited Jacqueline to do; to sleep, to dream, she went, — and to smile, in her dreaming, on the world that smiled on her.

Jacqueline sat by the window ; leaned from the window, and prayed ; her own prayer she prayed, as Antonine had said she must, if she would discover what she needed, and obtain an answer.

She thought of the dead, — her own. She pondered on the future. She recalled some lines of the hymn Antonine had repeated, and she wished — oh, how she wished ! — that, while the woman lived, and could reason and speak, she had told her about the letter she had received from the priest of Domrémy. Many a time it had been on her lips to tell, but she failed in courage to bring her poor affairs into that chamber and disturb that dying hour. Now she wished that she had done it. Now she felt that speech had been the merest act of justice to herself.

But there was Leclerc, the wool-comber, and his mother ; she might rely on them for the instruction she needed.

Old Antonine's faith had made a deep impression on the

strong-hearted and deep-thinking girl; as also had the prayers of John Leclerc, — especially that last prayer offered for Antonine. It seemed to authenticate, by its strong, un-faltering utterance, the poor old woman's evidence. "Jesus Christ, the same yesterday, to-day, and forever," were strong words that seemed about to take possession of the heart of Jacqueline.

Therefore, while Elsie slept, she prayed, — looking far-ther. than the city-streets and darkness, — looking farther than the shining stars. What she sought, poor girl, stood in her silent chamber, stood in her waiting heart. But she knew Him not, and her ear was heavy; she did not hear the voice, that she should answer Him, "Rabboni !"

IL

A FORTNIGHT from this night, after the harvesters had left the fields of M. Flaval, Jacqueline was lin-gering in the twilight.

The instant the day's work was done, the laborers set out for Meaux. Their haste suggested some unusual cause.

John Leclerc, wool-comber, had received that day his sentence. Report of the sentence had spread among the reapers in the field and all along the vineyards of the hill-sides. Not a little stir was occasioned by this sentence : three days of whipping through the public streets, to con-clude with branding on the forehead. For this Leclerc, it seemed, had profanely and audaciously declared that a man might in his own behalf deal with the invisible God, by the mediation of Christ, the sole Mediator beween God and man. Viewed in the light of his offence, his punish-ment certainly was of the mildest. Tidings of his sentence were received with various emotion ; by some as though they were maddened with new wine ; others wept openly ; many more were pained at heart ; some brutally rejoiced ; some were incredulous.

But now they were all on their way to Meaux ; the fields were quite deserted. Urged by one desire, to ascertain the facts of the trial, and the time when the sentence would be executed, the laborers were returning to the town.

Without demonstration of any emotion, Jacqueline Gabrie, quiet, silent, walked along the river-bank, until she came to the clump of chestnut-trees, whose shadow fell across the stream. Many a time, through the hot, dreadful day, her eyes turned wistfully to this place. In the morning Elsie Méril had promised Jacqueline that at twilight they would read together here the leaves the poor old mother of Leclerc gave Jacqueline last night : when they had read them, they would walk home by starlight together. But now the time had come, and Jacqueline was alone. Elsie had returned to town with other young harvesters.

"Very well," said Jacqueline, when Elsie told her she must go. It was not, indeed, inexplicable that she should prefer the many voices to the one, — excitement and company, rather than quiet, dangerous thinking.

But, thus left alone, the face of Jacqueline expressed both sorrow and indignation. She would exact nothing of Elsie ; but latterly how often had she expected of her companion more than she gave or could give !

Of course the young girl was equal to others in pity and surprise ; but there were people in the world beside the wool-comber and his mother. Nothing of *vast* import was suggested by his sentence to her mind. She did not see that spiritual freedom was threatened with destruction. If she heard the danger questioned, she could not apprehend it. Though she had listened to the preaching of Leclerc and had been moved by it, her sense of truth and of justice was not so acute as to lead her willingly to incur a risk in the maintaining of the same.

She would not look into Antonine's Bible, which Jacqueline had read so much during the last fortnight. She was not the girl to torment herself about her soul, when the

Church would save it for her by mere compliance with a few easy regulations.

More and more was Elsie disappointing Jacqueline. Day by day these girls were developing in ways which bade fair to separate them in the end. When now they had most need of each other, their estrangement was becoming more apparent and decided. The peasant-dress of Elsie would not content her always, Jacqueline said sadly to herself.

Jacqueline's tracts, indeed, promised poorly as entertainment for an hour of rest, — rest gained by hours of toil. The confusion of tongues and the excitement of the city pleased Elsie better. So she went along the road to Meaux, and was not talking, neither thinking, all the way, of the wrongs of John Leclerc, and the sorrows of his mother, — neither meditating constantly, and with deep-seated purpose, " I will not let thee go, except thou bless me !" — neither on this problem, agitated then in so many earnest minds, " What shall a man give in exchange for his soul ? "

Thus Jacqueline sat alone and thought that she would read by herself the tracts Leclerc had found it good to study. But unopened she held the little printed scroll, while she watched the home-returning birds, whose nests were in the mighty branches of the chestnut-trees.

She needed the repose more than the teaching even ; for all day the sun had fallen heavily on the harvesters, — and toiling with a troubled heart, under a burning sun, will leave the laborer not in the best condition for such work as Jacqueline believed she had to do.

But she had promised the old woman she would read these tracts, and this was her only time, for they must be returned that night : others were waiting for them with an eagerness and longing of which, haply, tract-dispensers see little now. Still she delayed in opening them. The news of Leclerc's sentence had filled her with dismay.

Did she dread to read the truth, — "the truth of Jesus Christ," as his mother styled it ? The frightful image of the bleeding, lacerated wool-comber would come between

her and the book in which that faith was written, for maintaining which this man must suffer. Strange contrast
between the heavy gloom and terror of her thoughts and
the peaceful "river flowing on"! How tranquil were the
fields that spread beyond her sight! But there is no rest
or joy in Nature to the agitated and foreboding spirit. Must
we not have conquered the world, if we serenely enter into
Nature's rest?

Fain would Jacqueline have turned her face and steps in
another direction that night than toward the road that led
to Meaux: to the village on the border of the Vosges, —
to the ancient Domrémy. Once her home was there; but
Jacqueline had passed forth from the old, humble, true defences: for herself must live and die.

Domrémy had a home for her no more. The priest, on
whom she had relied when all failed her, was still there,
it is true; and once she had thought, that, while he lived,
she was not fatherless, not homeless: but his authority had
ceased to be paternal, and she trusted him no longer.

She had two graves in the old village, and among the
living a few faces she never could forget. But on this earth
she had no home.

Musing on these dreary facts, and on the bleeding,
branded image of Leclerc, as her imagination rendered him
back to his friends, his fearful trial over, a vision more
familiar to her childhood than her youth opened to Jacqueline.

There was one who used to wander through the woods
that bordered the mountains in whose shadow stood
Domrémy, — one whose works had glorified her name in
the England and the France that made a martyr of her.
Jeanne d'Arc had ventured all things for the truth's sake:
was she, who also came forth from that village, by any
power commissioned?

Jacqueline laid the tracts on the grass. Over them she
placed a stone. She bowed her head. She hid her face.
She saw no more the river, trees, or home-returning birds;

heard not the rush of water or of wind, — nor, even now, the hurry and the shout that possibly to-morrow would follow the poor wool-comber through the streets of Meaux, — and on the third day they would brand him!.

She remembered an old cottage in the shadow of the forest-covered mountains. She remembered one who died there suddenly, and without remedy, — her father, unabsolved and unanointed, dying in fear and torment, in a moment when none anticipated death. She remembered a strong-hearted woman who seemed to die with him, — who died to all the interests of this life, and was buried by her husband ere a twelvemonth had passed, — her mother, who was buried by her father's side.

Burdened with a solemn care they left their child. The priest of Domrémy, and none beside him, knew the weight of this burden. How had he helped her bear it? since it is the *business* of the shepherd to look after the younglings of the flock. Her hard earnings paid him for the prayers he offered for the deliverance of her father from his purgatorial woes. Burdened with a dire debt of filial love, the priest had let her depart from Domrémy; his influence followed her as an oppression and a care, — a degradation also.

Her life of labor was a slavish life. All she did, and all she left undone, she looked at with sad-hearted reference to the great object of her life. Far away she put all allurement to tempting, youthful joy. What had she to do with merriment and jollity, while a sin remained unexpiated, or a moment of her father's suffering and sorrow could be anticipated?

How, probably, would these new doctrines, held fast by some through persecution and danger, these doctrines which brought liberty to light, be received by one so fast a prisoner of Hope as she? She had pledged herself, with solemn vows had promised, to complete the work her mother left unfinished when she died.

Some of the laborers in the field, Elsie among them, had

hoped, they said, that the wool-comber would retract from his dangerous position. Recalling their words, Jacqueline asked herself would *she* choose to have him retract? She reminded herself of the only martyr whose memory she loved, the glorious girl from Domrémy; and a lofty and stern spirit seemed to rouse within her as she answered that question. She believed that John had found and taught the truth; and was Truth to be sacrificed to Power that hated it? Not by a suicidal act, at least.

She took the tracts, so judging, from underneath the stone, wistfully looked them over, and, as she did so, recalled these words: "You cannot buy your pardon of a priest; he has no power to sell it; he cannot even give it. Ask of God, who giveth to all men liberally, upbraiding not. 'If ye, being evil, know how to give good gifts to your children, how much more shall your Heavenly Father give his Holy Spirit to them that ask him!'"

She could never forget these words. She could never forget the preacher's look when he used them; nor the solemnity of the assenting faith, as attested by the countenances of those around her in that "upper room."

But her father! What would this faith do for the departed?

Yet again she dared to pray, — here in this solitude, to ask for that Holy Spirit, the Enlightener. And it was truly with trembling, in the face of all presentiments of what the gift might possibly, must certainly, import to her. But what was she, that she could withstand God, or His gift, for any fear of the result that might attend the giving of the gift?

Divinely she seemed to be inspired with that courageous thought. She rose up, as if to follow the laborers who had already gone to Meaux. But she had not passed out from the shadow of the great trees when another shadow fell along her path.

III.

IT was Victor Le Roy who was so close at hand. He recognized Jacqueline; for, as he came down the road, now and then he caught a glimpse of her red peasant-dress. And he accepted his persuasion as it had been an assurance; for he believed that on such a night no other girl would linger alone near the place of her day's labor. Moreover, while passing the group of harvesters, he had observed that she was not among them.

The acquaintance of these young persons was but slight; yet it was of such a character as must needs increase. Within the last fortnight they had met repeatedly in the room of Leclerc's mother. On the last night of her son's preaching they had together listened to his words. The young student with manly aspirations, ambitious, courageous, inquiring, and the peasant girl who toiled in fields and vineyards, were on the same day hearkening to the call, " Ho, every one that thirsteth ! " with the consciousness that the call was meant for them.

When Victor Le Roy saw that Jacqueline perceived and recognized him, he also observed the tracts in her hand and the trouble in her countenance, and he wondered in his heart whether she could be ignorant of what had passed that day at Meaux, and if it could be possible that her manifest disturbance arose from any perplexity or disquietude independent of the sentence that had been passed on John Leclerc. His first words brought an answer that satisfied his doubt.

" She has chosen that good part which shall not be taken from her," said he, as he came near. " The country is so fair, could no one of them all except Jacqueline see that? Were they all drawn away by the bloody fascination of Meaux? even Elsie ? "

" It was the news that hurried her home with the rest," answered she, almost pleased at this disturbance of the solitude.

"Did that keep you here, Jacqueline?" he asked. "It sent me out of the city. The dust choked me. Every face looked like a devil's. To-morrow night, to-morrow night, the harvesters will hurry all the faster. Terrible curiosity! And if they find traces of his blood along the streets, there will be enough to talk about through the rest of the harvesting. Jacqueline, if the river could be poured through those streets, the sacred blood could never be washed out. 'T is not the indignity, nor the cruelty, I think of most, but the barbarous, wild sin. Shall a man's truest liberty be taken from him, as though, indeed, he were not a man of God, but the spiritual subject of his fellows? If that is their plan, they may light the fires, — there are many who will not shrink from sealing their faith with their blood."

These words, spoken with vehemence, were the first free utterance Victor Le Roy had given to his feelings all day. All day they had been concentrating, and now came from him fiery and fast.

It was time for him to know in whom and in what he believed.

Greatly moved by his words, Jacqueline said, giving him the tracts, —

"I came from Domrémy. I am free. No one can be hurt by what befalls me. I want to know the truth. I am not afraid. Did John Leclerc never give way for a moment? Is he really to be whipped through the streets, and on the third day to be branded? Will he not retract?"

"Never!" was the answer, — spoken not without a shudder. "He did not flinch through all the trial, Jacqueline. And his old mother says, 'Blessed be Jesus Christ and his witnesses!'"

"I came from Domrémy," seemed to be in the girl's thought again; for her eyes flashed when she looked at Victor Le Roy, as though she could believe the heavens would open for the enlightening of such believers.

"She gave me those to read," said she, pointing to the tracts she had given him.

"And have you been reading them here by yourself?"

"No. Elsie and I were to have read them together; but I fell to thinking."

"You mean to wait for her, then?"

"I was afraid I should not make the right sense of them."

"Sit down, Jacqueline, and let me read aloud. I have read them before. And I understand them better than Elsie does, or ever will."

"I am afraid that is true, sir. If you read, I will listen."

But he did not, with this permission, begin instantly.

"You came from Domrémy, Jacqueline," said he. "I came from Picardy. My home was within a stone's throw of the castle where Jeanne d'Arc was a prisoner before they carried her to Rouen. I have often walked about that castle and tried to think how it must have been with her when they left her there a prisoner. God knows, perhaps we shall all have an opportunity of knowing, how she felt when a prisoner of Truth. Like a fly in a spider's net she was, poor girl! Only nineteen! She had lived a life that was worth the living, Jacqueline. She knew she was about to meet the fate her heart must have foretold. Girls do not run such a course and then die quietly in their beds. They are attended to their rest by grim sentinels, and they light fagots for them. I have read the story many a time, when I could look at the window of the very room where she was a prisoner. It was strange to think of her witnessing the crowning of the King, with the conviction that her work ended there and then, — of the women who brought their children to touch her garments or her hands, to let her smile on them, or speak to them, or maybe kiss them. And the soldiers deemed their swords were stronger when they had but touched hers. And they knelt down to kiss her standard, that white standard, so often victorious! I have read many a time of that glorious day at Rheims."

"And she said, *that* day, 'O, why can I not die here?'" said Jacqueline, with a low voice.

"And when the Archbishop asked her," continued Victor, "'Where do you, then, expect to die?' she answered, 'I know not. I shall die where God pleases. I have done what the Lord my God commanded me; and I wish that He would now send me to keep my sheep with my mother and sister.'"

"Because she loved Domrémy, and her work was done," said Jacqueline, sadly. "And so many hated her! But her mother would be sure to love. Jeanne would never see an evil eye in Domrémy, and no one would lie in wait to kill her in the Vosges woods."

"It was such as you, Jacqueline, who believed in her, and comforted her. And to every one that consoled her Christ will surely say, 'Ye blessed of my Father, ye did it unto me!' Yes, to be sure, there were too many who stood ready to kill her in all France, — besides those who were afraid of her, and fought against our armies. Even when they were taking her to see the Dauphin, the guard would have drowned her, and lied about it, but they were restrained. It is something to have been born in Domrémy, — to have grown up in the very place where she used to play, a happy little girl. You have seen that fountain, and heard the bells she loved so much. It was good for you, I know."

"Her prayers were everywhere," Jacqueline replied. "Everywhere she heard the voices that called her to come and deliver France. But her father did not believe in her. He persecuted Jeanne."

"A man's foes are of his own household," said Victor. "You see the same thing now. It is the very family of Christ — yes! so they dare call it — who are going to tear and rend Leclerc to-morrow for believing the words of Christ. A hundred judges settled that Jeanne should be burned; and for believing such words as are in these books —"

"Read me those words," said Jacqueline.

So they turned from speaking of Joan and her work, to contemplate another style of heroism, and to question their own hearts.

Jacqueline Gabrie had lived through eighteen years of hardship and exposure. She was strong, contented, resolute. Left to herself, she would probably have suffered no disturbance of her creed, — would have lived and died conforming to the letter of its law. But thrown under the influence of those who did agitate the subject, she was brave and clear-headed. She listened now, while, according to her wish, her neighbor read, — listened with clear intelligence, intent on the truth. That, or any truth, accepted, she would hardly shrink from whatever it involved. This was the reason why she had really feared to ask the Holy Ghost's enlightenment! So well she understood herself! Truth was truth, and, if received, to be abided by. She could not hold it loosely. She could not trifle with it. She was born in Domrémy. She had played under the Fairy Oak. She knew the woods where Joan wandered when she sought her saintly solitude. The fact was acting on her as an inspiration, when Domrémy became a memory, when she labored far away from the wooded Vosges and the meadows of Lorraine.

She listened to the reading, as girls do not always listen when they sit in the presence of a reader such as young Le Roy.

And let it here be understood — that the conclusion bring no sorrow, and no sense of wrong to those who turn these pages, thinking to find the climax dear to half-fledged imagination, incapable from inexperience of any deeper truth, (I render them all homage!) — this story is not told for any sake but truth's.

This Jacqueline did listen to this Victor, thinking actually of the words he read. She looked at him really to ascertain whether her apprehension of these things was all the same as his. She questioned him, with the simple desire to learn what he could tell her. Her hands were very hard, so constant had been her dealing with the rough facts of this life; but the hard hand was firm in its clasp, and ready with its helpfulness. Her eyes were open, and very clear of dreams. There was room in them for tenderness as well as truth. Her voice was not the sweetest of all voices in this world; but it had the quality that would make it prized by others when heart and flesh were failing; for it would be strong to speak then with cheerful faith and an unfaltering courage.

Jacqueline sat there under the chestnut-trees, upon the river-bank, strong-hearted, high-hearted, a brave, generous woman. What if her days were toilsome? What if her peasant-dress was not the finest woven in the looms of Paris or of Meaux? Her prayers were brief, her toil was long, her sleep was sound, — her virtue firm as the ever-lasting mountains. Jacqueline, I have singled you from among hordes and tribes and legions upon legions of women, one among ten thousand, altogether lovely, — not for dalliance, not for idleness, not for dancing, which is well; not for song, which is better; not for beauty, which, perhaps, is best; not for grace, or power, or passion. There is an attribute of God which is more to His universe than all evidence of power. It is His truth. Jacqueline, it is for this your name shall shine upon my page.

And, manifestly, it is by virtue of this quality that her reader is moved and attracted at this hour of twilight on the river-bank.

Her intelligence is so quick! her apprehension so direct! her conclusions so true! He intended to aid her; but Mazurier himself had never uttered comments so entirely to the purpose as did this young girl, speaking from heart and brain. Better fortune, apparently, could not have be-fallen him than was his in this reading; for with every sentence almost came her comment, clear, earnest, to the point.

He had need of such a friend as Jacqueline seemed able to prove herself. His nearest living relative was an uncle, who had sent the ambitious and capable young student to Meaux; for he gave great promise, and was worth an experiment, the old man thought, — and was strong to be thrown out into the world, where he might ascertain the power of self-reliance. He had need of friends, and, of all friends, one like Jacqueline.

From the silence and retirement of his home in Picardy he had come to Meaux, — the town that was so astir, busy, thoroughly alive! Inexperienced in worldly ways he came. His face was beautiful with its refinement and power of expression. His eyes were full of eloquence; so also was his voice. When he came from Picardy to Meaux, his old neighbors prophesied for him. He knew their prophecies, and purposed to fulfil them. He ceased from dreaming, when he came to Meaux. He was not dreaming, when he looked on Jacqueline. He was aware of what he read, and how she listened, under those chestnut-trees.

The burden of the tracts he read to Jacqueline was salvation by faith, not of works, — an iconoclastic doctrine, that was to sweep away the great mass of Romish superstition, invalidating Papal power. Image-worship, shrine-frequenting sacrifices, indulgences, were esteemed and proved less than nothing worth in the work of salvation.

" Did you understand John, when he said that the priests deceived us and were full of robberies, and talked about the masses for the dead, and said the only good of them was to put money into the Church?" asked Jacqueline.

" I believe it," he replied, with spirit.

" That the masses are worth nothing?" she asked, — far from concealing that the thought disturbed her.

" What can they be worth, if a man has lived a bad life?"

" *That* my father did *not!*" she exclaimed.

" If a man is a bad man, why, then he is. He has gone where he must be judged. The Scripture says, As a tree falls, it must lie."

" My father was a good man, Victor. But he died of a sudden, and there was no time."

" No time for what, Jacqueline? No time for him to turn about, and be a bad man in the end ? "

" No time for confession and absolution. He died praying God to forgive him all his sins. I heard him. I wondered, Victor, for I never thought of his committing sins. And my mother mourned for him as a good wife should not mourn for a bad husband."

" Then what is your trouble, Jacqueline ? "

" Do you know why I came here to Meaux? I came to get money, — to earn it. I should be paid more money here than I got for any work at home, they said : that was the reason. When I had earned so much, — it was a large sum, but I knew I should get it, and the priest encouraged me to think I should, — he said that my heart's desire would be accomplished. And I could earn the money before winter is over, I think. But now if — "

" Throw it into the Seine, when you get it, rather than pay it to the liar for selling your father out of a place he was never in ! He is safe, believe me, if he was the good man you say. Do not disturb yourself, Jacqueline."

" He never harmed a soul. And we loved him that way a bad man could not be loved."

As Jacqueline said this, a smile more sad than joyful passed over her face, and disappeared.

" He rests in peace," said Victor Le Roy.

" It is what I must believe. But what if there should be a mistake about it ? It was all I was working for."

" Think for yourself, Jacqueline. No matter what Leclerc thinks or I think. Can you suppose that Jesus Christ requires any such thing as this of you, that you should make a slave of yourself for the expiation of your father? It is a monstrous thought. Doubt not it was love that took him away so quickly. And love can care for him. Long before this, doubtless, he has heard the words, ' Come, ye blessed of my father ! ' And what is required of you, do you ask? You shall be merciful to them that live ; and trust Him that He will care for those who have gone beyond your reach. Is it so? Do I understand you? You have been thinking to *buy* this good *gift* of God, eternal life for your father, when of course you could have nothing to do with it. You have been imposed upon, and robbed all this while, and this is the amount of it."

"Well, do not speak so. If what you say is true, — and I 'think it may be, — what is past is past."

"But won't you see what an infernal lie has been prac-'tised on you, and all the rest of us who had any conscience or heart in us, all this while? There *is* no purgatory; and it is nonsense to think, that, if there were, money could buy a man out of it. Jesus Christ is the one sole atonement for sin. And by faith in Him shall a man save his soul alive. That is the only way. If I lose my soul, and am gone, the rest is between me and God. Do you see it *should* be so, and must be so, Jacqueline?"

"He was a good man," said Jacqueline.

She did not find it quite easy to make nothing of all this matter, which had been the main-spring of her effort since her father died. She could not in one instant drop from her calculations that on which she had heretofore based all her activity. She had labored so long, so hard, to buy the rest and peace and heavenly blessedness of the father she loved, it was hardly to be expected that at once she would choose to see that in that rest and peace and blessedness, she, as a producing power, had no part whatever.

As she more than hinted, the purpose of her life seemed to be taken from her. She could not perceive that fact without some consternation; could not instantly connect it with another, which should enable her to look around her with the deliberation of a liberated spirit, choosing her new work. And in this she was acted upon by more than the fear arising from the influences of her old belief. Of course she should have been, and yet she was not, able to drop instantly and forever from recollection the constant sacrifices she had made, the deprivation she had endured, with heroic persistence, — the putting far away every per-

sonal indulgence whose price had a market value. Her
father was not the only person concerned in this work; the
priest; herself. She had believed in the pastor of Domrémy. Yet he had deceived her. Else he was self-deceived;
and what if the blind should strive to lead the blind?
Could she accept the new faith, the great freedom, with
perfect rejoicing?

Victor Le Roy seemed to have some suspicion of what
was passing in her thoughts. He did not need to watch
her changeful face in order to understand them.

"I advise you to still think of this," said he. "Recall
your father's life, and then ask yourself if it is likely that
He who is Love requires the sacrifice of your youth and
your strength before your father shall receive from Him
what He has promised to give to all who trust in Him.
Take God at his word, and you will be obliged to give up
all this priest-trash."

IV.

VICTOR LE ROY spoke these words quietly, as if
aware that he might safely leave them, as well as
any other true words, to the just sense of Jacqueline.

She was none the happier for them when she returned
that night to the little city room, the poor lodging whose
high window overlooked both town and country, city streets
and harvest-fields, and the river flowing on beyond the
borders of the town,—no happier through many a moment
of thinking, until, as it were by an instant illumination, she
began to see the truth of the matter, as some might wonder
she did not instantly perceive it, if they could omit from
observation this leading fact, that the orphan girl was
Jacqueline Gabrie, child of the Church, and not a wise and
generous person, who had never been in bondage to super-
stitions.

For a long time after her return to her lodging she was
alone. Elsie was in the street with the rest of the town,

talking, as all were talking, of the sight that Meaux should see to-morrow.

Besides Jacqueline, there was hardly another person in this great building, six stories high, every room of which had usually a tenant at this hour. She sat by her window, and looked at the dusky town, over which the moon was rising. But her thoughts were far away; over many a league they wandered.

Once more she stood on the play-ground of her toilsome childhood. She recalled many a year of sacrificing drudgery, which now she could not name such, — for another reason than that which had heretofore prevented her from calling it a sacrifice. She remembered these years of wrong and of extortion, — they received their proper name now, — years whose mirth and leisure she had quietly foregone, but during which she had borne a burden that saddened youth, while it also dignified it, — a burden which had made her heart's natural cheerfulness the subject of self-reproach, and her maiden dreams and wishes matter for tears, for shame, for confession, for prayer.

Now Victor Le Roy's words came to her very strangely; powerfully they moved her. She believed them in this solitude, where at leisure she could meditate upon them. A vision more fair and blessed than she had ever imagined rose before her. There was no suffering in it, and no sorrow; it was full of peace. Already, in the heaven to which she had hoped her toil would give him at length admission, her father had found his home. There was a glory in his rest not reflected from her filial love, but from the all-availing love of Christ.

Then — delay the rigor of your judgment! — she began, — yes, she, this Jacqueline, began to count the cost of what she had done. She was not a sordid soul, she had not a miserly nature. Before she had gone far in that strange computation, she paused abruptly, with a crimsoned face, and not with tearless eyes. Counting the cost! Estimating the sacrifice! Had, then, her purpose been less holy

because excited by falsehood and sustained through delusion? Was she less loving and less true, because deceived?
And was she to lament that Christ, the one and only Priest,
rather than another instrumentality, was the deliverer of
her beloved from the power of death?

No ritual was remembered, and no formula consulted,
when she cried out, — "It is so! and I thank Thee! Only
give me now, my Jesus, a purpose as holy as that Thou
hast taken away!"

But she had not come into her chamber to spend a
solitary evening there. Turning away from the window,
she bestowed a little care upon her person, smoothed away
the traces of her day's labor, and after all was done she
lingered yet longer. She was going out, evidently. Whither? To visit the mother of John Leclerc. She must carry
back the tracts the good woman had lent her. Their contents had firm lodgment in her memory.

Others might run to and fro in the streets, and talk about
the corners, and prognosticate with passion, and defy, in
the way of cowardice, where safety rather than the truth is
well assured. If one woman could console another, Jacqueline wished that she might console Leclerc's mother. And
if any words of wisdom could drop from the poor old
woman's lips while her soul was in this strait, Jacqueline
desired to hear those words.

Down the many flights of stairs she went across the court,
and then along the street, to the house where the wool-
comber lived.

A brief pause followed her knock for admittance. She
repeated it. Then was heard a sound from within, — a
step crossing the floor. The door opened, and there stood
the mother of Leclerc, ready to face any danger, the very
Fiend himself.

But when she saw that it was Jacqueline, only Jacqueline,
— an angel, as one might say, and not a devil, — the terrible look passed from her face ; she opened the door wide.

"Come in, child! come in!"

So Jacqueline went into the room where John had worked and thought, reasoned, argued, prayed.

This is the home of the man because of whom many are this night offended·in the city of Meaux. This is the place whence issued the power that has set the tongues to talking, and the minds to thinking, and the hearts to hoping, and the authorities to avenging.

A grain of mustard-seed is the kingdom of heaven in a figure ; the wandering winds a symbol of the Pentecostal power : a dove did signify the descent of God to man. This poor chamber, so pent in, and so lowly, so obscure, has its significance. Here has a life been lived ; and not the least does it import, that walls are rough and the ceiling low.

But the life of John Leclerc was not to be limited. A power has stood here which by its freedom has set at defiance the customary calculation of the worldly-wise. In high places and in low the people are this night disturbed because of him who has dared to lift his voice in the freedom of the speech of God. In drawing-rooms odorous with luxury the man's name has mention, and the vulgarity of his liberated speech and courageous faith is a theme to move the wonder and excite the reprobation of hearts whose languid beating keeps up their show of life, — to what sufficient purpose expect me not to tell. His voice is loud and harsh to echo through these music-loving halls ; it rends and tears, with almost savage strength, the dainty silences.

But busier tongues are elsewhere more vehement in speech ; larger hearts beat faster indignation ; grief and vulgarest curiosity are all manifesting themselves after their several necessity. In solitary places heroes pray throughout the night, wrestling like Jacob, agonizing like Saul, and with some of them the angel left his blessing ; for some the golden harp was struck that soothed their souls to peace. Angels of heaven had work to do that night. Angels of heaven and hell did prove themselves that night in Meaux ;

night of unrest and sleeplessness, or of cruel dreaming;
night of bloody visions, tortured by the apprehension óf a
lacerated body driven through the city streets, and of the
hooting shouts of Devildom ; night-haunted by a gory image, — the defiled temple of the Holy Ghost.

Did the prospect of torture keep *him* wakeful ? Could
the man bear the disgrace, the derision, shouting, agony ?
Was there nothing in this thought, that as a witness of
Jesus Christ he was to appear next day, that should soothe'
him even unto slumber ? Upon the silence of his guarded
chamber let none but ministering angels break. Sacred to
him, and to Him who watched the hours of the night, let
the night go !

But here — his mother, Jacqueline with her — we may
linger with these.

V.

WHEN the old woman saw that it was Jacqueline
Gabrie who stood waiting admittance, she opened
the door wider, as I said ; and the dark solemnity of her
countenance seemed to be, by so much as a single ray,
enlivened for an instant.

She at once perceived the tracts which Jacqueline had
brought. Aware of this, the girl said, —

"I stayed to hear them read, after I heard that for the
sake of the truth in them " — she hesitated — "this city
will invite God's wrath to-morrow."

And she gave the papers to the old woman, who took
them in silence.

By and by she asked, —

"Are you just home, Jacqueline ? "

"Since sunset, though it was nearly dark when I came
in," she answered. "Victor Le Roy was down by the
river-bank, and he read them for me."

"He wanted to get out of town, may be. You would
surely have thought it was a holiday, Jacqueline, if you

could have seen the people. Anything for a show; but some of them might well lament. Did you want to know the truth he pays so dear for teaching? But you have heard it, my child."

"We all heard what he must pay for it, in the fields at noon. Yes, mother, I wanted to know."

"But if you shall believe it, Jacqueline, it may lead you into danger, into sad straits," said the old woman, looking at the young girl with earnest pity in her eyes.

She loved this girl, and shuddered at the thought of exposing her to danger.

Jacqueline had nursed her neighbor, Antonine, and more than once, after a hard day's labor, which must be followed · by another, she had sat with her through the night; and she could pay this service only with love, and the best gift of her love was to instruct her in the truth. John and she had proved their grateful interest in her fortunes by giving her that which might expose her to danger, persecution, and they could not foresee to what extremity of evil.

And now the old woman felt constrained to say this to her, even for her love's sake, — "It may lead you into danger."

"But if truth is dangerous, shall I choose to be safe?" answered Jacqueline, with stately courage.

"It *is* truth. It *will* support him. Blessed be Jesus Christ and His witnesses! To-night, and to-morrow, and the third day, our Jesus will sustain him. They think John will retract. They do not know my son. They do not know how he has waited, prayed, and studied to learn the truth, and how dear it is to him. No, Jacqueline, they do not. But when they prove him, they will know. And if he is willing to witness, shall I not be glad? The people will understand him better afterward, — and the priests, maybe. 'I can do all things,' said he, 'Christ strengthening me'; and that was said long ago by one who was proved. Where shall you be, Jacqueline?"

"O," groaned Jacqueline, "I shall be in the fields at work,

away from these cruel people, and the noise and the sight.
But, mother, where shall you be?"

"With the people, child. With him, if I live. Yes, he
is my son; and I have never been ashamed of the brave
boy. I will not be ashamed to-morrow. I will follow John;
and when they bind him, I will let him see his mother's eyes
are on him, — blessing him, my child! — Hark! how they
talk through the streets! — Jacqueline, he was never a
coward. He is strong, too. They will not kill him, and
they cannot make him dumb. He will hold the truth the
faster for all they do to him. Jesus Christ on his side, do
you think he will fear the city, or all Paris, or all France?
He does not know what it is to be afraid. And when God
opened his eyes to the truth of his Gospel, which the priests
had hid, he meant that John should work for it; for he is
a working-man, whatever he sets about."

So this old woman tried, and not without success, to
comfort herself, and sustain her tender, proud, maternal
heart. The dire extremity into which she and her son had
fallen did not crush her; few were the tears that fell from
her eyes as she recalled for Jacqueline the years of her
son's boyhood, — told her of his courage, as in various
ways it had made itself manifest: how he had always been
fearless in danger, — a conqueror of pain, — seemingly re-
gardless of comfort, — fond of contemplation, — contented
with his humble state, — kindly, affectionate, generous, but
easily stirred to wrath by injustice, when manifested by the
strong toward the weak, or by cruelty, or by falsehood.

Many an anecdote of his career might she relate; for
his character, under the pressure of this trial, which was
as searching and severe a test of her faith as of his, seemed
to illustrate itself in manifold heroic ways, all now of the
highest significance. With more majesty and grandeur his
character arose before her; for now in all the past, as she
surveyed it, she beheld a living power, a capability, and a
necessity of new and grand significance, and her heart
reverenced the spirit she had nursed into being.

Removed to the distance of a prison from her sight, separated from her love by bolts and bars, and the wrath of tyranny and close-banded bigotry, he became a power, a hero, who moved her, as she recalled his sentence, and prophesied the morrow, to a feeling tears could not explain.

They passed the night together, the young woman and the old. In the morning, Jacqueline must go into the field again. She was in haste to go. Leaving a kiss on the old woman's cheek, she was about to steal away in silence; but as she laid her hand upon the latch, a thought arrested her, and she did not open the door, but went back and sat beside the window, and watched the mother of Leclerc through the sleep that must be brief. It was not in her heart to go away and leave those eyes to waken upon solitude. She must see a helpful hand and hopeful face, and, if it might be, hear a cheerful human voice, in the dawning of that day.

She had not long to wait; and the time she may have lost in waiting Jacqueline did not count or reckon, when she heard her name spoken, and could answer, "What wilt thou? here am I."

Not in vain had she lingered. What were wages, more or less, that they should be mentioned, thought of, when she might give and receive here what the world gives not, and never has to give, and what a mortal cannot buy, the treasure being priceless? Through the quiet of that morning hour, soothing words, and strong, she felt and knew to speak; and when at last she hurried away from the city to the fields, she was stronger than of nature, able to bear witness to the faith that speaks from the bewilderment of its distresses, "Though He slay me, yet will I trust in Him."

Not alone had her young, frank, loving eyes enlivened the dreary morning to the heart of Leclerc's mother. Grace for grace had she received. And words of the hymn that were always on John's lips had found echo from his mother's memory this morning: they lodged in the heart of Jacqueline. She went away repeating, —

> "In the midst of death, the jaws
> Of hell against us gape.
> Who from peril dire as this
> Openeth us escape?
> 'T is thou, O Lord, alone!
> Our bitter suffering and our sin
> Pity from thy mercy win,
> Holy Lord and God!
> Strong and holy God!
> Merciful and holy Saviour!
> Eternal God!
> Let us not despair
> For the fire that burneth there!
> Kyrie, eleison!"

Jacqueline met Elsie on her way to the fields. But the girls had not much to say to each other that morning in their walk. Elsie was manifestly conscious of some great constraint; she might have reported to her friend what she had heard in the streets last night, but she felt herself prevented from such communication, — seemed to be intent principally on one thing: she would not commit herself in any direction. She was looking with suspicion upon Jacqueline. Whatever became of her soul, her body she would save alive. She was waking to this world's enjoyment with vision alert, senses keen. Martyrdom in any degree was without attraction to her, and in Truth she saw no beauty that she should desire it. It was a root out of dry ground indeed, that gave no promise of spreading into goodly shelter and entrancing beauty.

As to Jacqueline, she was absorbed in her heroic and exalted thoughts. Her heart had almost failed her when she said farewell to John's mother; tearfully she had hurried on her way. One vast cloud hung between her and heaven; darkly rolled the river; every face seemed to bear witness to the tragedy that day should witness.

Not the least of her affliction was the consciousness of the distance increasing between herself and Elsie Méril

N

She knew that Elsie was rejoicing that she had in no way endangered herself yet; and sure was she that in no way would Elsie invite the fury of avenging tyranny and reckless superstition.

Jacqueline asked her no questions, — spoke few words to her, — was absorbed in her own thoughts. But she was kindly in her manner, and in such words as she spoke. So Elsie perceived two things, — that she should not lose her friend, neither was in danger of being seized by the heretical mania. It was her way of drawing inferences. Certain that she had not lost her friend, because Jacqueline did not look away, and refuse to recognize her; congratulating herself that she was not the object of suspicion, either justly or unjustly, among the dreadful priests.

But that friend whose steady eye had balanced Elsie was already sick at heart, for she knew that never more must she rely upon this girl who came with her from Domrémy.

As they crossed the bridge, lingering thereon a moment, the river seemed to moan in its flowing toward Meaux. The day's light was sombre; the birds' songs had no joyous sound, — plaintive was their chirping; it saddened the heart to hear the wind, — it was a wind that seemed to take the buoyancy and freshness out of every living thing, an ugly southeast wind. They went on together, — to the wheat-fields together. It was to be day of minutes to poor Jacqueline.

To be away from Meaux bodily was, it appeared, only that the imagination might have freer exercise. Yes, — now the people must be moving through the streets; shopmen were not so intent on profits this day as they were on other days. The priests were thinking with vengeful hate of the wrong to themselves which should be met and conquered that day. The people should be swiftly brought into order again! John in his prison was preparing, as all without the prison were.

The crowd was gathering fast. He would soon be led

forth. The shameful march was forming. Now the brutal hand of Power was lifted with scourges. The bravest man in Meaux was driven through the streets, — she saw with what a visage, — she knew with what a heart. Her heart was awed with thinking thereupon. A bloody mist seemed to fall upon the environs of Meaux; through that red horror she could not penetrate; it shrouded and it held poor Jacqueline.

Of the faith that would sustain him she began once more to inquire. It is not by a bound that mortals ever clear the heights of God. Step by step they scale the eminences, toiling through the heavenly atmosphere. Only around the summit shines the eternal sun.

So she must now recall the words that Victor Le Roy read for her last night; and the words he spoke from out his heart, — these also. And she did not fear now, as yesterday, to ask for light. Let the light dawn, — oh, let it shine on her!

The mother of Leclerc had uttered mysterious words which Jacqueline took for truth; the light was joyful and blessed, and of all things to be desired, though it smote the life from one like lightning. She waited alone with faith, watching till it should come, — left alone with this beam glimmering like a moth through darkness! — for thus was a believer, or one who resolved on believing, left in that day, when he turned from the machinery of the Church, and stood alone, searching for God without the aid of priestly intervention.

VI.

THERE was something awful in such loneliness. Jacqueline knew little of it until now, as she walked toward the fields, by the side of Elsie Méril.

She saw how she had depended on the priest of Domrémy, as he had been the lawgiver and the leader of her life. A spiritual life, to be sustained only by the invisible spirit, to be lived by faith, not in man, but in God, without intervention of saint or angel or Blessed Virgin, — was the world's life liberated by such freedom?

By faith, and not by sight, the just must live. Would He bow his heavens and come down to dwell with the contrite and the humble?

Wondrous strange it seemed, — incomprehensible, — more than she could manage or control. There are prisoners whose pardon proves the world too large for them: they find no rest until their prison-door is opened for them again.

Of this class was Elsie, — not Jacqueline. Elsie was afraid of freedom, — not equal to it, — unable to deal with it; satisfied with being a child, with being a slave, when it came to be a question whether she should accept and use her highest privilege and dignity. At this hour, and among all persuasions, you will find that Elsie does not stand alone. Little children there are, long as the world shall stand, — though not precisely such as we think of when we remember, " Of such is the kingdom of heaven."

It was enough for Elsie — it is enough for multitudes through all the reformations — that she had an earthly defence, even such as she relied on without trouble. She lived in the hour. She had never toiled to deliver her darling from the lions, — to redeem a soul from purgatory. She eased her conscience, when it was troubled, by such shallow discovery of herself as she deemed confession. She loved dancing, and all other amusements, — hated solitude, knew not the meaning of self-abnegation. And let her dance and enjoy herself ! — some service to the body is rendered thereby. She might do greatly worse, and is incapable of doing greatly better. Will you stint the idiots of comfort, — or rather build them decent habitations, and even vex yourself to feed and clothe them, in reverent confidence that the Future shall surely take them up and bless them, unstop their ears, open their eyes, give speech to them and absolute deliverance?

There are others beside Elsie who congratulate them-

selves on non-committal, — they covet not the advanced
and dangerous positions. Honorable, but dangerous positions! The head might be taken off, do you not see?
And could all eternity compensate for the loss of time?
Ah, the body might be mutilated, — the liberty restrained:
as if, indeed, a man's freedom were not eternally established,
when his enemies, howling around, must at least crucify
him! as if a divine voice were not ever heard through the
raging of the people, saying, "Come up higher!"

But a fern-leaf cannot grow into a mighty hemlock-tree.
From the ashes of a sparrow the phœnix shall not rise.
You will not to all eternity, by any artificial means, nor by
a miracle, bring forth an eagle from a mollusk.

There was not a sadder heart in all those fields of Meaux
than the heart of Jacqueline Gabrie. There was not a
stronger heart. Not a hand labored more diligently. Under
the broad-brimmed peasant-hat was a sad countenance, —
under the peasant-dress a heavily burdened spirit. Silent,
all day, she labored. She was alone at noon under the
river-bordered trees, eating her coarse fare without zest, but
with a conscience, — to sustain the body that was born to
toil. But in the maelstrom of doubt and anxiety was she
tossed and whirled, and she cared not for her life. To be
rid of it, now for the first time, she felt might be a blessing.
What purpose, indeed, had she? She turned her thought
from this question, but it would not let her alone. Again
and yet again she turned to meet it, and thus would surely
have at length its satisfying answer.

John Leclerc might pass through this ordeal, as from
the first she had expected of him. But she listened to the
speech of many of her fellow-laborers. Some prophecies
which had a sound incredible escaped them. She did not
credit them, but they tormented her. They contended with
one another. John, some foretold, would certainly retract.
One day of public whipping would suffice. When the
blood began to flow, he would see his duty clearer! The
men were prophesying from the depths and the abundance

of their self-consciousness. Others speculated on the final
result of the executed sentence. They believed that the
"obstinacy" and courage of the man would provoke his
judges, and the executors of his sentence ; that with rigor
they would execute it ; and that, led on by passion, and
provoked by such as would side with the victim, the sentence would terminate in his destruction. Sooner or láter,
nothing but his life would be found ultimately to satisfy his
enemies.

It might be so, thought Jacqueline Gabrie. What then ?
what then ? — she thought. There was inspiration to the
girl in that cruel prophecy. Her life-work was not ended.
If Christ was the One Ransom, and it did truly fall on
Him, and not on her, to care for those beloved, departed
from this life, her work was still for love.

John Leclerc disabled or dead, who should care then for
his aged mother ? Who should minister to him? Who,
indeed, but Jacqueline ?

Living or dying, she said to herself, with grand enthusiasm, — living or dying, let him do the Master's pleasure !
She also was here to serve that Master ; and while in
spiritual things he fed the hungry, clothed the naked, gave
the cup of living water, visited the imprisoned, and the
sick of sin, she would bind herself to minister to him and
his old mother in temporal things ; so should he live above
all cares save those of heavenly love. She could support
them all by her diligence, and in this there would be joy.

She thought this through her toil ; and the thought was
its own reward. It strengthened her like an angel, —
strengthened heart and faith. She labored as no other
peasant-woman did that day, — like a beast of burden,
unresisting, patient, — like a holy saint, so peaceful and
assured, so conscious of the present very God !

VII.

THE three days passed away. And every hour's progress was marked as it passed over the citizens of Meaux. Leclerc, and the doctrines for which he suffered, filled the people's thought; he was their theme of speech. Wonder softened into pity; unbelief was goaded by his stripes to cruelty; faith became transfigured, while he, followed by the hooting crowd, endured the penalty of faith. Some men looked on with awe that would become adoring; some with surprise that would take refuge in study and conviction. There were tears as well as exultation, solemn joy as well as execration, in his train. The mother of Leclerc followed him with her undaunted testimony, "Blessed be Jesus Christ and His Witnesses!"

By day, in the field, Jacqueline Gabrie thought over the reports she heard, through the harvesters, of the city's feeling, of its purpose, of its judgment; by night she prayed and hoped, with the mother of Leclerc; and wondrous was the growth her faith had in those days.

On the evening of the third day, Jacqueline and Elsie walked into Meaux together. This was not invariably their habit. Elsie had avoided too frequent conversation with her friend of late. She knew their paths were separate, and was never so persuaded of the fact as this night, when, of her own will, she sought to walk with Jacqueline. The sad face of her friend troubled her; it moved her conscience that she did not deeply share in her anxiety. When they came from Domrémy, she had relied on Jacqueline: there was safety in her counsel, — there was wisdom in it: but now, either?

"It made me scream outright, when I saw the play," said she; "but it is worse to see your face now-a-days, — it is more terrible, Jacqueline."

Jacqueline made no reply to this; and Elsie regarded the silence as sufficient provocation.

"You seem to think I have no feeling," said she. "I am as sorry about the poor fellows as you can be. But I cannot look as if I thought the day of judgment close at hand, when I don't, Jacqueline." ·

"Very well, Elsie. I am not complaining of your looks."

"But you are, — or you might as well."

"Let not that trouble you, Elsie. Your face is smooth, at least; and your voice does not sound like the voice of one who is in grief. Rejoice, — for, as you say, you have a right to yourself, with which I am not to interfere. We are old friends, — we came away from Lorraine together. Do not forget that. I never will forget it."

"But you are done with me. You say nothing to me. I might as well be dead, for all you care." ·

"Let us not talk of such things in this manner," said Jacqueline, mildly. But the dignity of her rebuke was felt, for Elsie said, —

"But I seem to have lost you, — and now we are alone together, I may say it. Yes, I have.lost you, Jacqueline !"

"This is not the first time we have been alone together in these dreadful three days."

"But now I cannot help speaking."

"You could help it before. Why, Elsie? You had not made up your mind. But now you have, or you would not speak, and insist on speaking. What have you to say, then ? "

"Jacqueline ! Are you Jacqueline ? "

"Am I not ? "

"You seem not to be."

"How is it, Elsie ? "

"You are silent and stern, and I think you are very unhappy, Jacqueline."

"I do not know, — not unhappy, I think. Perhaps I am silent, — I have been so busy. But for all it is so dreadful — no ! not unhappy, Elsie."

"Thinking of Leclerc all the while ? "

"Of him ? O, no ! I have not been thinking of him, —

not constantly. Jesus Christ will take care of him. His mother is quiet, thinking that. I, at least, can be as strong as she. I'm not thinking of the shame and cruelty, — but of what that can be worth which is so much to him, that he counts this punishment, as they call it, as nothing, as hardly pain, certainly not disgrace. The Truth, Elsie ! — if I have not as much to say, it is because I have been trying to find the Truth."

"But if you have found it, then I hope I never shall, — if it is the Truth that makes you so gloomy. I thought it was this business in Meaux."

"Gloomy ? when it may be I have found, or *shall* find — "

Here Jacqueline hesitated, — looked at Elsie. Grave enough was that look to expel every frivolous feeling from the heart of Elsie, — at least, so long as she remained under its influence. It was something to trust another as Jacqueline intended now to trust her friend. It was a touching sight to see her seeking her old confidence, and appearing to rely on it, while she knew how frail the reed was. But this girl, frivolous as was her spirit, this girl had come with her from the distant native village ; their childhood's recollections were the same. And Jacqueline determined now to trust her. For in times of blasting heat the shadow even of the gourd is not to be despised.

"You know what I have looked for so long, Elsie," she said ; "you ought to rejoice with me. I need work for that no longer."

"What is that, Jacqueline ? "

Even this question, betraying no such apprehension as Jacqueline's words seemed to intimate, did not disturb the girl. She was in the mood when, notwithstanding her show of dependence, she was really in no such necessity. Never was she stronger than now when she put off all show of strength. Elsie stood before her in place of the opposing world. To Elsie's question she replied as readily as though she anticipated the word, and had no expectation of better recollection, — not to speak of better apprehension.

10

" To bring him out of suffering he has never been made to endure, as surely as God lives. As if the Almighty judged men so! I shall send back no more money to Father La Croix. It is not his prayer, nor my earnings, that will have to do with the eternity of John Gabrie. — Do you hear me, Elsie ? "

" I seem to, Jacqueline."

"Have I any cause for wretched looks, then ? I am in sight of better fortune than I ever hoped for in this world."

" Then don't look so fearful. It is enough to scare one. You are not a girl to choose to be a fright, — unless this dreadful city has changed you altogether from what you were. You would frighten the Domrémy children with such a face as that ; they used not to fear Jacqueline."

" I shall soon be sailing on a smoother sea. As it is, do not speak of my looks. That is too foolish."

" But, O, I feel as if I must hold you, — hold you ! — you are leaving me ! "

" Come on, Elsie ! " exclaimed Jacqueline, as though she almost hoped this of her dear companion.

" But where ? " asked Elsie, not so tenderly.

"Where God leads. I cannot tell."

" I do not understand."

"You would not think the Truth worth buying at the price of your life ? "

" My life ? "

" Or such a price as he pays who — has been branded to-day ? "

" It was not the truth to your mother, — or to mine. It was not the truth to any one we ever knew, till we came here to Meaux."

" It is true to my heart, Elsie. It is true to my conscience. I know that I can live for it. And it may be — "

" Hush ! — do not ! O, I wish that I could get you back to Domrémy ! What is going to come of this ? Jacqueline, let us go home. Come, let us start to-night. We shall have the moon all night to walk by. There is nothing in Meaux for us. O, if we had never come away! It would have been better for you to work there for what you wanted, — for what you came here to do."

"No, let God's Truth triumph! What am I? Less than that rush! But if His breath is upon me, I will be moved by it, — I am not a stone."

Then they walked on in silence. Elsie had used her utmost of persuasion, but Jacqueline not her utmost of resistance. Her companion knew this, felt her weakness in such a contest, and was silent.

On to town they went together. They walked together through the streets, passing constantly knots of people who stood about the corners and among the shops, discussing what had taken place that day. They crossed the square where the noonday sun had shone on crowds of people, men and women, gathered from the four quarters of the town and the neighboring country, assembled to witness the branding of a heretic. They entered their court-yard together, — ascended the stairway leading to their lodging. But they were two, — not one.

Elsie's chief desire had been to get Jacqueline safely into the house ere she could find opportunity for expression of what was passing in her mind. Her fear was even greater than her curiosity. She had no desire to learn, under these present circumstances, the arguments and incidents which the knots of men and women were discussing with so much vehemence as they passed by. She could guess enough to satisfy her. So she had hurried along, betraying more eagerness than was common with her to get out of the street. Not often was she so overcome of weariness, — not often so annoyed by heat and dust. Jacqueline, without remonstrance, followed her. But they were two, — not one.

Once safe in their upper room, Elsie appeared to be, after all, not so devoid of interest in what was passing in the street as her hurried walk would seem to betoken. She had not quite yet lost her taste for excitement and display. For immediately she seated herself by the window, and was all eye and ear to what went on outside.

Jacqueline's demonstrations also were quite other than might have been anticipated. Each step she took in her chamber gave an indication that she had a purpose, and that she would perform it.

She removed from her dress the dust and stain of toil, arranged her hair, made herself clean and decent, to meet the sober gaze of others. Then she placed upon the table the remains of their breakfast; but she ate nothing.

VIII.

IT was nearly dark when Jacqueline said to Elsie, — "I am now going to see John and his mother. I must see with my own eyes, and hear with my own ears. I may be able to help them, — and I know they will be able to help me. John's word will be worth hearing, — and I want to hear it. He must have learned in these days more than we shall ever be able to learn for ourselves. Will you go with me?"

"No," cried Elsie, — as though she feared she might against her will be taken into such company. Then, not for her own sake, but for Jacqueline's, she added, almost as if she hoped that *she* might prove successful in persuasion, "I remember my father and mother. What they taught me. I believe. And that I shall live by. I shall never be wiser than they were. And I know I never can be happier. They were good and honest. Jacqueline, we shall never be as happy again as we were in Domrémy, when the pastor blessed us, and we hunted flowers for the altar, — never! — never!" And Elsie Méril, overcome by her recollections and her presentiments, burst into tears.

"It was the happiness of ignorance," said Jacqueline, after a solemn silence, full of hurried thought. "No, — I, for one, shall never be *as* happy as I was then. But my joy will be full of peace and bliss. It will be full of satisfaction, — very different, but such as belongs to me, such as I must not do without. God led us from Domrémy, and with me shall He do as seemeth good to Him. We were children then, Elsie; but now may we be children no longer!"

"I will be faithful to my mother. Go, Jacqueline, — let me alone."

Elsie said this with so much spirit that Jacqueline answered quickly, and yet very kindly, —

"I did not mean to trouble you, dear, — but — no matter now."

No sooner had Jacqueline left the house than Elsie went down to a church near by, where she confessed herself to the priest, and received such goodly counsel as was calculated to fortify her against Jacqueline in the future.

Jacqueline went to the house of the wool-comber, as of late had been her nightly custom, — but not, as heretofore, to lighten the loneliness and anxiety of the mother of Leclerc. Already she had said to the old woman, —

"I need not work now for my father's redemption. Then I will work for you, if your son is disabled. Let us believe that God brought me here for this. I am strong. You can lean on me. Try it."

Now she went to make repetition of the promise to Leclerc, if, perchance, he had come back to his mother sick and sore and helpless. For this reason, when she entered the humble home of the martyr, his eyes fell on her, and he saw her as she had been an angel; how serene was her countenance; and her courage was manifestly such as no mortal fear, no human affliction, could dismay.

Already in that room faithful friends had gathered to · congratulate the living man, and to refresh their strength from the abounding richness of his.

Martial Mazurier, the noted preacher, was there, and

Victor Le Roy; besides these, others, unknown by name
or presence to Jacqueline.

Among them was the wool-comber, — wounded with
many stripes, branded, a heretic! But a man still, it appeared, — a living man, — brave as any hero, determined
as a saint, — ready to proclaim now the love of God, and
from the couch where he was lying to testify to Jesus and
his Truth.

It was a goodly sight to see the tenderness of these men
here gathered; how they were forgetful of all inequalities
of station, such as worldlings live by, — meeting on a new
ground, and greeting one another in a new spirit.

They had come to learn of John. A halo surrounded
him; he was transfigured; and through that cloud of
glory they would fain penetrate. Perchance his eyes, as
Stephen's, had seen heaven open, when men had tried
their torments. At least, they had witnessed, when they followed the crowd, that his face, in contrast with theirs who
tormented, shone, as it had been the face of an angel.
They had witnessed his testimony given in the heroic endurance of physical pain. There was more to be learned
than the crowd were fit to hear or *could* hear. Broken
strains of the Lord's song they heard him singing through
the torture. Now they had come longing for the full
burden of that divinest melody.

Jacqueline entered the room quietly, scarcely observed.
She sat down by the door, and it chanced to be near the
mother of Leclerc, near Victor Le Roy.

To their conversation she listened as one who listens for
his life, — to the reading of the Scripture, — to the singing
of the psalm, — that grand old version, —

> "Out of the depths I cry to thee,
>   Lord God! O, hear my prayer!
> Incline a gracious ear to me,
>   And bid me not despair.
> If thou rememberest each misdeed,
> If each should have its rightful meed,
>   Lord, who shall stand before thee?

"Lord, through thy love alone we gain
  The pardon of our sin :
The strictest life is but in vain,
  Our works can nothing win,
That man should boast himself of aught,
But own in fear thy grace hath wrought
  What in him seemeth righteous.

"Wherefore my hope is in the Lord,
  My works I count but dust;
I build not there, but on his word,
  And in his goodness trust.
Up to his care myself I yield;
He is my tower, my rock, my shield;
  And for his help I tarry."

To the praying of the broken voice of John Leclerc she
listened. In his prayer she joined. To the eloquence of
Mazurier, whose utterances she laid up in her heart, — to
the fervor of Le Roy, which left her eyes not dry, her soul
not calm, but strong in its commotion, grasping fast the
eternal truths which he, too, would proclaim, she listened.

She was not only now among them, she was of them, —
of them forevermore. Though she should never again look
on those faces, nor listen to those voices, of them, of all
they represented, was she forevermore. Their God was
hers, — their faith was hers ; their danger would she share,
— their work would aid.

Their talk was of the Truth, and of the future of the
Truth. Well they understood that the spirit roused among
the people would not be quieted again, — that what of
ferocity in the nature of the bigot and the powerful had
been appeased had but for the moment been satisfied.
There would be unremitting watch for victims ; everywhere
the net for the unwary and the fearless would be laid.
Blood-thirstiness and lust and covetousness would make
grand their disguises, — broad would their phylacteries be
made, — shining with sacred gems, their breastplates.

Of course it was of the great God's honor these men
would be jealous. This heresy must needs be uprooted, or

no knowing where would .be the end of the wild growth. And, indeed, there was no disputing the fact that there was danger in open acceptance .of such doctrines as defy the authority of priestcraft, — ay, danger to falsehood, and death to falsehood!

Fanaticism, cowardice, cruelty, the spirit of persecution, the spirit of authority aroused, ignorance and vanity and foolishness would make themselves companions, no doubt. Should Truth succumb to these? Should Love retreat before the fierce onset. of Hate? These brave men said not so. And they looked above them and all human aid for succor, — Jacqueline with them.

When Mazurier and Victor Le Roy went away, they left Jacqueline with the wool-comber's mother, but they did not pass by her without notice. Martial lingered for a moment, looking down on the young girl.

" She is one of us," said the old woman.

Then the preacher laid his hand upon her head, and blessed her.

" Continue in prayer, and listen to the testimony of the Holy Ghost," said he. " Then shall you surely come deep into the blessed knowledge and. the dear love of Jesus Christ."

When he had passed on, Victor paused in turn.

" It is good to be here, Jacqueline," said he. " This is the house of God; this is the gate of heaven."

And he also went forth, whither Mazurier had gone.

Then beside the bed of the poor wool-comber, women like angels ministered, binding up his wounds, and soothing him with voices soft as ever spoke to man. And from the peasant whose toil was in harvest-fields and vineyards came offers of assistance which the poor can best give the poor.

But the wool-comber did not need the hard-earned pence of Jacqueline. When she said, " Let me serve you now, as a daughter and a sister, you two," — he made no mistake in regard to her words and offer. But he had no need of just such service as she stood prepared to render. In his toil he had looked forward to the seasons of adversity, had provided for a dark day's disablement; and he was able now to smile upon his mother and on Jacqueline, and to say, —

"I will, indeed, be a brother to you, and my mother will love you as if you were her child. But we shall not take the bread from your mouth to prove it. Our daughter and our sister in the Lord, we thank you and love you, Jacqueline. I know what you have been doing since I went away. The Lord love you, Jacqueline! You will no longer be a stranger and friendless in Meaux, while John Leclerc and his mother are alive, — nay, as long as a true man or woman lives in Meaux. Fear not."

"I will not fear," said Jacqueline.

And she sat by the side of the mother of Leclerc, and thought of her own mother in the heavens, and was tranquil, and prepared, she said to herself, to walk, if indeed she must, through the valley of the shadow of death, and would still fear no evil.

IX.

STRENGTHENED and inspired by the scenes of the last three days, Martial Mazurier began to preach with an enthusiasm, bravery, and eloquence unknown before to his hearers. He threw himself into the work of preaching the new revelation of the ancient eternal Truth, with an ardor that defied authority, that scorned danger, and with a recklessness that had its own reward.

Victor Le Roy was his ardent admirer, his constant follower, his loving friend, his servant. Day by day this youth was studying with indefatigable zeal the truths and doctrines adopted by his teacher. Enchanted by the wise man's eloquence, already a convert to the faith he magnified, he was prepared to follow wherever the preacher led. The fascination of danger he felt, and was allured by. Frowning faces had for him no terrors. He could defy evil.

Jacqueline and he might be called most friendly students. Often in the cool of the day the young man walked out from Meaux along the country-roads, and his face was always toward the setting sun, whence towards the east Jacqueline at that hour would be coming. The girls were living in the region of the vineyards now, and among the vines they worked.

It began to be remarked by some of their companions how much Jacqueline Gabrie and the young student from the city walked together. But the subject of their discourse, as they rested under the trees that fringed the river, was not within the range of common speculation; far enough removed from the ordinary use to which the peasants put their thought was the thinking of Le Roy and Jacqueline.

Often Victor went, carefully and with a student's precision, over the grounds of Martial's arguments, for the satisfaction of Jacqueline. Much pride as well as joy had he in the service; for he reverenced his teacher, and feared nothing so much, in these repetitions, as that this listener, this animated, thinking, feeling Jacqueline, should lose anything by his transmission of the preacher's arguments and eloquence.

And sometimes, on those special occasions which were now constantly occurring, she walked with him to the town, and hearkened for herself in the assemblages of those who were now one in the faith.

Elsie looked on and wondered, but did not jest with Jacqueline, as girls are wont to jest with one another on such points as seemed involved in this friendship between youth and youth, between man and woman.

Towards the conclusion of the girl's appointed labor in the vineyard, a week passed in which Victor Le Roy had not once come out from Meaux in the direction of the setting sun. He knew the time when the peasants' labor in the vineyard would be done ; Jacqueline had told him ; and with wonder, and with trouble, she lived through the days that brought no word from him.

At work early and late, Jacqueline had no opportunity of discovering what was going on in Meaux. But it chanced, on the last day of the last week in the vineyard, tidings reached her : Martial Mazurier had been arrested, and would be tried, the rumor said, as John Leclerc had been tried ; and sentence would be pronounced, doubtless, said conjecture, severe in proportion to the influence the man had acquired, to the position he held.

Hearing this, oppressed, troubled, yet not doubting, Jacqueline determined that she would go to Meaux that evening, and so ascertain the truth. She said nothing to Elsie of her purpose. She was careful in all things to avoid that which might involve her companion in peril in an unknown future ; but at nightfall she had made herself ready to set out for Meaux, when her purpose was changed in the first steps by the appearance of Victor Le Roy.

He had come to Jacqueline, — had but one purpose in his coming ; yet it was she who must say, —

"Is it true, Victor, that Martial Mazurier is in prison ?."

His answer surprised her.

"No, it is not true."

But his countenance did not answer the glad expression of her face with an equal smile. His gravity almost communicated itself to her. Yet this rebound from her recent dismay surely might demand an opportunity.

"I believe you," said she. "But I was coming to see if it could be true. It was hard to believe, and yet it has cost me a great deal to persuade myself against belief, Victor."

"It will cost you still more, Jacqueline. Martial Mazurier has recanted."

"He has been in prison, then ?"

"He has retracted, and is free again, — has denied himself. No more glorious words from him, Jacqueline, such

as we have heard! He has sold himself to the Devil, you
see."

" Mazurier ? "

" Mazurier has thought raiment better than life. *He* has
believed a man's life to consist in the abundance of the
things he possesseth," said the youth, bitterly. He continued, looking steadfastly at Jacqueline, " Probably I must
give up the Truth also. My uncle is dead: must I not
secure my possessions ? — for I am no longer a poor man ;
I cannot afford to let my life fall into the hands of those
wolves."

" Mazurier retracted ? I cannot believe it, Victor Le
Roy ! "

" Believe, then, that yesterday the man was in prison, and
to-day he is at large. Yes, he says that he can serve Jesus
Christ more favorably, more successfully, by complying
with the will of the bishop and the priests. You see the
force of his argument. If he should be silenced, or imprisoned long, or his life should be cut off, he would then
be able to preach no more at all in any way. He only does
not believe that whosoever will save his life, in opposition
to the law of the everlasting Gospel, must lose it."

" O, do you remember what he said to John, — what he
prayed in that room? O, Victor, what does it mean ? "

" It means what cannot be spoken, — what I dare not say
or think."

" Not that we are wrong, mistaken, Victor ? "

" No, Jacqueline, never ! it can never mean that ! Whatever we may do with the Truth, we cannot make it false.
We may act like cowards, unworthy, ungrateful, ignorant ;
but the truth will remain, Jacqueline."

" Victor, you could not desert it."

" How can I tell, Jacqueline ? The last time I saw
Martial Mazurier, he would have said nobler and more
loving words than I can command. But with my own eyes
I saw him walking at liberty in streets where liberty for
him to walk could be bought only at an infamous price."

"Is there such danger for all men who believe with John Leclerc, and with — with you, Victor?"

"Yes, there is danger, such danger."

"Then you must go away. You must not stay in Meaux," she said, quickly, in a low, determined voice.

"Jacqueline, I must remain in Meaux," he answered, as quickly, with flushed face and flashing eyes. The dignity of conscious integrity, and the "fear of fear," a beholder who could discern the tokens might have perceived in him.

"O, then, who can tell? Did he not pray that he might not be led into temptation?"

"Yes," Victor replied, more troubled than scornful, — "yes, and allowed himself to be led at last."

"But if you should go away —"

"Would not that be flying from danger?" he asked, proudly.

"Nay, might it not be doing with your might what you found to do, that you might not be led into temptation?"

"And you are afraid, that, if I stay here, I shall yield to them."

"You say you are not certain, Victor. You repeat Mazurier's words."

"Yet shall I remain. No, I will never run away."

The pride of the young fellow, and the consternation occasioned by the recreancy of his superior, his belief in the doctrines he had confessed with Mazurier, and the timeserving of the latter, had evidently thrown asunder the guards of his peace, and produced a sad state of confusion.

"It were better to run away," said Jacqueline, not pausing to choose the word, — "far better than to stay and defy the Devil, and then find that you could not resist him, Victor. O, if we could go, as Elsie said, back to Domrémy, anywhere away from this cruel Meaux!"

"Have you, then, gained nothing, Jacqueline?"

"Everything. But to lose it, — oh, I cannot afford that!"

"Let us stand together, then. Promise me, Jacqueline,"

he exclaimed, eagerly, as though he felt himself among defences here, with her.

"What shall I promise, Victor?" she asked, with the voice and the look of one who is ready for any deed of daring, for any work of love.

"I, too, have preached this word."

Her only comment was, "I know you preached it well."

"What has befallen others may befall me."

"Well." ,

So strongly, so confidently did she speak this word, that the young man went on, manifestly influenced by it, hesitating no more in his speech.

"May befall me," he repeated.

"'Whosoever believeth in me, though he were dead, yet shall he live,'" she answered, with lofty voice, repeating the divine word. "What is our life, that we should hold it at the expense of his Truth? Mazurier was wrong. He can never atone for the wrong he has done."

"I believe it!" exclaimed Victor, with a brightening countenance. The clouds of doubt rose from his face and floated away, as we see the mists ascending from the heights, when we are so happy as to live in the wild hillcountry. "You prize Truth more than life. Stand with me in this, Jacqueline. Speak of this Truth as it has come to me. You are all that I have left. I have lost Mazurier. Jacqueline, you are a woman, but you never, — yes! yes! though I dare not say as much of myself, I dare say it of you, — you never could have bought your liberty at such a price as Martial has paid. I know not how, even with the opportunity, he will ever gain the courage to speak of these things again, — those great mysteries which are hidden from the eyes of the covetous and worldly and unbelieving. Promise, stand with me, Jacqueline, and I will rely on you. Forsake me not."

"Victor, has He not said, who can best say it, 'I will never leave you nor forsake you'?"

"But, Jacqueline, I love you."

Having said these words, the face of the young man emerged wholly from the eclipse of the former shadow.

" What is this ? " said the brave peasant from Domrémy, manifestly doubting whether she had heard aright ; and her clear pure eyes were gazing full on Victor Le Roy, actually looking for an explanation of his words.

" I love you, Jacqueline," he repeated. " And I do not involve you in danger, oh, my friend ! Only let me have it to believe that my life is dear to Jacqueline, and I shall not be afraid then to lose it, if that testimony be required of me. Shall we not stand side by side, soldiers of Christ, stronger in each other than in all the world beside? Shall it not be so, Jacqueline ? True heart, answer me ! And if you will not love me, at least say, say you are my friend, you trust me. I will hold your safety sacred."

" I am your friend, Victor."

" Say my wife, Jacqueline. I honored you, that you came from Domrémy. You are my very dream of Joan, — as brave and as true, as beautiful. Jacqueline, it is not all for the Truth's sake, but for my love's sake. Is not our work one, moreover ? Are we not one in heart and purpose, Jacqueline ? You are alone ; let me protect you."

He needed no other answer than he had while his eyes constantly sought hers. Her calm look, the dignity and strength of her composure, assured him of all he longed to learn, — assured him that their hearts, even as their purposes and faith, were one.

" But speak one word," he urged.

The word she spoke was, " I can be true to you, Victor."

Won hardly by a word: too easily, you think ? She loved the youth, my friends, and she loved the Truth for which he dared not say that he could sacrifice himself.

" We are one, then," said Victor Le Roy. " It concerned me above all things to prove that, Jacqueline. So you shall have no more to do with these harvest-fields and vineyards henceforth, except to eat of the fruits, if God will. You have borne all the burden and heat of labor you shall ever bear. I can say that, with God's blessing. We shall sit under our own vine. Death in one direction has prepared for life in another. I inherit what my uncle can make use of no longer. We shall look out on our own fields, our harvests; for I think this city will keep us no longer than may be needful. We will go away into Picardy, and I will show you where our Joan was a prisoner; and we will go back to Domrémy, and walk in the places she loved, and pray God to bless us by that fountain, and in the graveyard where your father and mother sleep. O, Jacqueline, is it not all blessed and all fair?"

She could hardly comprehend all the brightness of this vision which Victor Le Roy would fain bring before her. The paths he pointed out to her were new and strange; but she could trust him, could believe that together they might walk without stumbling.

She had nothing to say of her unfitness, her unworthiness, to occupy the place to which he pointed. Not a doubt, not a fear, had she to express. He loved her, and that she knew; and she had no thought of depreciating his choice, its excellency, or its wisdom. Whatever excess of wonder she may have felt was not communicated. How know I that *she* marvelled at her lover's choice, though all the world might marvel?

Then remembering Mazurier, and thinking of her strength of faith, and her high-heartedness, he was eager that Jacqueline should appoint their marriage-day. And more than he, perhaps, supposed was betrayed by this haste. He made his words profoundly good. Strong woman that she was, he wanted her strength joined to his. He was secretly disquieted, secretly afraid to trust himself, since this defection of Martial Mazurier.

What did hinder them? They might be married on Sunday, if she would: they might go down together to the estate, which he must immediately visit.

Through the hurry of thought, and the agitation of heart, and the rush of seeming impossibilities, he brought out at length in triumph her consent.

She did consent. It should all be as he wished. And so they parted outside that town of Meaux on the fair summer evening, — plighted lovers, — hopeful man and woman. For them the evening sky was lovely with the day's last light ; for them the serene stars of night arose.

So they parted under the open sky : he going forward to the city, strengthened and refreshed in faith and holy courage ; she, adorned with holy hopes which never until now had found place among her visions. Neither was she prepared for them, until he brought them to a heart which, indeed, could never be dismayed by the approach and claim of love.

Love was no strange guest. Fresh and fair as Zephyrus, he came from the forest depths, and she welcomed him ; no stranger, though the breath that bore him was all heavenly, and his aspiration was remote from earthly sources. Yes, she so imagined.

She went back to the cottage where she and Elsie lodged now, to tell Elsie what had happened, — to thankfulness, — to gazing forward into a new world, — to aspiration, expectation, joy, humility, — to wonder, and to praise, — to all that my best reader will perceive must be true of Jacqueline on this great evening of her life.

X.

THAT same night Victor Le Roy was arrested on charge of heresy, — arrested and imprisoned. Watchmen were on the look-out when the lover walked forward with triumphant steps to Meaux.

"This fellow also was among the wool-comber's disciples," said they ; and their successful dealing with Mazurier encouraged the authorities to hope that soon all this evil would be overcome, trampled in the dust. This impudent insurrection of thought should certainly be stifled ; youth and age, high station, low, should be taught alike of Rome.

Tidings reached Martial Mazurier next day of what had befallen Victor Le Roy, and he went instantly to visit him in prison. It was an interview which the tender-hearted officials would have invited, had he not forestalled them by inviting himself to the duty. Mazurier had something to do in the matter of reconciling his conscience to the part he had taken, in his recent opportunity to prove himself equally a hero with Leclerc. He had recanted, done evil, in short, that good might come ; and was not content with having done this thing : how should he be ? Now that his follower was in the same position, he had but one wish, — that he should follow his example. He did not, perhaps, entirely ascertain his motive in this ; but it is hardly to be supposed that Mazurier was so persuaded of the justice of his course that he desired to have it imitated by another under the same circumstances.

No ! he was forever disgraced in his own eyes, when he remembered the valiant John Leclerc ; and it was not to be permitted that Victor Le Roy should follow the example of the wool-comber in preference to that he had given, — that politic, wise, blood-sparing, flesh-loving, truth-depreciating, God-defrauding example.

Accordingly he lost no time in seeking Victor in his cell. It was the very cell in which he himself had lately been imprisoned. Within those narrow walls he had meditated, prayed, and made his choice. There he had stood face to face with fate, with God, with Jesus, and had decided — not in favor of the flogging, and the branding, and the glorious infamy. There, in spite of eloquence and fervor and devotion, in spite of all his past vows and his hopes, he had decided to take the place and part of a timeserver ; for he feared disgrace and pain, and the hissing and scoff and persecution, more than he feared the blasting anger of insulted and forsaken Truth.

He found Victor within his cell, his bright face not over-cast with gloom, his eyes not betraying doubts, neither disappointed, astonished, nor in deep dejection. The mood

he deemed unfavorable for his special word, — poor, deceived, self-deceiving Mazurier !

He was not merely surprised at these indications, — he
was at a loss. A little trepidation, doubt, suspicion would
have better suited him. Alas ! and was *his* hour the extremity of another's weakness, not in the elevation of
another's spiritual strength ? Once when he preached the
Truth as moved by the Holy Ghost, it was not to the prudence or the worldly wisdom of his hearers he appealed,
but to the higher feelings and the noblest powers of men.
Then he called on them to praise God by their faith in all
that added to His glory and dominion. But now his eloquence was otherwise directed ; not full of the old fire and
enthusiasm ; not trustful in God, but dependent on prudence, as though all help were in man. He had to draw
from his own experience now, things new and old, — and
was not, by confession of the result of such experience,
humiliated !

"You are under a mistake," was his argument. "You
have not gone deep into these matters ; you have made
acquaintance only with the agitated surface of them." And
he proceeded to make good all this assertion, it was
so readily proven ! *He* also had been beguiled ; ah, had
he not ? He had been beguiled by the rude eloquence, the
insensibility to pain, the pride of opposition, the pride of
poverty, the pride of a rude nature, exhibited by John
Leclerc.

He acknowledged freely, with a fatal candor, that, until
he came to consider these things in their true light, when
shut away from all outward influences, until compelled to
quiet meditation beyond the reach and influence of mere
enthusiasm, he had believed with Leclerc, even as Victor
was believing now. He could have gone on, who might
tell to what fanatical length ? had it not been for that fortunate arrest which made a sane man of him !

Leclerc was not quite in the wrong ; not absolutely, —
but neither was he, as Mazurier had once believed, glo-

riously in the right. It was clearly apparent to him, that
Victor Le Roy, having now also like opportunity for calm
reflection, would come to like conclusions.

With such confident prophecy, Mazurier left the young
man. His visit was brief and hurried, — no duty that could
be waved should call him away from his friend at such
a time; but he would return; they would speak of this
again; and he kissed Victor, and blessed him, and went
out to bid the authorities delay yet before the lad was
brought to trial, for he was confident, that, if left to reflection, he would come to his senses, and choose wisely —
between God and Mammon? Mazurier expressed it in
another way.

In the street, Elsie Méril heard of Victor's arrest, and
she brought the news to Jacqueline. They had returned
to Meaux, to their old lodging, and a day had passed, during which, moment by moment, his arrival was anticipated.
Elsie went out to buy a gift for Jacqueline, a bit of fine
apparelling which she had coveted from the moment she
knew Jacqueline should be a bride. She stole away on her
errand without remark, and came back with the gift; but
also with that which made it valueless, unmentionable,
though it was a costly offering, purchased with the wages
of more than a week's labor in the fields.

It was almost dark when she returned to Jacqueline.
Her friend was sitting by the window, — waiting, — not for
her; and when she went in to her, it was silently, with no
mention of her errand or her love-gift. Quietly she sat
down, thankful that the night was falling, waiting for its
darkness before she should speak words which would make
the darkness to be felt.

" He does not come," said Jacqueline, at length.

" Did you think it was he, when I came up the stairs?"
inquired Elsie, tenderly.

" O, no ! I can tell your step from all the rest."

" His, too, I think."

"Yes, and his, too. My best friends. Strange, if I could not ! "

" O, I 'm glad you said that, Jacqueline ! "

" My best friends," repeated Jacqueline ; not merely to please Elsie. Love had opened wide her heart ; and Elsie, weak and foolish though she might be, — Elsie, her old companion, her playmate, her fellow-laborer, — Elsie, who should be to her a sister always, and share in her good-fortune, — Elsie had honorable place there.

" Could anything have happened, Jacqueline?" said Elsie, trembling : her tremulous voice betrayed it.

" O, I think not," was the answer.

" But he is so fearless ; he might have fallen into — into trouble."

" What have you heard, Elsie ? "

This question was quietly asked, but it struck to the heart of the questioned girl. Jacqueline suspected ! — and yet Jacqueline asked so calmly ! Jacqueline could hear it ; and yet how could this be declared?

Her hesitation quickened what was hardly suspicion into a conviction.

" What have you heard ? " Jacqueline again questioned, not so calmly as before ; and yet it was quite calm, even to the alarmed ear of Elsie Méril.

" They have arrested Victor, Jacqueline."

" For heresy ? "

" I heard it in the street."

Jacqueline arose, — she crossed the chamber, — her hand was on the latch. Instantly Elsie stood beside her.

" What will you do? I must go with you, Jacqueline."

" Where will you go ? " said Jacqueline.

" With you. Wait, — what is it you will do? Or, — no matter, go on, I will follow you, — and take the danger with you."

" Is there danger ? For him there is ! and there might be for you, — but none for me. Stay, Elsie. Where shall I go, in truth?"

Yet she opened the door, and began to descend the stairs
even while she spoke ; and Elsie followed her.

First to the house of the wool-comber. John was not at
home ; and his mother could tell them nothing, had heard
nothing of the arrest of Victor. Then to the place which
Victor had pointed out to her as the home of Mazurier.
Mazurier likewise they failed to find. Where, then, was
the prison of Le Roy's captivity ? That no man could tell
them ; so they came home to their lodging at length in the
dark night, there to wait through endless-seeming hours for
morning.

On the Sunday they had chosen for their wedding-day
Mazurier brought word of Victor to Jacqueline, — was really
a messenger, as he announced himself, when she opened
for him the door of her room in the fourth story of the
great lodging-house. He had come on that day with a
message ; but it was not in all things — in little beside the
love it was meant to prove — the message Victor had desired to convey. In want of more faithful, more trustworthy messenger, Le Roy sent word by this man of his
arrest, — and bade Jacqueline pray for him. and come to
him, if that were possible. He desired, he said, to serve
his Master, — and, of all things, sought the Truth.

To go to the prisoner, Mazurier assured Jacqueline, was
impossible, but she might send a message ; indeed, he was
here to serve his dear friends. Ah, poor girl, did she trust
the man by whom she sent into a prison words like these ? —

"Hold fast to the faith that is in you, Victor. Let
nothing persuade you that you have been mistaken. We
asked for light, — it was given us, — let us walk in it ; and
no matter where it leads, — since the light is from heaven.
Do not think of me, nor of yourself, but only of Jesus
Christ, who said, 'Whosoever would save his life shall
lose it.'"

Mazurier took this message. What did he do with it ?
He tossed it to the winds.

A week after, Le Roy was brought to trial, — and re-canted ; and so recanting, was acquitted and set at liberty.

Mazurier supposed that he meant all kindly in the exer-tion he made to save his friend. He would never have ceased from self-reproach, had he conveyed the words of Jacqueline to Victor ; for the effect of those words he could clearly foresee. And so far from attempting to bring about an interview between the pair, he would have striven to prevent it, had he seen a probability that it would be allowed. He set little value on such words as Jacqueline spoke, when her conscience and her love rose up against each other. The words she had committed to him he could account for by no supposition acceptable and reasonable to him. There was something about the girl he did not understand ; she was no fit guide for a man who had need of clear judgment, when such a decision was to be made as the court demanded of Le Roy.

Elsie Méril, between hope and fear, was dumb in these days ; but her presence and her tenderness, though not he-roic in action nor wise in utterance, had a value of which neither she nor Jacqueline was fully aware.

When Jacqueline learned the issue of the trial, and that Victor had falsified his faith, her first impulse was to fly, that she might never see his face again. For, the instant she heard his choice, her heart told her what she had been hoping during these days of suspense. She had tried to see Martial Mazurier, but without success, since he con-veyed, or promised to convey, her message to the prisoner. Of purpose he had avoided her. He guessed what strength she would by this time have attained ; and he was deter-mined to save both to each other, though it might be against their will.

XI.

VICTOR LE ROY'S first endeavor, on being liberated, was — of course to find Jacqueline? Not so. That was far from his first design. His impulse was to avoid the girl he had dared to love. Mazurier had, indeed, conveyed to his mind an impression that would have satisfied him, if anything of this character could do so. But this was impossible. The secret of his disquiet was far too profound for such easy removal.

He had not in himself the witness that he had fulfilled the will of God. He was disquieted, humiliated, wretched. He could not think of Leclerc, nor upon his protestations, except with shame and remorse, — remorse, already. In his heart, in spite of the impression Mazurier had contrived to convey, he believed not that Jacqueline would bless him to such work as he could henceforth perform, no longer a free man, no longer possessed of liberty of speech and thought.

He had no sooner renounced his liberty than he became persuaded, by an overwhelming reasoning, as he had never been convinced before, of the pricelessness of that he had sacrificed. When he went from the court-room, from the presence of his judges, he was not a free man, though the dignitaries called him so. Martial Mazurier walked arm in arm with him; but the world was a den of horrors, a blackened and accursed world, to the young man who came from prison, free to use his freedom — as the priests directed!

He went home from the prison with Mazurier. The world had conquered. Love had conquered, — Love, that in the conquest felt itself disgraced. He had sold the divine, he had received the human : it was the old pottage speculation over again. This privilege of liberty from his dungeon had looked so fair! — but now it seemed so worthless! This prospect of life so priceless in contemplation of its loss, — O, the beggar who crept past him was an enviable man compared with young Victor Le Roy, the heir of love and riches, the heir of liberty and life !

Yes, — he went home with Mazurier. Where else should he go ? Congratulations attended him. He was compelled to receive them with a countenance not too sombre, and a grace not all thankless, or — or — they would say it was of cowardice he had saved his precious body from the sentence of the judges, and given his precious LIFE up to the sentence of the JUDGE.

Yes, — Martial took him home. There they might talk at leisure of those things, — and ask a blessing on the testimony of Jesus, made and kept by them !

Victor Le Roy was too proud to complain now. He assented to all the preacher's sophistry. He allowed himself to be cheered. But this was no such evening as had been spent in the room of the wool-comber, when Leclerc's voice, strong, even through his weakness, called on God, and blessed and praised Him, and the spirit conquered the flesh gloriously, — the old mother of Leclerc sharing his joy, as she had also shared his anguish. Here was no Jacqueline to say to Victor, " Thou hast done well ! ' Glory be to Jesus Christ and His witnesses ! ' "

Mazurier thanked God for the deliverance of His servant ! He dedicated himself and Victor anew to the service of Truth, which they had shrunk from defending ! And his eloquence and fervor seemed to stamp the words with sincerity. He seemed not in the least to suspect or fear himself.

With Victor Le Roy such self-deception, such sophistry, was simply impossible.

Not of purpose did he meet Jacqueline that night. She had heard that Le Roy was at liberty, and alone now she applied at the door of Martial Mazurier for admittance, but in vain. The master had signified that his evening was not to be interrupted. Therefore she returned, from waiting near his door, to the street where she and Elsie lived.

Should her woman's pride have led her to her lofty lodging, and kept her there without a sign, till Victor himself came seeking her? She knew nothing of such pride, — but much of love ; and her love took her back to the post where she had waited many an hour since that disastrous arrest ; she would wait there till morning if she must, — at least, till one should enter, or come forth, who might tell her of Victor Le Roy.

The light in the preacher's study she could see from the door-step in a court-yard where she waited. Should Mazurier come with Victor, she would let them pass ; but if Victor came alone, she had a right to speak.

It was after midnight when the student came down from the preacher's study. She heard his voice when the door opened, — by the street-lamp saw his face. And she recognized also the voice of Mazurier, who, till the last moment of separation, seemed endeavoring to dissuade his friend from leaving him that night.

He heard footsteps following him, as he passed along the pavement, — observed that they gained on him. And could it be any other than Jacqueline who touched his arm, and whispered, "Victor"?

His fast-beating heart told him it was she. He took her hand, and drew it within his arm, and looked upon her face, — the face of his Jacqueline.

"Now where?" said he. "It is late. It is after midnight. Why are you alone in the street?"

"Waiting for you, Victor. I heard you were at liberty, and I supposed you were with him. I was safe."

"Yes, for you fear nothing. That is the only reason. You knew I was with the preacher, Jacqueline. Why? Because — because I *am* with him, of course."

"Yes," she said. "I heard it was so, Victor."

"Strange ! — strange ! — is it not? A prison is a better place to learn the truth than the pure air of liberty, it seems," said he, bitterly.

"What is that?" she asked. She seemed not to understand his meaning.

"Nothing. I am acquitted of heresy, you know. It seems, what we talked so bravely meant — nothing. O, I am safe now!"

"It was to preach none the less, to hold the truth none the less. But if he lost his life, there was an end of all; or if he lost his liberty, it was as bad. But he would keep both, and serve God so," said Jacqueline.

"Yes," cried Victor, "precisely what he said. I have said the same, you think?"

"If you are quite clear that Leclerc and the rest of us are all wrong, Victor."

"Jacqueline!"

"What is it, Victor?"

"'The rest of us,' you say. What would *you* have done in my place?"

"God knows. I pretend not to know anything more."

"But 'the rest of us,' you said. You think that you at least are with Leclerc?"

"That was the truth you taught me, Victor. But — I have not yet been tried."

"That is safe to say. What makes you speak so prudently, Jacqueline? Why do you not declare, 'Though all men deny Thee, yet will I never deny Thee'? Ah, you have not been tried! You are not yet in danger of the judgment, Jacqueline!"

"Do not speak so; you frighten me; it is not like you. How can I tell? I do not know but in this retirement, in this thought you have been compelled to, you have obtained more light than any one can have until he comes to just such a place."

"Ah, Jacqueline, why not say to me what you are thinking? Have you lost your courage? Say, 'Thou hast not lied unto men, but unto God.'"

"No, — oh, no! How could I say it, my poor Victor? How do you know?"

"Surely you cannot know, as you say. But from where you stand, that is what you are thinking. Jacqueline, confess! If you should speak your mind, it would be, 'Thou hast not lied unto men, but unto God, poor coward!' O, Jacqueline, Mazurier may deceive himself! I speak not for him; but what will you do with your poor Victor, my poor Jacqueline?"

She did not linger in the answer, — she did not sob or tremble, — he was by her side.

"Love him to the end. As He, when He loved His own."

"Your own, poor girl? No, no!"

"You gave yourself to me," she answered straightway, with resolute firmness clinging to the all she had.

"I was a man then," he answered. "But I will never give a liar and a coward to Jacqueline Gabrie. Everything but myself, Jacqueline! Take the old words and the old memory. But for this outcast, him you shall forget. My God! thou hast not brought this brave girl from Domrémy, and lighted her heart with a coal from Thine altar, that she should turn from Thee to me! If you love a liar and a coward, Jacqueline, you cannot help yourself, — he will make you one, too. And what I loved you for was your truth and purity and courage. I have given you a treasure which was greater than I could keep. Where is it that you live now, Jacqueline? I am not yet such a poltroon that I am afraid to conduct you. I think that I should have the courage to protect you to-night, if you were in any immediate danger. Come, lead the way."

"No," said Jacqueline. "I am not going home. I could not sleep; and a roof over my head — any save God's heaven — would suffocate me, I believe."

"Go, then, as you will. But where?"

Jacqueline did not answer, but walked quietly on; and so they passed beyond the city-borders to the river-bank, — far away into the country, through the fields, under the light of stars and of the waning moon.

"If I had been true!" said Victor, — "if I had not listened to him! But him I will not blame. For why should I blame him? Am I an idiot? And his influence could not have prevailed, had I not so chosen, when I stood before my judges and they questioned me. No, — I acquit Mazurier. Perhaps what I have denied never appeared to him so glorious as it did once to me; and so he was guiltless at least of knowing what it was I did. But I knew. And I could not have been deceived for a moment. No, — I think it impossible that for a moment I should have been deceived. They would have made a notable example of me, Jacqueline. I am rich, — I am a student. O, yes! Jesus Christ may die for me, and I accept the benefit; but when it comes to suffering for His sake, — you could not have expected that of such a poltroon, Jacqueline! We may look for it in brave men like Leclerc, whose very living depends on their ability to earn their bread, — to earn it by daily sweat; but men who need not toil, who have leisure and education, — of course you would not expect such testimony to the truth of Jesus from them! Bishop Briconnet recants, — and Martial Mazurier; and Victor Le Roy is no braver man, no truer man than these!"

With bitter shame and self-scorning he spoke. Poor Jacqueline had not a word to say. She sat beside him. She would help him bear his cross. Heavy-laden as he, she awaited the future, saying, in the silence of her spirit's dismal solitude, "O, teach us! O, help us!" But she called not on any name; her prayer went out in search of a God whom in that hour she knew not. The dark cloud and shadow of Satan that overshadowed him was also upon her.

"Mazurier is coming in the morning to take me with him, Jacqueline," said Victor. "We are to make a journey."

"What is it, Victor?" she asked, quietly.

There was nothing left for her but patience, — that she clearly saw, — nothing but patience, and quiet enduring of the will of God.

"He is afraid of me, — or of himself, — or of both, I believe. He thinks a change of scene would be good for both of us, poor lepers that we are."

"I must go with you, Victor Le Roy," said the resolute Jacqueline.

"Wherefore?" asked he.

"Because, when you were strong and happy, that was your desire, Victor; and now that you are sick and sorrowing, I will not give you to another: no! not to Mazurier, nor to any one that breathes, except myself, to whom you belong."

"I must stay here in Meaux, then?"

"That depends upon yourself, Victor."

"We were to have been married. We were going to look after our estate, now that the hard summer and the hard years of work are ended."

"Yes, Victor, it was so."

"But I will not wrong you. You were to be the wife of Victor Le Roy. You are his widow, Jacqueline. For you do not think that he lives any longer?"

"He lives, and he is free! If he has sinned, like Peter even, he weeps bitterly."

"Like Peter? Peter denied his Lord. But he did weep, as you say, — bitterly. Peter confessed again."

"And none served the Master with truer heart or greater courage afterward. Victor, you remember."

"Even so, — O, Jacqueline!"

"Victor! Victor! it was only Judas who hanged himself."

"Come, Jacqueline!"

She arose and went with him. At dawn they were married. Love did lead and save them.

I see two youthful students studying one page. I see two loving spirits walking through thick darkness. Along the horizon flicker the promises of day. They say, "O Holy Ghost, hast thou forsaken thine own temples?" Aloud they cry to God.

I see them wandering among Domrémy woods and meadows, — around the castle of Picardy, — talking of Joan. I see them resting by the graves they find in two ancient villages. I see them walk in sunny places; they are not called to toil: they may gather all the blossoms that delight their eyes. Their love grows beyond childhood, — does not die before it comes to love's best estate. Happy bride and bridegroom! But I see them as through a cloud whose fair hues are transient.

From the meadow-lands and the vineyards and the dark forests of the mountains, from study and from rest, I see them move with solemn faces and calm steps. Brave lights are in their eyes, and flowers that are immortal they carry in their hands. No distillation can exhaust the fragrance of those blooms.

What dost thou here, Victor? What dost thou here, Jacqueline?

This is the place of prisons. Here they light again, as they have often lighted, torch and fagot; — life must pay the cost! Angry crowds and hooting multitudes love this dreary square. O, Jacqueline and Victor, what is this I behold?

They come together from their prison, hand in hand. "The testimony of Jesus!" Stand back, Mazurier! Retire, Briconnet! Here is not your place, — this is not your hour! Yet here incendiaries fire the temples of the Holy Ghost!

The judges do not now congratulate. Jacqueline waits not now at midnight for the coming of Le Roy. Bride and bridegroom, there they stand; they face the world to give their testimony.

And a woman's voice, almost I deem the voice of Elsie Méril, echoes the mother's cry that followed John Leclerc when he fought the beasts at Meaux, —

"Blessed be Jesus Christ, and His witnesses."

So of the Truth were they borne up that day in a blazing chariot to meet their Lord in the air, to be forever with their Lord.

ELKANAH BREWSTER'S TEMPTATION.

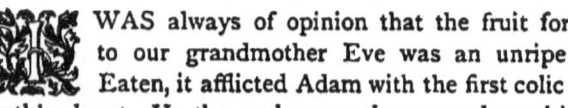 WAS always of opinion that the fruit forbidden to our grandmother Eve was an unripe apple. Eaten, it afflicted Adam with the first colic known to this planet. He, the weaker vessel, sorrowed over his transgression; but I doubt if Eve's repentance was thorough; for the plucking of unripe fruit has been, ever since, a favorite hobby of her sons and daughters, — until now our mankind has got itself into such a chronic state of colic, that even Dr. Carlyle declares himself unable to prescribe any Morrison's Pill or other remedial measure to allay the irritation.

Part of this irritation finds vent in a great cry about "legitimate ambition." Somehow, because any American *may* be President of the United States, almost every American feels himself bound to run for the office. A man thinks small things of himself, and his neighbors think less, if he does not find his heart filled with an insane desire, in some way, to attain to fame or notoriety, riches or bankruptcy. Nevertheless, we are not purse-proud, — nor, indeed, proud at all, more 's the pity, — and receive a man just as readily whose sands of life have been doled out to suffering humanity in the shape of patent pills, as one who has entered Fifth Avenue by the legitimate way of pork and cotton speculations, if only he have been successful, — which I call a very noble trait in the American character.

Now this is all very well, and, granted that Providence has placed us here to do what is best pleasing to ourselves, it is surely very noble and grand in us to please to serve nothing less than our country or our age. But let us not forget that the English language has such a little word as *duty*. A man's talents, and, perhaps, once in a great while, his wishes, would make him a great man (if wishes ever did such things, which I doubt), while duty imperatively demands that he shall remain a *little* man. What then? Let us see.

Elkanah Brewster was going to New York to-morrow.

"What for, boy?" asked old Uncle Shubael, meeting whom on the fish-wharf, he had bid him a cheery good-bye.

"To make my fortune," was the bold reply.

"Make yer fortin? You're a goose, boy! Stick to yer work here, — fishin' summers an' shoemakin' winters. Why, there is n't a young feller on the hull Cape makes as much as you. What's up? Gal gin ye the mitten? Or what?"

"I don't want to make shoes, nor fish neither, Uncle Shub," said Elkanah, soberly, looking the old fellow in the face, — "goin' down to the Banks year arter year in cold an' fish-gurry, an' peggin' away all winter, like mad. I want to be rich, like Captain Crowell; I want to be a gentleman, like that painter-chap that give me drawin'- lessons, last summer, when I stayed to home."

"Phew! Want to be rich an' a gentleman, eh? Gittin' tu big for yer boots, youngster? What's yer old man du but go down t' the Banks reg'lar every spring? You're no better 'n he, I guess! Keep yer trade, an' yer trade 'll keep you. A rollin' stun gethers no moss. Dry bread tu home's better 'n roast meat an' gravy abroad."

"All feet don't tread in one shoe, Uncle Shub," said young Brewster, capping the old fellow's proverbs with another. "Don't see why I should n't make money as well 's other fellers. It 's a free country, an' if a feller wants to try suthin' else 'sides fishin' uv it, what d'yer all want to be down on him fur? I don't want to slave all my days, when other folks ken live in big houses an' ride in 'ker- riges, an' all that."

11 *

" A'n't yer got bread enough to eat, an' a place to sleep ? an' what more's any on 'em got ? You stay here ; make yer money on the old Cape, where yer father an' grand'ther made it afore you. Use yer means, an' God 'll give the blessin'. Yer can't honestly git rich anywheres all tu once. Good an' quickly don't often meet. One nail drives out another. Slow an' easy goes fur in a day. Honor an' ease a'n't often bedfellows. Don't yer be a goose, I tell ye. What's to become of Hepsy Ann ? "

Having delivered himself of which last and hardest shot, Uncle Shubael shouldered his cod-craft, and, without await-ing an answer, tugged across the sand-beach for home.

Elkanah Brewster was a Cape-Cod boy, with a pedigree, if he had ever thought of it, as long as any on the Cape, — and they are the longest in the land. His forefathers had caught fish to the remotest generation known. The Cape boys take to the water like young ducks ; and are born with a hook and line in their fists, so to speak, as the Newfoundland codfish and Bay Chaleur mackerel know, to their cost. " Down on old Chatham " there is little question of a boy's calling, if he only comes into the world with the proper number of fingers and toes ; he swims as soon as he walks, knows how to drive a bargain as soon as he can talk, goes cook of a coaster at the mature age of eight years, and thinks himself robbed of his birthright, if he has not made a voyage to the Banks before his eleventh birthday comes round. There is good stuff in the Cape boys, as the South-Street ship-owners know, who don't sleep easier than when they have put a " Cape man " in charge of their best clipper. Quick of apprehension, fertile in resource, shrewd, enterprising, brave, prudent, and above all, lucky, — no better seamen sail the sea. Long may they keep their *prestige* and their sand !

They are not rich on the Cape, — in the Wall-Street sense of the word, that is to say. I doubt if Uncle Lew Baker, who was high line out of Dennis last year, and who, by the same token, had to work himself right smartly to achieve that honor, — I doubt if this smart and thoroughly wide-awake fellow took home more than three hundred dollars to his wife and children when old Obed settled the voyage. But then the good wife saves while he earns, and, what with a cow, and a house and garden-spot of his own, and a healthy lot of boys and girls, who, if too young to help, are not suffered to hinder, this man is more fore-handed and independent, gives more to the poor about him and to the heathen at the other end of the world, than many a city man who makes, and spends, his tens of thousands.

Uncle Abijah Brewster, the father of this Elkanah, was an old Banker, — which signifies here, not a Wall-Street broker-man, but a Grand-Bank fisherman. He had brought up a goodly family of boys and girls by his hook and line, and, though now a man of some fifty winters, still made his two yearly fares to the Banks, in his own trim little pinky, and prided himself on being the smartest and jol-liest man aboard. His boys had sailed with him till they got vessels of their own, had learned from his stout heart and strong arm their seamanship, their fisherman's acute-ness, their honest daring, and childlike trust in God's Providence. These poor fishermen are not rich, as I have said ; a dollar looks to them as big as a dinner-plate to us, and a moderately flush Wall-Street man might buy out the whole Cape, and not overdraw his bank-account. Also, they have but little book-learning among them, reading chiefly their Bible, Bowditch, and Nautical Almanac, and leaving theology mostly to the parson, on shore, who is paid for it. But they have a conscience, and; knowing a thing to be right, do it bravely, and against all odds. I have seen these men on Sunday, in a fleet of busy " Sun-day fishers," fish biting all around them, sitting faithfully, — ay, and contentedly, — with book in hand, sturdily re-fraining from what the mere human instinct of destruction would strongly impel them to, without counting the tempta-tion of dollars, — and this only because they had been

taught that Sunday was a day of rest and worship, wherein
no man should catch fish, and knew no theological quibble
or mercantile close-sailing by which to weather on God's
command.   It sounds little to us who have not been
tempted, or, if tempted, have gracefully succumbed, on the
plea that other people do so too; but how many stock-
speculators would see their fellows buying bargains and
making easy fortunes on Sunday morning, and not forget
the ring of Trinity chimes and go in for dollars ?   Or which
of us denies himself his Monday morning's paper ?

Elkanah had always been what his mother called a
strange boy.   He was, indeed, an odd sheep in her flock.
Restless, ambitious, dreamy, from his earliest youth, he
possessed, besides, a natural gift for drawing and sketching,
imitating and constructing, that bade fair, unless properly
directed, to make of him that saddest and most useless of
human lumber, a jack-at-all-trades.   He profited more by
his limited winter's schooling than his brothers and fellows,
and was always respected by the old man as "a boy that
took naterally to book-larnin', and would *be* suthin' some
day."   Of course he went to the Banks, and acquitted himself there with honor, — no man fishing more zealously or
having better luck.   But all the time he was dreaming of
his future, counting this present as nothing, and ready, as
soon as Fortune should make him an opening, to cast away
this life, and grasp — he had not settled what.

"*I* dun know what ails him," said his father; "but he
don't take kindly to the Banks.   Seems to me he kinder
despises the work, though he *does* it well enough.   And
then he makes the best shoes on the Cape ; but he a'n't
content, somehow."

And that was just it.   He was not contented.   He had
seen men — "no better than I," thought he, poor fool ! —
in Boston, living in big houses, wearing fine clothes, putting
fair, soft hands into smooth-fitting kid-gloves; "and why
not I ?" he cried to himself continually.   Year by year,
from his seventeenth to his twenty-first, he was pursued by

, this demon of "ambition," which so took possession of his heart as to crowd out nearly everything else, — father, mother, work, — even pretty Hepzibah Nickerson, almost, who loved him, and whom he also loved truly. They had almost grown up together, had long loved each other, and had been now two years betrothed. When Elkanah was out of his time and able to buy a share in a vessel, and had made a voyage to the Banks as captain, they were to be married.

The summer before this spring in which our story opens, Elkanah had stayed at home for two months, because of a rheumatism contracted by unusual exposure on the Banks in early spring ; and at this time he made the acquaintance of Mr. James Graves, N. A., from New York, spending part of his summer on the Cape in search of the picturesque, — which I hope he found. Elkanah had, as I have said, a natural talent for drawing, and some of his sketches had that in them which elicited the approval of Graves, who saw in the young fellow an untutored genius, or, at least, very considerable promise of future excellence. To him there could be but one choice between shoemaking and "Art"; and finding that young Brewster made rapid advances under his desultory tuition, he told him his thoughts, that he should not waste himself making sea-boots for fishermen, but enter a studio in Boston or New York, and make his career as a painter. It scarcely needed this, however ; for Elkanah took such delight in his new proficiency, and got from Graves's stories of artist life such exalted ideas of the unalloyed felicity of the gentleman of the brush, that, even had the painter said no word, he would have worked out that way himself.

"Only wait till next year, when I'm out of my time," said he to Graves ; and to himself, — "This is the opening for which I have been waiting."

That winter — "my last at shoemaking" — he worked more diligently than ever before, and more good-naturedly. Uncle Abijah was delighted at the change in his boy, and promised him great things in the way of a lift next year, to help him to a speedy wedding. Elkanah kept his own counsel, read much in certain books which Graves had left him, and looked impatiently ahead to the day when, twenty-one years of age, he should be a free man, — able to go whither he listed and do what he would, with no man authoritatively to say him nay.

And now the day had come; and with I don't know how few dollars in his pocket, his scant earnings, he had declared to his astounded parents his determination to fish and shoemake no longer, but to learn to be a painter.

"A great painter," — that was what he said.

"I don't see the use o' paintin' picters, for my part," said the old man, despairingly; "can't you learn that, an' fish tu?"

"Famous and rich too," said Elkanah half to himself, looking through the vista of years at the result he hoped for, and congratulating himself in advance upon it. And a proud, hard look settled in his eye, which froze the opposition of father and mother, and was hardly dimmed by encountering the grieved glance of poor Hepsy Ann Nickerson.

Poor Hepsy Ann! They had talked it all over, time and again. At first she was in despair; but when he laid before her all his darling hopes, and painted for her in such glowing colors the final reward which should come to him and her in return for his struggles, — when she saw him, her love and pride, before her already transfigured, as it were, by this rare triumph, clothed in honors, his name in all mouths, — dear, loving soul, her heart consented, "ay, if it should break meantime," thought she, as she looked proudly on him through her tears, and said, — "Go, in God's name, and God be with you!"

Perhaps we might properly here consider a little whether this young man did well thus to leave father, mother, home, his promised bride, sufficient bread-and-butter, healthy occupation, all, to attempt life in a new direction. Of course, your man who lives by bread alone will "pooh! pooh!" all such folly, and tell the young man to let well enough alone. But consider candidly, and decide: Should Elkanah have gone to New York?

On the whole, *I* think, *yes.* For, —

He had a certain talent, and gave good promise of excellence in his chosen profession.

He liked it, felt strongly impelled towards it. Let us not yet scrutinize too closely the main impelling forces. Few human actions originate solely in what we try to think the most exalted motives.

He would have been discontented for life, had he not had his way. And this should count for something, — for much, indeed. Give our boys liberty to try that to which their nature or fancy strongly drives them, — to burn their fingers, if that seem best.

Let him go, then; and God be with him! as surely He will be, if the simple, faithful prayers of fair, sad Hepsy Ann are heard. Thus will he, thus only can any, solve that sphinx-riddle of life which is propounded to each passer to-day, as of old in fable-lands, — failing to read which, he dies the death of rusting discontent, — solving whose mysteries, he has revealed to him the deep secret of his life, and sees and knows what best he may do here for himself and the world.

But *what, where, who,* is Elkanah Brewster's *world?*

While we stand reasoning, he has gone. In New York, his friend Graves assisted him to a place in the studio of an artist, whose own works have proved, no less than those of many who have gathered their most precious lessons from him, that he is truly a master of his art. But what are masters, teachers, to a scholar? It's very fine boarding at the Spread-Eagle Hotel; but even after you have feed the waiter, you have to chew your own dinner, and are benefited, not by the amount you pay for it, but only by so much of all that with which the bounteous mahogany is covered as you can thoroughly masticate, easily contain, and healthily digest. Elkanah began with the soup, so to speak. He brought all his Cape-Cod acuteness of observation to bear on his profession; lived closely, as well he might; studied attentively and intelligently; lost no hints, no precious morsels dropping from the master's board; improved slowly, but surely. Day by day he gained in that facility of hand, quickness of observation, accuracy of memory, correctness of judgment, patience of detail, felicity of touch, which, united and perfected and honestly directed, we call genius. He was above no drudgery, shirked no difficulties, and labored at the insignificant sketch in hand to-day as though it were indeed his masterpiece, to be hung up beside Raphael's and Titian's; meantime, keeping up poor Hepsy Ann's heart by letters full of a hope bred of his own brave spirit, rather than of any favoring circumstances in his life, and gaining his scant bread-and-butter by various honest drudgeries which I will not here recount.

So passed away three years; for the growth of a poor young artist in public favor, and that thing called fame, is fearfully slow. Oftenest he has achieved his best when the first critic speaks kindly or savagely of him. What, indeed, *at best*, do those blind leaders, but zealously echo a sentiment already in the public heart, — which they vainly endeavor to create (out of nothing) by any awe-inspiring formula of big words?

Men grow so slowly! But then so do oaks. And little matter, so the growth be straight.

Meantime Elkanah was getting, slowly and by hardest labor, to have some true conception of his art and his aims. He became less and less satisfied with his own performances; and, having with much pains and anxious prayers finished his first picture for the Academy, carefully hid it under the bed, and for that year played the part of independent critic at the Exhibition. Wherefrom resulted some increase of knowledge, — though chiefly negative.

For what positive lesson is taught to any by that yearly show of what we flatter ourselves by calling Art? Eight hundred and fifteen new paintings this year, shown by no less than two hundred and eighty-one painters. When you have gone patiently through and looked at every picture, see if you don't wish the critics *had* eyes, and a little common sense, too. How many of these two hundred and eighty-one, if they live to be a hundred, will ever solve their great riddle? and once solved, how many would honestly go back to shoemaking?

Why should they not paint? Because, unless some of them are poorer men than I think, that is not the thing they are like to do best; and a man is put into this world, not to do what he may think or hope will most speedily or effectually place him in the list of this world's illustrious benefactors, but honestly and against all devilish temptations to stick to that thing by which he can best serve and bless —

Whom? A city? A state? A republic? A king?

No, — but that person who is nearest to, and most dependent upon him. Look at Charles Lamb, and then at Byron and Shelley.

The growth of a poor young artist into public favor is slow enough. But even poor young artists have their temptations. When Elkanah hung his first picture in the Academy rooms, he thought the world must feel the acquisition. Now the world is a notoriously stupid world, and never does its duty ; but kind woman not seldom supplies its omissions. So it happened, that, though the world ignored the picture, Elkanah became at once the centre of admiration to a coterie of young ladies, who thought they were appreciating Art when they flattered an artist, and who, when they read in the papers the gratifying intelligence (invented by some sanguine critic, over a small bottle of Champagne cider) that the American people are rapidly growing in true love for the fine arts, blushingly owned to themselves that their virtuous labors in this direction were not going unrewarded.

Have you never seen them in the Academy, — these dear

Q

young ladies, who are so constantly foreseeing new Ra-
phaels, Claudes, and Rembrandts? Positively, in this year's
Exhibition they are better worth study than the paintings.
There they run, up and down, critical or enthusiastical, as
the humor strikes: Laura, with big blue eyes and a loud
voice, pitying Isidora because she "has never met" that
dear Mr. Herkimer, who paints such delicious, dreamy
landscapes ; and Emily dragging everybody off to see Mr.
Smith's great work, "The Boy and the Windmill," which —
so surprising is his facility — he actually painted in less
than twelve days, and which "promises so much for his
success and the future of American Art," says this sage
young critic, out of whose gray eyes look the garnered
experiences of almost eighteen summers.

Whoever desiderates cheap praise, let him cultivate a
beard and a sleepy look, and hang a picture in the Academy
rooms. Elkanah received it, you may be sure. It was
thought *so* romantic, that he, a fisherman, — the young
ladies sunk the shoemaker, I believe, — should be *so* devoted to Art. How splendidly it spoke for our civilization,
when even sailors left their vessels, and abjuring codfish,
took to canvas and brushes ! What admirable courage in
him, to come here and endeavor to work his way up from
the very bottom ! What praiseworthy self-denial, — "No ! !
is it *really* so ?" cried Miss Jennie, — when he had left
behind him a fair young bride !

It was as though it had been written, "Blessed is he who
forsaketh father, mother, and wife to paint pictures." But
it is not so written.

It was as if the true aim and glory of every man in a
civilized community should be to paint pictures. Which
has this grain of truth in it, that, in the highest form of
human development, I believe every man will be at heart
an artist. But then we shall be past picture-painting and
exhibitions. Don't you see, that, if the fruit be thoroughly
ripe, it needs no violent plucking ? or that, if a man is
really a painter, he *will* paint, — ay, though he were ten

times a shoemaker, and could never, never hope to hang his pictures on the Academy walls, to win cheap wonder from boarding-school misses, or just regard from judicious critics ?

Elkanah Brewster came to New York to make his career, — to win nothing less than fame and fortune. When he had struggled through five years of Art-study, and was now just beginning to earn a little money, he began also to think that he had somehow counted his chickens before they were hatched, — perhaps, indeed, before the eggs were laid. " Good and quickly come seldom together," said old Uncle Shubael. But then a man who has courage commonly has also endurance; and Elkanah, ardently pursuing from love now what he had first been prompted to by ambition, did not murmur nor despair. For, indeed, I must own that this young fellow had worked himself up to the highest and truest conception of his art, and felt, that, though the laborer is worthy of his hire, unhappy is the man who lowers his art to the level of a trade. In olden times, the priests did, indeed, eat of the sacrificial meats; but we live under a new and higher dispensation.

IL.

MEANTIME, what of Hepsy Ann. Nickerson? She had bravely sent her hero out, with her blessing on his aspirations. Did she regret her love and trust? I am ashamed to say that these five long, weary years had passed happily to this young woman. She had her hands full of work at home, where she reigned over a family of brothers and sisters, *vice* her mother, promoted. Hands busied with useful toils, head and heart filled with love and trust of Elkanah, there was no room for unhappiness. To serve and to be loved; this seems, indeed, to be the ˜bliss of the happiest women I have known, — and of the happiest men, too, for that matter. It does not sound logical, and I know of no theory of woman's rights which will satisfactorily account for the phenomenon. But then — there are the facts.

A Cape household is a simpler affair than you will meet with in the city. If any young marrying man waits for a wife who shall be an adept in the mysteries of the kitchen and the sewing-basket, let him go down to the Cape. Captain Elijah Nickerson, Hepsy Ann's father, was master and owner of the good schooner "Miranda," in which excellent, but rather strongly scented vessel, he generally made yearly two trips to the Newfoundland Banks, to draw thence his regular income ; and it is to be remarked, that his drafts, presented in person, were never dishonored in that foggy region. Uncle Elijah (they are all uncles, on the Cape, when they marry and have children, — and *boys* until then), Uncle Elijah, I say, was not uncomfortably off, as things go in those parts. The year before Elkanah went to New York, the old fellow had built himself a bran-new house, and Hepsy Ann was looked up to by her acquaintance as the daughter of a man who was not only brave and honest, but also lucky. "Elijah Nickerson's new house" — as it is still called, and will be, I suppose, until it ceases to be a house — was fitted up inside in a way which put you much in mind of a ship's cabin, and would have delighted the simple heart of good Captain Cuttle.

There was no spare space anywhere thrown away, nor anything suffered to lie loose. Beckets and cleats, fixed into the walls of the sitting-room, held and secured against any possible damage the pipes, fish-lines, dolphin-grains, and sou'westers of the worthy Captain ; and here he and his sat, when he was at home, through the long winter evenings, in simple and not often idle content. The kitchen, flanked by the compendious outhouses which make our New England kitchens almost luxurious in the comfort and handiness of every arrangement, was the centre of Hepsy Ann's kingdom, where she reigned supreme, and waged sternest warfare against dirt and disorder. Hence her despotic sway extended over the pantry, an awful, and fragrant sanctuary, whither she fled when household troubles, or a letter from Elkanah, demanded her entire seclusion from the outer world, and of whose interior the children got faint glimpses and sniffs only on special and long-remembered occasions; the west room, where her father slept when he was at home, and where the curious searcher might find store of old compasses, worn-out cod-hooks, condemned gurry-knives, and last year's fishing-mittens, all "stowed away against time-o'-need"; the spare room, sacred to the rites of hospitality; the "up-stairs," occupied by the children and Hepsy Ann's self; and finally, but most important of all, the parlor, a mysterious and hermetically sealed apartment, which almost seemed to me an unconsecrated spot in this little temple of the homely virtues and affections, — a room furnished in a style somewhat ostentatious and decidedly uncomfortable, swept and dusted on Saturday afternoons by Hepsy Ann's own careful hands, sat in by the Captain and her for an hour or two on Sundays in awkward state, then darkened and locked for the rest of the week.

As for the queen and mistress of so much neatness and comfort, I must say, that, like most queens whose likeness I have seen, she was rather plain than strictly beautiful, — though, no doubt, her loyal subjects, as in such cases commonly occurs, pictured her to themselves as a very Helen of Troy. If her cheeks had something of the rosy hue of health, cheeks, and arms, too, were well tanned by frequent exposure to the sun. Neither tall nor short, but with a lithe figure, a natural grace and sweet dignity of carriage, the result of sufficient healthy exercise, and a pure, untroubled spirit; hands and feet, mouth and nose, not such as a gentleman would particularly notice; and straight brown hair, which shaded the only *really* beautiful part of Hepsy Ann's face, — her clear, honest, brave blue eyes: eyes from which spoke a soul at peace with itself and with the outward world, — a soul yet full of love and trust, fearing nothing, doubting nothing, believing much good, and inclined to patient endurance of the human weaknesses it met with in daily life, as not perhaps altogether strange to itself. The Cape men are a brave, hardy race; and the Cape women, grave and somewhat silent, not demonstrative in joy or grief, reticent mostly of anxieties and sorrows, born to endure, in separation from fathers, brothers, lovers, husbands, in dangers not oftener fancied than real, griefs which more fortunate women find it difficult to imagine, — these Cape women are worthy mothers of brave men. Of such our Hepsy Ann was a fair example, — weaving her rather prosaic life into golden dreams in the quiet light of her pantry refuge, happy chiefly because she thought much and carefully for others and had little time for self-brooding; like most genuine heroines (except those of France), living an heroic life without in the least suspecting it.

And did she believe in Elkanah?

Utterly.

And did Elkanah believe in himself?

Yes, — but with certain grave doubts. Here is the difference: the woman's faith is intuition; the man must have a reason for the faith that is in him.

Yet Elkanah was growing. I think a man grows like the walls of a house, by distinct stages: so far the scaffolding reaches, and then a general stoppage while the outer shell is raised, the ladders lengthened, and the work squared off. Now I don't know, unhappily, the common process of growth of the artistic mind, and how far the light of to-day helps the neophyte to look into the indefinite twilight of to-morrow; but step by step was the slow rule of Elkanah's mind, and he had been now five years an artist, and was held in no despicable repute by those few who could rightly judge of a man's future by his past, when first it became very clear to him that he had yet to find his *specialty* in Art, — that truth which *he* might better represent than any other man. Don't think five years long to determine so trivial a point. The right man in the right place is still a rare phenomenon in the world; and some men spend a lifetime in the consideration of this very point, doubtless looking to take their chance of real work in the next world. I mean to say it took Elkanah just five years to discover, that, though he painted many things well, he did yet put his very soul into none, and that, unless he could now presently find this, *his* right place, he had, perhaps, better stop altogether.

Elkanah considered; but he also worked unceasingly, feeling that the best way to break through a difficulty is to pepper away at its outer walls.

Now while he was firing away wearily at this fortress, which held, he thought, the deepest secret of his life, Hepsy Ann sat in her pantry, her serene soul troubled by unwonted fears. Captain Elijah Nickerson had sailed out in his stanch schooner in earliest spring, for the Banks. The old man had been all winter meditating a surprise; and his crew were in unusual excitement, peering out at the weather, consulting almanacs, prophesying (to outsiders) a late season, and winking to each other a cheerful disbelief of their own auguries. The fact is, they were intending to slip off before the rest, and perhaps have half their fare of fish caught before the fleet got along. No plan could have succeeded better — up to a certain point. Captain Elijah got off to sea full twelve days earlier than anybody else, and was bowling merrily down towards the eternal fog-banks when his neighbors were yet scarce thinking of gathering up their mittens and sea-boots. By the time the last comers arrived on the fishing-ground, one who had spoken the "Miranda" some days before, anchored and fishing away, reported that they had, indeed, nearly *wet her salt*, — by which is meant that she was nearly filled with good, sound codfish. The men were singing as they dressed their fish, and Captain Elijah, sitting high up on the schooner's quarter, took his pipe out of his mouth, and asked, as the vessel rose on the sea, if they had any news to send home, for three days more like that would fill him up.

That was the last word of Captain Elijah Nickerson's ever heard by men now living. Whether the "Miranda" was sunk by an iceberg; whether run down in the dark and silent watches of the night by some monster packet or swift hurling steamer, little recking the pale fisher's light feebly glimmering up from the surface of the deep; or whether they went down at their anchors, in the great gale which set in on the third night, as many brave men have done before, looking their fate steadfastly in the face for long hours, and taking time to bid each other farewell ere the great sea swallowed them; — the particulars of their hapless fate no man may know, till the dread day when the sea shall give up its dead.

Vainly poor Hepsy Ann waited for the well-known signal in the offing, — daily walking to the shore, where kind old Uncle Shubael, now long superannuated, and idly busying himself about the fish-house, strove to cheer her fainting soul by store of well-chosen proverbs, and yarns of how, aforetimes, schooners not larger and not so stout as the "Miranda," starting early for the Banks, had been blown southward to the West Indies, and, when the second-fare men came in with their fish, had made their appearance laden with rich cargoes of tropical molasses and bananas. Poor Hepsy Ann! what need to describe the long-drawn agony which grew with the summer flowers, but did not wane with the summer sun? Hour after hour, day after day, she sat by her pantry-window, looking with wistful eyes out upon the sand, to that spot where the ill-fated "Miranda" had last been seen, but never should appear again, — another

> "poor lone Hannah,
> Sitting by the window, binding shoes," —

cheeks paling, eyes dimming, with that hope deferred which maketh the heart sick. Pray God you never may be so tried, fair reader! If, in these days, she had not had the children to keep and comfort, she has since told me, she could scarce have borne it. To calm their fears, to soothe their little sorrows, to look anxiously — more anxiously than ever before — after each one of her precious little brood, became now her chief solace.

Thus the long, weary days rolled away, each setting sun crushing another hope, until at last the autumn storms approached, the last Banker was safe home ; and by this time it was plain, even to poor Hepsy Ann's faithful heart. that her dead would not come back to her.

" If only Elkanah were here ! " she had sometimes sighed to herself ; — but in all these days she wrote him no word. And he — guessing nothing of her long, silent agony, him · self sufficiently bemired in his slough of despond, working away with sad, unsatisfied heart in his little studio, hoping yet for light to come to his night — was, in truth, so full of himself, that Hepsy Ann had little of his thoughts. Shall I go farther, and admit that sometimes this poor fellow dimly regretted his pledged heart, and faintly murmured, " If only I were free, *then* I might do something " ? If only the ship were rid of her helmsman, then indeed would she go — somewhere.

At last, — it was already near Thanksgiving, — the news reached Elkanah. " I thought you' d ha' been down afore this to see Hepsy Ann Nickerson in her trouble," said an old coasting-skipper to him, with mild reproach, handing him a letter from his mother, — of all persons in the world ! Whereupon, seeing ignorance in Elkanah's inquiring glance, he told the story.

Elkanah was as one in a maze. Going to his little room, he opened his mother's letter, half-dreading to find here a detailed repetition of what his heart had just taken in. But the letter was short.

" MY SON ELKANAH, —

" Do you not know that Captain Elijah Nickerson will never come home from the Banks, and that Hepsy Ann is left alone in the world ?

" ' For this cause shall a man leave his father and mother,

12

and be joined to his wife, and they two shall be one flesh.'"

That was all.

Elkanah sat on his stool, before his easel, looking vacantly at the unfinished picture, as one stunned and breathless. For the purport of this message was not to be mistaken. Nor did his conscience leave him in doubt as to his duty. O God! was this, indeed, the end? Had he toiled, and hoped and prayed, and lived the life of an anchorite these five years only for this? Was such faith, such devotion, *so* rewarded?

But had any one the right to demand this sacrifice of him? Was it not a devilish temptation to take him from his calling, from that work in which God had evidently intended him to work for the world? Had he a right to spoil his life, to belittle his soul, for any consideration? If Hepsy Ann Nickerson had claims, had not he also, and his Art? If he were willing, in this dire extremity, to sacrifice his love, his prospects of married bliss, might he not justly require the same of her? Was not Art his mistress? — Thus whispered the insidious devil of Selfishness to this poor, tempted, anguished soul.

"Yea," whispered another still, small voice; "but is not Hepsy Ann your promised wife?" And those fatal words sounded in his heart: "For this cause shall a man leave his father and mother, and be joined to his wife."

"Lord, inspire me to do what is right!" prayed poor amazed Elkanah, sinking on his knees at his cot-side.

But presently, through his blinding tears, "Lord, give me strength to do the right!"

And then, when he awoke next morning, the world seemed another world to him. The foundations of his life seemed broken loose. Tears were no longer, nor prayers. But he went about slowly, and with loving hands, packing up his brushes, pallets, paints, easel, — all the few familiar objects of a life which was his no longer, and on which he seemed to himself already looking as across some vast gulf of years. At last all was done. A last look about the dismantled garret, so long his workshop, his home, where he had grown out of one life into another, and a better, as he thought, — out of a narrow circle into a broader. And then, away for the Cape. No farewells, no explanations to friends, nothing that should hold out to his sad soul any faintest hope of a return to this garret, this toil, which now seemed to him more heaven than ever before. Thus this Adam left his paradise, clinging to his Eve.

It was the day before Thanksgiving when Elkanah arrived at home. Will any one blame him, if he felt little thankful? if the thought of the Thanksgiving turkey was like to choke him, and the very idea of giving thanks seemed to him a bitter satire? Poor fellow! he forgot that there were other hearts to whom Thanksgiving turkey seemed little tempting.

The Cape folk are not demonstrative. They have warm hearts, but the old Puritan ice has never quite melted away from the outer shell.

"Well, Elkanah, glad to see you, boy!" said his father, looking up from his corner by the stove; "how 's things in New York?" Father and son had not met for three years. But, going out into the kitchen, he received a warm grasp of the hand, and his mother said, in her low, sweet voice, "I knew you'd come." That was all. But it was enough.

How to take his sad face over to Elijah Nickerson's new house? But that must be done, too. Looking through the little sitting-room window, as he passed, he saw pale-faced Hepsy Ann sitting quietly by the table, sewing. The children had gone to bed. He did not knock; — why should he? — but, walking in, stood silent on the floor. A glad, surprised smile lit up the sad, wan face, as she recognized him, and, stepping to his side, said, "O, Elkanah! I knew you 'd come. How good of you!" Then, abashed to have so committed herself and him, she shrank to her chair again.

Let us not intrude further on these two. Surely Elkanah

Brewster had been less than man, had he not found his hard heart to soften, and his cold love to warm, as he drew from her the story of her long agony, and saw this weary heart ready to rest upon him, longing to be comforted in his strong arms.

The next day a small sign was put up at Abijah Brewster's door : —

BOOTS AND SHOES

MADE AND MENDED

BY

ELKANAH BREWSTER.

It was arranged that he should work at his trade all winter. In the spring, he was to have his father's vessel, and the wedding would be before he started for the Banks.

So the old life was put on again. I will not say that Elkanah was thoroughly content, — that there were no bitter longings, no dim regrets, no faint questionings of Providence. But hard work is a good salve for a sore heart ; and in his honest toils, in his care for Hepsy Ann and her little brood, in her kind heart, which acknowledged with such humility of love all he did for her and all he had cast away for her, he found his reward.

The wedding was over, — a quiet affair enough, — and Elkanah was anchored on the Banks, with a brave, skilful crew, and plenty of fish. His old luck had not deserted him ; wherever he dropped anchor, there the cod seemed to gather ; and, in the excitement of catching fish and guarding against the dangers of the Banks, the old New York life seemed presently forgotten ; and, once more, Elkanah's face wore the old, hopeful calm which belonged there. Art, that had been so long his tyrant mistress, was at last cast off.

Was she ?

As he sat, one evening, high on the quarter, smoking his pipe, in that calm, contemplative mood which is the smoker's reward for a day of toil, — the little vessel pitching bows under in the long, tremendous swell of the Atlantic, the low drifting fog lurid in the light of the setting sun, but bright stars twinkling out, one by one, overhead, in a sky of Italian clearness and softness, — it all came to him, — that which he had so long, so vainly sought, toiled for, prayed for in New York, — his destiny.

Why should he paint heads, figures, landscapes, objects with which his heart had never been really filled ?

But now, as in one flash of divinest intelligence, it was revealed to him ! — This sea, this fog, this sky, these stars, this old, old life, which he had been almost born into. O, blind bat indeed, not to have seen, long, long ago, that this was your birthright in Art ! not to have felt in your innermost heart, that this was indeed that thing, if anything, which God had called you to paint !

For this Elkanah had drunk in from his earliest youth, — this he understood to its very core; but the poor secret of that other life, which is so draped about with the artistic mannerisms and fashionable Art of New York, or any other civilized life, he had never rightly appreciated.

In that sunset-hour was born a *painter !*

III.

IT chanced, that, a few months ago, I paid my accustomed summer visit to an old friend, living near Boston, — a retired merchant he calls himself. He began life as a cabin-boy, — became, in time, master of an Indiaman, — then, partner in a China house, — and after many years' residence in Canton, returned some years ago, heart and liver whole, to spend his remaining days among olden scenes. A man of truest culture, generous heart, and rarely erring taste. I never go there without finding something new and admirable.

"What am I to see, this time?" I asked, after dinner, looking about the drawing-room.

"Come. I'll show you."

He led me up to a painting, — a sea-piece : — A schooner, riding at her anchor, at sunset, far out at sea, no land in sight, sails down, all but a little patch of storm-sail fluttering wildly in the gale, and heavily pitching in a great, grand, rolling sea ; around, but not closely enveloping her, a driving fog-bank, lurid in the yellow sheen of the setting sun ; above her, a few stars dimly twinkling through a clear blue sky ; on the quarter-deck, men sitting, wrapped in all the paraphernalia of storm-clothing, smoking and watching the roll of the sea.

"What do you think?" asked Captain Eastwick, interrupting my rapt contemplation.

"I never in my life saw so fine a sea-view. Whose can it be?"

"A Cape-Cod fisherman's."

"But he is a genius!" cried I, enthusiastically.

"A great, a splendid genius!" said my friend, quietly.

"And a fisherman?"

"Yes, and shoemaker."

"What a magnificent career he might make! Why don't you help him! What a pity to bury such a man in fish-boots and cod-livers!"

"My dear —," said Captain Eastwick, "you are a goose. The highest genius lives above the littleness of making a career. This man needs no Academy prizes or praises. To my mind, his is the noblest, happiest life of all."

Whereupon he told me the story which I have endeavored to relate.

THE QUEEN OF THE RED CHESSMEN.

HE box of chessmen had been left open all night. That was a great oversight! For everybody knows that the contending chessmen are but too eager to fight their battles over again by midnight, if a chance is only allowed them.

It was at the Willows, — so called, not because the house is surrounded by willows, but because a little clump of them hangs over the pond close by. It is a pretty place, with its broad lawn in front of the door-way, its winding avenue hidden from the road by high trees. It is a quiet place, too; the sun rests gently on the green lawn, and the drooping leaves of the willows hang heavily over the water.

No one would imagine what violent contests were going on under the still roof, this very night. It was the night of the first of May. The moon came silently out from the shadows; the trees were scarcely stirring. The box of chessmen had been left on the balcony steps by the draw-ing-room window, and the window, too, that warm night, had been left open. So, one by one, all the chessmen came out to fight over again their evening's battles.

It was a famously carved set of chessmen. The bishops wore their mitres, the knights pranced on spirited steeds, the castles rested on the backs of elephants, — even the pawns mimicked the private soldiers of an army. The skilful carver had given to each piece, and each pawn, too, a certain individuality. That night there had been a close contest. Two well-matched players had guided the game, and it had ended with leaving a deep irritation on the conquered side.

It was Isabella the Queen of the Red Chessmen, who had been obliged to yield. She was young and proud, and it was she, indeed, who held the rule ; for her father, the old Red King, had grown too imbecile to direct affairs ; he merely bore the name of sovereignty. And Isabella was loved by knights, pawns, and all ; the bishops were willing to die in her cause, the castles would have crumbled to earth for her. Opposed to her, stood the detested White Queen. All the Whites, of course, were despised by her ; but the haughty, self-sufficient queen angered her most.

The White Queen was reigning during the minority of her only son. The White Prince had reached the age of nineteen, but the strong mind of his mother had kept him always under restraint. A simple youth, he had always yielded to her control. He was pure-hearted and gentle, but never ventured to make a move of his own. He sought shelter under cover of his castles, while his more energetic mother went forth at the head of his army. She was dreaded by her subjects, — never loved by them. Her own pawn, it is true, had ventured much for her sake, had often with his own life redeemed her from captivity ; but it was loyalty that bound even him, — no warmer feeling of devotion or love.

The Queen Isabella was the first to come out from her prison.

" I will stay here no longer," she cried ; " the blood of the Reds grows pale in this inactivity."

She stood upon the marble steps ; the May moon shone down upon her. She listened a moment to a slight murmuring within the drawing-room window. The Spanish lady, the Murillo-painted Spanish lady, had come down from her frame that bound her against the wall. Just for this one night in the year, she stepped out from the canvas to walk up and down the rooms majestically. She would not exchange a word with anybody; nobody understood her language. She could remember when Murillo looked at her, watched over her, created her with his pencil. She could have nothing to say to little paltry shepherdesses, and other articles of *virtù*, that came into grace and motion just at this moment.

The Queen of the Red Chessmen turned away, down into the avenue. The May moon shone upon her. Her feet trod upon unaccustomed ground; no black or white square hemmed her in; she felt a new liberty.

"My poor old father!" she exclaimed, "I will leave him behind; better let him slumber in an ignoble repose than wander over the board, a laughing-stock for his enemies. We have been conquered, — the foolish White Prince rules!"

A strange inspiration stole upon her; the breath of the May night hovered over her; the May moon shone upon her. She could move without waiting for the will of another; she was free. She passed down the avenue; she had left her old prison behind.

Early in the morning, — it was just after sunrise, — the kind Doctor Lester was driving home, after watching half the night out with a patient. He passed the avenue to the Willows, but drew up his horse just as he was leaving the entrance. He saw a young girl sitting under the hedge. She was without any bonnet, in a red dress, fitting closely and hanging heavily about her. She was so very beautiful, she looked so strangely lost and out of place here at this early hour, that the Doctor could not resist speaking to her.

"My child, how came you here?"

The young girl rose up, and looked round with uncertainty.

"Where am I?" she asked.

She was very tall and graceful, with an air of command, but with a strange, wild look in her eyes.

"The young woman must be slightly insane," thought the Doctor; "but she cannot have wandered far."

"Let me take you home," he said aloud. "Perhaps you come from the Willows?"

"O, don't take me back there!" cried Isabella, "they will imprison me again! I had rather be a slave than a conquered queen!"

"Decidedly insane!" thought the Doctor. "I must take her back to the Willows."

He persuaded the young girl to let him lift her into his chaise. She did not resist him; but when he turned up the avenue, she leaned back in despair. He was fortunate enough to find one of the servants up at the house, just sweeping the steps of the hall-door. Getting out of his chaise, he said confidentially to the servant, —

"I have brought back your young lady."

"Our young lady!" exclaimed the man, as the Doctor pointed out Isabella.

"Yes, she is a little insane, is she not?"

"She is not our young lady," answered the servant; "we have nobody in the house just now, but Mr. and Mrs. Fogerty, and Mrs. Fogerty's brother, the old geologist."

"Where did she come from?" inquired the Doctor.

"I never saw her before," said the servant, "and I certainly should remember. There's some foreign folks live down in the cottage, by the railroad; but they are not the like of her!"

The Doctor got into his chaise again, bewildered.

"My child," he said, "you must tell me where you came from."

"O, don't let me go back again!" said Isabella, clasping her hands imploringly. "Think how hard it must be never to take a move of one's own! to know how the game might be won, then see it lost through folly! O, that last game, lost through utter weakness! There was that one move! Why did he not push me down to the king's row? I might have checkmated the White Prince, shut in by his own castles and pawns, — it would have been a direct checkmate! Think of his folly! he stopped to take the queen's pawn with his bishop, and within one move of a check-mate!"

"Quite insane!" repeated the Doctor. "But I must have my breakfast. She seems quiet; I think I can keep her till after breakfast, and then I must try and find where the poor child's friends live. I don't know what Mrs. Lester will think of her."

They rode on. Isabella looked timidly round.

"You don't quite believe me," she said, at last. "It seems strange to you."

"It does," answered the Doctor, "seem very strange."

"Not stranger than to me," said Isabella, — "it is so very grand to me! All this motion! Look down at that great field there, not cut up into squares! If I only had my knights and squires there! I would be willing to give *her* as good a field, too; but I would show her where the true bravery lies. What a place for the castles, just to defend that pass!"

The Doctor whipped up his horse.

Mrs. Lester was a little surprised at the companion her husband had brought home to breakfast with him.

"Who is it?" she whispered.

"That I don't know, — I shall have to find out," he answered, a little nervously.

"Where is her bonnet?" asked Mrs. Lester; this was the first absence of conventionality she had noticed.

"You had better ask her," answered the Doctor.

But Mrs. Lester preferred leaving her guest in the parlor while she questioned her husband. She was somewhat disturbed when she found he had nothing more satisfactory to tell her.

"An insane girl! and what shall we do with her?" she asked.

"After breakfast I will make some inquiries about her," answered the Doctor.

"And leave her alone with us? that will never do! You must take her away directly, — at least to the Insane

Asylum, — somewhere! What if she should grow wild while you were gone? She might kill us all! I will go in and tell her that she cannot stay here."

On returning to the parlor, she found Isabella looking dreamily out of the window. As Mrs. Lester approached, she turned.

"You will let me stay with you a little while, will you not?"

She spoke in a quiet tone, with an air somewhat commanding. It imposed upon nervous little Mrs. Lester. But she made a faint struggle.

"Perhaps you would rather go home," she said.

"I have no home now," said Isabella; "some time I may recover it; but my throne has been usurped."

Mrs. Lester looked round in alarm, to see if the Doctor were near.

"Perhaps you had better come in to breakfast," she suggested.

She was glad to place the Doctor between herself and their new guest.

Celia Lester, the only daughter, came down stairs. She had heard that her father had picked up a lost girl in the road. As she came down in her clean morning dress, she expected to have to hold her skirts away from some little squalid object of charity. She started when she saw the elegant-looking young girl who sat at the table. There was something in her air and manner that seemed to make the breakfast equipage, and the furniture of the room about her, look a little mean and poor. Yet the Doctor was very well off, and Mrs. Lester fancied she had everything quite in style. Celia stole into her place, feeling small in the presence of the stranger.

After breakfast, when the Doctor had somewhat refreshed himself by its good cheer from his last night's fatigue, Isabella requested to speak with him.

"Let me stay with you a little while," she asked, beseechingly; "I will do everything for you that you desire. You shall teach me anything ; — I know I can learn all that you will show me, all that Mrs. Lester will tell me."

" Perhaps so, — perhaps that will be best," answered the Doctor, " until your friends inquire for you ; then I must send you back to them."

" Very well, very well," said Isabella, relieved. " But I must tell you they will not inquire for me. I see you will not believe my story. If you only would listen to me, I could tell it all to you."

" That is the only condition I can make with you," answered the Doctor, " that you will not tell your story, — that you will never even think of it yourself. I am a physician. I know that it is not good for you to dwell upon such things. Do not talk of them to me, nor to my wife or daughter. Never speak of your story to any one who comes here. It will be better for you."

" Better for me," said Isabella, dreamily, " that no one should know ! Perhaps so. I am, in truth, captive to the White Prince ; and if he should come and demand me, — I should be half afraid to try the risks of another game."

" Stop, stop ! " exclaimed the doctor, " you are already forgetting the condition. I shall be obliged to take you away to some retreat, unless you promise me — "

" O, I will promise you anything," interrupted Isabella ; " and you will see that I can keep my promise."

Meanwhile Mrs. Lester and Celia had been holding a consultation.

" I think she must be some one in disguise," suggested Celia.

Celia was one of the most unromantic of persons. Both she and her mother had passed their lives in an unvarying routine of duties. Neither of them had ever found time from their sewing even to read. Celia had her books of history laid out, that she meant to take up when she should get through her work ; but it seemed hopeless that this time would ever come. It had never come to Mrs. Lester, and she was now fifty years old. Celia had never read any novels. She had tried to read them, but never was interested in them. So she had a vague idea of what romance was, conceiving of it only as something quite different from her every-day life. For this reason the unnatural event that was taking place this very day was gradually appearing to her something possible and natural. Because she knew there was such a thing as romance, and that it was something quite beyond her comprehension, she was the more willing to receive this event quietly from finding it incomprehensible.   •

"We can let her stay. here to-day, at least," said Mrs. Lester. "We will keep John at work in the front door-yard, in case we should want him. And I will set Mrs. Anderson's boy to weeding in the border; we can call him, if we should want to send for help."

She was quite ashamed of herself, when she had uttered these words, and Isabella walked into the room, so composed, so refined in her manners.

"The Doctor says I may stay here a little while, if you will let me," said Isabella, as she took Mrs. Lester's hands.

"We will try to make you comfortable," replied Mrs. Lester.

"He says you will teach me many things, — I think he said, how to sew."

"How to sew! Was it possible she did not know how to sew?" Celia thought to herself, "How many servants she must have had, never to have learned how to sew, herself!"

And this occupation was directly provided, while the Doctor set forth on his day's duties, and at the same time to inquire about the strange apparition of the young girl. He was so convinced that there was a vein of insanity about her, that he was very sure that questioning her only excited her the more. Just as he had parted from her, some compunction seized her, and she followed him to the door.

"There is my father," said she.

"Your father! where shall I find him?" asked the Doctor.

"O, he could not help me," she replied; "it is a long time since he has been able to direct affairs. He has scarcely been conscious of my presence, and will hardly feel my absence, his mind is so weak."

"But where can I find him?" persisted the Doctor.

"He did not come out," said Isabella; "the White Queen would not allow it, indeed."

"Stop, stop!" exclaimed the Doctor, "we are on forbidden ground."

He drove away.

"So there is insanity in the family," he thought to himself. "I am quite interested in this case. A new form of monomania! I should be quite sorry to lose sight of it. I shall be loath to give her up to her friends."

But he was not yet put to that test. No one could give him any light with regard to the strange girl. He went first to the Willows, and found there so much confusion that he could hardly persuade any one to listen to his questions. Mrs. Fogerty's brother, the geologist, had been riding that morning, and had fallen from his horse and broken his leg. The Doctor arrived just in time to be of service in setting it. Then he must linger some time to see that the old gentleman was comfortable, so that he was obliged to stay nearly the whole morning. He was much amused at the state of disturbance in which he left the family. The whole house was in confusion, looking after some lost chessmen.

"There was nothing," said Mrs. Fogerty, apologetically, "that would soothe her brother so much as a game of chess. That, perhaps, might keep him quiet. He would be willing to play chess with Mr. Fogerty by the day together. It was so strange! they had a game the night before, and now some of the pieces could not be found. Her brother had lost the game, and to-day he was so eager to take his revenge!"

"How absurd!" thought the Doctor; "what trifling things people interest themselves in! Here is this old man more disturbed at losing his game of chess than he is at breaking his leg. It is different in my profession, where one deals with life and death. Here is this young girl's fate in my hands, and they talk to me of the loss of a few paltry chessmen!"

The "foreign people" at the cottage knew nothing of Isabella. No one had seen her the night before, or at any time. Dr. Lester even drove ten miles to Dr. Giles's Retreat for the Insane, to see if it were possible that a patient could have wandered away from there. Dr. Giles was deeply interested in the account Dr. Lester gave. He would very gladly take such a person under his care.

"No," said Dr. Lester, "I will wait awhile. I am interested in the young girl. It is not possible but that I shall in time find out from her, by chance, perhaps, who her friends are, and where she came from. She must have wandered away in some delirium of fever, — but it is very strange, for she appears perfectly calm now. Yet I hardly know in what state I shall find her."

He returned to find her very quiet and calm, learning from his wife and daughter how to sew. She seemed deeply interested in this new occupation, and had given all her time and thought to it. Celia and her mother privately confided to the Doctor their admiration of their strange guest. Her ways were so graceful and beautiful! all that she said seemed so new and singular! The Doctor, before he went away, had exhorted Mrs. Lester and Celia to ask her no questions about her former life, and everything had gone on very smoothly. And everything went on as smoothly for some weeks. Isabella seemed willing to be as silent as the Doctor upon all exciting subjects. She appeared to be quite taken up with her sewing, much to Mrs. Lester's delight.

"She will turn out quite as good a seamstress as Celia," said she to the Doctor. "She sews steadily all the time, and nothing seems to please her so much as to finish a piece of work. She will be able to do much more than her own sewing, and may prove quite a help to us."

"I shall be very glad," said the Doctor, "if anything can be a help, to prevent you and Celia from working yourselves to death. I shall be glad if you can ever have done with that eternal sewing. It is time that Celia should do something about cultivating her mind."

"Celia's mind is so well regulated," interrupted Mrs. Lester.

"We won't discuss that," continued the Doctor, — "we never come to an agreement there. I was going on to say that I am becoming so interested in Isabella, that I feel towards her as if she were my own. If she is of help to the family, that is very well, — it is the best thing for her to be able to make herself of use. But I don't care to make any profit to ourselves out of her help. Somehow I begin to think of her as belonging to us. Certainly she belongs to nobody else. Let us treat her as our own child. We have but one, yet God has given us means enough to care for many more. I confess I should find it hard to give Isabella up to any one else. I like to find her when I come home, — it is pleasant to look at her."

"And I, too, love her," said Mrs. Lester. "I like to see her as she sits quietly at her work."

So Isabella went on learning what it was to be one of the family, and becoming, as Mrs. Lester remarked, a very experienced seamstress. She seldom said anything as she sat at her work, but seemed quite occupied with her sewing; while Mrs. Lester and Celia kept up a stream of conversation, seldom addressing Isabella, as, indeed, they had few topics in common.

One day, Celia and Isabella were sitting together.

"Have you always sewed?" asked Isabella.

"O, yes," answered Celia, — "since I was quite a child."

"And do you remember when you were a child?" asked Isabella, laying down her work.

"O, yes, indeed," said Celia; "I used to make all my doll's dresses myself."

"Your doll's dresses!" repeated Isabella.

"O, yes," replied Celia, — "I was not ashamed to play with dolls in that way."

"I should like to see some dolls," said Isabella.

"I will show you my large doll," said Celia; "I have always kept it, because I fitted it out with such a nice set of clothes. And I keep it for children to play with."

She brought her doll, and Isabella handled it and looked at it with curiosity.

"So you dressed this, and played with it," said Isabella, inquiringly, "and moved it about as one would move a piece at chess?"

Celia started at this word "chess." It was one of the forbidden words. But Isabella went on : —

"Suppose this doll should suddenly have begun to speak, to move, and walk round, would not you have liked it?"

"O, no!" exclaimed Celia. "What! a wooden thing speak and move! It would have frightened me very much."

"Why should it not speak, if it has a mouth, and walk, if it has feet?" asked Isabella.

"What foolish questions you ask!" exclaimed Celia, "of course it has not life."

"O, life, — that is it!" said Isabella. "Well what is life?"

"Life! why it is what makes us live," answered Celia. "Of course you know what life is."

"No, I don't know," said Isabella, "But I have been thinking about it lately, while I have been sewing, — what it is."

"But you should not think, you should talk more, Isabella," said Celia. "Mamma and I talk while we are at work, but you are always very silent."

"But you think sometimes?" asked Isabella.

"Not about such things," replied Celia. "I have to think about my work."

" But your father thinks, I suppose, when he comes home and sits in his study alone ? "

" O, he reads when he goes into his study, — he reads books and studies them," said Celia.

" Do you know how to read ? " asked Isabella.

" Do I know how to read ! " cried Celia, angrily.

" Forgive me," said Isabella, quickly, " but I never saw you reading. I thought perhaps — women are so different here ! "

She did not finish her sentence, for she saw Celia was really angry. Yet she had no idea of hurting her feelings. She had tried to accommodate herself to her new circumstances. She had observed a great deal, and had never been in the habit of asking questions. Celia was disturbed at having it supposed that she did not know how to read ; therefore it must be a very important thing to know how to read, and she determined she must learn. She applied to the Doctor. He was astonished at her entire ignorance, but he was very glad to help her. Isabella gave herself up to her reading, as she had done before to her sewing. The Doctor was now the gainer. All the time he was away, Isabella sat in his study, poring over her books ; when he returned, she had a famous lesson to recite to him. Then he began to tell her of books that he was interested in. He made Celia come in, for a history class. It was such a pleasure to him to find Isabella interested in what he could tell her of history !

" All this really happened," said Isabella to Celia once, — " these people really lived ! "

" Yes, but they died," responded Celia, in an indifferent tone, — " and ever so long ago, too ! "

" But did they die," asked Isabella, " if we can talk about them, and imagine how they looked ? They live for us as much as they did then."

" That I can't understand," said Celia. " My uncle saw Napoleon when he was in Europe, long ago. But I never saw Napoleon. He is dead and gone to me, just as much as Alexander the Great."

"Well, who does live, if Alexander the Great, if Napoleon, and Columbus do not live?" asked Isabella, impatiently.

"Why, papa and mamma live," answered Celia, "and you —"

"And the butcher," interrupted Isabella, "because he brings you meat to eat; and Mr. Spool, because he keeps the thread store. Thank you for putting me in, too! Once —"

"Once!" answered Celia, in a dignified tone, "I suppose once you lived in a grander circle, and it appears to you we have nobody better than Mr. Spool and the butcher."

Isabella was silent, and thought of her "circle," her former circle. The circle here was large enough, the circumference not very great, but there were as many points in it as in a larger one. There were pleasant, motherly Mrs. Gibbs, and her agreeable daughters, — the Gresham boys, just in college, — the Misses Tarletan, fresh from a New York boarding-school, — Mr. Lovell, the young minister, — and the old Misses Pendleton, that made raspberry-jam, — together with Celia's particular friends, Anna and Selina Mountfort, who had a great deal of talking with Celia in private, but not a word to say to anybody in the parlor. All these, with many others in the background, had been speculating upon the riddle that Isabella presented, — "Who was she? and where did she come from?"

Nobody found any satisfactory answer. Neither Celia nor her mother would disclose anything. It is a great convenience in keeping a secret, not to know what it is. One can't easily tell what one does not know.

"The Doctor really has a treasure in his wife and daughter," said Mrs. Gibbs, "they keep his secrets so well! Neither of them will lisp a word about this handsome Isabella."

"I have no doubt she is the daughter of an Italian refugee," said one of the Misses Tarletan. "We saw a number of Italian refugees in New York."

This opinion became prevalent in the neighborhood.

That Dr. Lester should be willing to take charge of an unknown girl did not astonish those who knew of his many charitable deeds. It was not more than he had done for his cousin's child, who had no especial claim upon him. He had adopted Lawrence Egerton, educated him, sent him to college, and was giving him every advantage in his study of the law. In the end Lawrence would probably marry Celia and the pretty property that the Doctor would leave behind for his daughter.

"She is one of my patients," the Doctor would say, to any one who asked him about her.

The tale that she was the daughter of an Italian refugee became more rife after Isabella had begun to study Italian. She liked to have the musical Italian words linger on her tongue. She quoted Italian poetry, read Italian history. In conversation, she generally talked of the present, rarely of the past or of the future. She listened with wonder to those who had a talent for reminiscence. How rich their past must be, that they should be willing to dwell in it! Her own she thought very meagre. If she wanted to live in the past, it must be in the past of great men, not in that of her own little self. So she read of great painters and great artists, and because she read of them she talked of them. Other people, in referring to by-gone events, would say, "When I was in Trenton last summer," — "In Cuba the spring that we were there"; but Isabella would say, "When Raphael died, or when Dante lived." Everybody liked to talk with her, — laughed with her at her enthusiasm. There was something inspiring, too, in this enthusiasm; it compelled attention, as her air and manner always attracted notice. By her side, the style and elegance of the Misses Tarletan faded out; here was a moon that quite extinguished the light of their little tapers. She became the centre of admiration; the young girls admired her, as they are prone to admire some one particular star. She never courted attention, but it was always given.

"Isabella attracts everybody," said Celia to her mother.

"Even the old Mr. Spencers, who have never been touched by woman before, follow her, and act just as she wills."

Little Celia, who had been quite a belle hitherto, sunk into the shade by the side of the brilliant Isabella. Yet she followed willingly in the sunny wake that Isabella left behind. She expanded somewhat, herself, for she was quite ashamed to know nothing of all that Isabella talked about so earnestly. The sewing gave place to a little reading, to Mrs. Lester's horror. The Mountforts and the Gibbses met with Isabella and Celia to read and study, and went into town with them to lectures and to concerts.

A winter passed away and another summer came. Still Isabella was at Dr. Lester's; and with the lapse of time the harder did it become for the Doctor to question her of her past history, — the more, too, was she herself weaned from it.

The young people had been walking in the garden one evening.

"Let me sit by you here in the porch," said Lawrence Egerton to Celia, — "I want rest, for body and spirit. I am always in a battle-field when I am talking with Isabella. I must either fight with her or against her. She insists on my fighting all the time. I have to keep my weapons bright, ready for use, every moment. She will lead me, too, in conversation, sends me here, orders me there. I feel like a poor knight in chess, under the sway of a queen — "

"I don't know anything about chess," said Celia, curtly.

"It is a comfort to have you a little ignorant," said Lawrence. "Please stay in bliss awhile. It is repose, it is refreshment. Isabella drags one into the company of her heroes, and then one feels completely ashamed not to be on more familiar terms with them all. Her Mazzinis, her Tancreds, heroes false and true, — it makes no difference to her, — put one into a whirl between history and story. What a row she would make in Italy, if she went back there!"

"What could we do without her?" said Celia; "it was so quiet and commonplace before she came!"

"That is the trouble," replied Lawrence, "Isabella won't let anything remain commonplace. She pulls everything out of its place, — makes a hero or heroine out of a piece of clay. I don't want to be in heroics all the time. Even Homer's heroes ate their suppers comfortably. I think it was a mistake in your father, bringing her here. Let her stay in her sphere queening it, and leave us poor mortals to our bread and butter."

"You know you don't think so," expostulated Celia; "you worship her shoe-tie, the hem of her garment."

"But I don't want to," said Lawrence, — "it is a compulsory worship. I had rather be quiet."

"Lazy Lawrence!" cried Celia, "it is better for you. You would be the first to miss Isabella. You would find us quite flat without her brilliancy, and would be hunting after some other excitement."

"Perhaps so," said Lawrence. "But here she comes to goad us on again. Queen Isabella, when do the bull-fights begin?"

"I wish I were Queen Isabella!" she exclaimed. "Have you read the last accounts from Spain? I was reading them to the Doctor to-day. Nobody knows what to do there. Only think what an opportunity for the Queen to show herself a queen! Why will not she make of herself such a queen as the great Isabella of Castile was?"

"I can't say," answered Lawrence.

"Queens rule in chess," said Horace Gresham. "I always wondered that the king was made such a poor character there. He is not only ruled by his cabinet, bishops, and knights, but his queen is by far the more warlike character."

"Whoever plays the game rules, — you or Mr. Egerton," said Isabella, bitterly; "it is not the poor queen. She must yield to the power of the moving hand. I suppose it is so with us women. We see a great aim before us, but have not the power."

" Nonsense ! " exclaimed Lawrence, " it is just the reverse. With some women, — for I won't be personal, — the aim, as you call it, is very small, — a poor amusement, another dress, a larger house — "

" You may stop," interrupted Isabella, " for you don't believe this. At least, keep some of your flings for the women that deserve them ; Celia and I don't accept them."

" Then we 'll talk of the last aim we were discussing, — the ride to-morrow."

The next winter was passed by Mrs. Lester, her daughter, and Isabella in Cuba. Lawrence Egerton accompanied them thither, and the Doctor hoped to go for them in the spring. They went on Mrs. Lester's account. She had worn herself out with her household labors, — very use- lessly, the Doctor thought, — so he determined to send her away from them. Isabella and Celia were very happy all this winter and spring. With Isabella, Spanish took the place of Italian studies. She liked talking in Spanish. They made some friends among the residents, as well as among the strangers, particularly the Americans. Of these last, they enjoyed most the society of Mrs. Blanchard and her son, Otho, who were at the same hotel with them.

The opera, too, was a new delight to Isabella, and even Celia was excited by it.

" It is a little too absurd, to see the dying scene of Romeo and Juliet sung out in an opera ! " remarked Lawrence Egerton, one morning ; " all the music of the spheres could not have made that scene, last night, otherwise than su- premely ridiculous."

" I am glad you did not sit by us, then," replied Celia ; " Isabella and I were crying."

" I dare say," said Lawrence. " I should be afraid to take you to see a tragedy well acted. You would both be in hysterics before the killing was over."

" I should be really afraid," said Celia, " to see Romeo and Juliet finely performed. It would be too sad."

" It would be much better to end it up comfortably,"

said Lawrence. "Why should not Juliet marry her Romeo in peace?"

"It would be impossible!" exclaimed Isabella, — "impossible to bring together two such hostile families! Of course the result must be a tragedy."

"In romances," answered Lawrence, "that may be necessary; but not in real life."

"Why not in real life?" asked Isabella. "When two thunder-clouds meet, there must be an explosion."

"But we don't have such hostile families arrayed against each other now-a-days," said Lawrence. "The Bianchi and the Neri have died out; unless the feud lives between the whites and the blacks of the present day."

"Are you sure that it has died out everywhere?" asked Isabella.

"Certainly not," said Otho Blanchard; "my mother, Bianca Bianco, inherits her name from a long line of ancestry, and with it come its hatreds as well as its loves."

"You speak like an Italian or Spaniard," said Lawrence. "We are cold-blooded Yankees, and in our slow veins such passions do die out. I should have taken you for an American from your name."

"It is our name Americanized; we have made Americans of ourselves, and the Bianchi have become the Blanchards."

"The romance of the family, then," persisted Lawrence, "must needs become Americanized too. If you were to meet with a lovely young lady of the enemy's race, I think you would be willing to bury your sword in the sheath for her sake."

"I hope I should not forget the honor of my family," said Otho. "I certainly never could, as long as my mother lives; her feelings on the subject are stronger even than mine."

"I cannot imagine the possibility of such feelings dying out," said Isabella. "I cannot imagine such different elements amalgamating. It would be like fire and water

13   S

uniting. Then there would be no longer any contest ; the game of life would be over."

"Why will you make out life to be a battle always?" exclaimed Lawrence ; "won't you allow us any peace ? I do not find such contests all the time, — never, except when I am fighting with you."

"I had rather fight with you than against you," said Isabella, laughing. "But when one is not striving, one is sleeping."

"That reminds me that it is time for our siesta," said Lawrence ; "so we need not fight any longer."

Afterwards Isabella and Celia were talking of their new friend Otho.

"He does not seem to me like a Spaniard," said Celia, "his complexion is so light ; then, too, his name sounds German."

"But his passions are quick," replied Isabella. "How he colored up when he spoke of the honor of his family ! "

"I wonder that you like him," said Celia ; "when he is with his mother, he hardly ventures to say his soul is his own."

"I don't like his mother," said Isabella ; "her manner is too imperious and unrefined, it appears to me. No wonder that Otho is ill at ease in her presence. It is evident that her way of talking is not agreeable to him. He is afraid that she will commit herself in some way."

"But he never stands up for himself," answered Celia ; "he always yields to her. Now I should not think you would like that."

"He yields because she is his mother," said Isabella ; "and it would not be becoming to contradict her."

"He yields to you, too," said Celia ; "how happens that ?"

"I hope he does not yield to me more than is becoming," answered Isabella, laughing ; "perhaps that is why I like him. After all, I don't care to be always sparring, as I am with Lawrence Egerton. With Otho I find that I agree wonderfully in many things. Neither of us yields to the other, neither of us is obliged to convince the other."'

"Now I should think you would find that stupid," said Celia. "What becomes of this desire of yours never to rest, always to be struggling after something?"

"We might strive together, we might struggle together," responded Isabella.

She said this musingly, not in answer to Celia, but to her own thoughts,—as she looked away, out from everything that surrounded her. The passion for ruling had always been uppermost in her mind; suddenly there dawned upon her the pleasure of being ruled. She became conscious of the pleasure of conquering all things for the sake of giving all to another. A new sense of peace stole upon her mind. Before, she had felt herself alone, even in the midst of the kindness of the home that had been given her. She had never dared to think or to speak of the past, and as little of the future. She had gladly flung herself into the details of every-day life. She had given her mind to the study of all that it required. She loved the Doctor, because he was always leading her on to fresh fields, always exciting her to a new knowledge. She loved him, too, for himself, for his tenderness and kindness to her. With Mrs. Lester and Celia she felt herself on a different footing. They admired her, but they never came near her. She led them, and they were always behind her.

With Otho she experienced a new feeling. He seemed, very much as she did herself, out of place in the world just around him. He was a foreigner,—was not yet acclimated to the society about him. He was willing to talk of other things than every-day events. He did not talk of "things," indeed, but he speculated, as though he lived a separate life from that of mere eating and drinking. He was not content with what seemed to every-day people possible, but was willing to believe that there were things not dreamed of in their philosophy.

"It is a satisfaction," said Lawrence once to Celia, "that

Isabella has found somebody who will go high enough into the clouds to suit her. Besides, it gives me a little repose."

"And a secret jealousy at the same time; is it not so?" asked Celia. "He takes up too much of Isabella's time to please you."

"The reason he pleases her," said Lawrence, "is because he is more womanly than manly, and she thinks women ought to rule the world. Now if the world were made up of such as he, it would be very easily ruled. Isabella loves power too well to like to see it in others. Look at her when she is with Mrs. Blanchard! It is a splendid sight to see them together!"

"How can you say so? I am always afraid of some outbreak."

These families were, however, so much drawn together, that, when the Doctor came to summon his wife and daughter and Isabella home, Mrs. Blanchard was anxious to accompany them to New England. She wondered if it were not possible to find a country-seat somewhere near the Lesters, that she could occupy for a time. The Doctor knew that the Willows was to be vacant this spring. The Fogertys were all going to Europe, and would be very willing to let their place.

So it was arranged after their return. The Fogertys left for Europe, and Mrs. Blanchard took possession of the Willows. It was a pleasant walking distance from the Lesters, but it was several weeks before Isabella made her first visit there. She was averse to going into the house, but, in company with Celia, Lawrence, and Otho, walked about the grounds. Presently they stopped near a pretty fountain that was playing in the midst of the garden.

"That is a pretty place for an Undine," said Otho.

"The idea of an Undine makes me shiver," said Lawrence. "Think what a cold-blooded, unearthly being she would be!"

"Not after she had a soul!" exclaimed Isabella.

"An Undine with a soul!" cried Lawrence. "I conceive of them as malicious spirits, who live and die as the bubbles of water rise and fall."

"You talk as if there were such things as Undines," said Celia. "I remember once trying to read the story of Undine, but I never could finish it."

"It ends tragically," remarked Otho.

"Of course all such stories must," responded Lawrence; "of course it is impossible to bring the natural and the unnatural together."

"That depends upon what you call the natural," said Otho.

"We should differ, I suppose," said Lawrence, "if we tried to explain what we each call the natural. I fancy your 'real life' is different from mine."

"Pictures of real life," said Isabella, "are sometimes pictures of horses and dogs, sometimes of children playing, sometimes of fruits of different seasons heaped upon one dish, sometimes of watermelons cut open."

"That is hardly your picture of real life," said Lawrence, laughing, — "a watermelon cut open! I think you would rather choose the picture of the Water Fairies from the Düsseldorf Gallery."

"Why not?" said Isabella. "The life we see must be very far from being the only life that is."

"That is very true," answered Lawrence; "but let the fairies live their life by themselves, while we live our life in our own way. Why should they come to disturb our peace, since we cannot comprehend them, and they certainly cannot comprehend us?"

"You do not think it well, then," said Isabella, stopping in their walk, and looking down, — "you do not think it well that beings of different natures should mingle?"

"I do not see how they can," replied Lawrence. "I am limited by my senses; I can perceive only what they show me. Even my imagination can picture to me only what my senses can paint."

"Your senses!" cried Otho, contemptuously, — "it is

very true, as you confess, you are limited by your senses. Is all this beauty around you created merely for you, — and the other insects about us? I have no doubt it is filled with invisible life."

"Do let us go in!" said Celia. "This talk, just at twilight, under the shade of this shrubbery, makes me shudder. I am not afraid of the fairies. I never could read fairy stories when I was a child; they were tiresome to me. But talking in this way makes one timid. There might be strollers or thieves under all these hedges."

They went into the house, through the hall, and different apartments, till they reached the drawing-room. Isabella stood transfixed upon the threshold. It was all so familiar to her! — everything as she had known it before! Over the mantel-piece hung the picture of the scornful Spanish lady; a heavy bookcase stood in one corner; comfortable chairs and couches were scattered round the room; beautiful landscapes against the wall seemed like windows cut into foreign scenery. There was an air of ease in the room, an old-fashioned sort of ease, such as the Fogertys must have loved.

"It is a pretty room, is it not?" said Lawrence. "You look at it as if it pleased you. How much more comfort there is about it than in the fashionable parlors of the day? It is solid, substantial comfort."

"You look at it as if you had seen it before," said Otho to Isabella. "Do you know the room impressed me in that way, too?"

"It is singular," said Lawrence, "the feeling, that 'all this has been before,' that comes over one at times. I have heard it expressed by a great many people."

"Have you, indeed, ever had this feeling?" asked Isabella.

"Certainly," replied Lawrence; "I say to myself sometimes, 'I have been through all this before!' and I can almost go on to tell what is to come next, — it seems so much a part of my past experience."

" It is strange it should be so with you, — and with you too," she said, turning to Otho.

" Perhaps we are all more alike than we have thought," said Otho.

Otho's mother appeared, and the conversation took another turn.

Isabella did not go to the Willows again, until all the Lester family were summoned there to a large party that Mrs. Blanchard gave. She called it a house-warming, although she had been in the house some time. It was a beautiful evening. A clear moonlight made it as brilliant outside on the lawn as the lights made the house within. There was a band of music stationed under the shrubbery, and those who chose could dance. Those who were more romantic wandered away down the shaded walks, and listened to the dripping of the fountain.

Lawrence and Isabella returned from a walk through the grounds, and stopped a moment on the terrace in front of the house. Just then a dark cloud appeared in the sky, threatening the moon. The wind, too, was rising, and made a motion among the leaves of the trees.

" Do you remember," asked Lawrence, " that child's story of the Fisherman and his Wife ? how the fisherman went down to the sea-shore, and cried out, —

> " 'O man of the sea,
> Come listen to me !
> For Alice, my wife,
> The plague of my life,
> Has sent me to beg a boon of thee !'

The sea muttered and roared ; — do you remember? There was always something impressive to me in the descriptions, in the old story, of the changes in the sea, and of the tempest that rose up, more and more fearful, as the fisherman's wife grew more ambitious and more and more grasping in her desires, each time that the fisherman went down to the sea-shore. I believe my first impression of the sea came from that. The coming on of a storm is always as-

sociated with it. I always fancy that it is bringing with it
something beside the tempest, — that there is something
ruinous behind it."

"That is more fanciful than you usually are," said Isabella ; "but, alas! I cannot remember your story, for I
never read it."

"That is where your education and Celia's was fearfully
neglected," said Lawrence ; "you were not brought up on
fairy stories and Mother Goose. You have not needed
the first, as Celia has ; but Mother Goose would have
given a tone to your way of thinking, that is certainly
wanting."

A little while afterwards, Isabella stood upon the balcony
steps leading from the drawing-room. Otho was with her.
The threatening clouds had driven almost every one into
the house.   There was distant thunder and lightning ;
but through the cloud-rifts, now and then, the moonlight
streamed down.   Isabella and Otho had been talking
earnestly, — so earnestly, that they were quite unobservant
of the coming storm, of the strange lurid light that hung
around.

"It is strange that this should take place here !" said
Isabella, — "that just here I should learn that you love
me! Strange that my destiny should be completed in this
spot ! "

"And this spot has its strange associations with me,"
said Otho, "of which I must some time speak to you.
But now I can think only of the present. Now, for the
first time, do I feel what life is, — now that you have
promised to be mine ! "

Otho was interrupted by a sudden cry. He turned to
find his mother standing behind him.

"You are here with Isabella ! she has promised herself
to you ! " she exclaimed. " It is a fatality, a terrible fatality !
Listen, Isabella ! You are the Queen of the Red Chessmen ; and he, Otho, is the King of the White Chessmen, —
and I, their Queen. Can there be two queens ? Can there

be a marriage between two hostile families? Do you not see, if there were a marriage between the Reds and the Whites, there were no game? Look! I have found our old prison! The pieces would all be here, — but we, we are missing! Would you return to the imprisonment of this poor box, — to your old mimic life? No, my children, go back! Isabella, marry this Lawrence Egerton, who loves you. You will find what life is, then. Leave Otho, that he may find this same life also."

Isabella stood motionless.

"Otho, the White Prince! Alas! where is my hatred? But life without him! Even stagnation were better! I must needs be captive to the White Prince!"

She stretched out her hand to Otho. He seized it passionately. At this moment there was a grand crash of thunder. A gust of wind extinguished at once all the lights in the drawing-room. The terrified guests hurried into the hall, into the other rooms.

"The lightning must have struck the house!" they exclaimed.

A heavy rain followed; then all was still. Everybody began to recover his spirits. The servants relighted the candles. The drawing-room was found untenanted. It was time to go; yet there was a constraint upon all the party, who were eager to find their hostess and bid her good-bye.

But the hostess could not be found! Isabella and Otho, too, were missing! The Doctor and Lawrence went everywhere, calling for them, seeking them in the house, in the grounds. They were nowhere to be found, — neither that night, nor the next day, nor ever afterwards!

The Doctor found in the balcony a box of chessmen fallen down. It was nearly filled; but the red queen, and the white king and queen, were lying at a little distance. In the box was the red king, his crown fallen from his head, himself broken in pieces. The Doctor took up the red queen, and carried it home.

13*

" Are you crazy ? " asked his wife.   " What are you going to do with that red queen ? "

But the Doctor placed the figure on his study-table, and often gazed at it wistfully.

Whenever, afterwards, as was often the case, any one suggested a new theory to account for the mysterious disappearance of Isabella and the Blanchards, the Doctor looked at the carved image on his table and was silent.

MISS LUCINDA.

UT that Solomon is out of fashion I should quote him, here and now, to the effect that there is a time for all things; but Solomon is obsolete, and never, no, never, will I dare to quote a dead language, "for raisons I have," as the exiles of Erin say. Yet, in spite of Solomon and Horace, I may express my own less concise opinion, that even in hard times, and dull times, and war times, there is yet a little time to laugh, a brief hour to smile and love and pity, just as through this dreary easterly storm, bringing clouds and rain, sobbing against casement and door with the inarticulate wail of tempests, there comes now and then the soft shine of a sun behind it all, a fleeting glitter, an evanescent aspect of what has been.

But if I apologize for a story that is nowise tragic, nor fitted to "the fashion of these times," possibly somebody will say at its end that I should also have apologized for its subject, since it is as easy for an author to treat his readers to high themes as vulgar ones, and velvet can be thrown into a portrait as cheaply as calico; but of this apology I wash my hands. I believe nothing in place or circumstance makes romance. I have the same quick sympathy for Biddy's sorrows with Patrick that I have for the Empress of France and her august, but rather grim lord and master. I think words are often no harder to bear than "a blue bating," and I have a reverence for poor old maids as great as for the nine Muses. Commonplace people are only commonplace from character, and no position affects that. So forgive me once more, patient reader, if I offer to you no tragedy in high life, no sentimental history of fashion and wealth, but only a little story about a woman who could not be a heroine.

Miss Lucinda Jane Ann Manners was a lady of unknown age, who lived in a place I call Dalton, in a State of these Disuniting States, which I do not mention for good cause. I have already had so many unconscious personalities visited on my devoted head, that but for lucidity I should never mention persons or places, inconvenient as it would be. However, Miss Lucinda did live, and lived by the aid of "means," which, in the vernacular, is money. Not a great deal, it is true, — five thousand dollars at lawful interest, and a little wooden house, do not imply many luxuries even to a single-woman; and it is also true that a little fine sewing taken in helped Miss Manners to provide herself with a few small indulgences otherwise beyond her reach. She had one or two idiosyncrasies, as they are politely called, that were her delight. Plenty of dish-towels were necessary to her peace of mind; without five pair of scissors she could not be happy; and Tricopherous was essential to her well-being: indeed, she often said she would rather give up coffee than Tricopherous, for her hair was black and wiry and curly, and caps she abhorred, so that of a winter's day her head presented the most irrelevant and volatile aspect, each particular hair taking a twist on its own responsibility, and improvising a wild halo about her unsaintly face, unless subdued into propriety by the aforesaid fluid.

I said Miss Lucinda's face was unsaintly, — I mean unlike ancient saints as depicted by contemporary artists: modern and private saints are after another fashion. I met one yesterday, whose green eyes, great nose, thick lips, and sallow wrinkles, under a bonnet of fifteen years' standing, further clothed upon by a scant merino cloak and cat-skin tippet, would have cut a sorry figure in the gallery of the

Vatican or the Louvre, and put the tranquil Madonna of San Sisto into a state of stunning antithesis; but if Saint Agnes or Saint Catharine was half as good as my saint, I am glad of it!

No, there was nothing sublime and dolorous about Miss Manners; her face was round, cheery, and slightly puckered, with two little black eyes sparking and shining under dark brows, a nose she unblushingly called pug, and a big mouth, with eminently white and regular teeth, which she said were such a comfort, for they never ached, and never would to the end of time. Add to this physiognomy a small and rather spare figure, dressed in the cleanest of calicoes, always made in one style, and rigidly scorning hoops, — without a symptom of a collar, in whose place (or it may be over which) she wore a white cambric handkerchief, knotted about her throat, and the two ends brought into subjection by means of a little angular-headed gold pin, her sole ornament, and a relic of her old father's days of widowhood, when buttons were precarious tenures. So much for her aspect. Her character was even more quaint.

She was the daughter of a clergyman, one of the old school, the last whose breeches and knee-buckles adorned the profession, who never "outlived his usefulness," nor lost his godly simplicity. Parson Manners held rule over an obscure and quiet village in the wilds of Vermont, where hard-handed farmers wrestled with rocks and forests for their daily bread, and looked forward to heaven as a land of green pastures and still waters, where agriculture should be a pastime, and winter impossible. Heavy freshets from the mountains that swelled their rushing brooks into annual torrents, and snow-drifts that covered five-rail fences a foot above the posts and blocked up the turnpike-road for weeks, caused this congregation fully to appreciate Parson Manners's favorite hymns, —

> "There is a land of pure delight,"

and —

> "On Jordan's stormy banks I stand."

Indeed, one irreverent, but " pretty smart feller," who lived on the top of a hill known as Drift Hill, where certain adventurous farmers dwelt for the sake of its smooth sheep-pastures, was heard to say, after a mighty sermon by Parson Manners about the seven-times heated furnaces of judgment reserved for the wicked, that " Parson had n't better try to skeer Drift-Hillers with a hot place ; 't would n't more 'n jest warm 'em through down there, arter a real snappin' winter."

In this out-of-the-way nook was Lucinda Jane Ann born and bred. Her mother was like her in many things, — just such a cheery, round-faced little body, but with no more mind than found ample scope for itself in superintending the affairs of house and farm, and vigorously " seeing to " her husband and child. So, while Mrs. Manners baked, and washed, and ironed, and sewed, and knit, and set the sweetest example of quiet goodness and industry to all her flock, without knowing she *could* set an example, or be followed as one, the Parson amused himself, between sermons of powerful doctrine and parochial duties of a more human interest, with educating Lucinda, whose intellect was more like his own than her mother's. A strange training it was for a young girl, — mathematics, metaphysics, Latin, theology of the driest sort ; and after an utter failure at Greek and Hebrew, though she had toiled patiently through seven books of the " Æneid," Parson Manners mildly sniffed at the inferiority of the female mind, and betook himself to teaching her French, which she learned rapidly, and spoke with a pure American accent, perhaps as pleasing to a Parisian ear as the hiss of Piedmont or the gutturals of Switzerland. Moreover, the minister had been brought up, himself, in the most scrupulous refinement of manner ; his mother was a widow, the last of an " old family," and her dainty, delicate observances were inbred, as it were, in her only son. This sort of elegance is perhaps the most delicate test of training and descent, and all these things Lucinda was taught from the grateful recollection of a son who never forgot his mother, through all the solitary labors and studies of a long life. So it came to pass, that, after her mother died, Lucinda grew more and more like her father, and, as she became a woman, these rare refinements separated her more and more from those about her, and made her necessarily solitary. As for marriage, the possibility of such a thing never crossed her mind; there was not a man in the parish who did not offend her sense of propriety and shock her taste, whenever she met one; and though her warm, kind heart made her a blessing to the poor and sick, her mother was yet bitterly regretted at quiltings and tea-drinkings, where she had been so "sociable-like."

It is rather unfortunate for such a position as Lucinda's, that, as Deacon Stowell one day remarked to her father, "Natur' will be Natur' as much on Drift Hill as down to Bosting"; and when she began to feel that "strong necessity of loving" that sooner or later assails every woman's heart, there was nothing for it to overflow on, when her father had taken his share. Now Lucinda loved the Parson most devoutly. Ever since the time when she could just remember watching through the dusk his white stockings, as they glimmered across the road to evening-meeting, and looked like a supernatural pair of legs taking a walk on their own responsibility, twilight concealing the black breeches and coat from mortal view, Lucinda had regarded her father with a certain pleasing awe. His long abstractions, his profound knowledge, his grave, benign manners, and the thousand daily refinements of speech and act that seemed to put him far above the sphere of his pastorate, — all these things inspired as much reverence as affection; and when she wished with all her heart and soul she had a sister or a brother to tend and kiss and pet, it never once occurred to her that any of those tender familiarities could be expended on her father: she would as soon have thought of caressing any of the goodly angels whose stout legs, flowing curls, and impossible draperies sprawled among the pictures in the big Bible, and who excited her wonder as much by their garments as their turkey-wings and brandishing arms. So she betook herself to pets, and growing up to the old-maidenhood of thirty-five before her father fell asleep, was by that time the centre of a little world of her own, — hens, chickens, squirrels, cats, dogs, lambs, and sundry transient guests of stranger kind; so that, when she left her old home, and removed to the little house in Dalton that had been left her by her mother's aunt, and had found her small property safely invested by means of an old friend of her father's, Miss Manners made one more journey to Vermont to bring in safety to their future dwelling a cat and three kittens, an old blind crow, a yellow dog of the true cur breed, and a rooster with three hens, "real creepers," as she often said, "none of your longlegged, screaming creatures."

Lucinda missed her father, and mourned him as constantly and faithfully as ever a daughter could; but her temperament was more cheerful and buoyant than his, and when once she was quietly settled in her little house, her garden and her pets gave her such full occupation that she sometimes blamed herself for not feeling more lonely and unhappy. A little longer life or a little more experience would have taught her better: power to be happy is the last thing to regret. Besides, it would have been hard to be cheerless in that sunny little house, with its queer old furniture of three-legged tables, high-backed chairs, and chintz curtains where red mandarins winked at blue pagodas on a deep-yellow ground, and birds of insane ornithology pecked at insects that never could have been hatched, or perched themselves on blossoms totally unknown to any mortal flora. Old engravings of Bartolozzi, from the stiff elegances of Angelica Kaufman and the mythologies of Reynolds, adorned the shelf; and the carpet in the parlor was of veritable English make, older than Lucinda herself, but as bright in its fading and as firm in its usefulness as she. Up stairs the tiny chambers were decked with spotless white dimity, and rush-bottomed chairs stood in each window, with a strip of the same old carpet by either bedside ; and in the kitchen the blue settle that had stood by the Vermont fireside now defended this lesser hearth from the draught of the door, and held under the seat thereof sundry ironing-sheets, the blanket belonging to them, and good store of ticking and worsted holders. A half-gone set of egg-shell china stood in the parlor-closet, —cups, and teapot, and sugar-bowl, rimmed with brown and gold in a square pattern, and a shield without blazon on the side; the quaint tea-caddy with its stopper stood over against the pursy little cream-pot, and held up in its lumps of sparkling sugar the oddest sugar-tongs, also a family relic ; — beside this, six small spoons, three large ones, and a little silver porringer comprised all the "plate" belonging to Miss Manners, so that no fear of burglars haunted her, and but for her pets she would have lived a life of profound and monotonous tranquillity. But this was a vast exception; in her life her pets were the great item now ; — her cat had its own chair in the parlor and kitchen ; her dog, a rug and a basket never to be meddled with by man or beast; her old crow, its special nest of flannel and cotton, where it feebly croaked as soon as Miss Lucinda began to spread the little table for her meals; and the three kittens had their own playthings and their own saucer as punctiliously as if they had been children. In fact, Miss Manners had a greater share of kindness for beasts than for mankind. A strange compound of learning and unworldliness, of queer simplicity, native penetration, and common sense, she had read enough books to despise human nature as it develops itself in history and theology, and she had not known enough people to love it in its personal development. She had a general idea that all men were liars, and that she must be on her guard against their propensity to cheat and annoy a lonely and helpless woman ; for, to tell the truth, in her good father's over-anxiety to defend her from the snares of evil men after his

T

death, his teachings had given her opinion this bias, and
he had forgotten to tell her how kindly and how true he
had found many of his own parishioners, how few inclined to
harm or pain him. So Miss Lucinda made her entrance
into life at Dalton, distrustful, but not, suspicious; and
after a few attempts on the part of the women who were
her neighbors to be friendly or intimate, they gave her up
as impracticable: not because she was impolite or unkind:
they did not themselves know why they failed, though she
could have told them; for, old maid as she was, poor and
plain and queer, she could not bring herself to associate
familiarly with people who put their teaspoons into the
sugar-bowl, helped themselves with their own knives and
forks, gathered up bits of uneaten butter and returned them
to the plate for next time, or replaced on the dish pieces of
cake half eaten or cut with the knives they had just introduced into their mouths. Miss Lucinda's code of minor
morals would have forbidden her to drink from the same
cup with a queen, and have considered a pitchfork as suitable as a knife to eat with, nor would she have offered to a
servant the least thing she had touched with her own lips
or her own implements of eating; and she was too delicately bred to look on in comfort where such things were
practised. Of course these women were not ladies; and
though many of them had kind hearts and warm impulses
of goodness, yet that did not make up to her for their social
misdemeanors, and she drew herself more into her own
little shell, and cared more for her garden and her chickens,
her cats and her dog, than for all the humanity of Dalton
put together.

Miss Manners held her flowers next dearest to her pets,
and treated them accordingly. Her garden was the most
brilliant bit of ground possible. It was big enough to hold
one flourishing peach-tree, one Siberian crab, and a solitary
egg-plum; while under these fruitful boughs bloomed moss-
roses in profusion, of the dear old-fashioned kind, every
deep pink bud with its clinging garment of green breathing

out the richest odor; close by, the real white rose, which fashion has banished to country towns, unfolded its cups of pearl flushed with yellow sunrise to the heart; and by its side its damask sister waved long sprays of bloom and perfume. Tulips, dark-purple and cream-color, burning scarlet and deep-maroon, held their gay chalices up to catch the dew; hyacinths, blue, white, and pink, hung heavy bells beneath them; spiced carnations of rose and garnet crowded their bed in July and August, heart's-ease fringed the walks, May honeysuckles clambered over the board-fence, and monthly honeysuckles overgrew the porch at the back-door, making perpetual fragrance from their moth-like horns of crimson and ivory. Nothing inhabited those beds that was not sweet and fair and old-fashioned. Gray-lavender-bushes sent up purple spikes in the middle of the garden and were duly housed in winter, but these were the sole tender plants admitted, and they pleaded their own cause in the breath of the linen-press and the bureau-drawers that held Miss Lucinda's clothes. Beyond the flowers, utility blossomed in a row of bean-poles, a hedge of currant-bushes against the farther fence, carefully tended cauliflowers, and onions enough to tell of their use as sparing as their number; a few deep-red beets and golden carrots were all the vegetables beside : Miss Lucinda never ate potatoes or pork.

Her housekeeping, but for her pets, would have been the proper housewifery for a fairy. Out of her fruit she annually conserved miracles of flavor and transparence, — great plums like those in Aladdin's garden, of shining topaz, — peaches tinged with the odorous bitter of their pits, and clear as amber, — crimson crabs floating in their own ruby sirup, or transmuted into jelly crystal clear, yet breaking with a grain, — and jelly from the acid currants to garnish her dinner-table or refresh the fevered lips of a sick neighbor. It was a study to visit her tiny pantry, where all these "lucent sirops" stood in tempting array, — where spices, and sugar, and tea, in their small jars, flanked the sweetmeats, and a jar of glass showed its store of whitest honey, and another stood filled with crisp cakes. Here always a loaf or two of home-made bread lay rolled in a snowy cloth, and another was spread over a dish of butter; pies were not in favor here, — nor milk, save for the cats; salt fish Miss Manners never could abide, — her savory taste allowed only a bit of rich old cheese, or thin scraps of hung beef, with her bread and butter; sauces and spices were few in her repertory, but she cooked as only a lady can cook, and might have asked Soyer himself to dinner. For, verily, after much meditation and experience, I have divined that it takes as much sense and refinement and talent to cook a dinner, wash and wipe a dish, make a bed as it should be made, and dust a room as it should be dusted, as goes to the writing of a novel or shining in high society.

But because Miss Lucinda Manners was reserved and " unsociable," as the neighbors pronounced her, I did not, therefore, mean to imply that she was inhuman. No neighbor of hers, local or Scriptural, fell ill, without an immediate offer of aid from her: she made the best gruel known to Dalton invalids, sent the ripest fruit and the sweetest flowers: and if she could not watch with the sick, because it interfered with her duties at home in an unpleasant and inconvenient way, she would sit with them hour after hour in the day-time, and wait on all their caprices with the patient tenderness of a mother. Children she always eyed with strange wistfulness, as if she longed to kiss them, but did n't know how; yet no child was ever invited across her threshold, for the yellow cur hated to be played with, and children always torment kittens.

So Miss Lucinda wore on happily toward the farther side of the middle ages. One after another of her pets passed away and was replaced, the yellow cur barked his last currish signal, the cat died and her kittens came to various ends of time or casualty, the crow fell away to dust and was too old to stuff, and the garden bloomed and faded ten times over, before Miss Manners found herself to be forty-six years old, which she heroically acknowledged one fine day to the census-taker. But it was not this consciousness, nor its confession, that drew the dark brows so low over Miss Lucinda's eyes that day ; it was quite another trouble, and one that wore heavily on her mind, as we shall proceed to explain. For Miss Manners, being, like all the rest of her sex, quite unable to do without some masculine help, had employed, for some seven years, an old man by the name of Israel Slater, to do her " chores," as the vernacular hath it. It is a mortifying thing, and one that strikes at the roots of Women's Rights terribly sharp blows, but I must even own it, that one might as well try to live without one's bread-and-butter as without the aid of the dominant sex. When I see women split wood, unload coal-carts, move wash-tubs, and roll barrels of flour and apples handily down cellar-ways or up into carts, then I shall believe in the sublime theories of the strong-minded sisters ; but as long as I see before me my own forlorn little hands, and sit down on the top stair to recover breath, and try in vain to lift the water-pitcher at table, just so long I shall be glad and thankful that there are men in the world, and that half a dozen of them are my kindest and best friends. It was rather an affliction to Miss Lucinda to feel this innate dependence, and at first she resolved to employ only small boys, and never any one of them more than a week or two. She had an unshaped theory that an old maid was a match for a small boy, but that a man would cheat and domineer over her. Experience sadly put to flight these notions ; for a succession of boys in this cabinet-ministry for the first three years of her stay in Dalton would have driven her into a Presbyterian convent, had there been one at hand. Boy Number One caught the yellow cur out of bounds one day, and shaved his plumy tail to a bare stick, and Miss Lucinda fairly shed tears of grief and rage when Pink appeared at the door with the denuded appendage tucked between his little legs, and his funny yellow eyes casting sidelong looks of apprehension at his mistress. Boy Number One was despatched directly. Number Two did pretty well for a month, but his integrity and his appetite conflicted, and Miss Lucinda found him one moonlight night perched in her plum-tree devouring the half-ripe fruit. She shook him down with as little ceremony as if he had been an apple; and though he lay at Death's door for a week with resulting cholera-morbus, she relented not. So the experiment went on, till a list of casualties that numbered in it fatal accidents to three kittens, two hens and a rooster, and at last Pink himself, who was sent into a decline by repeated drenchings from the watering-pot, put an end to her forbearance, and she instituted in her viziership the old man who had now kept his office so long, — a queer, withered, slow, humorous old creature, who did "chores" for some six or seven other households, and got a living by sundry "jobs" of wood-sawing, hoeing corn, and other like works of labor, if not of skill. Israel was a great comfort to Miss Lucinda: he was efficient counsel in the maladies of all her pets, had a sovereign cure for the gapes in chickens, and could stop a cat's fit with the greatest ease; he kept the tiny garden in perfect order, and was very honest, and Miss Manners favored him accordingly. She compounded liniment for his rheumatism, herb-sirup for his colds, presented him with a set of flannel shirts, and knit him a comforter; so that Israel expressed himself strongly in favor of "Miss Lucindy," and she said to herself he really was "quite good for a man."

But just now, in her forty-seventh year, Miss Lucinda had come to grief, and all on account of Israel and his attempts to please her. About six months before this census-taking era, the old man had stepped into Miss Manners's kitchen with an unusual radiance on his wrinkles and in his eyes, and began without his usual morning greeting, —

"I 've got so'thin' for you naow, Miss Lucindy. You 're a master-hand for pets, but I 'll bet a red cent you ha'n't an idee what I 've got for ye naow!"

" I 'm sure I can't tell, Israel," said she ; " you 'll have to let me see it."

" Well," said he, lifting up his coat and looking carefully behind him as he sat down on the settle, lest a stray kitten or chicken should preoccupy the bench, " you see I was down to Orrin's abaout a week back, and he hed a litter o' pigs, — eleven on 'em. Well, he could n't raise the hull on 'em, — 't a'n't good to raise more 'n nine, — an' so he said, ef I 'd 'a' had a place o' my own, I could 'a' had one on 'em, but, as 't was, he guessed he 'd hev to send one to market for a roaster. I went daown to the barn to see 'em, an' there was one, the cutest little critter I ever sot eyes on, and I 've seen more 'n four pigs in my day, — 't was a little black-spotted one, as spry as an ant, and the dreffullest knowin' look out of its eyes ! I fellowshipped it right off, and I said, says I, ' Orrin, ef you 'll let me hev that 'ere little spotted feller, I 'll git a place for him, for I do take to him consarnedly.' So he said I could, and I fetched him hum, and Miss Slater and me we kinder fed him up for a few days back, till he got sorter wonted, and I 'm a-goin' to fetch him to you."

" But, Israel, I have n't any place to put him in."

" Well, that a'n't nothin' to hender. I 'll jest fetch out them old boards out of the wood-shed, and knock up a little sty right off, daown by the end o' the shed, and you ken keep your swill that I 've hed before, and it 'll come handy."

" But pigs are so dirty ! "

" I don't know as they be ; they ha'n't no great conveniences for washin' ginerally ; but I never heerd as they was dirtier 'n other critters, where they run wild. An' beside, that a'n't goin' to hender, nuther ; I calculate to make it one o' the chores to take keer of him ; 't won't cost no more to you ; and I ha'n't no great opportunities to do things for folks that 's allers a-doin' for me ; so 't you need n't be afeard, Miss Lucindy : I love to."

Miss Lucinda's heart got the better of her judgment. A nature that could feel so tenderly for its inferiors in the scale could not be deaf to the tiny voices of humanity, when they reached her solitude ; and she thanked Israel for the pig so heartily that the old man's face brightened still more, and his voice softened from its cracked harshness, as he said, clicking up and down the latch of the back-door, —

"Well, I 'm sure you 're as welcome as you are obleeged, and I 'll knock up that 'ere pen right off; he sha'n't pester ye any, — that 's a fact."

Strange to say, — yet perhaps it might have been expected from her proclivities, — Miss Lucinda took an astonishing fancy to the pig. Very few people know how intelligent an animal a pig is; but when one is regarded merely as pork and hams, one's intellect is apt to fall into neglect : a moral sentiment which applies out of Pigdom. This creature would not have passed muster at a county fair; no Suffolk blood compacted and rounded him; he belonged to the "racers," and skipped about his pen with the alacrity of a large flea, wiggling his curly tail as expressively as a dog's, and "all but speakin'," as Israel said. He was always glad to see Miss Lucinda, and established a firm friendship with her dog Fun, a pretty, sentimental, German spaniel. Besides, he kept tolerably clean by dint of Israel's care, and thrust his long nose between the rails of his pen for grass, or fruit, or carrot- and beet-tops, with a knowing look out of his deep-set eyes that was never to be resisted by the soft-hearted spinster. Indeed, Miss Lucinda enjoyed the possession of one pet who could not tyrannize over her. Pink's place was more than filled by Fun, who was so oppressively affectionate that he never could leave his mistress alone. If she lay down on her bed, he leaped up and unlatched the door, and stretched himself on the white counterpane beside her with a grunt of satisfaction; if she sat down to knit or sew, he laid his head and shoulders across her lap, or curled himself up on her knees; if she was cooking, he whined and coaxed round her till she hardly knew whether she fried or broiled her steak; and if she turned him out and buttoned the door, his cries were so pitiful she could never be 'resolute enough to keep him in exile five minutes,' — for it was a prominent article in her creed, that animals have feelings that are easily wounded, and are of "like passions" with men, only incapable of expression. Indeed, Miss Lucinda considered it the duty of human beings to atone to animals for the Lord's injustice in making them dumb and four-legged. She would have . been rather startled at such an enunciation of her practice, but she was devoted to it as a practice: she would give her own chair to the cat and sit on the settle herself; get up at midnight, if a mew or a bark called her, though the thermometer was below zero ; the tenderloin of her steak or the liver of her chicken was saved for a pining kitten or an ancient and toothless cat ; and no disease or wound daunted her faithful nursing, or disgusted her devoted tenderness. It was rather hard on humanity, and rather reversive of Providence, that all this care and pains should be lavished on cats and dogs, while little morsels of flesh and blood, ragged, hungry, and immortal, wandered up and down the streets. Perhaps that they were immortal was their defence from Miss Lucinda ; one might have hoped that her "other-worldliness" accepted that fact as enough to outweigh present pangs, if she had not openly declared, to Israel Slater's immense amusement and astonishment, that *she* believed creatures had souls, — little ones perhaps, but souls after all, and she did expect to see Pink again some time or other.

"Well, I hope he 's got his tail feathered out ag'in," said Israel, dryly. "I do'no' but what hair 'd grow as well as feathers in a speretooal state, and I never see a pictur' of an angel but what hed consider'ble many feathers."

Miss Lucinda looked rather confounded. But humanity had one little revenge on her in the shape of her cat, a beautiful Maltese, with great yellow eyes, fur as soft as velvet, and silvery paws as lovely to look at as they were thistly to touch. Toby certainly pleaded hard for Miss

14

Lucinda's theory of a soul; but his was no good one: some tricksy and malign little spirit had lent him his share of intellect, and he used it to the entire subjugation of Miss Lucinda. When he was hungry, he was as well-mannered and as amiable as a good child, — he would coax, and purr, and lick her fingers with his pretty red tongue, like a "perfect love"; but when he had his fill, and needed no more, then came Miss Lucinda's time of torment. If she attempted to caress him, he bit and scratched like a young tiger, he sprang at her from the floor and fastened on her arm with real fury; if he cried at the window and was not directly let in, as soon as he had achieved entrance his first manœuvre was to dash at her ankles and bite them, if he could, as punishment for her tardiness. This skirmishing was his favorite mode of attack; if he was turned out of the closet, or off the pillow up stairs, he retreated under the bed and made frantic sallies at her feet, till the poor woman got actually nervous, and if he was in the room made a flying leap as far as she could to her bed, to escape those keen claws. Indeed, old Israel found her more than once sitting in the middle of the kitchen-floor with Toby crouched for a spring under the table, his poor mistress afraid to move, for fear of her unlucky ankles. And this literally cat-ridden woman was hazed about and ruled over by her feline tyrant to that extent that he occupied the easiest chair, the softest cushion, the middle of the bed, and the front of the fire, not only undisturbed, but caressed. This is a veritable history, beloved reader, and I offer it as a warning and an example: if you will be an old maid, or if you can't help it, take to petting children, or donkeys, or even a respectable cow, but beware of domestic tyranny in any shape but man's!

No wonder Miss Lucinda took kindly to the pig, who had a house of his own, and a servant, as it were, to the avoidance of all trouble on her part, — the pig who capered for joy when she or Fun approached, and had so much expression in his physiognomy that one almost expected to see him smile. Many a sympathizing conference Miss Lucinda held with Israel over the perfections of Piggy, as he leaned against the sty and looked over at his favorite after this last chore was accomplished.

"I say for 't," exclaimed the old man, one day, "I b'lieve that cre'tur' knows enough to be professor in a college. Why, he talks! he re'lly doos: a leetle through his nose, maybe, but no more 'n Dr. Colton allers doos, — 'n' I declare he appears to have abaout as much sense. I never see the equal of him. I thought he 'd 'a' larfed right out yesterday, when I gin him that mess o' corn: he got up onto his forelegs on the trough, an' he winked them knowin' eyes o' his'n, an' waggled his tail, an' then he set off an' capered round till he come bunt up ag'inst the boards. I tell *you*, — that sorter sobered him; he gin a growlin' grunt, an' shook his ears, an' looked sideways at me, and then he put to and eet up that corn as sober as a judge. I swan! he does beat the Dutch!"

But there was one calculation forgotten both by Miss Lucinda and Israel: the pig would grow, — and in consequence, as I said before, Miss Lucinda came to grief; for when the census-taker tinkled her sharp little door-bell, it called her from a laborious occupation at the sty, — no more and no less than trying to nail up a board that Piggy had torn down in struggling to get out of his durance. He had grown so large that Miss Lucinda was afraid of him; his long legs and their vivacious motion added to the shrewd intelligence of his eyes, and his nose seemed as formidable to this poor little woman as the tusk of a rhinoceros: but what should she do with him? One might as well have proposed to her to kill and cut up Israel as to consign Piggy to the "fate of race." She could not turn him into the street to starve, for she loved him; and the old maid suffered from a constancy that might have made some good man happy, but only embarrassed her with the pig. She could not keep him forever, — that was evident; she knew enough to be aware that time would increase his

disabilities as a pet, and he was an expensive one now, —
for the corn-swallowing capacities of a pig, one of the
"racer" breed, are almost incredible, and nothing about
Miss Lucinda wanted for food even to fatness.   Besides, he
was getting too big for his pen, and so "cute" an animal
could not be debarred from all out-door pleasures, and
tantalized by the sight of a green and growing garden
before his eyes continually, without making an effort to
partake of its delights.   So, when Miss Lucinda indued
herself with her brown linen sack and sun-bonnet to go
and weed her carrot-patch, she was arrested on the way by
a loud grunting and scrambling in Piggy's quarter, and
found to her distress that he had contrived to knock off the
upper board from his pen.   She had no hammer at hand;
so she seized a large stone that lay near by and pounded
at the board till the twice-tinkling bell recalled her to the
house, and as soon as she had made confession to the
census-taker she went back, — alas, too late! Piggy had
redoubled his efforts, another board had yielded, and he
was free !   What a thing freedom is ! how objectionable in
practice, how splendid in theory !   More people than Miss
Lucinda have been put to their wits' end when "Hoggie"
burst his bonds and became rampant instead of couchant.
But he enjoyed it; he made the tour of the garden on a
delightful canter, brandishing his tail with an air of defiance that daunted his mistress at once, and regarding her
with his small bright eyes as if he would before long taste
her and see if she was as crisp as she looked.   She retreated
forthwith to the shed and caught up a broom with which
she courageously charged upon Piggy, and was routed entirely ; for, being no way alarmed by her demonstration,
the creature capered directly at her, knocked her down,
knocked the broom out of her hand, and capered away
again to the young carrot-patch.

"O dear !" said Miss Manners, gathering herself up
from the ground, — " if there only was a man here !"

Suddenly she betook herself to her heels, — for the ani-

mal looked at her, and stopped eating : that was enough
to drive Miss Lucinda off the field. And now, quite desperate, she rushed through the house and out of the front-
door, actually in search of a man ! Just down the street
she saw one. Had 'she been composed, she might have
noticed the threadbare cleanliness of his dress, the odd
cap that crowned his iron-gray locks, and the peculiar
manner of his walk ; for our little old maid had stumbled
upon no less a person than Monsieur Jean Leclerc, the
dancing-master of Dalton. Not that this accomplishment
was much in vogue in the embryo city; but still there were
a few who liked to fit themselves for firemen's balls and
sleighing-party frolics, and quite a large class of children
were learning betimes such graces as children in New
England receive more easily than their elders. Monsieur
Leclerc had just enough scholars to keep his coat threadbare and restrict him to necessities ; but he lived, and was
independent. All this Miss Lucinda was ignorant of ; she
only saw a man, and, with the instinct of the sex in trouble
or danger, she appealed to him at once.

"O, sir ! won't you step in and help me ? My pig has
got out, and I can't catch him, and he is ruining my garden !"

" Madame, I shall ! " replied the Frenchman, bowing low,
and assuming the first position.

So Monsieur Leclerc followed Miss Manners, and supplied himself with a mop that was hanging in the shed as
his best weapon. Dire was the battle between the pig and
the Frenchman. They skipped past each other and back
again as if they were practising for a cotillon. Piggy had
four legs, which gave him a certain advantage; but the
Frenchman had most brain, and in the long run brain gets
the better of legs. A weary dance they led each other, but
after a while the pet was hemmed in a corner, and Miss
Lucinda had run for a rope to tie him, when, just as she
returned, the beast made a desperate charge, upset his
opponent, and, giving a leap in the wrong direction, to his

manifest astonishment, landed in his own sty! Miss Lucinda's courage rose; she forgot her prostrate friend in need, and, running to the pen, caught up hammer and nailbox on her way, and, with unusual energy, nailed up the bars stronger than ever, and then bethought herself to thank the stranger. But there he lay quite still and pale.

"Dear me!" said Miss Manners, "I hope you have n't hurt yourself, sir?"

"I have fear that I am hurt, Madame," said he, trying to smile. "I cannot to move but it pains me."

"Where is it? Is it your leg or your arm? Try and move one at a time," said Miss Lucinda, promptly.

The left leg was helpless, it could not answer to the effort, and the stranger lay back on the ground pale with the pain. Miss Lucinda took her lavender-bottle out of her pocket and softly bathed his head and face; then she took off her sack and folded it up under his head, and put the lavender beside him. She was good at an emergency, and she showed it.

"You must lie quite still," said she; "you must not try to move till I come back with help, or your leg will be hurt more."

With that she went away, and presently returned with two strong men and the long shutter of a shop-window. To this extempore litter she carefully moved the Frenchman, and then her neighbors lifted him and carried him into the parlor, where Miss Lucinda's chintz lounge was already spread with a tight-pinned sheet to receive the poor man, and while her helpers put him to bed she put on her bonnet and ran for the doctor.

Doctor Colton did his best for his patient, but pronounced it an impossibility to remove him till the bone should be joined firmly, as a thorough cure was all-essential to his professional prospects. And now, indeed, Miss Lucinda had her hands full. A nurse could not be afforded, but Monsieur Leclerc was added to the list of old Israel's "chores," and what other nursing he needed Miss Lucinda

was glad to do; for her kind heart was full of self-re-
proaches to think it was her pig that had knocked down
the poor man, and her mop-handle that had twisted itself
across and under his leg, and aided, if not caused, its
breakage. So Israel came in four or five times a day to do
what he could, and Miss Lucinda played nurse at other
times to the best of her ability. Such flavorous gruels and
porridges as she concocted! such *tisanes* after her guest's
instructions! such dainty soups, and sweetbreads, and cut-
lets, served with such neatness! After his experience of
a second-rate boarding-house, Monsieur Leclerc thought
himself in a gastronomic paradise. Moreover, these tiny
meals were garnished with flowers, which his French taste
for color and decoration appreciated: two or three stems
of lilies-of-the-valley in their folded green leaves, cool and
fragrant; a moss-rosebud and a spire of purple-gray lavender bound together with ribbon-grass; or three carnations
set in glittering myrtle-sprays, the last acquisition of the
garden.

Miss Lucinda enjoyed nursing thoroughly, and a kindlier
patient no woman ever had. Her bright needle flew faster
.than ever through the cold linen and flaccid cambric of the
shirts and cravats she fashioned, while he told her, in his
odd idioms, stories of his life in France, and the curious
customs both of society and *cuisinerie*, with which last he
showed a surprising acquaintance. Truth to tell, when
Monsieur Leclerc said he had been a member of the Duc
de Montmorenci's household, he withheld the other half
of this truth, — that he had been his *valet-de-chambre:* but
it was an hereditary service, and seemed to him as different
a thing from common servitude as a peer's office in the
bedchamber differs from a lackey's. Indeed, Monsieur
Leclerc was a gentleman in his own way, — not of blood,
but of breeding; and while he had faithfully served the
"aristocrats," as his father had done before him, he did
not limit that service to their prosperity, but in their greatest need descended to menial offices, and forgot that he

could dance and ride and fence almost as well as his young
master. But a bullet from a barricade put an end to his
duty there, and he hated utterly the democratic rule that
had overturned for him both past and future, so he escaped,
and came to America, the grand resort of refugees, where
he had labored, as he best knew how, for his own support,
and kept to himself his disgust at the manners and customs
of the barbarians. Now, for the first time, he was at
home and happy. Miss Lucinda's delicate fashions suited
him exactly; he adored her taste for the beautiful, which
she was unconscious of; he enjoyed her cookery, and
though he groaned within himself at the amount of debt
he was incurring, yet he took courage from her kindness
to believe she would not be a hard creditor, and, being
naturally cheerful, put aside his anxieties and amused himself as well as her with his stories, his quavering songs, his
recipes for *pot-au-feu, tisane,* and *pâtés,* at once economi-
cal and savory. Never had a leg of lamb or a piece of
roast beef gone so far in her domestic experience, a chicken
seemed almost to outlive its usefulness in its various forms
of reappearance, and the salads he devised were as wonderful as the omelets he superintended, or the gay dances he
played on his beloved violin, as soon as he could sit up
enough to manage it. Moreover, — I should say *most-
over,* if the word were admissible, — Monsieur Leclerc
lifted a great weight before long from Miss Lucinda's mind.
He began by subduing Fun to his proper place by a mild
determination that completely won the dog's heart. "Women and spaniels," the world knows, "like kicking"; and
though kicks were no part of the good man's Rareyfaction
of Fun, he certainly used a certain amount of coercion,
and the dog's lawful owner admired the skill of the teacher
and enjoyed the better manners of the pupil thoroughly;
she could do twice as much sewing now, and never were
her nights disturbed by a bark, for the dog crouched by
his new friend's bed in the parlor and lay quiet there.
Toby was next undertaken, and proved less amenable to

discipline; he stood in some slight awe of the man who tried to teach him, but still continued to sally out at Miss Lucinda's feet, to spring at her caressing hand when he felt ill-humored, and to claw Fun's patient nose and his approaching paws when his misplaced sentimentality led him to caress the cat; but after a while a few well-timed slaps administered with vigor cured Toby of his worst tricks, though every blow made Miss Lucinda wince, and almost shook her good opinion of Monsieur Leclerc: for in these long weeks he had wrought out a good opinion of himself in her mind, much to her own surprise; she could not have believed a man could be so polite, so gentle, so patient, and above all so capable of ruling without tyranny. Miss Lucinda was puzzled.

One day, as Monsieur Leclerc was getting better, just able to go about on crutches, Israel came into the kitchen, and Miss Manners went out to see him. She left the door open, and along with the odor of a pot of raspberry-jam scalding over the fire, sending its steams of leaf-and-insect fragrance through the little house, there came in also the following conversation.

"Israel," said Miss Lucinda, in a hesitating and rather forlorn tone, "I have been thinking,— I don't know what to do with Piggy. He is quite too big for me to keep. I 'm afraid of him, if he gets out; and he eats up the garden.'

"Well, that *is* a consider'ble swaller for a pig, Miss Lucindy; but I b'lieve you 're abaout right abaout keepin' on him. He *is* too big,— that 's a fact; but he 's so like a human cre'tur', I 'd jest abaout as lieves slarter Orrin. I declare, I don't know no more'n a taown-haouse goose what to do with him!"

"If I gave him away, I suppose he would be fatted and killed, of course?"

"I guess he 'd be killed, likely; but as for fattenin' on him, I 'd jest as soon undertake to fatten a salt codfish. He 's one o' the racers, an' they 're as holler as hogsheads:

you can fill 'em up to their noses, ef you're a mind to spend your corn, and they'll caper it all off their bones in twenty-four haours. I b'lieve, ef they was tied neck an' heels an' stuffed, they'd wiggle thin betwixt feedin'-times. Why, Orrin, he raised nine on 'em, and every darned critter's as poor as Job's turkey, to-day : they a'n't no good. I'd as lieves ha' had nine chestnut rails, — an' a little lieveser, 'cause they don't eat nothin'."

"You don't know of any poor person who'd like to have a pig, do you ? " said Miss Lucinda, wistfully.

"Well, the poorer they was, the quicker they'd eat him up, I guess, — ef they could eat such a razor-back."

"O, I don't like to think of his being eaten ! I wish he could be got rid of some other way. Don't you think he might be killed in his sleep, Israel ? "

This was a little too much for Israel. An irresistible flicker of laughter twitched his wrinkles and bubbled in his throat.

"I think it's likely 't would wake him up," said he, demurely. "Killin' 's killin', and a cre'tur' can't sleep over it's though 't was the stomach-ache. I guess he'd kick some, ef he *was* asleep, — and screech some, too ! "

"Dear me ! " said Miss Lucinda, horrified at the idea. "I wish he could be sent out to run in the woods. Are there any good woods near here, Israel ? "

"I don't know but what he'd as lieves be slartered to once as to starve, an' be hunted down out in the lots. Besides, there a'n't nobody as I knows of would like a hog to be a-rootin' round amongst their turnips and young wheat."

"Well, what I shall do with him I don't know ! " despairingly exclaimed Miss Lucinda. "He was such a dear little thing when you brought him, Israel ! Do you remember how pink his pretty little nose was, — just like a rose-bud, — and how bright his eyes looked, and his cunning legs ? And now he's grown so big and fierce ! But I can't help liking him, either."

"He's a cute critter, that's sartain; but he does too much rootin' to have a pink nose now, I expect; — there's consider'ble on 't, so I guess it looks as well to have it gray. But I don't know no more 'n you do what to do abaout it."

"If I could only get rid of him without knowing what became of him!" exclaimed Miss Lucinda, squeezing her fore-finger with great earnestness, and looking both puzzled and pained.

"If Mees Lucinda would pairmit?" said a voice behind her.

She turned round to see Monsieur Leclerc on his crutches, just in the parlor-door.

"I shall, Mees, myself dispose of Piggee, if it please. I can. I shall have no sound; he shall to go away like a silent snow, to trouble you no more, never!"

"O, sir! if you could! But I don't see how!"

"If Mees was to see, it would not be to save her pain. I shall have him to go by *magique* to fiery land."

Fairy-land, probably! But Miss Lucinda did not perceive the *équivoque*.

"Nor yet shall I trouble Meester Israyel. I shall have the aid of myself and one good friend that I have; and some night when you rise of the morning, he shall not be there."

Miss Lucinda breathed a deep sigh of relief.

"I am greatly obliged, — I shall be, I mean," said she.

"Well, I'm glad enough to wash my hands on 't," said Israel. "I shall hanker arter the critter some, but he's a-gettin' too big to be handy; 'n' it's one comfort abaout critters, you ken get rid on' em somehaow when they're more plague than profit. But folks has got to be let alone, excep' the Lord takes 'em; an' He don't allers see fit."

What added point and weight to these final remarks of old Israel was the well-known fact that he suffered at home from the most pecking and worrying of wives, and had been heard to say in some moment of unusual frankness that he "did n't see how 't could be sinful to wish Miss

Slater was in heaven, for she'd be lots better off, and other folks too!"

Miss Lucinda never knew what befell her pig one fine September night; she did not even guess that a visit paid to Monsieur by one of his pupils, a farmer's daughter just out of Dalton, had anything to do with this *enlèvement;* she was sound asleep in her bed up stairs, when her guest shod his crutches with old gloves, and limped out to the garden-gate by dawn, where he and the farmer tolled the animal out of his sty and far down the street by tempting red apples, and then Farmer Steele took possession of him, and he was seen no more. No, the first thing Miss Lucinda knew of her riddance was when Israel put his head into the back-door that same morning, some four hours afterward, and said, with a significant nod, —

"He's gone!"

After all his other chores were done, Israel had a conference with Monsieur Leclerc, and the two sallied into the garden, and in an hour had dismantled the low dwelling, cleared away the wreck, levelled and smoothed its site, and Monsieur, having previously provided himself with an Isabella-grape-vine, planted it on this forsaken spot, and trained it carefully against the end of the shed : strange to say, though it was against all precedent to transplant a grape in September, it lived and flourished. Miss Lucinda's gratitude to Monsieur Leclerc was altogether disproportioned, as he thought, to his slight service. He could not understand fully her devotion to her pets, but he respected it, and aided it whenever he could, though he never surmised the motive that adorned Miss Lucinda's table with such delicate superabundance after the late departure, and laid bundles of lavender-flowers in his tiny portmanteau till the very leather seemed to gather fragrance.

Before long, Monsieur Leclerc was well enough to resume his classes, and return to his boarding-house ; but the latter was filled, and only offered a prospect of vacancy in some three weeks after his application ; so he returned home somewhat dejected, and as he sat by the little parlor-fire after tea, he said to his hostess, in a reluctant tone, —

"Mees Lucinda, you have been of the kindest to the poor alien. I have it in my mind to relieve you of this care very rapidly, but it is not in the Fates that I do. I have gone to my house of lodgings, and they cannot to give me a chamber as yet. I have fear that I must yet rely me on your goodness for some time more, if you can to entertain me so much more of time?"

"Why, I shall like to, sir," replied the kindly, simple-hearted old maid. "I 'm sure you are not a mite of trouble, and I never can forget what you did for my pig."

A smile flitted across the Frenchman's thin, dark face, and he watched her glittering needles a few minutes in silence before he spoke again.

"But I have other things to say of the most unpleasant to me, Mees Lucinda. I have a great debt for the goodness and care you to me have lavished. To the angels of the good God we must submit to be debtors, but there are also of mortal obligations. I have lodged in your mansion for more of ten weeks, and to you I pay yet no silver, but it is that I have it not at present. I must ask of your goodness to wait."

The old maid's shining black eyes grew soft as she looked at him.

"Why!" said she, "I don't think you owe me much of anything, Mr. Leclerc. I never knew things last as they have since you came. I really think you brought a blessing. I wish you would please to think you don't owe me anything."

The Frenchman's great brown eyes shone with suspicious dew.

"I cannot to forget that I owe to you far more than any silver of man repays; but I should not think to forget that I also owe to you silver, or I should not be worthy of a man's name. No, Mees! I have two hands and legs. I will not let a woman most solitary spend for me her good self."

"Well," said Miss Lucinda, "if you will be uneasy till you pay me, I would rather have another kind of pay than money. I should like to know how to dance. I never did learn, when I was a girl, and I think it would be good exercise."

Miss Lucinda supported this pious fiction through with a simplicity that quite deceived the Frenchman. He did not think it so incongruous as it was. He had seen women of sixty, rouged, and jewelled, and furbelowed, foot it deftly in the halls of the Faubourg St. Germain in his earliest youth ; and this cheery, healthy woman, with lingering blooms on either cheek, and uncapped head of curly black hair but slightly strewn with silver, seemed quite as fit a subject for the accomplishment. Besides, he was poor, — and this offered so easy a way of paying the debt he had so dreaded ! Well said Solomon, — " The destruction of the poor is their poverty ! " For whose moral sense, delicate sensitiveness, generous longings, will not sometimes give way to the stringent need of food and clothing, the gall of indebtedness, and the sinking consciousness of an empty purse and threatening possibilities ?

Monsieur Leclerc's face brightened.

"Ah ! with what grand pleasure shall I teach you the dance ! "

But it fell dark again as he proceeded, —

" Though not one, nor two, nor three, nor four quarters shall be of value sufficient to achieve my payment."

"Then, if that troubles you, why, I should like to take some French lessons in the evening, when you don't have classes. I learned French when I was quite a girl, but not to speak it very easily ; and if I could get some practice and the right way to speak, I should be glad."

"And I shall give you the real *Parisien* tone, Mees Lucinda ! " said he proudly. " I shall be as if it were no more an exile when I repeat my tongue to you ! "

And so it was settled. Why Miss Lucinda should learn French any more than dancing was not a question in Mon-

sieur Leclerc's mind. It is true, that Chaldaic would, in all
probability, be as useful to our friend as French; and the
flying over poles and hanging by toes and fingers, so elo-
quently described by the Apostle of the Body in these
"Atlantic" pages, would have been as well adapted to
her style and capacity as dancing; — but his own language,
and his own profession! what man would not have regarded these as indispensable to improvement, particularly
when they paid his board?

During the latter three weeks of Monsieur Leclerc's stay
with Miss Lucinda he made himself surprisingly useful.
He listed the doors against approaching winter breezes, —
he weeded in the garden, — trimmed, tied, trained, wherever
either good office was needed, — mended china with an
infallible cement, and rickety chairs with the skill of a
cabinet-maker; and whatever hard or dirty work he did,
he always presented himself at table in a state of scrupulous neatness: his long brown hands showed no trace of
labor; his iron-gray hair was reduced to smoothest order;
his coat speckless, if threadbare; and he ate like a gentleman, an accomplishment not always to be found in the
"best society," as the phrase goes, — whether the best in
fact ever lacks it is another thing. Miss Lucinda appreciated these traits, — they set her at ease; and a pleasanter
home-life could scarce be painted than now enlivened the
little wooden house. But three weeks pass away rapidly;
and when the rusty portmanteau was gone from her spare
chamber, and the well-worn boots from the kitchen-corner,
and the hat from its nail, Miss Lucinda began to find herself wonderfully lonely. She missed the armfuls of wood
in her wood-box, that she had to fill laboriously, two sticks
at a time; she missed the other plate at her tiny round
table, the other chair beside her fire; she missed that dark,
thin, sensitive face, with its rare and sweet smile; she
wanted her story-teller, her yarn-winder, her protector, back
again. Good gracious! to think of an old lady of forty-
seven entertaining such sentiments for a man!

Presently the dancing-lessons commenced. It was thought advisable that Miss Manners should enter a class, and, in the fervency of her good intentions, she did not demur. But gratitude and respect had to strangle with persistent hands the little serpents of the ridiculous in Monsieur Leclerc's soul, when he beheld his pupil's first appearance. What reason was it, O rose of seventeen, adorning thyself with cloudy films of lace and sparks of jewelry before the mirror that reflects youth and beauty, that made Miss Lucinda array herself in a brand-new dress of yellow muslin-de-laine strewed with round green spots, and displace her customary handkerchief for a huge tamboured collar, on this eventful occasion? Why, O why did she tie up the roots of her black hair with an unconcealable scarlet string? And most of all, why was her dress so short, her slipper-strings so big and broad, her thick slippers so shapeless by reason of the corns and bunions that pertained to the feet within? The "instantaneous rush of several guardian angels" that once stood dear old Hepzibah Pynchon in good stead was wanting here, — or perhaps they stood by all-invisible, their calm eyes softened with love deeper than tears, at this spectacle so ludicrous to man, beholding in the grotesque dress and adornments only the budding of life's divinest blossom, and in the strange skips and hops of her first attempts at dancing only the buoyancy of those inner wings that goodness and generosity and pure self-devotion were shaping for a future strong and stately flight upward. However, men, women, and children do not see with angelic eyes, and the titterings of her fellow-pupils were irrepressible: one bouncing girl nearly choked herself with her handkerchief trying not to laugh, and two or three did not even try. Monsieur Leclerc could not blame them, — at first he could scarce control his own facial muscles; but a sense of remorse smote him, as he saw how unconscious and earnest the little woman was, and remembered how often those knotty hands and knobbed feet had waited on his need or his comfort. Presently he tapped on his violin for a few moments' respite, and approached Miss Lucinda as respectfully as if she had been a queen.

"You are ver' tired, Mees Lucinda ? " said he.

"I am a little, sir," said she, out of breath. "I am not used to dancing ; it's quite an exertion."

"It is that truly. If you are too much tired, is it better to wait ? I shall finish for you the lesson till I come to-night for a French conversation ?"

. "I guess I will go home," said the simple little lady. "I am some afraid of getting rheumatism ; but use makes perfect, and I shall stay through next time, no doubt."

"So I believe," said Monsieur, with his best bow, as Miss Lucinda departed and went home, pondering all the way what special delicacy she should provide for tea.

"My dear young friends," said Monsieur Leclerc, pausing with the uplifted bow in his hand, before he recommenced his lesson, "I have observe that my new pupil does make you much to laugh. I am not so surprise, for you do not know all, and the good God does not robe all angels in one manner ; but she have taken me to her mansion with a leg broken, and have nursed me like a saint of the blesséd, nor with any pay of silver except that I teach her the dance and the French. They are pay for the meat and the drink, but she will have no more for her good patience and care. I like to teach you the dance, but she could teach you the saints' ways which are better. I think you will no more to laugh."

"No ! I guess we *won't !*" said the bouncing girl with great emphasis, and the color rose over more than one young face.

After that day Miss Lucinda received many a kind smile and hearty welcome, and never did anybody venture even a grimace at her expense. But it must be acknowledged that her dancing was at least peculiar. With a sanitary view of the matter, she meant to make it exercise, and fearful was the skipping that ensued. She chasséd on tiptoe, and balancéd with an indescribable hopping twirl, that made one think of a chickadee pursuing its quest of food on new-ploughed ground; and some late-awakened feminine instinct of dress, restrained, too, by due economy, indued her with the oddest decorations that woman ever devised. The French lessons went on more smoothly. If Monsieur Leclerc's Parisian ear was tortured by the barbarous accent of Vermont, at least he bore it with heroism, since there was nobody else to hear; and very pleasant, both to our little lady and her master, were these long winter evenings, when they diligently waded through Racine, and even got as far as the golden periods of Chateaubriand. The pets fared badly for petting in these days; they were fed and waited on, but not with the old devotion; it began to dawn on Miss Lucinda's mind that something to talk to was preferable, as a companion, even to Fun, and that there might be a stranger sweetness in receiving care and protection than in giving it.

Spring came at last. Its softer skies were as blue over Dalton as in the wide fields without, and its footsteps as bloom-bringing in Miss Lucinda's garden as in mead or forest. Now Monsieur Leclerc came to her aid again at odd minutes, and set her flower-beds with mignonette borders, and her vegetable-garden with salad herbs of new and flourishing kinds. Yet not even the sweet season seemed to hurry the catastrophe that we hope, dearest reader, thy tender eyes have long seen impending. 'No, for this quaint alliance a quainter Cupid waited, — the chubby little fellow with a big head and a little arrow, who waits on youth and loveliness, was not wanted here. Lucinda's God of Love wore a lank, hard-featured, grizzly shape, no less than that of Israel Slater, who marched into the garden one fine June morning, earlier than usual, to find Monsieur in his blouse, hard at work weeding the cauliflower-bed.

"Good mornin', sir! good mornin'!" said Israel, in answer to the Frenchman's greeting. "This is a real slick little garden-spot as ever I see, and a pooty house, and a real clever woman too. I'll be skwitched, ef it a'n't a fust-rate consarn, the hull on 't. Be you ever a-goin' back to France, Mister ? "

" No, my goot friend. I have nobody there. I stay here ; I have friend here : but there, — *oh, non ! je ne reviendrai pas ! ah, jamais ! jamais !*"

" Pa's dead, eh ? or shamming ? Well, I don't understand your lingo ; but ef you 're a-goin' to stay here, I don't see why you don't hitch hosses with Miss Lucindy."

Monsieur Leclerc looked up astonished.

" Horses, my friend ? I have no horse ! "

" Thunder 'n' dry trees ! I did n't say you hed, did I ? But that comes o' usin' what Parson Hyde calls figgurs, I s'pose. I wish 't he 'd use one kind o' figgurin' a leetle more ; he 'd pay me for that wood-sawin'. I did n't mean nothin' about horses. I sot out fur to say, Why don't ye marry Miss Lucindy ? "

" I ? " gasped Monsieur, — " I, the foreign, the poor ? I could not to presume so ! "

" Well, I don't see 's it 's sech drefful presumption. Ef you 're poor, she 's a woman, and real lonesome too ; she ha'n't got nuther chick nor child belongin' to her, and you 're the only man she ever took any kind of a notion to. I guess 't would be jest as much for her good as yourn."

" Hush, good Is-ray-el ! it is good to stop there. She would not to marry after such years of goodness : she is a saint of the blessèd."

" Well, I guess saints sometimes fellerships with sinners ; I 've heerd tell they did ; and ef I was you, I 'd make trial for 't. Nothin' ventur', nothin' have."

Whereupon Israel walked off, whistling. ·

Monsieur Leclerc's soul was perturbed within him by these suggestions ; he pulled up two young cauliflowers and reset their places with pigweeds ; he hoed the nicely-sloped border of the bed flat to the path, and then flung the hoe across the walk, and went off to his daily occupation with a new idea in his head. Nor was it an unpleasant one. The idea of a transition from his squalid and pinching boarding-house to the delicate comfort of Miss Lucinda's *ménage*, the prospect of so kind and good a wife to care for his hitherto dreaded future, — all this was pleasant. I cannot honestly say he was in love with our friend; I must even confess that whatever element of that nature existed between the two was now all on Miss Lucinda's side, little as she knew it. Certain it is, that, when she appeared that day at the dancing-class in a new green calico flowered with purple, and bows on her slippers big enough for a bonnet, it occurred to Monsieur Leclerc, that, if they were married, she would take no more lessons! However, let us not blame him; he was a man, and a poor one; one must not expect too much from men, or from poverty; if they are tolerably good, let us canonize them even, it is so hard for the poor creatures! And to do Monsieur Leclerc justice, he had a very thorough respect and admiration for Miss Lucinda. Years ago, in his stormy youth-time, there had been a pair of soft-fringed eyes that looked into his as none would ever look again, — and they murdered her, those mad wild beasts of Paris, in the chapel where she knelt at her pure prayers, — murdered her because she knelt beside an aristocrat, her best friend, the Duchess of Montmorenci, who had taken the pretty peasant from her own estate to bring her up for her maid. Jean Leclerc had lifted that pale shape from the pavement and buried it himself; what else he buried with it was invisible; but now he recalled the hour with a long, shuddering sigh, and, hiding his face in his hands, said softly, "The violet is dead, — there is no spring for her. I will have now an amaranth, — it is good for the tomb."

Whether Miss Lucinda's winter dress suggested this floral metaphor let us not inquire. Sacred be sentiment, when there is even a shadow of reality about it! — when it becomes a profession, and confounds itself with millinery and shades of mourning, it is — "bosh," as the Turkeys say.

So that very evening Monsieur Leclerc arrayed himself in his best, to give another lesson to Miss Lucinda. But,

somehow or other, the lesson was long in beginning; the
little parlor looked so home-like and so pleasant, with its
bright lamp and gay bunch of roses on the table, that it
was irresistible temptation to lounge and linger. Miss
Lucinda had the volume of Florian in her hands, and was
wondering why he did not begin, when the book was drawn
away, and a hand laid on both of hers.

"Lucinda!" he began, "I give you no lesson to-night.
I have to ask. Dear Mees, will you to marry your poor
slave?"

"O dear!" said Miss Lucinda.

Don't laugh at her, Miss Tender-eyes! You will feel
just so yourself some day, when Alexander Augustus says,
"Will you be mine, loveliest of your sex?" only you won't
feel it half so strongly, for you are young, and love is
Nature to youth, but it is a heavenly surprise to age.

Monsieur Leclerc said nothing. He had a heart after all,
and it was touched now by the deep emotion that flushed
Miss Lucinda's face, and made her tremble so violently, —
but presently he spoke.

"Do not!" said he. "I am wrong. I presume. Forgive the stranger!"

"O dear!" said poor Lucinda again, — "O, you know
it is n't that! but how can you like *me*?"

There, Mademoiselle! there's humility for you! *you* will
never say that to Alexander Augustus!

Monsieur Leclerc soothed this frightened, happy, incredulous little woman into quiet before very long; and if he
really began to feel a true affection for her from the moment
he perceived her humble and entire devotion to him, who
shall blame him? Not I. If we were all heroes, who
would be *valet-de-chambre?* if we were all women, who
would be men? He was very good as far as he went; and
if you expect the chivalries of grace out of Nature, you
"may expect," as old Fuller saith. So it was peacefully
settled that they should be married, with a due amount of
tears and smiles on Lucinda's part, and a great deal of

tender sincerity on Monsieur's. She missed her dancing-lesson next day, and when Monsieur Leclerc came in the evening he found a shade on her happy face.

"O dear!" said she, as he entered.

"O dear!" was Lucinda's favorite aspiration. Had she thought of it as an Anglicizing of "*O Dieu!*" perhaps she would have dropped it; but this time she went on head-long, with a valorous despair, —

"I have thought of something! I'm afraid I can't! Monsieur, are n't you a Romanist?"

"What is that?" said he, surprised.

"A Papist, — a Catholic!"

"Ah!" he returned, sighing, "once I was *bon Catholique*, — once in my gone youth; after then I was nothing but the poor man who bats for his life; now I am of the religion that shelters the stranger and binds up the broken poor."

Monsieur was a diplomatist. This melted Miss Lucinda's orthodoxy right down; she only said, —

"Then you will go to church with me?"

"And to the skies above, I pray," said Monsieur, kissing her knotty hand like a lover.

So in the earliest autumn they were married, Monsieur having previously presented Miss Lucinda with a delicate plaided gray silk for her wedding attire, in which she looked almost young; and old Israel was present at the ceremony, which was briefly performed by Parson Hyde in Miss Manners's parlor. They did not go to Niagara, nor to Newport; but that afternoon Monsieur Leclerc brought a hired rockaway to the door, and took his bride a drive into the country. They stopped beside a pair of bars, where Monsieur hitched his horse, and, taking Lucinda by the hand, led her into Farmer Steele's orchard, to the foot of his biggest apple-tree. There she beheld a little mound, at the head and foot of which stood a daily rose-bush shedding its latest wreaths of bloom, and upon the mound itself was laid a board on which she read, — "Here lie the bones of poor Piggy."

Mrs. Lucinda burst into tears, and Monsieur, picking a bud from the bush, placed it in her hand, and led her tenderly back to the rockaway.

That evening Mrs. Lucinda was telling the affair to old Israel with so much feeling that she did not perceive at all the odd commotion in his face, till, as she repeated the epitaph to him, he burst out with, — " He did n't say what became o' the flesh, did he ? " — and therewith fled through the kitchen-door. For years afterward Israel would entertain a few favored auditors with his opinion of the matter, screaming till the tears rolled down his cheeks, —

" That was the beateree of all the weddin'-towers I ever heerd tell on. Goodness ! it 's enough to make the Wanderin' Jew die o' larfin' ! "

THE DENSLOW PALACE.

T is the privilege of authors and artists to see and to describe; to "see clearly and describe vividly" gives the pass on all state occasions. It is the "cap of darkness" and the *talaria*, and wafts them whither they will. The doors of boudoirs and senate-chambers open quickly, and close after them, — excluding the talentless and staring rabble. I, who am one of the humblest of the seers, — a universal admirer of all things beautiful and great, — from the commonwealths of Plato and Solon, severally, expulsed, as poet without music or politic, and a follower of the great, — I, from my dormitory, or nest, of twelve feet square, can, at an hour's notice, or less, enter palaces, and bear away, unchecked and unquestioned, those *imagines* of Des Cartes which emanate or are thrown off from all forms, — and this, not in imagination, but in the flesh.

Whether it was the "tone of society" which pervaded my "Florentine letters," or my noted description of the boudoir of Egeria Mentale, I could not just now determine; but these, and other humble efforts of mine, made me known in palaces as a painter of beauty and magnificence; and I have been in demand, to do for wealth what wealth cannot do for itself, — namely, make it live a little, or, at least, spread as far, in fame, as the rings of a stone-plash on a great pond.

I enjoy friendships and regards which would satisfy the most fastidious. Are not the Denslows enormously rich?

Is not Dalton a sovereign of elegance? It was I who gave the fame of these qualities to the world, in true colors, not flattered. And *they* know it, and love me. Honoria Denslow is the most beautiful and truly charming woman of society. It was I who first said it; and she is my friend, and loves me. I defy poverty; the wealth of all the senses is mine, without effort. I desire not to be one of those who mingle as principals and sufferers; for they are less causes than effects. As the Florentine in the Inferno saw the souls of unfortunate lovers borne upon a whirlwind, so have I seen all things fair and precious, — outpourings of wealth, — all the talents, — all the offerings of duty and devotion, — angelic graces of person and of soul, — borne and swept violently around on the circular gale. Wealth is only an enlargement of the material boundary, and leaves the spirit free to dash to and fro, and exhaust itself in vain efforts. But I am philosophizing, — oddly enough, — when I should describe.

An exquisite little note from Honoria, sent at the last moment, asking me to be present that evening at a "select" party, which was to open the "new house," — the little palace of the Denslows, — lay beside me on the table. It was within thirty minutes of nine o'clock, the hour I had fixed for going. A howling winter out of doors, a clear fire glowing in my little grate. My arm-chair, a magnificent present from Honoria, shaming the wooden fixtures of the poor room, invited to meditation, and perhaps the composition of some delicate periods. They formed slowly. Time, it is said, devours all things; but imagination, in turn, devours time, — and, indeed, swallowed my half-hour at a gulp. The neighboring church-clock tolled nine. I was belated, and hurried away.

It was a *réunion* of only three hundred invitations, selected by my friend Dalton, the intimate and adviser of Honoria. So happy were their combinations, scarce a dozen were absent or declined.

At eleven, the guests began to assemble. Introductions

15   v

were almost needless. Each person was a recognized member of "society." One half of the number were women, — many of them young, beautiful, accomplished, — heiresses, "charming widows," poetesses of real celebrity, and, rarer still, of good repute, — wives of millionnaires, flashing in satin and diamonds. The men, on their side, were of all professions and arts, and of every grade of celebrity, from senator to merchant, — each distinguished by some personal attribute or talent; and in all was the gift, so rare, of manners and conversation. It was a company of undoubted gentlemen, as truly entitled to respect and admiration as if they stood about a throne. They were the untitled nobility of Nature, wealth, and genius.

As I stood looking, with placid admiration, from a recess, upon a brilliant *tableau* of beautiful women and celebrated men that had accidentally arranged itself before me, Dalton touched my arm.

"I have seen," said he, "aristocratic and republican *réunions* of the purest mode in Paris, the court and the banker's circle of London, *conversazioni* at Rome and Florence. Every face in this room is intelligent, and nearly all either beautiful, remarkable, or commanding. Observe those five women standing with Denslow and Adonaïs, — grandeur, sweetness, grace, form, purity; each has an attribute. It is a rare assemblage of superior human beings. The world cannot surpass it. And, by the by, the rooms are superb."

They were indeed magnificent: two grand suites, on either side a central hall of Gothic structure, in white marble, with light, aërial staircases and gilded balconies. Each suite was a separate miracle: the height, the breadth, the columnal divisions; the wonderful delicacy of the arches, upon which rested ceilings frescoed with incomparable art. In one compartment the arches and caryatides were of black marble; in another, of snowy Parian; in a third, of wood, exquisitely carved, and joined like one piece, as if it were a natural growth; vines rising at the bases of the walls, and spreading under the roof. There was no forced consistency. Forms suitable only for the support of heavy masses of masonry, or for the solemn effects of church interiors, were not here introduced. From straight window-cornices of dark wood, slenderly gilt, but richly carved, fell cataracts of gleaming satin, softened in effect with laces of rare appreciation.

The frescoes and panel-work were a study by themselves, uniting the classic and modern styles in allegorical subjects. The paintings, selected by the taste of Dalton, to over-power the darkness of the rooms by intensity of color, were incorporated with the walls. There were but few mirrors. At the end of each suite, one, of fabulous size, without frame, made to appear, by a cunning arrangement of dark draperies, like a transparent portion of the wall itself, extended the magnificence of the apartments.

Not a flame nor a jet was anywhere visible. Tinted vases, pendent, or resting upon pedestals, distributed har-monies and thoughts of light rather than light itself; and yet all was visible, effulgent. The columns which separated the apartments seemed to be composed of masses of richly-colored flames, compelled, by some ingenious alchemy, to assume the form and office of columns.

In New York, *par excellence* the city of private gorgeous-ness and *petite* magnificence, nothing had yet been seen equal to the rooms of the glorious Denslow Palace. Even Dalton, the most capricious and critical of men, whose nice vision had absorbed the elegancies of European taste, pro-nounced them superb. The upholstery and ornamentation were composed under the direction of celebrated artists. Palmer was consulted on the marbles. Page (at Rome) advised the cartoons for the frescoes, and gave laws for the colors and disposition of the draperies. The paintings, panelled in the walls, were modern, triumphs of the art and genius of the New World.

Until the hour for dancing, prolonged melodies of themes modulated in the happiest moments of the great composers floated in the perfumed air from a company of unseen musicians, while the guests moved through the vast apartments, charmed or exalted by their splendor, or conversed in groups, every voice subdued and intelligent.

At midnight began the modish music of the dance, and groups of beautiful girls moved like the atoms of Chladni on the vibrating crystal, with their partners, to the sound of harps and violins, in pleasing figures or inebriating spirals.

When supper was served, the ivory fronts of a cabinet of gems divided itself in the centre, — the two halves revolving upon silver hinges, — and discovered a hall of great height and dimensions, walled with crimson damask, supporting pictures of all the masters of modern art. The dome-like roof of this hall was of marble variously colored, and the floor tessellated and mosaicked in grotesque and graceful figures of Vesuvian lavas and painted porcelain.

The tables, couches, chairs, and *vis-a-vis* in this hall were of plain pattern and neutral dead colors, not to overpower or fade the pictures on the walls, or the gold and Parian service of the cedar tables.

But the chief beauty of this unequalled supper-room was an immense bronze candelabrum, which rose in the centre from a column of black marble. It was the figure of an Italian elm, slender and of thin foliage, embraced, almost enveloped, in a vine, which reached out and supported itself in hanging from all the branches; the twigs bearing fruit, not of grapes, but of a hundred little spheres of crimson, violet, and golden light, whose combination produced a soft atmosphere of no certain color.

Neither Honoria, Dalton, nor· myself remained long in the gallery. We retired with a select few, and were served in an antechamber, separated from the grand reception-room by an arch, through which, by putting aside a silk curtain, Honoria could see, at a distance, any that entered, as they passed in from the hall.

My own position was such that I could look over her

shoulder and see as she saw. *Vis-a-vis* with her, and consequently with myself, was Adonaïs, a celebrated author,
and person of the *beau monde*. On his left, Dalton, always
mysteriously elegant and dangerously witty. Denslow and
Jeffrey Lethal, the critic, completed our circle. The conversation was easy, animated, personal.

"You are fortunate in having a woman of taste to
manage your entertainments," said Lethal, in answer to a
remark of Denslow's, — "but in bringing these people together she has made a sad blunder."

"And what may that be ?" inquired Dalton, mildly.

"Your guests are too well behaved, too fine, and on their
guard; there are no butts, no palpable fools or vulgarians,
and, worse, there are many distinguished, but no one great
man, — no social or intellectual sovereign of the occasion."

Honoria looked inquiringly at Lethal. "Pray, Mr. Lethal,
tell me who he is? I thought there was no such person in
America," she added, with a look of reproachful inquiry at
Dalton and myself, as if we should have found this sovereign and suggested him.

"You are right, my dear queen; Lethal is joking," responded Dalton; "we are a democracy, and have only a
queen of —"

"Water ices," interrupted Lethal; "but, as for the king
you seek, as democracies finally come to that —"

"Good Heavens !" exclaimed Honoria, raising the curtain, "it must be he that is coming in."

Honoria frowned slightly, rose, and advanced to meet a
new-comer, who had entered unannounced, and was advanc-
ing alone. Dalton followed to support her. I observed
their movements, — Lethal and Adonaïs using my face as a
mirror of what was passing beyond the curtain.

The masses of level light from the columns on the left
seemed to envelop the stranger, who came toward us from
the entrance, as if he had divined the presence of Honoria
in the alcove.

He was about the middle height, Napoleonic in form and

bearing, with features of marble paleness, firm, and sharply
defined.   His hair and magnificent Asiatic beard were jetty
black, curling, and naturally disposed.   Under his dark and
solid brows gleamed large eyes of abysmal blackness and
intensity.

"Is it Lord N——?" whispered Lethal, moved from his
habitual coldness by the astonishment which he read in my
face.

"Senator D——, perhaps," suggested Denslow, whose
ideas, like his person, aspired to the senatorial.

"Dumas," hinted Adonaïs, an admirer of French literature. "I heard he was expected."

"No," I answered, "but certainly in appearance the most
noticeable man living.   Let us go out and be introduced."

"Perhaps," said Lethal, "it is the d——."

All rose instantly at the idea, and we went forward, urged
by irresistible curiosity.

As we drew near the stranger, who was conversing with
Honoria and Dalton, a shudder went through me.   It was
a thrill of the universal Boswell; I seemed to feel the
presence of "the most aristocratic man of the age."

Honoria introduced me.   "My Lord Duke, allow me to
present my friend, Mr. De Vere; Mr. De Vere, the Duke
of Rosecouleur."

Was I, then, face to face with, nay, touching the hand of
a highness, — and that highness the monarch of the *ton?*
And is this a ducal hand, white as the albescent down of
the eider-duck, which presses mine with a tender touch, so
haughty and so delicately graduated to my standing as
"friend" of the exquisite Honoria?   It was too much; I
could have wept; my senses rather failed.

Dalton fell short of himself; for, though his head stooped
to none, unless conventionally, the sudden and unaccount-
able presence of the Duke of Rosecouleur annoyed and
perplexed him.   His own sovereignty was threatened.

Lethal stiffened himself to the ordeal of an introduction;
the affair seemed to exasperate him.   Denslow alone, of

the men, was in his element. Pompous and soft, he "cot-
toned" to the grandeur with the instinct of a born satellite,
and his eyes grew brighter, his body more shining and
rotund, his back more concave. His *bon-vivant* tones, jolly
and conventional, sounded a pure barytone to the clear
soprano of Honoria, in the harmony of an obsequious welcome.

The Duke of Rosecouleur glanced around him approv-
ingly upon the apartments. I believed that he had never
seen anything more beautiful than the *petite* palace of
Honoria, or more ravishing than herself. He said little,
in a low voice, and always to one person at a time. His
answers and remarks were simple and well-turned.

Dalton allowed the others to move on, and by a slight
sign drew me to him.

"It is unexpected," he said, in a thoughtful manner, looking me full in the eyes.

"You knew the Duke of Rosecouleur in Europe?"

"At Paris, yes, — and in Italy he was a travel friend;
but we heard lately that he had retired upon his estates in
England; and certainly, he is the last person we looked for
here."

"Unannounced."

"That is a part of the singularity."

"His name was not in the published list of arrivals; but
he may have left England incognito. Is a mistake possible?"

"No! there is but one such man in Europe; — a hand-
somer or a richer does not live."

"An eye of wonderful depth."

"Hands exquisite."

"Feet, ditto."

"And his dress and manner."

"Unapproachable!"

"Not a shadow of pretence; — the essence of good-
breeding founded upon extensive knowledge, and a thorough
sense of position and its advantages; — in fact, the Napoleon of the parlor."

" But, Dalton," said I, nervously, " no one attends him."

" No, — I thought so at first ; but do you see that Me-phistophelean figure, in black, who follows the Duke a few paces behind, and is introduced to no one ? "

" Yes. A singular creature, truly ! — how thin he is ! "

" That shadow that follows his Highness is, in fact, the famous valet, Rêve de Noir, — the prince of servants. The Duke goes nowhere without this man as a shadow. He asserts that Rêve de Noir has no soul ; and I believe him. The face is that of a demon. It is a separate creation, equally wonderful with the master, but not human. He was condensed out of the atmosphere of the great world."

As we' were speaking, we observed a crowd of distin-guished persons gathered about and following his Highness, as he moved. He spoke now to one, now to another. Honoria, fascinated, her beauty every instant becoming more radiant, just leaned, with the lightest pressure, upon the Duke's arm. They were promenading through the rooms. The music, soft and low, continued, but the groups of dancers broke up, the loiterers in the gallery came in, and as the sun draws his fifty, perhaps his hundreds .of planets, circling around and near him, this noble luminary centred in himself the attention of all. If they could not speak with him, they could at least speak of him. If they could not touch his hand, they could pass before him and give one glance at his eyes. The less aristocratic were even satisfied for the moment with watching the singular being, Rêve de Noir, — who caught no one's eye, seemed to see no one but his master, — and yet was not here nor there, nor in any place, — never in the way, a thing of air, and not tangible, but only black.

At a signal, he would advance and present to his master a perfume, a laced handkerchief, a rose of rubies, a diamond clasp ; of many with whom he spoke the liberal Duke begged the acceptance of some little token, as an earnest of his esteem. After interchanging a few words with Jeffrey Lethal, — who dared not utter a sarcasm, though he chafed visibly under the restraint, — the Duke's tasteful generosity suggested a seal ring, with an intaglio head of Swift cut in opal, the mineral emblem of wit, which dulls in the sunlight of fortune, and recovers its fiery points in the shade of adversity; — Rêve de Noir, with a movement so slight, 't was like the flitting of a bat, placed the seal in the hand of the Duke, who, with a charming and irresistible grace, compelled Lethal to receive it.

To Denslow, Honoria, Dalton, and myself he offered nothing. Strange ? — Not at all. Was he not the guest, and had not I been presented to him by Honoria as her "friend ?" — a word of pregnant meaning to a Duke of Rosecouleur !

To Adonaïs he gave *a lock of hair* of the great novelist, Dumas, in a locket of yellow tourmaline, — a stone usually black. Lethal smiled at this. He felt relieved. " The Duke," thought he, " must be a humorist."

From my coarse way of describing this, you would suppose that it was a farcical exhibition of vulgar extravagance, and the Duke a madman or an impostor ; but the effect was different. It was done with grace, and, in the midst of so much else, it attracted only that side regard, at intervals, which is sure to surprise and excite awe.

Honoria had almost ceased to converse with us. It was painful to her to talk with any person. She followed the Duke with her eyes. When, by some delicate allusion or attention, he let her perceive that she was in his thoughts, a mantling color overspread her features, and then gave way to paleness, and a manner which attracted universal remark. It was then Honoria abdicated that throne of conventional purity which hitherto she had held undisputed. Women who were plain in her presence outshone Honoria, by meeting this ducal apparition, that called itself Rosecouleur, — and which might have been, for aught they knew, a fume of the Infernal, shaped to deceive us all, — with calm and haughty propriety.

The sensation did not subside. The music of the waltz

15 *

invited a renewal of that intoxicating whirl which isolates friends and lovers, in whispering and sighing pairs, in the midst of a great assemblage. All the world looked on, when Honoria Denslow placed her hand upon the shoulder of the Duke of Rosecouleur, and the noble and beautiful forms began silently and smoothly turning, with a dream-like motion. Soon she lifted her lovely eyes and steadied their rays upon his. She leaned wholly upon his arm, and the gloved hands completed the magnetic circle. At the close of the first waltz, she rested a moment, leaning upon his shoulder, and his hand still held hers, — a liberty often assumed and permitted, but not to the nobles and the monarchs of society. She fell farther, and her ideal beauty faded into a sensuous.

Honoria was lost. Dalton saw it. We retired together to a room apart. He was dispirited; called for and drank rapidly a bottle of Champagne; — it was insufficient.

"De Vere," said he, "affairs go badly."

"Explain."

"This cursed thing that people call a duke — it kills me."

"I saw."

"Of course you did; — the world saw; the servants saw. Honoria has fallen to-night. I shall transfer my allegiance."

"And Denslow?"

"A born sycophant; — he thinks it natural that his wife should love a duke, and a duke love his wife."

"So would you, if you were any other than you are."

"Faugh! it is human nature."

"Not so; would you not as soon strangle this Rosecouleur for making love to your wife in public, as you would another man?"

"Rather."

"Pooh! I give you up. If you had simply said, 'Yes,' it would have satisfied me."

Dalton seemed perplexed. He called a servant and sent

him with an order for Nalson, the usher, to come instantly
to him.

Nalson appeared with his white gloves and mahogany
face.

"Nalson, you were a servant of the Duke in England?"

"Yes, sir."

"Is the person now in the rooms the Duke of Rosecouleur?"

"I have not seen him, sir."

"Go immediately, study the man well, — do you hear? —
and come to me. Let no one know your purpose."

Nalson disappeared.

I was alarmed. If "the Duke" should prove to be an
impostor, we were indeed ruined.

In five minutes, — an hour, it seemed, — Nalson stood
before us.

"Is it he?" said Dalton, looking fixedly upon the face of
the usher.

No reply.

"Speak the truth; you need not be afraid."

"I cannot tell, sir."

"Nonsense! go and look again."

"It is of no use, Mr. Dalton; you, who are as well acquainted with the personal appearance of his Highness as
I am, you have been deceived, — if I have."

"Nalson, do you believe that this person is an impostor?"
said Dalton pointing at myself.

"Who? Mr. De Vere, sir?"

"If, then, you know at sight that this gentleman is my
friend Mr. De Vere, why do you hesitate about the other?"

"But the imitation is perfect. And there is Rêve de
Noir."

"Yes, did Rêve de Noir recognize you?"

"I have not caught his eye. You know, sir, that this
Rêve is not, and never was like other men; he is a devil.
One knows, and one does not know him."

"Were you at the door when the Duke entered?"

"I think not; at least—I cannot tell. When I first saw him, he was in the room, speaking with Madam Denslow."

"Nalson, you have done wrong; no one should have entered unannounced. Send the doorkeeper to me."

The doorkeeper came; a gigantic negro, magnificently attired.

"Jupiter, you were at the door when the Duke of Rosecouleur entered?"

"Yes, sir."

"Did the Duke and his man come in a carriage?"

"Yes, sir,—a hack."

"You may go. They are not devils," said Dalton musingly, "or they would not have come in a carriage."

"You seem to have studied the spiritual mode of locomotion," said I.

Dalton frowned. "This is serious, De Vere."

"What mean you?"

"I mean that Denslow is a bankrupt."

"Explain yourself."

"You know what an influence he carries in political circles. The G——rs, the S——es, and their kind, have more talent, but Denslow enjoys the secret of popularity."

"Well, I know it."

"In the middle counties, where he owns vast estates, and has been liberal to debtors and tenants, he carries great favor; both parties respect him for his ignorance and pomposity, which they mistake for simplicity and power, as usual. The estates are mortgaged three deep, and will not hold out a year. The shares of the Millionnaire's Hotel and the Poor Man's Bank in the B——y are worthless. Denslow's railroad schemes have absorbed the capital of those concerns."

"But he had three millions."

"Nominally. This palace has actually sunk his income."

" Madness ! "

" Wisdom, if you will listen.'

" I am all attention."

" The use of money is to create and hold power. Denslow was certain of the popular and county votes; he
needed only the aristocratic support, and the A——people
would have made him Senator."

" Fool, why was he not satisfied with his money ? "

" Do you call the farmer fool, because he is not satisfied
with the soil, but wishes to grow wheat thereon ? Money
is the soil of power. For much less than a million one may
gratify the senses ; great fortunes are not for sensual luxuries, but for those of the soul. To the facts, then. The
advent of this mysterious duke, — whom I doubt, — hailed
by Denslow and Honoria as a piece of wonderful good-fortune, has already shaken him and ruined the *prestige* of his
wife. They are mad and blind."

" Tell me, in plain prose, the *how* and the *why.*"

" De Vere, you are dull. There are three hundred people in the rooms of the Denslow Palace; these people
are the 'aristocracy.' They control the sentiments of the
' better class.' Opinion, like dress, descends from them.
They no longer respect Denslow, and their women have
seen the weakness of Honoria."

" Yes, but Denslow still has ' the people.' "

" That is not enough. I have calculated the chances, and
mustered all our available force. We shall have no support
among the ' better class ' since we are disgraced with the
' millionnaires.' "

At this moment Denslow came in.

" Ah ! Dalton, — like you ! I have been looking for you
to show the pictures. Devil a thing I know about them.
The Duke wondered at your absence."

" Where is Honoria ? "

" Ill, ill, — fainted. The house is new; smell of new
wood and mortar; deused disagreeable in Honoria. If it
had not been for the Duke, she would have fallen. That's

a monstrous clever fellow, that Rosecouleur. Admires Honoria vastly. Come, — the pictures."

"Mr. John Vanbrugen Denslow, you are an ass ! "

The large, smooth, florid millionnaire, dreaming only of senatorial honors, the shouts of the multitude, and the adoration of a party press, cowered like a dog under the lash of the " man of society."

"Rather rough, — ha, De Vere ? What have *I* done ? Am I an ass because I know nothing of pictures ? Come, Dalton, you are harsh with your old friend."

"Denslow, I have told you a thousand times never to concede position."

"Yes, but this is a duke, man, — a prince ! "

" This from you ? By Jove, De Vere, I wish you and I could live a hundred years, to see a republican aristocrat. We are still mere provincials," added Dalton, with a sigh.

Denslow perspired with mortification.

"You use me badly, — I tell you, Dalton, this Rosecouleur is a devil. Condescend to him ! be haughty and — what do you call it ? — urbane to him ! I defy *you* to do it, with all your impudence. Why, his valet, that shadow that glides after him, is too much for me. Try him yourself, man."

"Who, the valet ? "

" No, the master, — though I might have said the valet."

" Did I yield in Paris ? "

" No, but you were of the embassy, and — and — *no one really knew us*, you know."

Dalton pressed his lips hard together.

"Come," said he, " De Vere, let us try a fall with this Titan of the carpet."

Denslow hastened back to the Duke. I followed Dalton; but as for me, bah ! I am a cipher.

The room in which we were adjoined Honoria's boudoir, from which a secret passage led down by a spiral to a panel behind hangings ; raising these, one could enter the drawing-room unobserved. Dalton paused midway in the secret passage, and through a loop or narrow window, concealed by architectural ornaments, and which overlooked the great drawing-rooms, made a *reconnoissance* of the field.

Nights of Venice ! what a scene was there ! The vine-branch chandeliers, crystal-fruited, which depended from the slender ribs of the ceiling, cast a rosy dawn of light, deepening the green and crimson of draperies and carpets, making an air like sunrise in the bowers of a forest. Form and order were everywhere visible, though unobtrusive. Arch beyond arch, to fourth apartments, lessening in dimension, with increase of wealth ; — groups of beautiful women, on either hand, seated or half reclined ; the pure or rich hues of their robes blending imperceptibly, or in gorgeous contrasts, with the soft outlines and colors of their supports ; a banquet for the eyes and the mind ; the perfect work of art and culture ; — gliding about and among these, or, with others, springing and revolving in that monarch of all measures, which blends luxury and purity, until it is either the one or the other, moved the men.

"That is my work," exclaimed Dalton, unconsciously.

"Not *all*, I think."

"I mean the combinations, — the effect. But see ! Honoria will again accept the Duke's invitation. He is coming to her. Let us prevent it."

He slipped away ; and I, remaining at my post of observation, saw him, an instant later, passing quickly across the floor among the dancers, toward Honoria. The Duke of Rosecouleur arrived at the same instant before her. She smiled sorrowfully upon Dalton, and held out her hand in a languid manner toward the Duke, and again they floated away upon the eddies of the music. I followed them with eyes fixed in admiration. It was a vision of the orgies of Olympus, — Zeus and Aphrodite circling to a theme of Chronos.

Had Honoria tasted of the Indian drug, the weed of paradise ? Her eyes, fixed upon the Duke's, shone like molten sapphires. A tress of chestnut hair, escaping from the diamond coronet, sprang lovingly forward and twined itself

over her white shoulder and still fairer bosom. Tints like
flitting clouds, Titianic, the mystery and despair of art, disclosed to the intelligent eye the feeling that mastered her
spirit and her sense. Admirable beauty ! Unrivalled, unhappy ! The Phidian idol of gold and ivory, into which
a demon had entered, overthrown, and the worshippers
gazing on it with a scorn unmixed with pity !

The sullen animal rage of battle is nothing to the livor,
the burning hatred of the drawing-room. Dalton, defeated,
cast a glance of deadly hostility on the Duke. Nor was it
lost. While the waltz continued, for ten minutes, he stood
motionless. Fearing some untoward event, I came down
and took my place near him.

The Duke led Honoria to a sofa. But for his arm she
would again have fallen. Dalton had recovered his courage
and natural haughtiness. The tone of his voice, rich, tender, and delicately expressive, did not change.

" Honoria, you sent for *me;* and the Duke wishes to see
the pictures. The air of the gallery will relieve your faintness."

He offered his arm, which she, rising mechanically, accepted. A deep blush crimsoned her features, at the allusion to her weakness. Several of the guests moved after
us, as we passed into the gallery. The Duke's shadow,
Rêve de Noir, following last, closed the ivory doors. We
passed through the gallery,— where pyramids of sunny
fruits, in baskets of fine porcelain, stood relieved by gold
and silver services for wine and coffee, disposed on the
tables, — and thence entered another and smaller room,
devoid of ornament, but the crimson tapestried walls were
covered with works or copies of the great masters of Italy.

Opposite the entrance there was a picture of a woman
seated on a throne, behind which stood a demon whispering
in her ear, and pointing to a handsome youth in the circle
of the courtiers. The design and color were in the style
of Correggio. Denslow stood close behind me. In advance were Honoria, Dalton, and the Duke, whose conver-

sation was adressed alternately to her and Dalton. The lights of the gallery burst forth in their full refulgence as we approached the picture.

The glorious harmony of its colors, — the force of the shadows, which seemed to be converging in the rays of a single unseen source of light, — the unity of sentiment, which drew all the groups together, in the idea ; — I had seen all this before, but with the eyes of supercilious criticism. Now the picture smote us with awe.

"I have the original of this excellent work," said the Duke, "in my house at A——, but your copy is nearly as good."

The remark, intended for Honoria, reached the pride of her companion, who blandly replied, —

"Your Highness's exquisite judgment is for once at fault. The piece is original. It was purchased from a well-known collection in Italy, where there are none others of the school."

Honoria was gazing upon the picture, as I was, in silent astonishment.

"If this," said she, "is a copy, what must have been the genuine work? Did you never before notice the likeness between the queen, in that picture, and myself?" she asked, addressing Dalton.

The remark excited general attention. Every one murmured, "The likeness is perfect."

"And the demon behind the queen," said Denslow, insipidly, "resembles your Highness's valet."

There was another exclamation. No sooner was it observed, than the likeness to Rêve de Noir seemed to be even more perfect.

The Duke made a sign.

Rêve de Noir placed himself near the canvas. His profile was the counterpart of that in the painting. He seemed to have stepped out of it.

"It was I," said the Duke, in a gentle voice, and with a smile which just disclosed the ivory line under the black

W

moustache, "who caused this picture to be copied and altered. The beauty of the Hon. Mrs. Denslow, whom it was my highest pleasure to know, seemed to me to surpass that of the queen of my original. I first, with great secrecy, unknown to your wife," continued the Duke, turning to Denslow, "procured a portrait from the life by memory, which was afterwards transferred to this canvas. The resemblance to my attendant is, I confess, remarkable and inexplicable."

"But will you tell us by what accident this copy happened to be in Italy ?" asked Dalton.

"You will remember," replied the Duke, coldly, "that at Paris, noticing your expressions of admiration for the picture, which you had seen in my English gallery, I gave you a history of its purchase at Bologna by myself. I sent my artist to Bologna, with orders to place the copy in the gallery and to introduce the portrait of the lady; it was a freak of fancy; I meant it for a surprise; as I felt sure, that, if you saw the picture, you would secure it."

"It seems to me," replied Dalton, "that the *onus* of proof rests with your Highness."

The Duke made a signal to Rêve de Noir, who again stepped up to the canvas, and, with a short knife or stiletto, removed a small portion of the outer layer of paint, disclosing a very ancient ground of some other and inferior work, over which the copy seemed to have been painted. The proof was unanswerable.

"Good copies," remarked the Duke, "are often better than originals."

He offered his arm to Honoria, and they walked through the gallery, — he entertaining her, and those near him, with comments upon other works. The crowd followed them, as they moved on or returned, as a cloud of gnats follow up and down, and to and fro, a branch tossing in the wind.

"Beaten at every point," I said, mentally, looking on the pale features of the defeated Dalton.

"Yes," he replied, seeing the remark in my face; "but

there is yet time. ˙ I am satisfied this is the man with whom we travelled; none other could have devised such a plan, or carried it out. He must have fallen in love with Honoria at that time; and simply to see her is the object of his visit to America. He is a connoisseur in pictures as in women; but he must not be allowed to ruin us by his arrogant assumptions."

"Excepting his manner and extraordinary personal advantages, I find nothing in him to awe or astonish."

"His wealth is incalculable; he is used to victories; and that manner which you affect to slight, — that is everything. 'T is power, success, victory. This man· of millions, this prince, does not talk; he has but little use for words. It is manner, and not words, that achieves social and amatory conquests."

"Bah! You are like the politicians, who mistake accidents for principles. But even you are talking, while this pernicious foreigner is acting. See! they have left the gallery, and the crowd of fools is following them. You cannot stem such a tide of folly."

"I deny that they are fools. Why does that sallow wretch, Lethal, follow them? or that enamelled person, Adonaïs? They are at a serpent-charming, and Honoria is the bird-of-paradise. They watch with delight, and sketch as they observe, the struggles of the poor bird. The others are indifferent or curious, envious or amused. It is only Denslow who is capped and antlered, and the shafts aimed at his foolish brow glance and wound us.

We were left alone in the gallery. Dalton paced back and forth, in his slow, erect, and graceful manner; there was no hurry or agitation.

"How quickly," said he, as his moist eyes met mine, " how like a dream, this glorious vision, this beautiful work, will fade and be forgotten! Nevertheless, I made it," he added, musingly. "It was I who moulded and expanded the sluggish millions."

"You will still be what you are, Dalton, — an artist, more

than a man of society. You work with a soft and perishable material."

"A distinction without a difference. Every *man* is a politician, but only every artist is a gentleman."

"Denslow, then, is ruined."

"Yes and no ; — there is nothing in him to ruin. It is I who am the sufferer."

"And Honoria ?"

"It was I who formed her manners, and guided her perceptions of the beautiful. It was I who married her to a mass of money, De Vere."

"Did you never love Honoria ?'

He laughed.

"Loved ? Yes ; as Praxiteles may have loved the clay he moulded, — for its smoothness and ductility under the hand."

"The day has not come for such men as you, Dalton.'

"Come, and gone, and coming. It has come in dreamland. Let us follow your fools."

The larger gallery was crowded. The pyramids of glowing fruit had disappeared ; there was a confused murmur of pairs and parties, chatting and taking wine. The master of the house, his wife, and guest were nowhere to be seen. Lethal and Adonaïs stood apart, conversing. As we approached them unobserved, Dalton checked me. "Hear what these people are saying," said he.

"My opinion is," said Lethal, holding out his crooked forefinger like a claw, "that this *soi-disant* duke — what the deuse is his name ?"

"Rosecouleur," interposed Adonaïs, in a tone of society.

"Right, — Couleur de Rose is an impostor, — an impostor, a sharper. Everything tends that way. What an utter sell it would be !"

"You were with us at the picture scene ?" murmured Adonaïs.

"Yes. Dalton looked wretchedly cut up, when that devil of a valet, who must be an accomplice, scraped the new paint

The picture must have been got up in New York by

off. The picture must have been got up in New York by Dalton and the Denslows."

"Perhaps the Duke, too, was got up in New York, on the same principle," suggested Adonaïs. "Such things are possible. Society is intrinsically rotten, you know, and Dalton — "

"Is a fellow of considerable talent," sneered Lethal, — "but has enemies, who may have planned a duke."

Adonaïs coughed in his cravat, and hinted, — "How would it do to call him 'Barnum Dalton'?"

Adonaïs appeared shocked at himself, and swallowed a minim of wine to cleanse his vocal apparatus from the stain of so coarse an illustration.

"Do you hear those creatures?" whispered Dalton. "They are arranging scandalous paragraphs for the 'Illustration.'"

A moment after, he was gone. I spoke to Lethal and Adonaïs.

"Gentlemen, you are in error about the picture and the Duke; they are as they now appear: the one, an excellent copy, purchased as an original, — no uncommon mistake; the other, a genuine highness. How does he strike you?"

Lethal cast his eyes around to see who listened.

"The person," said he, "who is announced here to-night as an English duke seemed to me, of all men I could select, least like one."

"Pray, what is your ideal of an English duke, Mr. Lethal?" asked Adonaïs, with the air of a connoisseur, sure of himself, but hating to offend.

"A plain, solid person, well dressed, but simple; mutton-chop whiskers; and the manners of a — a — "

"Bear!" said a soft female voice.

"Precisely, — the manners of a bear; a kind of gentlemanly bear, perhaps, — but still, ursine and heavy; while this person, who seems to have walked out of —— or a novel, affects me, by his ways and appearance, like a — a — h'm — "

"Gambler!" said the same female voice, in a conclusive tone.

There was a general soft laugh. Everybody was pleased. All admired, hated, and envied the Duke. It was settled beyond a doubt that he was an impostor, — and that the Denslows were either grossly taken in, or were "selling" their friends. In either case, it was shocking and delightful.

"The fun of the thing," continued Lethal, raising his voice a little, "is, that the painter who got up the old picture must have been as much an admirer of the Hon. Mrs. Denslow as — his — Highness ; for, in touching in the queen, he has unconsciously made it a portrait."

The blow was final. I moved away, grieved and mortified to the soul, cursing the intrusion of the mysterious personage whose insolent superiority had overthrown the hopes of my friends.

At the door of the gallery I met G——, the painter, just returned from London. I drew him with me into the inner gallery, to make a thorough examination of the picture. I called his attention to the wonderful resemblance of the queen to Honoria. He did not see it; we looked together, and I began to think that it might have been a delusion. I told the Duke's story of the picture to G——. He examined the canvas, tested the layers of color, and pronounced the work genuine and of immense value. We looked again and again at the queen's head, viewing it in every light. The resemblance to Honoria had disappeared ; nor was the demon any longer a figure of the Duke's valet.

"One would think," said G——, laughing, "that you had been mesmerized. If you had been so deceived in a picture, may you not be equally cheated in a man? I am loath to offend ; but, indeed, the person whom you call Rosecouleur cannot be the Duke of that title, whom I saw in England. I had leave to copy a picture in his gallery. He was often present. His manners were mild and unassuming, — not at all like those of this man, to whom, I acknowledge, the personal resemblance is surprising. I am afraid our good friends, the Denslows, and Mr. Dalton, — whom I esteem for their patronage of art, — have been taken in by an adventurer."

"But the valet, Rêve de Noir ?"

"The Duke had a valet of that name who attended him, and who may, for aught I know, have resembled this one ; but probability is against concurrent resemblances. There is also an original of the picture in the Duke's gallery ; in fact, the artist, as was not unusual in those days, painted two pictures of the same subject. Both, then, are genuine."

Returning my cordial thanks to the good painter for his timely explanation, I hastened to find Dalton. Drawing him from the midst of a group whom he was entertaining, I communicated G——'s account of the two pictures, and his suspicions in regard to the Duke.

His perplexity was great. "Worse and worse, De Vere ! To be ruined by a common adventurer is more disgraceful even than the other misfortune. Besides, our guests are leaving us. At least a hundred of them have gone away with the first impression, and the whole city will have it. The journal reporters have been here. Denslow's principal creditors were among the guests to-night ; they went away soon, just after the affair with the picture ; to-morrow will be our dark day. If it had not been for this demon of a duke and his familiar, whoever they are, all would have gone well. Now we are distrusted, and they will crush us. Let us fall facing the enemy. Within an hour I will have the truth about the Duke. Did I ever tell you what a price Denslow paid for that picture ?"

"No, I do not wish to hear."

"You are right. Come with me."

The novel disrespect excited by the scandal of Honoria and the picture seemed to have inspired the two hundred people who remained with a cheerful ease. Eating, drinking excessively of Denslow's costly wines, dancing to music which grew livelier and more boisterous as the musicians, imbibed more of the inspiriting juice, and, catching scraps of the scandal, threw out significant airs, the company of young persons, deserted by their scandalized seniors, had converted the magnificent suite of drawing-rooms into a carnival theatre. Parties of three and four were junketing in corners; laughing servants rushed to and fro as in a *café;* the lounges were occupied by reclining beauties or languid fops overpowered with wine, about whom lovely young women, flushed with champagne and mischief, were coquetting and frolicking.

"I warrant you, these people know it is our last night," said Dalton; "and see what a use they make of us! Denlow's rich wines poured away like water; everything soiled, smeared, and overturned; our entertainment, at first stately and gracious as a queen's drawing-room, ending with the loss of *prestige*, in the riot of a *bal masqué.* So fades ambition! But to this duke."

Denslow, who had passed into the polite stage of inebriation, evident to close observers, had arranged a little exclusive circle, which included three women of fashionable reputation, his wife, the Duke, Jeffrey Lethal, and Adonaïs. Rêve de Noir officiated as attendant. The *fauteuils* and couches were disposed around a pearl table, on which were liquors, coffee, wines, and a few delicacies for Honoria, who had not supped. They were in the purple recess adjoining the third drawing-room. Adonaïs talked· with the Duke about Italy; Lethal criticised; while Honoria, in the full splendor of her beauty, outshining and overpowering, dropped here and there a few musical words, like servicenotes, to harmonize.

There is no beauty like the newly-enamored. Dalton seemed to forget himself, as he contemplated her, for a moment. Spaces had been left for us; the valet placed chairs.

"Dalton," cried Lethal, "you are in time to decide a question of deep interest; — your friend, De Vere, will assist you. His Highness has given preference to the women of America over those of Italy. Adonaïs, the exquisite and mild, settles his neck-tie against the Duke, and objects in that bland but firm manner which is his. I am the Duke's bottle-holder; Denslow and wife accept that function for the chivalrous Adonaïs."

"I am of the Duke's party," replied Dalton, in his most agreeable manner. "To be in the daily converse and view of the most beautiful women in America, as I have been for years, is a privilege in the cultivation of a pure taste. I saw nothing in Italy, except on canvas, comparable with what I see at this moment. The Duke is right; but in commending his judgment, I attribute to him also sagacity. Beauty is like language; its use is to conceal. One may, under rose-colored commendations, a fine manner, and a flowing style, conceal, as Nature does with personal advantages in men, the gross tastes and vulgar cunning of a charlatan."

Dalton, in saying this, with a manner free from suspicion or excitement, fixed his eyes upon the Duke's.

"You seem to have no faith in either men or women," responded the rich barytone voice of his Highness, the dark upper lip disclosing, as before, the row of square, sharp, ivory teeth.

"Little, very little," responded Dalton, with a sigh. "Your Highness will understand me, — or if not now, presently."

Lethal trod upon Adonaïs's foot; I saw him do it. Adonaïs exchanged glances with a brilliant hawk-faced lady who sat opposite. The lady smiled and touched her companion. Honoria, who saw everything, opened her magnificent eyes to their full extent. Denslow was oblivious.

"In fact," continued Dalton, perceiving the electric flash he had excited, "scepticism is a disease of my intellect. Perhaps the most noticeable and palpable fact of the moment is the presence and identity of the Duke who is opposite to me; and yet, doubting as I sometimes do my own existence, is it not natural, that, philosophically speak-

16

ing, the presence and identity of your Highness are at moments a subject of philosophical doubt?"

"In cases of this kind," replied the Duke, "we rest upon circumstantial evidence."

So saying, he drew from his finger a ring and handed it to Dalton, who went to the light and examined it closely, and passed it to me. It was a minute cameo, no larger than a grain of wheat, in a ring of plain gold; a rare and beautiful work of microscopic art.

"I seem to remember presenting the Duke of Rosecouleur with a similar ring, in Italy," said Dalton, resuming his seat; "but the coincidence does not resolve my philosophic doubt, excited by the affair of the picture. We all supposed that we saw a portrait of the Hon. Mrs. Denslow in yon picture; and we seemed to discover, under the management of your valet, that Denslow's picture, a genuine duplicate of the original by the author, was a modern copy. Since your Highness quitted the gallery, those delusions have ceased. The picture appears now to be genuine. The likeness to Mrs. Denslow has vanished."

An exclamation of surprise from all present, except the Duke, followed this announcement.

"And so," continued Dalton, "it may be with this ring, which now seems to be the one I gave the Duke at Rome, but to-morrow may be different."

As he spoke, Dalton gave back the ring to the Duke, who received it with his usual grace.

"Who knows," said Lethal, with a deceptive innocence of manner, "whether aristocracy itself be not founded in mesmerical deceptions?"

"I think, Lethal," observed Adonaïs, "you push the matter. It would be impossible, for instance, even for his Highness, to make Honoria Denslow appear ugly."

We all looked at Honoria, to whom the Duke leaned over and said, —

"Would you be willing for a moment to lose that exquisite beauty?"

" For my sake, Honoria," said Dalton " refuse him.'

The request, so simply made, was rewarded by a ravisning smile.

"Edward, do you know that you have not spoken a kind word to me to-night, until now ? "

Their eyes met, and I saw that Dalton trembled with a deep emotion. " I will save you yet," he murmured.

A tall, black hound, of the slender breed, rose up near Honoria, and placing his fore-paws upon the edge of the pearl table, turned and licked her face and eyes.

It was the vision of a moment. The dog sprang upon the sofa by the Duke's side, growling and snapping.

" Rêve de Noir," cried Lethal and Adonaïs, "drive the dog away ! "

The valet had disappeared.

"I have no fear of him, gentlemen," said the Duke, patting the head of the hound ; "he is a faithful servant, and has a faculty of reading thoughts. Go bring my servant, Demon," said the Duke.

The hound sprang away with a great bound, and in an instant Rêve de Noir was standing behind us. The dog did not appear again.

Honoria looked bewildered. "Of, what dog were you speaking, Edward ? "

" The hound that licked your face.'

" You are joking. I saw no hound."

"See, gentlemen," exclaimed Lethal, "his Highness shows us tricks. He is a wizard."

The three women gave little shrieks, — half pleasure, half terror.

Denslow, who had fallen back in his chair asleep, awoke and rubbed his eyes.

"What is all this, Honoria ? "

" That his Highness is a wizard," she said, with a forced laugh, glancing at Dalton.

" Will his Highness do us the honor to lay aside the mask,

and appear in his true colors?" said Dalton, returning Honória's glance with an encouraging look.

"Gentlemen," said the Duke, haughtily, "I am your guest, and by hospitality protected from insult."

"Insult, most noble Duke!" exclaimed Lethal, with a sneer,—"impossible, under the roof of our friend, the Honorable Walter Denslow, in the small hours of the night, and in the presence of the finest women in the world. Dalton, pray, reassure his Highness!"

"Edward! Edward!" murmured Honoria, "have a care,—even if it be as you think."

Dalton remained bland and collected.

"Pardon, my Lord, the effect of a little wine, and of those wonderful fantasies you have shown us. Your dog, your servant, and yourself interest us equally; the picture, the ring,—all are wonderful. In supposing that you had assumed a mask, and one so noble, I was led into an error by these miracles, expecting no less than a translation of yourself into the person of some famous wonder-worker. It is, you know, a day of miracles, and even kings have their salaried seers, and take counsel of the spiritual world. More! —let us have more!"

The circle were amazed; the spirit of superstitious curiosity seized upon them.

"Rêve de Noir," said the Duke, "a *carafe*, and less light."

The candelabra became dim. The Duke took the *carafe* of water from the valet, and, standing up, poured it upon the air; it broke into flames, which mounted and floated away, singly or in little crowds. Still the Duke poured, and dashing up the water with his hand, by and by the ceiling was illuminated with a thousand miniature tongues of violet-colored fire. We clapped our hands, and applauded,—"Beautiful! marvellous! wonderful, Duke!—your Highness is the only magician,"—when, on a sudden, the flames disappeared and the lights rose again.

"The world is weary of scepticism," remarked Lethal;

"there is no chemistry for that. It is the true magic, doubtless, — recovered from antiquity by his Highness. Are the
wonders exhausted ? "

The Duke smiled again. He stretched out his hand
toward Honoria, and she slept. It was the work of an instant.

" I have seen that before," said Dalton.

" Not as *we* see it," responded his Highness. " Rêve de
Noir, less light ! "

The room was dark in a moment. Over the head of Honoria appeared a cloud, at first black, and soon in this a
nucleus of light, which expanded and shaped itself into an
image and took the form of the sleeper, nude and spiritual,
a belt of rosy mist enveloping and concealing all but a head
and bust of ravishing beauty. The vision gazed with languid and beseeching eyes upon Dalton, and a sigh seemed
to heave the bosom. In scarce a breathing-time, it was
gone. Honoria waked, unconscious of what had passed.

Deep terror and amazement fell upon us all.

"I have seen enough," said Dalton, rising slowly, and
drawing a small riding-whip, "to know now that this person
is no duke, but either a charlatan or a devil. In either case,
since he has intruded here, to desecrate and degrade, I find
it proper to apply a magic more material."

At the word, all rose exclaiming, —" For God's sake, Dalton ! " He pressed forward and laid his hand upon the
Duke. A cry burst from Rêve de Noir which rent our very
souls ; and a flash followed, unspeakably bright, which revealed the demoniacal features of the Duke, who sat motionless, regarding Dalton's uplifted arm. A darkness followed
profound and palpable. I listened in terror. There was no
sound. Were we transformed ? Silence, darkness, still. I
closed my eyes, and opened them again. A pale, cold light
became slowly perceptible, stealing through a crevice, and
revealing the walls and ceiling of my narrow room. The
dream still oppressed me. I went to the window, and let
in reality with the morning light. Yet, for days after, the

images of the real Honoria and Dalton, my friends, remained separated from the creatures of the vision ; and the Denslow palace of dream-land, the pictures, the revelry, and the magic of the Demon Duke, haunted my memory, and kept with them all their visionary splendors and regrets.

FRIEND ELI'S DAUGHTER.

I.

THE mild May afternoon was drawing to a close, as
Friend Eli Mitchenor reached the top of the long
hill, and halted a few minutes, to allow his horse
time to recover breath. He also heaved a sigh of satisfaction, as he saw again the green, undulating valley of the
Neshaminy, with its dazzling squares of young wheat, its
brown patches of corn-land, its snowy masses of blooming
orchard, and the huge, fountain-like jets of weeping-willow,
half concealing the gray stone fronts of the farm-houses.
He had been absent from home only six days, but the time
seemed almost as long to him as a three-years' cruise to a
New-Bedford whaleman. The peaceful seclusion and pas-
toral beauty of the scene did not consciously appeal to his
senses; but he quietly noted how much the wheat had
grown during his absence, that the oats were up and looking well, that Friend Comly's meadow had been ploughed,
and Friend Martin had built his half of the line-fence along
the top of the hill-field. If any smothered delight in the
loveliness of the spring-time found a hiding-place anywhere
in the well-ordered chambers of his heart, it never relaxed
or softened the straight, inflexible lines of his face. As
easily could his collarless drab coat and waistcoat have
flushed with a sudden gleam of purple or crimson.

Eli Mitchenor was at peace with himself and the world,
—that is, so much of the world as he acknowledged. Be-

yond the community of his own sect, and a few personal
friends who were privileged to live on its borders, he neither
knew, nor cared to know, much more of the human race
than if it belonged to a planet farther from the sun. In the
discipline of the Friends he was perfect; he was privileged
to sit on the high seats, with the elders of the Society; and
the travelling brethren from other States, who visited Bucks
County, invariably blessed his house with a family-meeting.
His farm was one of the best on the banks of the Neshaminy, and he also enjoyed the annual interest of a few
thousand dollars, carefully secured by mortgages on real
estate. His wife, Abigail, kept even pace with him in the
consideration she enjoyed within the limits of the sect;
and his two children, Moses and Asenath, vindicated the
paternal training by the strictest sobriety of dress and
conduct. Moses wore the plain coat, even when his ways
led him among "the world's people"; and Asenath had
never been known to wear, or to express a desire for, a
ribbon of a brighter tint than brown or fawn-color. Friend
Mitchenor, had thus gradually ripened to his sixtieth year
in an atmosphere of life utterly placid and serene, and
looked forward with confidence to the final change, as a
translation into a deeper calm, a serener quiet, a prosperous
eternity of mild voices, subdued colors, and suppressed
emotions.

He was returning home, in his own old-fashioned "chair,"
with its heavy square canopy and huge curved springs,
from the Yearly Meeting of the Hicksite Friends, in Philadelphia. The large bay farm-horse, slow and grave in his
demeanor, wore his plain harness with an air which made
him seem, among his fellow-horses, the counterpart of his
master among men. He would no more have thought of
kicking than the latter would of swearing a huge oath.
Even now, when the top of the hill was gained, and he
knew that he was within a mile of the stable which had
been his home since colthood, he showed no undue haste
or impatience, but waited quietly, until Friend Mitchenor,

by a well-known jerk of the lines, gave him the signal to go on. Obedient to the motion, he thereupon set forward once more, jogging soberly down the eastern slope of the hill,— across the covered bridge, where, in spite of the tempting level of the hollow-sounding floor, he was as careful to abstain from trotting as if he had read the warning notice, — along the wooded edge of the green meadow, where several cows of his acquaintance were grazing, — and finally, wheeling around at the proper angle, halted squarely in front of the gate which gave entrance to the private lane.

The old stone house in front, the spring-house in a green little hollow just below it, the walled garden, with its clumps of box and lilac, and the vast barn on the left, all joined in expressing a silent welcome to their owner, as he drove up the lane. Moses, a man of twenty-five, left his work in the garden, and walked forward in his shirt-sleeves.

" Well, father, how does thee do ? " was his quiet greeting, as they shook hands.

" How 's mother, by this time ? " asked Eli.

" O, thee need n't have been concerned," said the son. " There she is. Go in : I 'll 'tend to the horse."

Abigail and her daughter appeared on the piazza. The mother was a woman of fifty, thin and delicate in frame, but with a smooth, placid beauty of countenance which had survived her youth. She was dressed in a simple dove-colored gown, with book-muslin cap and handkerchief, so scrupulously arranged that one might have associated with her for six months without ever discovering a spot on the former or an uneven fold in the latter. Asenath, who followed, was almost as plainly attired, her dress being a dark-blue calico, while a white pasteboard sun-bonnet, with broad cape, covered her head.

" Well, Abigail, how art thou ? " said Eli, quietly giving his hand to his wife.

" I 'm glad to see thee back," was her simple welcome.

No doubt they had kissed each other as lovers, but

16 * x

Asenath had witnessed this manifestation of affection but once in her life, — after the burial of a younger sister. The fact impressed her with a peculiar sense of sanctity and solemnity: it was a caress wrung forth by a season of tribulation, and therefore was too earnest to be profaned to the uses of joy. So, far, therefore, from expecting a paternal embrace, she would have felt, had it been given, like the doomed daughter of the Gileadite, consecrated to sacrifice.

Both she and her mother were anxious to hear the proceedings of the Meeting, and to receive personal news of the many friends whom Eli had seen; but they asked few questions until the supper-table was ready and Moses had come in from the barn. The old man enjoyed talking, but it must be in his own way and at his own good time. They must wait until the communicative spirit should move him. With the first cup of coffee the inspiration came. Hovering, at first, over indifferent details, he gradually approached those of more importance, — told of the addresses which had been made, the points of discipline discussed, the testimony borne, and the appearance and genealogy of any new Friends who had taken a prominent part therein. Finally, at the close of his relation, he said, —

"Abigail, there is one thing I must talk to thee about. Friend Speakman's partner — perhaps thee's heard of him, Richard Hilton — has a son who is weakly. He's two or three years younger than Moses. His mother was consumptive, and they're afraid he takes after her. His father wants to send him into the country for the summer, — to some place where he'll have good air, and quiet, and moderate exercise, and Friend Speakman spoke of us. I thought I'd mention it to thee, and if thee thinks well of it, we can send word down next week, when Josiah Comly goes."

"What does *thee* think?" asked his wife, after a pause.

"He's a very quiet, steady young man, Friend Speakman says, and would be very little trouble to thee. I thought perhaps his board would buy the new yoke of oxen we must

have in the fall, and the price of the fat ones might go to
help set up Moses. But it's for thee to decide."

"I suppose we could take him," said Abigail, seeing that
the decision was virtually made already; "there's the cor-
ner-room, which we don't often use. Only, if he should get
worse on our hands " ——

"Friend Speakman says there's no danger. He's only
weak-breasted, as yet, and clerking is n't good for him. I
saw the young man at the store. If his looks don't belie
him, he's well-behaved and orderly."

So it was settled that Richard Hilton the younger was
to be an inmate of Friend Mitchenor's house during the
summer.

II.

A T the end of ten days he came.
In the under-sized, earnest, dark-haired, and dark-eyed
young man of three-and-twenty Abigail Mitchenor at once
felt a motherly interest. Having received him as a tempo-
rary member of the family, she considered him entitled to the
same watchful care as if he were in reality an invalid son.
The ice over an hereditary Quaker nature is but a thin crust,
if one knows how to break it; and in Richard Hilton's case,
it was already broken before his arrival. His only embarrassment, in fact, arose from the difficulty which he naturally experienced in adapting himself to the speech and
address of the Mitchenor family. The greetings of old Eli,
grave, yet kindly, of Abigail, quaintly familiar and tender,
of Moses, cordial and slightly condescending, and finally of
Asenath, simple and natural to a degree which impressed
him like a new revelation in woman, at once indicated to
him his position among them. His city manners, he felt,
instinctively, must be unlearned, or at least laid aside for a
time. Yet it was not easy for him to assume, at such short
notice, those of his hosts. Happening to address Asenath
as "Miss Mitchenor," Eli turned to him with a rebuking
face.

"We do not use compliments, Richard," said he; "my daughter's name is Asenath."

"I beg pardon. I will try to accustom myself to your ways, since you have been so kind as to take me for a while," apologized Richard Hilton.

"Thee's under no obligation to us," said Friend Mitchenor, in his strict sense of justice; "thee pays for what thee gets."

The finer feminine instinct of Abigail led her to interpose.

"We'll not expect too much of thee, at first, Richard," she remarked, with a kind expression of face, which had the effect of a smile; "but our ways are plain and easily learned. Thee knows, perhaps, that we're no respecters of persons."

It was some days, however, before the young man could overcome his natural hesitation at the familiarity implied by these new forms of speech. "Friend Mitchenor" and "Moses" were not difficult to learn, but it seemed a want of respect to address as "Abigail" a woman of such sweet and serene dignity as the mother, and he was fain to avoid either extreme by calling her, with her cheerful permission, "Aunt Mitchenor." On the other hand, his own modest and unobtrusive nature soon won the confidence and cordial regard of the family. He occasionally busied himself in the garden, by way of exercise, or accompanied Moses to the cornfield or the woodland on the hill, but was careful never to interfere at inopportune times, and willing to learn silently, by the simple process of looking on.

One afternoon as he was idly sitting on the stone wall which separated the garden from the lane, Asenath, attired in a new gown of chocolate-colored calico, with a double-handled willow work-basket on her arm, issued from the house. As she approached him, she paused and said, —

"The time seems to hang heavy on thy hands, Richard. If thee's strong enough to walk to the village and back, it might do thee more good than sitting still."

Richard Hilton at once jumped down from the wall.

"Certainly I am able to go," said he, "if you will allow it."

"Have n't I asked thee?" was her quiet reply.

"Let me carry your basket," he said, suddenly, after they had walked, side by side, some distance down the lane.

"Indeed, I shall not let thee do that. I 'm only going for the mail, and some little things at the store, that make no weight at all. Thee must n't think I 'm like the young women in the city, who, — I 'm told, — if they buy a spool of cotton, must have it sent home to them. Besides, thee must n't over-exert thy strength."

Richard Hilton laughed merrily at the gravity with which she uttered the last sentence.

"Why, Miss — Asenath, I mean — what am I good for, if I have not strength enough to carry a basket?"

"Thee 's a man, I know, and I think a man would almost as lief be thought wicked as weak. Thee can't help being weakly-inclined, and it 's only right that thee should be careful of thyself. There 's surely nothing in that that thee need be ashamed of."

While thus speaking, Asenath moderated her walk, in order, unconsciously to her companion, to restrain his steps.

"O, there are the dog's-tooth violets in blossom!" she exclaimed, pointing to a shady spot beside the brook; "does thee know them?"

Richard immediately gathered and brought to her a handful of the nodding yellow bells, trembling above their large, cool, spotted leaves.

"How beautiful they are!" said he; "but I should never have taken them for violets."

"They are misnamed," she answered. "The flower is an *Erythronium;* but I am accustomed to the common name, and like it. Did thee ever study botany?"

Not at all. I can tell a geranium, when I see it, and I know a heliotrope by the smell. I could never mistake a red cabbage for a rose, and I can recognize a hollyhock or a sunflower at a considerable distance. The wild-flowers are all strangers to me; I wish I knew something about them."

"If thee's fond of flowers, it would be very easy to learn. I think a study of this kind would pleasantly occupy thy mind. Why could n't thee try? I would be very willing to teach thee what little I know. It's not much, indeed, but all thee wants is a start. See, I will show thee how simple the principles are."

Taking one of the flowers from the bunch, Asenath, as they slowly walked forward, proceeded to dissect it, explained the mysteries of stamens and pistils, pollen, petals, and calyx, and, by the time they had reached the village, had succeeded in giving him a general idea of the Linnæan system of classification. His mind took hold of the subject with a prompt and profound interest. It was a new and wonderful world which suddenly opened before him. How surprised he was to learn that there were signs by which a poisonous herb could be detected from a wholesome one, that cedars and pine-trees blossomed, that the gray lichens on the rocks belonged to the vegetable kingdom! His respect for Asenath's knowledge thrust quite out of sight the restraint which her youth and sex had imposed upon him. She was teacher, equal, friend; and the simple, candid manner which was the natural expression of her dignity and purity thoroughly harmonized with this relation.

Although, in reality, two or three years younger than he, Asenath had a gravity of demeanor, a calm self-possession, a deliberate balance of mind, and a repose of the emotional nature, which he had never before observed, except in much older women. She had had, as he could well imagine, no romping girlhood, no season of careless, light-hearted dalliance with opening life, no violent alternation even of the usual griefs and joys of youth. The social calm in which she had expanded had developed her nature as gently and securely as a sea-flower is unfolded below the reach of tides and storms.

She would have been very much surprised, if any one had called her handsome ; yet her face had a mild, unobtrusive beauty, which seemed to grow and deepen from day to day. Of a longer oval than the Greek standard, it was yet as harmonious in outline ; the nose was fine and straight, the dark-blue eyes steady and untroubled, and the lips calmly, but not too firmly closed. Her brown hair, parted over a high white forehead, was smoothly laid across the temples, drawn behind the ears, and twisted into a simple knot. The white cape and sun-bonnet gave her face a nun-like character, which set her apart, in the thoughts of "the world's people " whom she met, as one sanctified for some holy work. She might have gone around the world, repelling every rude word, every bold glance, by the protecting atmosphere of purity and truth which inclosed her.

The days went by, each bringing some new blossom to adorn and illustrate the joint studies of the young man and maiden. For Richard Hilton had soon mastered the elements of botany, as taught by Priscilla Wakefield, — the only source of Asenath's knowledge, — and entered, with her, upon the text-book of Gray, a copy of which he procured from Philadelphia. Yet, though he had overtaken her in his knowledge of the technicalities of the science, her practical acquaintance with plants and their habits left her still his superior. Day by day, exploring the meadows, the woods, and the clearings, he brought home his discoveries to enjoy her aid in classifying and assigning them to their true places. Asenath had generally an hour or two of leisure from domestic duties in the afternoons, or after the early supper of summer was over ; and sometimes, on "Seventh-days," she would be his guide to some locality where the rarer plants were known to exist. The parents saw this community of interest and exploration without a thought of misgiving. They trusted their daughter as themselves ; or, if any possible fear had flitted across their hearts, it was allayed by the absorbing delight with which Richard Hilton pursued his study. An earnest discussion as to whether a certain leaf was ovate or lanceolate, whether a certain plant belonged to the species *scandens* or *canadensis*, was, in their eyes, convincing proof that the young brains were touched, and therefore *not* the young hearts.

But love, symbolized by a rose-bud, is emphatically a botanical emotion. A sweet, tender perception of beauty, such as this study requires, or develops, is at once the most subtile and certain chain of communication between impressible natures. Richard Hilton, feeling that his years were numbered, had given up, in despair, his boyish dreams, even before he understood them : his fate seemed to preclude the possibility of love. But, as he gained a little strength from the genial season, the pure country air, and the release from gloomy thoughts which his rambles afforded, the end was farther removed, and a future — though brief, perhaps, still a *future* — began to glimmer before him. If this could be his life, — an endless summer, with a search for new plants every morning, and their classification every evening, with Asenath's help, on the shady portico of Friend Mitchenor's house, — he could forget his doom, and enjoy the blessing of life unthinkingly.

The azaleas succeeded to the anemones, the orchis and trillium followed, then the yellow gerardias and the feathery purple pogonias, and finally the growing gleam of the golden-rods along the wood-side and the red umbels of the tall eupatoriums in the meadow announced the close of summer. One evening, as Richard, in displaying his collection, brought to view the blood-red leaf of a gum-tree, Asenath exclaimed, —

"Ah, there is the sign ! It is early, this year."

"What sign ?" he asked.

"That the summer is over. We shall soon have frosty nights, and then nothing will be left for us except the asters and gentians and golden-rods."

Was the time indeed so near? A few more weeks, and this Arcadian life would close. He must go back to the city, to its rectilinear streets, its close brick walls, its artificial, constrained existence. How could he give up the peace, the contentment, the hope he had enjoyed through the summer? The question suddenly took a more definite form in his mind: How could he give up Asenath? Yes, —the quiet, unsuspecting girl, sitting beside him, with her lap full of the September blooms he had gathered, was thenceforth a part of his inmost life. Pure and beautiful as she was, almost sacred in his regard, his heart dared to say, —"I need her and claim her!"

"Thee looks pale to-night, Richard," said Abigail, as they took their seats at the supper-table. "I hope thee has not taken cold."

III.

"WILL thee go along, Richard? I know where the rudbeckias grow," said Asenath, on the following "Seventh-day" afternoon.

They crossed the meadows, and followed the course of the stream, under its canopy of magnificent ash and plane-trees, into a brake between the hills. It was an almost impenetrable thicket, spangled with tall autumnal flowers. The eupatoriums, with their purple crowns, stood like young trees, with an undergrowth of aster and blue spikes of lobelia, tangled in a golden mesh of dodder. A strong, mature odor, mixed alike of leaves and flowers, and very different from the faint, elusive sweetness of spring, filled the air. The creek, with a few faded leaves dropped upon its bosom, and films of gossamer streaming from its bushy fringe, gurgled over the pebbles in its bed. Here and there, on its banks, shone the deep yellow stars of the flower they sought.

Richard Hilton walked as in a dream, mechanically plucking a stem of rudbeckia, only to toss it, presently, into the water.

"Why, Richard! what's thee doing?" cried Asenath; "thee has thrown away the very best specimen."

"Let it go," he answered, sadly. "I am afraid everything else is thrown away."

"What does thee mean?" she asked, with a look of surprised and anxious inquiry.

"Don't ask me, Asenath. Or—yes, I *will* tell you. I must say it to you now, or never afterwards. Do you know what a happy life I've been leading since I came here?— that I've learned what life is, as if I'd never known it before? I want to live, Asenath,—and do you know why?"

"I hope thee will live, Richard," she said, gently and tenderly, her deep-blue eyes dim with the mist of unshed tears.

"But, Asenath, how am I to live without you? But you can't understand that, because you do not know what you are to me. No, you never guessed that all this while I've been loving you more and more, until now I have no other idea of death than not to see you, not to love you, not to share your life!"

"O, Richard!"

"I knew you would be shocked, Asenath. I meant to have kept this to myself. You never dreamed of it, and I had no right to disturb the peace of your heart. The truth is told now,—and I cannot take it back, if I wished. But if you cannot love, you can forgive me for loving you,— forgive me now, and every day of my life."

He uttered these words with a passionate tenderness, standing on the edge of the stream, and gazing into its waters. His slight frame trembled with the violence of his emotion. Asenath, who had become very pale as he commenced to speak, gradually flushed over neck and brow as she listened. Her head drooped, the gathered flowers fell from her hands, and she hid her face. For a few minutes no sound was heard but the liquid gurgling of the water, and the whistle of a bird in the thicket beside them.

Richard Hilton at last turned, and, in a voice of hesitating entreaty, pronounced her name, —

"Asenath!"

She took away her hands and slowly lifted her face. She was pale, but her eyes met his with a frank, appealing, tender expression, which caused his heart to stand still a moment. He read no reproach, no faintest thought of blame; but — was it pity? — was it pardon? — or ——

"We stand before God, Richard," said she, in a low, sweet, solemn tone. "He knows that I do not need to forgive thee. If thee requires it, I also require His forgiveness for myself."

Though a deeper blush now came to cheek and brow, she met his gaze with the bravery of a pure and innocent heart. Richard, stunned with the sudden and unexpected bliss, strove to take the full consciousness of it into a being which seemed too narrow to contain it. His first impulse was to rush forward, clasp her passionately in his arms, and hold her in the embrace which encircled, for him, the boundless promise of life; but she stood there, defenceless, save in her holy truth and trust, and his heart bowed down and gave her reverence.

"Asenath," said he, at last, "I never dared to hope for this. God bless you for those words! Can you trust me? — can you indeed love me?"

"I can trust thee, — I *do* love thee!"

They clasped each other's hands in one long, clinging pressure. No kiss was given, but side by side they walked slowly up the dewy meadows, in happy and hallowed silence. Asenath's face became troubled as the old farm-house appeared through the trees.

"Father and mother must know of this, Richard," said she. "I am afraid it may be a cross to them."

The same fear had already visited his own mind, but he answered, cheerfully, —

"I hope not. I think I have taken a new lease of life, and shall soon be strong enough to satisfy them. Besides, my father is in prosperous business."

"It is not that," she answered; "but thee is not one of us."

It was growing dusk when they reached the house. In the dim candle-light Asenath's paleness was not remarked; and Richard's silence was attributed to fatigue.

The next morning the whole family attended meeting at the neighboring Quaker meeting-house, in the preparation for which, and the various special occupations of their "First-day" mornings, the unsuspecting parents overlooked that inevitable change in the faces of the lovers which they must otherwise have observed. After dinner, as Eli was taking a quiet walk in the garden, Richard Hilton approached him.

"Friend Mitchenor," said he, "I should like to have some talk with thee."

"What is it, Richard?" asked the old man, breaking off some pods from a seedling radish, and rubbing them in the palm of his hand.

"I hope, Friend Mitchenor," said the young man, scarcely knowing how to approach so important a crisis in his life, "I hope thee has been satisfied with my conduct since I came to live with thee, and has no fault to find with me as a man."

"Well," exclaimed Eli, turning around and looking up, sharply, "does thee want a testimony from me? I've nothing, that I know of, to say against thee."

"If I were sincerely attached to thy daughter, Friend Mitchenor, and she returned the attachment, could thee trust her happiness in my hands?"

"What?" cried Eli, straightening himself and glaring upon the speaker, with a face too amazed to express any other feeling.

"Can you confide Asenath's happiness to my care? I love her with my whole heart and soul, and the fortune of my life depends on your answer."

The straight lines in the old man's face seemed to grow deeper and more rigid, and his eyes shone with the chill glitter of steel. Richard, not daring to say a word more, awaited his reply in intense agitation.

"So !" he exclaimed at last, "this is the way thee 's repaid me ! I did n't expect *this* from thee ! Has thee spoken to her ?"

"I have."

"Thee has, has thee ? And I suppose thee 's persuaded her to think as thee does. Thee 'd better never have come here. When I want to lose my daughter, and can't find anybody else for her, I 'll let thee know."

"What have you against me, Friend Mitchenor ?" Richard sadly asked, forgetting, in his excitement, the Quaker speech he had learned.

"Thee need n't use compliments now ! Asenath shall be a Friend while *I* live ; thy fine clothes and merry-makings and vanities are not for her. Thee belongs to the world, and thee may choose one of the world's women."

"Never !" protested Richard ; but Friend Mitchenor was already ascending the garden-steps on his way to the house.

The young man, utterly overwhelmed, wandered to the nearest grove and threw himself on the ground. Thus, in a miserable chaos of emotion, unable to grasp any fixed thought, the hours passed away. Towards evening, he heard a footstep approaching, and sprang up. It was Moses.

The latter was engaged, with the consent of his parents, and expected to "pass meeting " in a few weeks. He knew what had happened, and felt a sincere sympathy for Richard, for whom he had a cordial regard. His face was very grave, but kind.

"Thee 'd better come in, Richard," said he ; "the evenings are damp, and I 've brought thy overcoat. I know everything, and I feel that it must be a great cross for thee. But thee won't be alone in bearing it."

"Do you think there is no hope of your father relenting ?" he asked, in a tone of despondency which anticipated the answer.

"Father 's very hard to move," said Moses ; "and when

mother and Asenath can't prevail on him, nobody else need try. I 'm afraid thee must make up thy mind to the trial. I 'm sorry to say it, Richard, but I think thee 'd better go back to town."

"I 'll go to-morrow, — go and die!" he muttered hoarsely, as he followed Moses to the house.

Abigail, as she saw his haggard face, wept quietly. She pressed his hand tenderly, but said nothing. Eli was stern and cold as an Iceland rock. Asenath did not make her appearance. At supper, the old man and his son exchanged a few words about the farm-work to be done on the morrow, but nothing else was said. Richard soon left the room and went up to his chamber to spend his last, his only unhappy night at the farm. A yearning, pitying look from Abigail accompanied him.

"Try and not think hard of us!" was her farewell the next morning, as he stepped into the old chair, in which Moses was to convey him to the village where he should meet the Doylestown stage. So, without a word of comfort from Asenath's lips, without even a last look at her beloved face, he was taken away.

IV.

TRUE and firm and self-reliant as was the nature of Asenath Mitchenor, the thought of resistance to her father's will never crossed her mind. It was fixed, that she must renounce all intercourse with Richard Hilton; it was even sternly forbidden her to see him again during the few hours he remained in the house; but the sacred love, thus rudely dragged to the light and outraged, was still her own. She would take it back into the keeping of her heart, and if a day should ever come when he would be free to return and demand it of her, he would find it there, unwithered, with all the unbreathed perfume hoarded in its folded leaves. If that day came not, she would at the last give it back to God, saying, "Father, here is Thy most precious gift: bestow it as Thou wilt."

As her life had never before been agitated by any strong emotion, so it was not outwardly agitated now. The placid waters of her soul did not heave and toss before those winds of passion and sorrow; they lay in dull, leaden calm, under a cold and sunless sky. What struggles with herself she underwent no one ever knew. After Richard Hilton's departure, she never mentioned his name, or referred, in any way, to the summer's companionship with him. She performed her household duties, if not cheerfully, at least as punctually and carefully as before ; and her father congratulated himself that the unfortunate attachment had struck no deeper root. Abigail's finer sight, however, was not deceived by this external resignation. She noted the faint shadows under the eyes, the increased whiteness of the temples, the unconscious traces of pain which sometimes played about the dimpled corners of the mouth, and watched her daughter with a silent, tender solicitude.

The wedding of Moses was a severe test of Asenath's strength, but she stood the trial nobly, performing all the duties required by her position with such sweet composure that many of the older female Friends remarked to Abigail, "How womanly Asenath has grown !" Eli Mitchenor noted, with peculiar satisfaction, that the eyes of the young Friends — some of them of great promise in the sect, and well endowed with worldly goods — followed her admiringly. "It will not be long," he thought, "before she is consoled."

Fortune seemed to favor his plans, and justify his harsh treatment of Richard Hilton. There were unfavorable accounts of the young man's conduct. His father had died during the winter, and he was represented as having become very reckless and dissipated. These reports at last assumed such a definite form that Friend Mitchenor brought them to the notice of his family.

"I met Josiah Comly in the road," said he one day at dinner. "He's just come from Philadelphia, and brings bad news of Richard Hilton. He's taken to drink, and is spending in wickedness the money his father left him. His friends have a great concern about him, but it seems he's not to be reclaimed."

Abigail looked imploringly at her husband, but he either disregarded or failed to understand her look. Asenath, who had grown very pale, steadily met her father's gaze, and said, in a tone which he had never yet heard from her lips, —

"Father, will thee please never mention Richard Hilton's name when I am by?"

The words were those of entreaty, but the voice was that of authority. The old man was silenced by a new and unexpected power in his daughter's heart; he suddenly felt that she was not a girl, as heretofore, but a woman, whom he might persuade, but could no longer compel.

"It shall be as thee wishes, Asenath," he said; "we had best forget him."

Of their friends, however, she could not expect this reserve, and she was doomed to hear stories of Richard which clouded and embittered her thoughts of him. And a still severer trial was in store. She accompanied her father, in obedience to his wish, and against her own desire, to the Yearly Meeting in Philadelphia. It has passed into a proverb, that the Friends on these occasions, always bring rain with them; and the period of her visit was no exception to the rule. The showery days of "Yearly Meeting Week" glided by, until the last, and she looked forward with relief to the morrow's return to Buck's County, glad to have escaped a meeting with Richard Hilton, which might have confirmed her fears, and could but have given her pain in any case.

As she and her father joined each other, outside the meeting-house, at the close of the afternoon meeting, a light rain was falling. She took his arm, under the capacious umbrella, and they were soon alone in the wet streets, on their way to the house of the Friends who entertained them. At a crossing, where the water, pouring down the gutter towards the Delaware, caused them to halt, a man, plashing through the flood, staggered towards them. ' Without an umbrella, with dripping, disordered clothes, yet with a hot, flushed face, around which the long black hair hung wildly, he approached, singing to himself, with maudlin voice, a song which would have been sweet and tender in a lover's mouth. Friend Mitchenor drew to one side, lest his spotless drab should be brushed by the unclean reveller; but the latter, looking up, stopped suddenly, face to face with them.

"Asenath!" he cried, in a voice whose anguish pierced through the confusion of his senses, and struck down into the sober quick of his soul.

"Richard!" she breathed, rather than spoke, in a low, terrified voice.

It was indeed Richard Hilton who stood before her, or rather — as she afterwards thought, in recalling the interview — the body of Richard Hilton, possessed by an evil spirit. His cheeks burned with a more than hectic red, his eyes were wild and bloodshot, and though the recognition had suddenly sobered him, an impatient, reckless devil seemed to lurk under the set mask of his features.

"Here I am, Asenath," he said at length, hoarsely. "I said it was death, did n't I? Well, it 's worse than death, I suppose; but what matter? You can 't be more lost to me now than you were already. This is *thy* doing, Friend Eli!" he continued, turning to the old man, with a sneering emphasis on the "*thy.*" "I hope thee 's satisfied with thy work?"

Here he burst into a bitter, mocking laugh, which it chilled Asenath's blood to hear.

The old man turned pale. "Come away, child!" said he, tugging at her arm. But she stood firm, strengthened for the moment by a solemn feeling of duty which trampled down her pain.

"Richard," she said, with the music of an immeasurable sorrow in her voice, "O Richard, what has thee done?

Where the Lord commands resignation, thee has been re-
bellious; where he chasteneth to purify, thee turns blindly
to sin. I had not expected this of thee, Richard; I thought
thy regard for me was of the kind which would have helped
and uplifted thee, — not through me, as an unworthy object,
but through the hopes and the pure desires of thy own heart.
I expected that thee would so act as to justify what I felt
towards thee, not to make my affection a reproach, — O
Richard, not to cast over my heart the shadow of thy
sin!"

The wretched young man supported himself against the
post of an awning, buried his face in his hands, and wept
passionately. Once or twice he essayed to speak, but his
voice was choked by sobs, and, after a look from the streaming eyes which Asenath could scarcely bear to meet, he
again covered his face. A stranger, coming down the street,
paused out of curiosity. "Come, come!" cried Eli, once
more, eager to escape from the scene. His daughter stood
still, and the man slowly passed on.

Asenath could not thus leave her lost lover, in his despairing grief. She again turned to him, her own tears
flowing fast and free.

"I do not judge thee, Richard, but the words that passed
between us give me a right to speak to thee. It was hard
to lose sight of thee then, but it is still harder for me to see
thee now. If the sorrow and pity I feel could save thee, I
would be willing never to know any other feelings. I would
still do anything for thee except that which thee cannot ask,
as thee now is, and I could not give. Thee has made the
gulf between us so wide that it cannot be crossed. But I
can now weep for thee and pray for thee as a fellow-crea-
ture whose soul is still precious in the sight of the Lord.
Fare thee well!"

He seized the hand she extended, bowed down, and
showered mingled tears and kisses upon it. Then, with a
wild sob in his throat, he started up and rushed down the
street, through the fast-falling rain. The father and daugh-

ter walked home in silence. Eli had heard every word that
was spoken, and felt that a spirit whose utterances he dared
not question had visited Asenath's tongue.

She, as year after year went by, regained the peace and
patience which give a sober cheerfulness to life. The pangs
of her heart grew dull and transient; but there were two
pictures in her memory which never blurred in outline or
faded in color: one, the break of autumn flowers, under the
bright autumnal sky, with bird and stream making accordant
music to the new voice of love; the other, a rainy street,
with a lost, reckless man leaning against an awning-post,
and staring in her face with eyes whose unutterable woe,
when she dared to recall it, darkened the beauty of the
earth, and almost shook her trust in the providence of God.

V.

YEAR after year passed by, but not without bringing
change to the Mitchenor family. Moses had moved
to Chester County soon after his marriage, and had a good
farm of his own. At the end of ten years Abigail died;
and the old man, who had not only lost his savings by an
unlucky investment, but was obliged to mortgage his farm,
finally determined to sell it and join his son. He was getting too old to manage it properly, impatient under the
unaccustomed pressure of debt, and depressed by the loss
of the wife to whom, without any outward show of tenderness, he was, in truth, tenderly attached. He missed her
more keenly in the places where she had lived and moved
than in a neighborhood without the memory of her presence.
The pang with which he parted from his home was weak-
ened by the greater pang which had preceded it.

It was a harder trial to Asenath. She shrank from the
encounter with new faces, and the necessity of creating
new associations. There was a quiet satisfaction in the
ordered, monotonous round of her life, which might be the

same elsewhere, but here alone was the nook which held all the morning sunshine she had ever known. Here still lingered the halo of the sweet departed summer,—here still grew the familiar wild-flowers which *the first* Richard Hilton had gathered. This was the Paradise in which the Adam of her heart had dwelt, before his fall. Her resignation and submission entitled her to keep those pure and perfect memories, though she was scarcely conscious of their true charm. She did not dare to express to herself, in words, that one everlasting joy of woman's heart, through all trials and sorrows, — "I have loved, I have been beloved."

On the last "First-day" before their departure, she walked down the meadows to the lonely brake between the hills. It was the early spring, and the black buds of the ash had just begun to swell. The maples were dusted with crimson bloom, and the downy catkins of the swamp-willow dropped upon the stream and floated past her, as once the autumn leaves. In the edges of the thickets peeped forth the blue, scentless violet, the fairy cups of the anemone, and the pink-veined bells of the miskodeed. The tall blooms through which the lovers walked still slept in the chilly earth; but the sky above her was mild and blue, and the remembrance of the day came back to her with a delicate, pungent sweetness, like the perfume of the trailing arbutus in the air around her. In a sheltered, sunny nook, she found a single erythronium, lured forth in advance of its proper season, and gathered it as a relic of the spot, which she might keep without blame. As she stooped to pluck it, her own face looked up at her out of a little pool filled by the spring rains. Seen against the reflected sky, it shone with a soft radiance, and the earnest eyes met hers, as if it were her young self, evoked from the past, to bid her farewell. "Farewell!" she whispered, taking leave at once, as she believed, of youth and the memory of love.

During those years she had more than once been sought in marriage, but had steadily, though kindly, refused. Once, when the suitor was a man whose character and position made the union very desirable in Eli Mitchenor's eyes, he ventured to use his paternal influence. Asenath's gentle resistance was overborne by his arbitrary force of will, and her protestations were of no avail.

"Father," she finally said, in the tone which he had once heard and still remembered, "thee can take away, but thee cannot give."

He never mentioned the subject again.

Richard Hilton passed out of her knowledge shortly after her meeting with him in Philadelphia. She heard, indeed, that his headlong career of dissipation was not arrested, — that his friends had given him up as hopelessly ruined, — and, finally, that he had left the city. After that, all reports ceased. He was either dead, or reclaimed and leading a better life, somewhere far away. Dead, she believed, — almost hoped ; for in that case might he not now be enjoying the ineffable rest and peace which she trusted might be her portion ? It was better to think of him as a purified spirit, waiting to meet her in a holier communion, than to know that he was still bearing the burden of a soiled and blighted life. In any case, her own future was plain and clear. It was simply a prolongation of the present, — an alternation of seed-time and harvest, filled with humble duties and cares, until the Master should bid her lay down her load and follow Him.

Friend Mitchenor bought a small cottage adjacent to his son's farm, in a community which consisted mostly of Friends, and not far from the large old meeting-house in which the Quarterly Meetings were held. He at once took his place on the upper seat, among the elders, most of whom he knew already, from having met them, year after year, in Philadelphia. The charge of a few acres of ground gave him sufficient occupation ; the money left to him after the sale of his farm was enough to support him comfortably ; and a late Indian summer of contentment seemed now to have come to the old man. He was done with the earnest business of life. Moses was gradually taking his place, as

father and Friend; and Asenath would be reasonably provided for at his death. As his bodily energies decayed, his
imperious temper softened, his mind became more accessi-
ble to liberal influences, and he even cultivated a cordial
friendship with a neighboring farmer who was one of "the
world's people." Thus, at seventy-five, he was really younger, because tenderer of heart and more considerate than he
had been at sixty.

Asenath was now a woman of thirty-five, and suitors had
ceased to approach her. Much of her beauty still remained,
but her face had become thin and wasted, and the inevitable
lines were beginning to form around her eyes. Her dress
was plainer than ever, and she wore the scoop-bonnet of
drab silk, in which no woman can seem beautiful, unless
she be very old. She was calm and grave in her demeanor,
save that her perfect goodness and benevolence shone
through and warmed her presence; but, when earnestly interested, she had been known to speak her mind so clearly
and forcibly that it was generally surmised among the
Friends that she possessed "a gift," which might, in time,
raise her to honor among them. To the children of Moses
she was a good genius, and a word from " Aunt 'Senath "
oftentimes prevailed when the authority of the parents was
disregarded. In them she found a new source of happiness; and when her old home on the Neshaminy had been
removed a little farther into the past, so that she no longer
looked, with every morning's sun, for some familiar feature
of its scenery, her submission brightened into a cheerful
content with life.

It was summer, and Quarterly-Meeting Day had arrived.
There had been rumors of the expected presence of " Friends
from a distance," and not only those of the district, but
most of the neighbors who were not connected with the
sect, attended. By the by-road through the woods, it was
not more than half a mile from Friend Mitchenor's cottage
to the meeting-house, and Asenath, leaving her father to be
taken by Moses in his carriage, set out on foot. It was a

sparkling, breezy day, and the forest was full of life. Squirrels chased each other along the branches of the oaks, and
the air was filled with fragrant odors of hickory-leaves,
sweet-fern, and spice-wood. Picking up a flower here and
there, Asenath walked onward, rejoicing alike in shade and
sunshine, grateful for all the consoling beauty which the
earth offers to a lonely heart. That serene content which
she had learned to call happiness had filled her being until
the dark canopy was lifted and the waters took back their
transparency under a cloudless sky.

Passing around to the "women's side" of the meeting-
house, she mingled with her friends, who were exchanging
information concerning the expected visitors. Micajah
Morrill had not arrived, they said, but Ruth Baxter had
spent the last night at Friend Way's, and would certainly
be there. Besides, there were Friend Chandler, from Nine
Partners, and Friend Carter, from Maryland: they had
been seen on the ground. Friend Carter was said to have
a wonderful gift, — Mercy Jackson had heard him once, in
Baltimore. The Friends there had been a little exercised
about him, because they thought he was too much inclined
to "the newness," but it was known that the Spirit had
often manifestly led him. Friend Chandler had visited
Yearly Meeting once, they believed. He was an old man,
and had been a personal friend of Elias Hicks.

At the appointed hour they entered the house. After the
subdued rustling which ensued upon taking their seats,
there was an interval of silence, shorter than usual, because
it was evident that many persons would feel the promptings
of the Spirit. Friend Chandler spoke first, and was followed by Ruth Baxter, a frail little woman, with a voice of
exceeding power. The not unmelodious chant in which she
delivered her admonitions rang out, at times, like the peal
of a trumpet. Fixing her eyes on vacancy, with her hands
on the wooden rail before her, and her body slightly sway-
ing to and fro, her voice soared far aloft at the commencement of every sentence, gradually dropping, through a me-

lodious scale of tone, to the close. She resembled an inspired prophetess, an aged Deborah, crying aloud in the valleys of Israel.

The last speaker was Friend Carter, a small man, not more than forty years of age. His face was thin and intense in its expression, his hair gray at the temples, and his dark eye almost too restless for a child of "the stillness and the quietness." His voice, though not loud, was clear and penetrating, with an earnest, sympathetic quality, which arrested, not the ear alone, but the serious attention of the auditor. His delivery was but slightly marked by the peculiar rhythm of the Quaker preachers; and this fact, perhaps, increased the effect of his words, through the contrast with those who preceded him.

His discourse was an eloquent vindication of the law of kindness, as the highest and purest manifestation of true Christian doctrine. The paternal relation of God to man was the basis of that religion which appealed directly to the heart: so the fraternity of each man with his fellow was its practical application. God pardons the repentant sinner: we can also pardon, where we are offended; we can pity, where we cannot pardon. Both the good and the bad principles generate their like in others. Force begets force; anger excites a corresponding anger; but kindness awakens the slumbering emotions even of an evil heart. Love may not always be answered by an equal love, but it has never yet created hatred. The testimony which Friends bear against war, he said, is but a general assertion, which has no value except in so far as they manifest the principle of peace in their daily lives, — in the exercise of pity, of charity, of forbearance, and Christian love.

The words of the speaker sank deeply into the hearts of his hearers. There was an intense hush, as if in truth the Spirit had moved him to speak, and every sentence was armed with a sacred authority. Asenath Mitchenor looked at him, over the low partition which divided her and her sisters from the men's side, absorbed in his rapt earnestness and truth. She forgot that other hearers were present: he spake to her alone. A strange spell seemed to seize upon her faculties and chain them at his feet: had he beckoned to her, she would have arisen and walked to his side.

Friend Carter warmed and deepened as he went on. "I feel moved to-day," he said, — "moved, I know not why, but I hope for some wise purpose, — to relate to you an instance of Divine and human kindness which has come directly to my own knowledge. A young man of delicate constitution, whose lungs were thought to be seriously affected, was sent to the house of a Friend in the country, in order to try the effect of air and exercise."

Asenath almost ceased to breathe, in the intensity with which she gazed and listened. Clasping her hands tightly in her lap to prevent them from trembling, and steadying herself against the back of the seat, she heard the story of her love for Richard Hilton told by the lips of a stranger! —not merely of his dismissal from the house, but of that meeting in the street, at which only she and her father were present! Nay, more, she heard her own words repeated, she heard Richard's passionate outburst of remorse described in language that brought his living face before her! She gasped for breath, — his face *was* before her! The features, sharpened by despairing grief, which her memory recalled, had almost anticipated the harder lines which fifteen years had made, and which now, with a terrible shock and choking leap of the heart, she recognized. Her senses faded, and she would have fallen from her seat but for the support of the partition against which she leaned. Fortunately, the women near her were too much occupied with the narrative to notice her condition. Many of them wept silently, with their handkerchiefs pressed over their mouths.

The first shock of death-like faintness passed away, and she clung to the speaker's voice, as if its sound alone could give her strength to sit still and listen further.

"Deserted by his friends, unable to stay his feet on the evil path," he continued, "the young man left his home and

17 *

went to a city in another State. But here it was easier to find associates in evil than tender hearts that might help him back to good. He was tired of life, and the hope of a speedier death hardened him in his courses. But, my friends, Death never comes to those who wickedly seek him. The Lord withholds destruction from the hands that are madly outstretched to grasp it, and forces His pity and forgiveness on the unwilling soul. Finding that it was the principle of *life* which grew stronger within him, the young man at last meditated an awful crime. The thought of self-destruction haunted him day and night. He lingered around the wharves, gazing into the deep waters, and was restrained from the deed only by the memory of the last loving voice he had heard. One gloomy evening, when even this memory had faded, and he awaited the approaching darkness to make his design secure, a hand was laid on his arm. A man in the simple garb of the Friends stood beside him, and a face which reflected the kindness of the Divine Father looked upon him. 'My child,' said he, 'I am drawn to thee by the great trouble of thy mind. Shall I tell thee what it is thee meditates?' The young man shook his head. 'I will be silent, then, but I will save thee. I know the human heart, and its trials and weaknesses, and it may be put into my mouth to give thee strength.' He took the young man's hand, as if he had been a little child, and led him to his home. He heard the sad story, from beginning to end ; and the young man wept upon his breast, to hear no word of reproach, but only the largest and tenderest pity bestowed upon him. They knelt down, side by side, at midnight ; and the Friend's right hand was upon his head while they prayed.

"The young man was rescued from his evil ways, to acknowledge still further the boundless mercy of Providence. The dissipation wherein he had recklessly sought death was, for him, a marvellous restoration to life. His lungs had become sound and free from the tendency to disease. The measure of his forgiveness was almost more than he could bear. He bore his cross thenceforward with a joyful resignation, and was mercifully drawn nearer and nearer to the Truth, until, in the fulness of his convictions, he entered into the brotherhood of the Friends.

"I have been powerfully moved to tell you this story," Friend Carter concluded, "from a feeling that it may be needed, here, at this time, to influence some heart trembling in the balance. Who is there among you, my friends, that may not snatch a brand from the burning? O, believe that pity and charity are the most effectual weapons given into the hands of us imperfect mortals, and leave the awful attribute of wrath in the hands of the Lord!"

He sat down, and dead silence ensued. Tears of emotion stood in the eyes of the hearers, men as well as women, and tears of gratitude and thanksgiving gushed warmly from those of Asenath. An ineffable peace and joy descended upon her heart.

When the meeting broke up, Friend Mitchenor, who had not recognized Richard Hilton, but had heard the story with feelings which he endeavored in vain to control, approached the preacher.

"The Lord spoke to me this day through thy lips," said he ; "will thee come to one side, and hear me a minute ?"

"Eli Mitchenor!" exclaimed Friend Carter; "Eli! I knew not thee was here! Does n't thee know me ?"

The old man stared in astonishment. "It seems like a face I ought to know," he said, "but I can't place thee."

They withdrew to the shade of one of the poplars. Friend Carter turned again, much moved, and, grasping the old man's hands in his own, exclaimed, —

"Friend Mitchenor, I was called upon to-day to speak of myself. I am — or, rather, I *was* — the Richard Hilton whom thee knew."

Friend Mitchenor's face flushed with mingled emotions of shame and joy, and his grasp on the preacher's hands tightened.

"But thee calls thyself Carter ?" he finally said.

"Soon after I was saved," was the reply, "an aunt on the mother's side died, and left her property to me, on condition that I should take her name. I was tired of my own then, and to give it up seemed only like losing my former self; but I should like to have it back again now."

"Wonderful are the ways of the Lord, and past finding out!" said the old man. "Come home with me, Richard, — come for my sake, for there is a concern on my mind until all is clear between us. Or, stay, — will thee walk home with Asenath, while I go with Moses?"

"Asenath?"

"Yes, there she goes, through the gate. Thee can easily overtake her. I'm coming, Moses!" — and he hurried away to his son's carriage, which was approaching.

Asenath felt that it would be impossible for her to meet Richard Hilton there. She knew not why his name had been changed; he had not betrayed his identity with the young man of his story; he evidently did not wish it to be known, and an unexpected meeting with her might surprise him into an involuntary revelation of the fact. It was enough for her that a saviour had arisen, and her lost Adam was redeemed, — that a holier light than the autumn sun's now rested, and would forever rest, on the one landscape of her youth. Her eyes shone with the pure brightness of girlhood, a soft warmth colored her cheek and smoothed away the coming lines of her brow, and her step was light and elastic as in the old time.

Eager to escape from the crowd, she crossed the highway, dusty with its string of returning carriages, and entered the secluded lane. The breeze had died away, the air was full of insect-sounds, and the warm light of the sinking sun fell upon the woods and meadows. Nature seemed penetrated with a sympathy with her own inner peace.

But the crown of the benignant day was yet to come. A quick footstep followed her, and erelong a voice, near at hand, called her by name.

She stopped, turned, and for a moment they stood silent, face to face.

" I knew thee, Richard ! " at last she said, in a trembling voice ; "may the Lord bless thee ! "

Tears were in the eyes of both.

" He has blessed me," Richard answered, in a reverent tone ; "and this is His last and sweetest mercy. Asenath, let me hear that thee forgives me."

" I have forgiven thee long ago, Richard, — forgiven, but not forgotten."

The hush of sunset was on the forest, as they walked on- ward, side by side, exchanging their mutual histories. Not a leaf stirred in the crowns of the tall trees, and the dusk, creeping along between their stems, brought with it a richer woodland odor. Their voices were low and subdued, as if an angel of God were hovering in the shadows, and listen- ing, or God Himself looked down upon them from the violet sky.

At last Richard stopped.

" Asenath," said he, "does thee remember that spot on the banks of the creek, where the rudbeckias grew ? "

" I remember it," she answered, a girlish blush rising to her face.

" If I were to say to thee now what I said to thee there, what would be thy answer ? "

Her words came brokenly.

" I would say to thee, Richard, — ' I can trust thee, — I *do* love thee ! ' "

" Look at me, Asenath."

Her eyes, beaming with a clearer light than even then when she first confessed, were lifted to his. She placed 'her hands gently upon his shoulders, and bent her head upon his breast. He tenderly lifted it again, and, for the first time, her virgin lips knew the kiss of man.

A HALF–LIFE AND HALF A LIFE.

"On garde longtemps son premier amant, quand on n'en prend point de second." — *Maximes Morales du Duc de la Rochefoucauld.*

T is not suffering alone that wears out our lives. We sometimes are in a state when a sharp pang would be hailed almost as a blessing, — when, rather than bear any longer this living death of calm stagnation, we would gladly rush into action, into suffering, to feel again the warmth of life restored to our blood, to feel it at least coursing through our veins with something like a living swiftness.

This death-in-life comes sometimes to the most earnest men, — to those whose life is fullest of energy and excitement. It is the reaction, the weariness which they name Ennui, foul fiend that eats fastest into the heart's core, that shakes with surest hand the sands of life, that makes the deepest wrinkles on the cheeks and deadens most surely the lustre of the eyes.

But what are the occasional visits of this life-consumer, this vampire that sucks out the blood, to his constant, never-failing presence? There are those who feel within themselves the power of living fullest lives, of sounding every chord of the full diapason of passion and feeling, yet who have been so hemmed around, so shut in by adverse and narrowing circumstances, that never, no, not once in their half-century of years which stretch from childhood to old age, have they been free to breath out, to speak aloud the heart that was in them. Ever the same wasting indifference to the things that are, the same ill-repressed longing for the things that might be. Long days of wearisome repetition of duties in which there is no life, followed by restless nights, when Imagination seizes the reins in her own hands, and paints the out-blossoming of those germs of happiness and fulness of being of whose existence within us we carry about always the aching consciousness.

And such things I have known from the moment when I first stepped from babyhood into childhood, from the time when life ceased to be a play and came to have its duties and its sufferings. Always the haunting sense of a happiness which I was capable of feeling, faint glimpses of a paradise of which I was a born denizen, — and always, too, the stern knowledge of the restraints which held me prisoner, the idle longings of an exile. But would no strong effort of will, no energy of heart or mind, break the bonds that held me down, — no steady perseverance of purpose win me a way out of darkness into light? No, for I was a woman, an ugly woman, whose girlhood had gone by without affection, and whose womanhood was passing without love, — a woman, poor and dependent on others for daily bread, and yet so bound by conventional duties to those around her that to break from them into independence would be to outrage all the prejudices of those who made her world.

I could plan such escape from my daily and yearly narrowing life, could dream of myself walking steadfast and unshaken through labor to independence, could picture a life where, if the heart were not fed, at least the tastes might be satisfied, could strengthen myself through all the imaginary details of my going forth from the narrow surroundings which made my prison-walls ; but when the time came to take the first step, my courage failed. I could not go out into that world which looked to me so wide and lonely ; the necessity for love was too strong for me, I must dwell among mine own people. There, at least, was the bond of custom, there was the affection which grows out of habit ; but in the world what hope had I to win love from strangers, with my repellent looks, awkward movements, and want of personal attractions?

Few persons know that within one hundred and fifty miles of the Queen City of the West, bounded on both sides by highly cultivated tracts of country, looking out westwardly on the very garden of Kentucky, almost in the range of railroad and telegraph, in the very geographical centre of our most populous regions, there lie some thousand square miles of superb woodland, rolling, hill above hill, in the beautiful undulations which characterize the country bordering on the Ohio, watered by fair streams which need only the clearing away of the few obstructions incident to a new country to make them navigable, and yet a country where the mail passes only once a week, where all communication is by horse-paths or by the slow course of the flat-boat, where schools are not known and churches are never seen, where the Methodist itinerant preacher gives all the religious instruction, and a stray newspaper furnishes all the political information. Does any one doubt my statement? Then let him ask a passage up-stream in one of the flat-boats that supply the primitive necessities of the small farmers who dwell on the banks of the Big Sandy, in that debatable border-land which lies between Kentucky and Virginia; or let him, if he have a taste for adventure, hire his horse at Catlettsburg, at the mouth of the river, and lose his way among the blind bridle-paths that lead to Louisa and to Prestonburg. If he stops to ask a night's lodging at one of the farm-houses that are to be found at the junction of the creeks with the rivers, log-houses with their primitive out-buildings, their half-constructed rafts of lumber ready to float down-stream with the next rise, their "dug-outs" for the necessities of river-intercourse, and their rough ox-carts for hauling to and from the mill, he will see before him such a home as that in which I passed the first twenty years of my life.

I had little claim on the farmer with whom I lived. I was the child by a former marriage of his wife, who had brought me with her into this wilderness, a puny, ailing creature of four years, and into the three years that followed was compressed all the happiness I could remember. The free life in the open air, the nourishing influence of the rich natural scenery by which I was surrounded, the grand, silent trees with their luxuriant foliage, the fresh, strong growth of the vegetation, all seemed to breathe health into my frame, and with health came the capacity for enjoyment. I was happy in the mere gift of existence, happy in the fulness of content, with no playmate but the kindly and lovely mother Earth from whose bosom I drew fulness of life.

But in my seventh year my mother died, worn out by the endless, unvarying round of labors which break down the constitutions of our small farmers' wives. She grew sallow and thin under repeated attacks of chills and fever, brought into the world, one after another, three puny infants, only to lay them away from her breast, side by side, under the sycamore that overshadowed our cornfield, and visibly wasted away, growing more and more feeble, until, one winter morning, we laid her, too, at rest by her babies. Before the year was out, my father (so I called him) was married again.

My step-mother was a good woman, and meant to do her duty by me. Nay, she was more than that: she was, as far her poor light went, a Christian. She had experienced religion in the great revival of 18—, which was felt all through Western Kentucky, under the preaching of the Reverend Peleg Dawson, and when she married my father and went to bury herself in the wilds of "Up Sandy" was a shining light in the Methodist Church, a class-leader who had had and had told experiences.

But all that glory was over now; it had flashed its little day: for there is a glow in the excitement of our religious revivals as potent in its effect on the imaginations of women and young men as ever were the fastings and penances which brought the dreams and reveries, the holy visions and· the glorious revealings, of the Catholic votaries. In this short, triumphant time of spiritual pride lay the whole romance of my step-mother's life. Perhaps it was well for her soul that she was taken from the scene of her triumphs and brought again to the hard realities of life. The self-exaltation, the *un*godly pride passed away; but there was left the earnest, prayerful desire to do her duty in her way and calling, and the first path of duty which opened to her zeal was that which led to the care of a motherless child, the saving of an immortal soul. And in all sincerity and uprightness did she strive to walk in it. But what woman of five-and-thirty, who has outlived her youth and womanly tenderness in the loneliness and hardening influences of a single life, and who marries at last for a shelter in old age, knows the wants of a little child? Indeed, what but a mother's love has the long-enduring patience to support the never-ceasing calls for forbearance and perseverance which a child makes upon a grown person? Those little ones need the nourishment of love and praise, but such milk for babes can come only from a mother's breast. I got none of it. On the contrary, my dearly loved independence, my wild-wood life, where Nature had become to me my nursing-mother, was exchanged for one of never-ceasing supervision. " Little girls must learn to be useful," was the phrase that greeted my unwilling ears fifty times a day, which pursued me through my daily round of dish-washings, floor-sweepings, bed-making and potato-peeling, to overtake me at last in the very moment when I hoped to reap the reward of my diligence in a free afternoon by the river-side in the crotch of the water-maple that hung over the stream, clutching me and fastening me down to the hated square of patchwork, which bore, in the spots of red that defaced its white purity in following the line of my stitches, the marks of the wounds that my awkward hands inflicted on themselves with their tiny weapon.

And so the years went on. It was a pity that no babies came to soften our hearts, my step-mother's and mine, and to draw us nearer together as only the presence of children

can. A household without children is always hard and angular, even when surrounded by all the softening influences
of refinement and education. What was ours with its poverty
and roughness, its every-day cares and its endless discom-
forts? One day was like all the rest, and in their wearying
succession they rise up in my memory like ghosts of the
past coming to lay their cold, death-like hands on the feebly
kindling hopes of the present. I see myself now, as I look
back, a tall, awkward girl of fifteen, with my long, straggling,
sunburnt hair, my sallow, yet pimply complexion, my small,
weak-looking blue eyes, that every exposure to the sun and
wind would redden, and my long, lean hands and arms, that
offended my sense of beauty constantly, as I dwelt on their
hopelessly angular turns. I had one beauty; so my little
paper-framed glass, that rested on the rough rafter that
edged the sloping roof of my garret, told me, whenever I
took it down to gaze in it, which, but for that beauty, would
have been but seldom. It was a finely cut and firmly set
mouth and chin. There was, and I felt it, beauty and character in the curves of the lips, in the rounding of the chin;
there was even a healthy ruddiness in the lips, and something of delicacy in the even, well-set teeth that showed
themselves when they parted.

The gazing at these beauties gave me great pleasure, not
for any effect they might ever produce in others, — what did
I know of that? — but because I had in myself a strong love
of the beautiful, a passion for grace of form and brilliancy
of color which made doubly distasteful to me our bare,
uncouth walls, with their ugly straight-backed chairs, and
their frightfully painted yellow or red tables and chests of
drawers.

My step - mother's appearance, too, was a constant offence to my beauty-loving eye, — with her lank, tall figure,
round which clung those narrow skirts of "bit" calico, dingy red or dreary brown, — her feet shod in the heavy store-
shoes which were brought us from Catlettsburg by the returning flat-boat men, — her sharp-featured face, the fore-

head and cheeks covered with brown, mouldy-looking spots, the eyes deep-set, with a livid dyspeptic ring around them, and the lips thin and pinched, — the whole face shaded by the eternal sun-bonnet, which never left her head from early sunrise till late bedtime (no Sandy woman is ever seen without her sun-bonnet). All these were perpetual annoyances to me ; they made me discontented without knowing why ; they filled me with disgust, a disgust which my respect for her good qualities could not overcome.

And then our life, how dreary ! The rising in the cold, gray dawn to prepare the breakfast of corn-dodgers and bacon for my father and his men, — the spreading the table-cloth, stained with the soil-spots of yesterday's meal, — the putting upon it the ugly unmatched crockery, — the straggling in of the unwashed, uncombed men in their coarse working-clothes, redolent of the week's unwholesome toil, — their washings, combings, and low talk close by my side, — the varied uses to which our household utensils were put, — the dipping of dirty knives into the salt and of dirty fingers into the meat-dish, — all filled me then, and fill me now, with loathing.

There was a relief when the men left the house ; but then came the dreary "slicking-up," almost more disgusting, in its false, superficial show of cleanliness, than had been the open carelessness of the workmen.

But there was no time for rest ; my step-mother's sharp, high-pitched voice was heard calling, "Janet !" and I followed her to the garden to dig the potatoes from the hills or to the cornfield to pull and husk the three dozen ears of corn which made our chief dish at dinner. Then came the week's washing, the apple-peeling, the pork-salting, work varied only with the varying season, until the blowing of the horn at twelve brought back the men to dinner, after which came again the clearing up, again the day's task, and again the supper.

I often thought that the men around us were always more cheerful and merry than the women. They worked as hard, they endured as many hardships, but they had, certainly, more pleasures. There was the evening lounge by the fire in winter, the sitting on the fence or at the door-step in summer, when, pipe or cigar in mouth, knife and whittling-stick in hand, jest and gibe would pass round among them, and the boisterous laugh would go up, reaching me, as I lay, tired out, on my little cot, or leaned disconsolate at my garret-window, looking with longing eyes far out into the darkness of the woods. No such gatherings-together of the women did I ever see. If one of our neighbors dragged her weary steps to our kitchen, and sat herself down, baby in lap, on the upturned tub or flag-bottomed chair that I dusted off with my apron, it was to commence the querulous complaint of the last week's chill or the heavy washing of the day before, the ailing baby, or the troublesome child, all told in the same whining voice. Even the choice bit of gossip which roused us at rare intervals always had its dark side, on which these poor women dwelt with a perverse pleasure.

In short, life was too hard for them; it brought its constant cares without any alleviating pleasures. Their homes were only places of monotonous labor, — their husbands so many hard taskmasters, who exacted from them more than their strength could give, — their children, who should have been the delight of their mothers' hearts, so many additional burdens, the bearing and nursing of which broke down their poor remaining health; the glorious and lavish Nature in which they lived only brought to them added labor, and shut them out from the few social enjoyments that they knew of.

I was old enough to feel all this, — not to reason on it as I can now, but to rebel against it with all the violence of a vehement nature which feels its strength only in the injuries it inflicts upon itself in its useless struggles for freedom. Bitter tears did I shed sometimes, as I lay with my head on my arms, leaning on that narrow window-sill, — tears of passionate regret that I was not a boy, a man, that I might, by the very force of my right arm, hew my way out of that encircling forest into the world of which I dreamed, — tears, too, that, being as I was, only an ugly, ignorant girl, I could not be allowed to care only for myself, and dream away my life in this same forest, which charmed me while it hemmed me in.   My rude, chaotic nature had something of force in it, strength which I knew would stand me in good stead, could I ever find an outlet for it; it had also a power of enjoyment, keen, vivid, could I ever get leave to enjoy.

At length came the opening, the glimpse of sunlight.   I remember, as if it were but yesterday, that afternoon which first showed to my physical sight something of that full life of which my imagination had framed a rude, faint sketch. I was standing at the end of the meadow, just where the rails had been thrown down for the cows, when, looking up the path that led through the wood by the river, I saw, almost at my side, a man on horseback. He stopped, and, half raising his hat, a motion I had never seen before, said, —

" Is this Squire Boarders's place ? "

I pushed back my sun-bonnet, and looked up at him.   I see him now as I saw him then; for my quick, startled glance took in the whole face and figure, which daguerrotyped themselves on my memory.   A frank, open face, with well-cut and well-defined features and large hazel eyes, set off by curling brown hair, was smiling down upon me, and, throwing himself from his horse, a young man of about five-and-twenty stood beside me.   He had to repeat his question before I gained presence of mind enough to answer him.

" Is this Squire Boarders's house, and do you think I could get a night's lodging here ? "

It was no unusual thing for us to give a night's lodging to the boatmen from the river, or to the farmers from the back-country, as they passed to or from Catlettsburg ; but what accommodation had we for such a guest as here presented ? I walked before him up the path to the house, and, shyly pointing to my step-mother, who stood on the porch, said, —

" That 's Miss Boarders ; you can ask her."

And then, before he had time to answer, I fled in an agony of bashfulness to my refuge under the water-maple behind the house. I lingered there as long as I dared, — longer, indeed, than I had any right to linger, for I heard my mother's voice crying, "Janet!" and I well knew that there was nobody but myself to mix the corn-cake, spread the table, or run the dozen errands that would be needed. I slipped in by the back-door, and, escaping my step-mother's peevish complaints, passed into the little closet which served us for pantry, and, scooping up the meal, began diligently to mix it.

The window by which I stood opened on the porch. My father and his men had come in, and, tipping their chairs against the wall, or mounted on the porch-railing, were smoking their cigars, laughing, joking, talking, — and there in the midst of them sat the stranger, smoking too, and joining in their talk with an easy earnestness that seemed to win them at once. Our country-people do not spare their questions. My father took the lead, the men throwing in a remark now and then.

"I calculate you have never been in these parts before?"

"No, never. You have a beautiful country here."

"The country's well enough, if we could clear off some of them trees that stop a man every way he turns. Did you come up from Lowiza to-day?"

"No ; I have only ridden from the mouth of Blackberry, I believe you call it. I have left a boat and crew there, who will be up in the morning."

"What truck have you got on your boat?"

"Lumber and so forth, and plenty of tools of one sort or other."

"Damn me if I don't believe you're the man who is coming up here to open the coal mines on Burgess's land!" And the whole crowd gathered round him.

He laughed good-naturedly.

"Yes, I am coming to live among you. I hope you'll give me a welcome."

There was a cheery sound of welcome from the men, but my father shook his head.

"We don't like no new-fangled notions, noways, up here, and I 'll not say that I 'm glad you 're bringing them in; but, at any rate, you 're welcome here to-night."

The young man held out his hand.

"We are to be close neighbors, Squire Boarders, and I hope we shall be good friends; but I ought to tell you all about myself. Mr. Burgess's land has been bought by a company, who intend to open the coal mines, as you know and I am sent up here as their agent, to make ready for the miners and the workmen. We shall clear away a little, and put up some rough shanties, to make our men comfortable before we go to work. We shall bring a new set of people among you, those Scotch and Welsh miners; but I believe they are a peaceable set, and we 'll try to be friendly with each other."

The frank speech and the free, open face seemed to mollify my father.

"And how do you call yourself, stranger, when you are at home?"

"My name is George Hammond."

"Well, as I was telling you, you 're welcome here to-night, and I don't know as I 've anything against your settling over the river on Burgess's land. The people round here have been telling me your coming will be a good thing for us farmers, because you 'll bring us a market for our corn and potatoes; but I don't see no use of raising more corn than we want for ourselves. We have enough selling to do with our lumber, and you 'll be thinning out the trees. — But there 's my old woman 's got her supper ready."

I listened as I waited on the table. The talk varied from farming to mining and the state of the river, merging at last into the politics of the country, and through the whole of it I watched the stranger: noticed how different was his language from anything I had ever heard before; marked the clear tones of his voice, and the distinctness of his utterance, contrasting with the heavy, thick gutturals, the running of words into each other, the slovènly drawl of my father and his men ; watched his manner of eating, his neat disposition of his food on his plate ; saw him move his chair back with a slight expression of annoyance, unmarked by any one else, as Will Foushee spit on the floor beside him. All this I observed, in a mood half envious, half sullen, — a mood which pursued me that night into my little attic, as I peevishly questioned with myself wherein lay the difference between us.

"Why is this man any better than Will Foushee or Ned Burgess ? He is no stronger nor better able to do a day's work. Why am I afraid of him, when I don't care an acorn for the others ? Why do my father and the men listen to him and crowd round him ? What makes him stand among them as if he did not belong to them, even when he talks of what they know better than he ? There is not a man round Sandy that could make me feel as ashamed as that gentleman did when he spoke to me this afternoon. Is it because he is a gentleman ?" And sullenly I resolved that I would be put down by no airs. I was as good as he, and would show him to-morrow morning that I felt so. Then came the bitter acknowledgment. "I am not as good as he is. I am a stupid, ugly girl, who knows nothing but hateful housework and a little of the fields and trees ; and he, — I suppose he has been to school, and read plenty of books, and lived among quality." And I cried myself to sleep before I had made up my mind fully to acknowledge his superiority.

It was one of my greatest pleasures to get up early. Our people were not early risers, except when work pressed upon them, and I often secured my only leisure hour for the day by stealing down the staircase, out into the woods, by early sunrise, when, wrapped in an old shawl, and sheltered from the dew by climbing into the lower branches of my pet maple, I would watch the fog reaching up the opposite hills, putting forth as it were an arm, by which, stretched

18

far out over the trees, it seemed to lift itself from the valley,
— or, perhaps carrying with me one of the few books which
made my library, I would spell out the sentences and attempt to extract their meaning.

They were a strange medley, my books ; some belonging
to my step-mother, and others borrowed or begged from the
neighbors, or brought to me by the men, with whom I was
a favorite, and who knew my passion for reading. My
mother's books were mostly religious : a life of Brainerd,
the missionary, whose adventures rouscd within me a gleam
of religious enthusiasm ; some sermons of the leading Methodist clergy, which, to her horror, I pronounced stupid ; and
a torn copy of the " Imitation of Christ," a book which she
threatened to take from me, because she believed it had
something to do with the Papists, but to which, for that
very reason, I clung with a tenacity and read with an earnestness which brought at last its own beautiful fruits.
Then, there was the " Scottish Chiefs," a treasure-house
of delight to me, — two or three trashy novels, given me by
Tom Salyers, of which my mother knew nothing, — and
(the only poetry I had ever seen) a song-book, which had,
scattered among its vulgarisms and puerilities, some gems
of Burns and Moore. These, my natural, unvitiated taste
had singled out, and I would croon them over to myself, set
them to a tune of my own composing, and half sing, half
chant them, when at work out-of-doors, till my mother declared I was going crazy.

This morning I did not read. I sat looking down into
the water from my perch, carrying on the inward discussion
of the night before, and wishing that breakfast-time were
come, that I might try my strength and show that I was
not to be put down by any assumption of superiority, when
suddenly a voice near me made me start so that I almost
lost my balance. Mr. Hammond was standing beneath.
He laughed, and held out his hand to help me down ; but
I sprang past him and was on my way to the house, when
suddenly my brave resolutions came back to my mind, and

I stood still with a feeling of defiance. I wondered what he would dare to say. Would he tell me how stupid he thought us all, how like the very pigs we lived? or would he describe his own grand house and the great places he had seen? I scowled up sullenly.

"Will you tell me where to find a towel, that I may wash my face here by the river-side?"

I laughed aloud, and with that laugh fled my sullenness. He looked a little puzzled, but went on, —

"I went to bed so early that I cannot sleep any longer; and if I could only find some way of getting across the river, I could get things under way a little before my men come up."

There were ways, then, in which I could help him, — he was not so immeasurably above me, — and down went my defiant spirit. The towel, a crash roller, luckily clean, was brought at once, and gathering courage as I stood by and saw him finish his washing, I said, —

"I can scull you over the river in a few minutes, if you will go in our skiff."

"You? can you manage that shell of a thing? will your father let you take it, Miss Boarders?"

"My name is Janet Rainsford, and Squire Boarders is not my father," said I, some of my sullenness returning.

"If you will take me, Janet," said he, with the frank, open-hearted tone which had won my step-father the night before, — a tone before which my sullenness melted.

I jumped in, and, letting him pass me before I threw off the rope, sculled the little dug-out into the middle of the river. No boatman on the Sandy was more skilful than I in the management of the little vessel, for in it most of my leisure time had been passed for the last year or two. My step-mother had scolded, my father grumbled, and the farmers' wives and daughters had shaken their heads and "allowed that Janet Rainsford would come to no good, if she was let fool about here and there, like a boy." But on that point I was incorrigible; the boat was my one escape from

my daily drudgery, and late at night and early in the morning I went up and down among the shoals and bars, under
the trees and over the ripples, till every turn of the current
was familiar to me.   I knew all the boatmen, too, up and
down the river, would pull along-side their rafts or pushing-
boats, and get from them a slice of their corn-bread or a
cup of coffee, or at least a pleasant word or jest.   And none
but pleasant words did I ever receive from the rough, but
honorable men whom I met.   They respected, as the rough-
est men will always do, my lonely girlhood, and felt a sort
of pride in the daring, adventurous spirit that I showed.

My knowledge of the river stood Mr. Hammond in good
stead that morning, as soon as I understood that he was
looking for a place where his men could land easily.   It was
only to sweep round a small bluff that jutted into the river,
and carry the skiff into the mouth of Nat's Creek, where
the bank sloped gradually down to the water from a level
bit of meadow-land that extended back some rods before
the hills began to rise.   Mr. Hammond leaped out.

"The very place, — and here, on this point shall be my
saw-mill.   I'll run the road through here and up the creek
to the mining-ground, and build my store under the ledge
there, and my shanties on each side of the road."

I caught his enthusiasm, and my shyness all gone, I
found myself listening and suggesting; more than that, I
found my suggestions attended to.   I knew the river well;
I knew what points of land would be overflowed in the
June rise; I knew how far the backwater would reach up
the creek; I knew the least obstructed paths through the
woods; I could even tell where the most available timber
was to be found.   I felt, too, that my knowledge was appreciated.   George Hammond had that one best gift that belongs to all successful leaders, whether of armies, colonies,
or bands of miners; he recognized merit when he saw it.
From that morning a feeling of self-respect dawned upon
me, I was not so altogether ignorant as I had thought myself, I had some available knowledge; and with that feeling

came the determination to raise myself out of that slough of despond into which I had fallen the night before.

From that time a sort of friendship sprang up between George Hammond and myself. Every morning I rowed him across the river, and, in the early morning light, before the workmen were out of bed, he talked over, partly to himself and partly to me, his plans for the day and his vexations of the day before, until I began to offer advice and make suggestions, which made him laughingly call me his little counsellor.

Then in the evenings (he slept at my father's) he would pick up my books and amuse himself with talking to me about them, laugh at my crude enthusiasms, clear up some difficult passage, prune away remorselessly the trash that had crept into my little collection, until, one day, returning from Cincinnati, where business had called him, he brought with him a store of books inexhaustible to my inexperienced eyes, and declared himself my teacher for the winter.

"Never mind Janet's knitting and mending, Mrs. Boarders," said he, in reply to my mother's complaints; "she is a smart girl, and may be a schoolmistress yet, and earn more money than any women on Sandy."

"But I am afraid," my step-mother answered, "that the books she reads are not godly, and have no grace in them. They look to me like players' trash. I 've tried to do my duty to Janet," she continued, plaintively; "but I hope the Lord won't hold me accountable for her headstrong ways."

Meantime, as I read in one of my books, and repeated to myself over and over again in my fulness of content, —

"How happily the days
Of Thalaba went by!"

How rapidly fled that winter, and how soon came the spring, that would bring me, I thought, new hopes, new interests, new companions!

How changed a scene did I look upon, that bright April morning, when I went over the river to see that all was in

readiness for the boats from below which were to bring
Esther Hammond to her new home! She was to keep her
brother's house ; and furniture, books, and pictures, such as
I had never dreamed of, had been sent up by the last-re-
turning boatmen, all of which I had helped Mr. Hammond
to arrange in the little two-story cottage which stood on the
first rise of the hill behind the store.

A little plat of ground was hedged in with young Osage-
orange shrubs, and within it one of the miners, who had
formerly been an under-gardener in a great house in Scot-
land, had already prepared some flower-beds and sodded
carefully the little lawn, laying down the walks with bright-
colored tan, which contrasted pleasantly with the lively
green of the grass. From the gate one might look up and
down the road, bordered on one side by the trees that hung
over the river, and on the other by the miners' houses, one-
story cottages, each with its small enclosure, and showing
every degree of cultivation, from the neat vegetable-patch
and whitewashed porch of the Scotch families to the neglected waste ground and slovenly potato-patch of the Irishmen. There were some Sandians among the hands, but
they never could be made to take one of the houses prepared for the miners. They lived back on the creek, generally on their own lands, raised their corn and tobacco, cut
their lumber, and hunted or rode the country, taking jobs
only when they felt so inclined, but showing themselves
fully able to compete with the best hands both in skill and
in endurance, when they were willing to work.

On the side of the hill across the creek could be seen the
entrance to the mines, and down that hill were passing constantly the cars, loaded with earth and stone taken from the
tunnel, which fell with a thundering sound into the valley
beneath. Below me was the store, gay with its multifarious
goods, which supplied all the needs of the miners and their
wives, from the garden-tools and seeds for the afternoon-
work to the gay-colored dresses for the Sunday leisure, —
where, too, on Saturday night, whiskey was to be had in

exchange for the scrip in which their wages were paid, and where, sometimes, the noise waxed fast and furious, till Mr. Hammond would cut off the supply of liquor, as the readiest means of stilling the tumult.

On this side the river all was changed. But as I looked that morning across the stream towards my step-father's farm, my own home, everything there lay as wild and unimproved as I had known it since the first day my mother brought me there, comfortless and disorderly as it was when, child as I was, I could remember the tears of fatigue and discouragement which she dropped upon my face as she put me for the first time into my little crib ; but there, too, were still (and my heart exulted as I saw them) the glorious water-maples, the giant sycamores, and the bright-colored chestnut-trees, which I had known and loved so long. Would Miss Hammond see how beautiful they were ? would she praise them as her brother had done ? would she listen as kindly to my rhapsodies about them ? and would she say, as he had said, that I was a poet by nature, with a poet's quick appreciation of beauty and the poet's gift of enthusiastic expression ? I could not tell whether Esther Hammond would be to me the friend her brother had been, with the added blessing, that, being a woman, I could go freely to her with my deficiencies in sure dependence upon her aid and sympathy, — or if she would come to stand between me and him, to take away from me my friend and teacher. Time alone would show ; and meanwhile I must be busy with my preparations, for the boats were expected at noon, and Mr. Hammond, who had ridden down to Louisa to meet them, had said that he depended upon me to have things cheerful and in order when they arrived.

Two hours' hard work saw everything in its place, the furniture arranged to the best of my ability, but wanting, as I sorely felt, the touch of a mistress's hand to give it a home-like look. I had done my best, but what did I know of the arrangement of a lady's house ? I hardly knew the use of half the things I touched. But I *would* not let my old spirit of discontent creep over me now; so, betaking myself to the woods, which were full of the loveliest spring flowers, I brought back such a profusion of violets, spring-beauties, and white bloodroot-blossoms, that the whole room was brightened with their beauty, while their faint, delicate perfume filled the air.

"Surely these must please her," I said to myself, as I put the last saucerful on the table, and stepped back to see the result of my work.

"They certainly will, Janet," said George Hammond, who had entered behind me. "How well you have worked, and how pleasant everything looks! Esther will be so much obliged to you. She is just below, in the boat. Will you not come with me and help her up the bank?"

But I hung back, bashful and frightened, while he called some of the men to his assistance, and, hurrying down to the river, landed the boat, and was presently seen walking toward the house with a lady leaning upon his arm. I saw her from the window. A tall, dignified woman, with a face, — yes, beautiful, certainly, for there were the regular features, the dark eyes, with their straight brows, the heavy, dark hair, parted over the fair, smooth forehead, but so quiet, so cold, so almost haughty, that my heart stood still with an undefined alarm.

She came in and sat down in one of the chairs without taking the least notice of me. Mr. Hammond spoke, —

"This is Janet Rainsford, my little friend that I told you of, Esther. I hope you will be as good friends as we have been. She will show you every beautiful place around the country, and make you acquainted with the people, too."

Miss Hammond looked at me with a steadiness of gaze under which my eyes sank.

"I shall not trouble the young person much, since I shall only walk when you can go with me; and as for the people, it is not necessary for me to know them, I suppose."

George Hammond bit his lip.

"Janet has taken great pains to put everything in order

for us here. I should hardly know the room, it is so improved since I left it this morning."

"She is very kind," said his sister, languidly; "but, George, how horribly this furniture is arranged, — the sofa across the window, the centre-table in the corner!"

"O, you will have plenty of time to arrange it, Esther. Come, let me show you your own room; you will want to rest while your Dutch girl — what's her name? Catrine? — gets us something to eat."

Miss Hammond followed her brother to her room, while, mortified and angry with her, with myself, I escaped from the house, jumped into my skiff, and hardly stopped to breathe till I had reached my own little garret. I flung myself on my bed, and burst into bitter tears of resentment and despair. So, after all my pains, after my endeavors to improve myself, after all I had done, I was not worth the notice of a real lady. I supposed I was an uncouth, awkward girl, disagreeable enough to her; she would not want to see me near her. All I had done was miserable; it would have been better to let things alone. I never would go near her again, — that was certain, — she should not be troubled by me; — and my tears fell hot and fast upon my pillow. Then came my old sullenness. Why was she any better than I? Her brother thought me worth talking to; could she not find me worthy of at least a kind look? Perhaps she knew more than I did of books: but what of that? She had not half the useful knowledge wherewith to make her way here in the woods. And what right had she to bring her haughty looks and proud ways here among our people? My sullenness gave way before my bitter disappointment and my offended pride. I was only a child of sixteen, sensitive and distrustful of myself, and her cold looks and colder words had keenly wounded me.

A week passed, in which I gave myself most earnestly to the household tasks, going through them with dogged pertinacity, and accomplishing an amount of work which made my step-mother declare that Janet was coming back to her senses after all. It was only my effort to forget my disappointment.

On the Saturday evening when I sat tired out with my exertions, Mr. Hammond came up the path. How my heart leaped at seeing him! How good he was to come! His sister had not taught him to despise me. But when he asked me to come over the next day, and see what he had done to his house and garden, the demon of sullen pride took possession of me again. I would not go. I had too much to do ; my mother would want me to get the dinner. In short, I could not go. He bore it good-naturedly, though I think he understood it, and, leaving with me a package of books which he had promised me, said he must go, as Esther would be waiting tea for him.

Many another endeavor did George Hammond make to bring his sister and myself together, but the first impression had been too strong for me, and Miss Hammond made no effort to remove it. I do not believe it ever crossed her mind to try to do so. Little was it to her whether or no she made herself pleasant to a stupid, ugly girl. She had her books, her light household cares, her letter-writing, her gardening, her walks and drives with her brother, and she felt and showed little interest in anything else. Very unpopular she was among the people around her, who contrasted her cold reserve with her brother's frank cordiality ; but she troubled herself not at all about her unpopularity. For me, I kept shyly out of her way, and fell back into my old habits.

I had not lost my friend, Mr. Hammond. He did not read with me regularly as before, but he kept me supplied with books, and the very infrequency of his lessons stimulated me to redoubled effort, that I might surprise him by my progress when we met again. Then there was scarcely a day that some business did not take him past our house, or that I did not meet him by the river-bank or at the store. Sometimes he would ask me to row him down the stream on some errand, sometimes he would take me with him in his rides. I was a fearless horsewoman, and Miss Hammond did not ride. In all those meetings he was frank and kind as ever ; he told me of his plans, his annoyances, his projects. No, I had not lost my friend, as I had feared, and when assured of this, I could do without Miss Hammond.

And so the weeks glided into months, and the months into years, and I was nineteen years old. Four years had passed since the morning when George Hammond first awakened my self-esteem, first gave me the impulse to raise myself out of my awkwardness and ignorance, to make of myself something better than one of the worn, depressed, dispirited women I saw around me. Had I done anything for myself ? I asked. I was not educated, I had no acquirements, so-called ; but I had read, and read well, some good and famous books, and I knew that I had made their contents my own. I was richer for their beauties and excellencies. With my self-respect had come, too, a desire to improve my surroundings, and, as far as they lay under my control, they had been improved. Our household was more orderly ; some little attempt at neatness and decoration was to be seen around and in the house, and my own room, where I had full sway, was beautiful in its rustic adornment.

My glass, too, the poor little three-cornered, paper-framed companion of my girlhood, showed me some change. The complexion had cleared, the hair had taken a decided brown, and the angular figure had rounded and filled. It was hardly a week since, standing in Miss Hammond's kitchen counting over with her servant-girl the basketful of fresh eggs which were sent from our house every week, I had overheard Mr. Hammond say to his sister, —

"Really, Janet Rainsford has improved so much that she is almost pretty. Her brown hair tones so well with her quiet eyes ; and as to her mouth, it is really lovely, so finely cut, and with so much character in it."

What was it to me that Miss Hammond's cold voice answered, —

"I think you make a fool of yourself, George, and of that girl, too, going on as you do about her. She will be entirely unfitted for her state of life, and for the people she must live with."

Her words had hardly time to chill my heart when it bounded again, as I turned hurriedly away and passed under the window on my way out, at hearing her brother's answer : —

"There is too much in her to be spoiled. I like her. She has talent and character, and I cannot understand, Esther, why you are so prejudiced against her."

There were others besides Mr. Hammond who thought me improved and who liked me. Tom Salyers never let an evening pass without dropping into our house on his way home from the store, where he was a sort of overseer or salesman, — never failed to bring in its season the earliest wild-flower or the freshest fruit, — had thoroughly searched Catlettsburg for books to please me, — nay, had once sent an indefinite order to a Cincinnati bookseller to put up twenty dollars' worth of the best books for a lady, which order was filled by a collection of the Annuals of six years back and a few unsalable modern novels. I read them all most conscientiously and gratefully, and would not listen for a moment to Mr. Hammond's jests about them : but, a few weeks afterwards, I almost repented of my complaisance, when Tom Salyers took me at an advantage while rowing me down to Louisa one afternoon, and, seeing a long stretch of river before him without shoal or sand-bar, leisurely laid up his oars, and, letting the boat float with the stream, asked me, abruptly, to marry him, and go with him up into the country to a new place which he meant to clear and farm.

I laughed at him at first, but he persisted till I was forced to believe him in earnest ; and then I told him how foolish he was to fancy an ugly, sallow-looking girl like me, who had no father nor mother, when he might take one of John Mills's rosy daughters, or go down to Catlettsburg and get somebody whose father would give him a farm already cleared.

"You are laughing at me, Janet," he said. "I know I am not smart enough for you, nor hardly fit to keep company with you, now that Hammond has taught you so many things that are proper for a lady to know; but I love you true, and if you can only fancy me, I 'll work so hard that you 'll be able to keep a hired girl and have all your time for reading and going about the woods as you like to do. And you 'll be in your own house, instead of under Squire Boarders and his sharp-spoken wife. Could n't you fancy me after a while? I 'd do anything you said to make myself agreeable and fit company for you."

"You are very fit company for me now, Tom," I said, "and you are of a great deal more use in the world than I am; you know more that is worth knowing than I do. Only let us be good friends, as we have always been, and do not talk about anything else."

"I will not talk any more of it now," said he, "if so be it don't please you, and if you 'll promise never to say any more to me about the Mills gals, or any of them critters down in Catlettsburg, — I can't abide the sight of them, — and if you 'll let me come and see you all the same, and row you about and take you to the mill when you want flour."

I held out my hand to Tom with the earnest assurance that I always liked to see him and talk to him, and that there was nobody whom I would sooner ask to do me a kindness.

The poor fellow choked a little as he thanked me, and then, recovering himself, rowed a few strokes in silence, when, looking round as if to assure himself that there was nothing near us but the quiet trees, he said suddenly, —

"I 'll tell you what, Janet, I 've a great mind to tell you something, seeing how you 're not a woman that can't hold her tongue, and then you think so much of Hammond."

I started with a quick sense of alarm, but Tom went doggedly on.

"You know what a hard winter we 've had, with this low

water and no January rise, and all that ice in the Ohio. They say they 're starving for coal down in Cincinnati, and here we 've no end of it stacked up. Well, Hammond, he 's had hard work enough to keep the men along through the winter. Many another man would have turned them off, but he would n't do it; so he 's shinned here and shinned there to get money to pay them their wages, and they 've had scrip, and we 've fairly brought goods up to the store overland, on horseback and every kind of way, just for their convenience; and now the damned Irish rascals, with some of the Sandy boys for leaders, have made up their minds to strike for higher wages the minute we have a rise, just when we 'll need all hands to get the coal off, and all those boats laying at the mouth, too. I heard it day before yesterday, by chance like, when Jim Foushee and the two O'Learys were sitting smoking on the fence behind the store. The O'Learys were tight with the Redeye they had aboard, and let it out in their stupid 'colloguing,' as they call it; but Jim Foushee saw me standing at the window, and right away called in two or three of the Sandy men and threatened my life if I told Hammond. They have watched me like a cat ever since, and never left me and Hammond alone together. They are with Hammond now, launching a coal-boat, or I 'd never have got off with you."

I sat breathless. I knew it was ruin to let the expected rise pass without getting the coal-boats down; but what could be done?

"Don't look so pale, Janet. You can tell Hammond, you know, and he 'll find a way to circumvent them. And it was to tell you all this that I brought you out here this afternoon, only my unlucky tongue would talk of what I see it 's too soon to talk of yet. But here 's Louisa, right ahead. Make haste and get your traps, while I settle my business, and we 'll be back, perhaps, in time for you to manage some way to see Hammond to-night. Nobody knows you went with me, and you 'll never be suspected."

Not Tom Salyers's most rapid and vigorous rowing could make our little skiff keep pace with my impatience; but, thanks to his efforts, the sun was still high when he landed me in the little cove behind our house, where I could run up through the woods to our back-door, while he pulled boldly up to the store-landing and called some of the men to help him carry his purchases up the bank. I did not stop for a word with my step-mother, but passing rapidly through the house, threw my parcels on the bed in the sitting-room, and, running down the walk to the maple-tree under which my dug-out was always tied, jumped into it and sculled out into the river. The coal-boat had just been launched, and George Hammond was standing on the bank superintending the calking of the seams which the water made visible. I pushed up to the bank, and called to him as I neared, —

"Can you not come, Mr. Hammond, a little way up-stream with me? I have found those young tulip-trees that you want for your garden; they are just round the bend above Nat's Creek. Jim Foushee will see to that work, and I have just time to show them to you before supper."

I was a favorite with Jim Foushee. He laughed a joking welcome to me, as he said, —

"I'll see to this, sir, if you want to go with Janet Rains-ford. She's the gal that knows the woods. A splendid Sandy wife you'll make some young fellow, Janet, if you don't get too book-learned."

In five minutes we were off and had rounded the point out of sight and hearing. In a few hurried words I told my story, but at first Mr. Hammond would not believe it.

"Those men that I've done so much for and worked so hard for this winter!"

At last, convinced, his face set with the determined look that I had seen on it once or twice before.

"I'll not raise the wages of a single man, and, what's more, I'd turn them all off the place, if only I could find others. But those boats at Catlettsburg, they are the most important. The company would send me up men from Cincinnati, if only I could get word to them; but these rascals will stop any letter I send. Those Sandians are capable of it, — or rather they are capable of putting the Irishmen up to doing their dirty work for them."

"A letter would be safe, if it once reached Catlettsburg?" I asked.

"Certainly. But how to get it there?"

"I can take it. Nobody will suspect me. Give me the letter to-night, and I will go to-morrow."

"You, Janet? you are crazy!"

"No, indeed. I often ride to Louisa; what is to hinder me from having errands to Catlettsburg. I could go down there in one day, and take two days back, if my father thinks it is too much for old Bill to take it through in one."

"O, you could borrow Swiftfoot. I have often lent him to you, and he would carry you safely and surely. I don't believe any harm would come to you, and so much depends upon it."

I turned the skiff decidedly.

"You have only to get your letter ready and give it to me when I come over in the morning to borrow Swiftfoot. I will take care of all the rest."

And, sculling rapidly, we were at the wharf again before he had time to raise objections. I knew that I could persuade my mother into letting me go to Louisa again the next day, for we needed all our spring purchases, — and once there it was easy to find it necessary to go to the mouth. I had never been alone, but often with my father or some of our hands; besides, I was too well able to take care of myself, too accustomed to have my own way, to anticipate any anxiety about my not returning.

And so it proved. The next morning saw me mounted on Swiftfoot, the letter safe in my bosom, and a long list of articles wanted in my pocket. What a lovely ride that was, with the gentle, spirited horse of which I was so fond for a companion, and my own beautiful forests in all their loveliest spring green around me, with just enough of mystery and danger in the expedition to add an exhilarating excitement, and with the happy consciousness that I was doing something for Mr. Hammond, who had done so much for me, to urge me on! I cantered merrily past Jim Foushee's cornfield, and, nodding to him, as he stood in the door of his log-house, I enjoyed telling him that I was going to Louisa on a shopping expedition. "Should I get anything for him? He could see that Mr. Hammond had lent me Swift-foot, so that I should soon be back, if I could buy all I wanted in Louisa; if not, I did believe I should go on to Catlettsburg : the ride would be so glorious !"

And glorious it was. I was happy in myself, happy in my thoughts of my friend, happy in the physical enjoyment of the air, the woods, the sun, the shade. Let me dwell on that ride. I have not had many happy days, but that was one which had its fulness of content. And I succeeded in putting Mr. Hammond's letter into the Catlettsburg post-office, made my little purchases, and turned my horse's head homeward, reaching the end of my journey before my father or step-mother had time to be anxious for me, and having a chance to whisper, "All right," to Tom Salyers, as he took my horse from me at the door of the store.

The long-expected rise came, and the strike came, Jim Foushee heading it, and standing sullen and determined in the midst of his party. Mr. Hammond was prepared for them. The malcontents came to him in the store, where he was filling Tom's place ; for he had sent Tom to Catlettsburg, avowedly to prepare the boats there to meet the rise, really to have him out of the way. Their first word was met coolly enough.

"You will not work another stroke, unless I give you higher wages, I understand, Foushee? And these men say the same thing? You are their spokesman? Very well, I am satisfied ; you can quit work to-morrow. I have other hands at the mouth for the boats there, and there is no hurry about the coal that lies here."

Foushee burst out with an oath, —

"That damned Salyers is the traitor! mean, cowardly rascal!"

But Mr. Hammond would not tell me more of what passed; perhaps he was afraid of frightening me. This only he told me that night, when thanking me with glance, voice, and pressure of the hand for all I had done for him. The blood rushed quick and hot through my veins, I was delirious with an undreamed-of happiness, which took away from me all power of answering, of even raising my eyes to his face, and the same delirium followed me to my pillow. He had called me his friend, his little Janet, who was so quick and ready, so fertile in invention, so brave in execution: what should he have done without me? I repeated his words to myself till they lost all their meaning; they were only replete with blissful content, and filled me with their music till I dropped asleep for very weariness in saying them over.

The next morning, before I waked, George Hammond had gone. He had left for Catlettsburg to direct the new hands. The works lay idle, the men (those who had been dismissed) lounged around gloomy and sullen, and so passed the week. Then came the news that Mr. Hammond and Tom Salyers had gone to Cincinnati, and would not return for the present, and that such men as were satisfied with the former wages were to be put to work again. Readily did the miners come back to their duty, all but a few of the Sandy men, who returned to their own homes, and all fell into the usual train.

And I? There was first the calm sense of happy security, then the impatience to test again its reality, then the longing homesickness of the heart. As weeks passed on and I saw nothing of him, as I heard of his protracted stay, as I saw Miss Hammond make her preparations to join him, as I watched the boat which carried her away, my sense of loneliness became too heavy for me, and the same pillow on which I had known those happy slumbers was wet with tears of bitter despondency.

And yet I understood neither the happiness nor the tears. I did not know (how should I ?) what were the new feelings which made my heart beat at George Hammond's name. I did not know why I yearned towards his sister with a warmth of love that would fain show itself in kindly word or deed. I did not know why the news that he was coming again, which greeted me after long weeks of weariness, brightened with joyful radiance everything that I saw, and glorified the aspect of my little garret, as I had seen a brilliant bunch of flowers glorify and refine with a light of beauty the every-day ugliness of our sitting-room.

I sang my merriest songs that night, and my feet kept time to their music in almost dancing measures. The next day, yes, by noon he would be at home. I could see his boat land from my little window, and then, giving Miss Hammond time to be safely housed, I would row myself over to the store and meet him there. How much I should have to tell him, how much to hear!

The morning came, and with it came a nervous bashfulness. I should never dare to go over to see him. No, I would wait quietly until night, when he would surely come himself to see me. Still I could watch his boat. And nervously did I stand, my face pressed against the window-pane, through the long morning hours, my sewing dropped neglected in my lap at the risk of a scolding from my mother, watching the slow-passing river, and the leaves hanging motionless over it in the stillness of the summer noon. At last there was a stir on the opposite shore. Yes, the boat must be in sight; I could even hear the shouts of the boatmen; and there, rounding the bluff, she was; there, too, was Mr. Hammond in the stern, with the rudder in his hand; there sat Miss Hammond, book in hand, with her usual look of listless disdain. But whose was that girlish face raised towards Mr. Hammond, while he pointed out so eagerly the surrounding objects? whose that slight, girlish figure, crowned with the light garden-hat, with its wealth of golden hair escaping from under it?

A sharp pang shot through me. Some one was coming to disturb my happy hours with my teacher and friend; and the chill of disappointment was on me already. I saw the boat land, saw George Hammond assist carefully every step of the strange girl, saw an elderly gentleman step also upon the bank and give his hand to Miss Hammond, and in two minutes the trees of the landing hid them from my sight.

And how slowly went the hours of that afternoon! how nervously I listened to every tread, to every click of the gate! nay, my sharpened hearing took note of every sway of the branches. But the day passed, the night, and no one came. The next morning brought with it an impatience which mastered me. I *must* go, I must see him, and in five minutes I was pushing my boat from its cove under the water-maple.

But I needed not to have left my room; my visit would be useless; for, lifting my eyes, as my boat came out from under the leaves, there, on the path by the river-side opposite, I saw the strange lady mounted on Swiftfoot, her light figure set off by a cloth riding-habit such as I had never seen before, the graceful folds of which struck me even then with a sense of beauty and fitness. I could even distinguish the golden curls again, which fell close on George Hammond's face, as he stood by her side arranging her stirrup, his own horse's bridle over his arm. A backward motion of the oar sent my boat under the branches again, and I sat motionless, watching them as they rode away.

Two hours afterward they stopped at our gate, and I heard George Hammond's voice calling me. The blood rushed to my forehead. Had I been alone, I would not have heard; but my mother was in the room, and I had no excuse for not going forward. He leaned from his horse and shook hands cordially, while, at the same time, he said,—

"I have brought Miss Worthington to see you, Janet. She has heard so much of your kindness to me, and of your courage last spring, that she was anxious to know you.

"This is Janet Rainsford, Amy," he continued, turning to her.

The lovely, bright young face was bent towards me, the tiny hand stretched out to mine, and I heard a gentle voice say, —

"Mr. Hammond has told me so much of you, Janet, (I may call you Janet, may I not?) that I was determined to come and see you. I hope we shall know each other."

A great fear seized me then, — a fear which seemed to clutch my heart and stop its beatings, leaving me without any power of reply. I only stammered a few words, and Mr. Hammond, pitying what he thought my bashfulness, rode on with a nod of farewell and some words, I could not take in their sense, which seemed to be requests that I would teach Miss Worthington all that I knew of the woods and the country.

I sat down with a stunned feeling, dizzied with the knowledge that seemed to blaze upon me with that horrid fear. Yes, I knew now what it all meant, — the happiness, the loneliness of the past weeks, the shrinking bashfulness of yesterday morning, and the chill that fell upon me when I first saw the stranger in the boat.

I loved George Hammond, — I, the country-girl, without one beauty, one accomplishment, so ignorant, so beneath him. I had been fool enough to fling away my heart, — and now, now that it was gone from me, there came this terrible fear. What was this young girl to him? Were my intuitions right? Did he love her? Would she take him away from me? take away even that poor friendship which was all I asked?

That night, — I cannot tell of it, — the rapid, wearying walk from side to side of my little garret, the despairing flinging myself on the bed, the restlessness that would bring me to my feet again, the pressing my hot face against the cool window-pane, the convulsive sobs with which the struggle ended, the heavy, unrefreshing sleep that came at last, and the dull wakening in the morning, when nothing seemed left about my heart but a dead weight of insensibility. But with the brightening hours came again the restlessness. I would at least know the worst ; let me face all my wretchedness ; it could not be but strength would come to me when the worst was over.

And so I went doggedly through my morning tasks, and the early afternoon saw me at the store. I would not go to Miss Hammond's house, but I was sure to hear something of the new-comers among the gossiping miners and work-men, — or, if not there, I had only to drop into some of the cottages to learn from their wives all that they knew or im-agined. How little I learned, — how little compared to what my fierce, craving heart asked !

" Miss Worthington was here with her father; they had come to see the mines, so they said ; but who knows the truth ? More like it was to be a wedding between the young folks, and the father wanted to see the Sandy country before he let his daughter come into it. She was a sweet-spoken young thing, — not like Miss Hammond, with her proud, quality airs."

But all this was only conjecture, and I must have cer-tainty. The certainty came that evening. Mr. Hammond passed the store as I was standing by the counter, and in-sisted that I should go home to tea with him. I had often done so before, and had no excuse, even when he said, —

" I want so much to make Miss Worthington like our Sandy people, Janet. I want her father to see that there are people worth knowing even here. You will tell her of all the pleasures we have, — our walks, our rides. You cannot be afraid of her, dear Janet, — she is so gentle, so lovely."

A strange feeling seized me, one mingled of gentleness and bitterness. Yes, for his sake, I would help him. I would do all I could to welcome to his home her who was to be its blessing, and (here my good angel left me and some evil one whispered) I would show her, too, that I was not so altogether to be contemned ; she should see that I was not merely the poor country-girl she thought me. And all I had of thought or feeling, all that George Hammond had called my inborn poetry, came out that evening. I talked, I talked well, for I was talking of what I understood, —of my own forests and streams, of the flowers whose haunts I knew so well, of the changing seasons in their varying beauty, — nay, as I gained courage, as I saw that I commanded attention, the books that I had read so well, the thoughts of those great writers that I had made my own, came to my aid, and quotation and allusion pressed readily to my lips.

I saw Esther Hammond's cold look fixed upon my face, but I dared it back again, and my color rose and my eye sparkled from the excitement. I felt my triumph when I saw the surprise on Mr. Hammond's face, when I heard the patronizing tone of Mr. Worthington's voice changed to one of equality, as he said, —

"You are a worthy champion of Sandy life, Miss Janet. I believe Amy will be tempted to try it."

There was a quick blush on Amy's face as I turned to look at it, and a glance of proud affection towards her from George Hammond, which took away my false strength as I stood, leaving me, weak and trembling, to seek my home in the evening twilight.

That evening's short-lived triumph cost me dear. It betrayed my scarcely self-acknowledged secret to another. Miss Hammond's woman's-eye had read the poor fool who laid her heart open before her. I was made to feel my weakness before her the next morning, when, walking into our kitchen, she asked, with her hard, yet dignified calmness, that I should gather for her some of the Summer Sweetings that hung so thick on the tree behind our house.

She followed me to the orchard. I gathered the apples diligently and spoke no word, but not for that did I escape. She stood calmly looking on till I had finished, then began with that terrible opening from which we all shrink.

"I should like to speak to you a few moments, Janet."

I quailed before her, for I had somehow a perception of what she was going to say, though I scarcely dreamed of the hardness with which it would be said. The blow came, however.

" My brother has been in the habit of taking notice of you ever since he has been on the Sandy, and he has been of great advantage to you ; but you must be aware that such notice as he gave you when you were a mere child cannot be continued now that you are a woman."

I bowed my head, and my lips formed something like a " Yes."

She went on.

" I say this to you because I was surprised to find by your behavior last night that you had allowed yourself to presume upon that notice, and I do not suppose you know how unbecoming this is, from a person in your position, especially before Miss Worthington."

I was stung into a reply.

" What is Miss Worthington to me ? " came out sullenly from my lips.

" Nothing to you, certainly, nor can she ever be : but as the future wife of my brother, she is something to me."

It was true, then ; but so fully had I felt the truth before that this certainty gave me no added pang. From its very depths of despair I drew strength, and, my courage rising, I had power even to look full at Miss Hammond, and say, —

" You may be sure I shall never intrude myself on Mr. Hammond's wife or sister, nor upon him, unless he desires it, except, indeed, to wish him happiness."

My unexpected calmness roused her worst feelings, her pride, her jealousy, and, with a woman's keen aim, she sent the next dart home. So calmly she spoke, too, with such command of herself, — with a lady-like self-control that I, alas ! knew not how to reach.

" I am happy to hear you say so, for there have been times when your singular manner has made me fear that you nourished some very false and idle dreams, — follies that I have sometimes thought it my duty as a woman to warn you against " ; and with one keen look at my burning face, she took up the basket and walked away.

I think at that moment I could have killed her, so bitter was the hatred which I felt towards her; but the next brought its crushing shame, taking away from me all but the desire to hide myself from every eye. Where should I go? Somewhere where nobody could find me, where I could be insured perfect solitude. It was not difficult to bury myself in the forest that pressed around me on every side, and a few minutes saw me struggling with the embarrassments of the tangled vines which obstructed the path up our steepest hill. There was in the very difficulties to be overcome something that seemed to bring me relief; they forced my mind from myself. On, on I went, as if my life depended upon my struggles, till, breathless and utterly exhausted, I had reached the top of the hill, the highest point for miles around.

I sank down on the cool grass, the fresh wind blowing on my face, and, too wearied to think, shut my eyes against the beautiful Nature around me, alive only to my own overpowering misery. How long I lay there I never knew. I was safe and alone. I could be wretched as I pleased, away from Miss Hammond's mocking eye, away from the sight of George Hammond's happiness. But, strangely enough, out of the very freedom to be miserable came at last a sense of relief. I looked my wretchedness full in the face. Could I not bear it? And there rose within me a strength I had not known before. I was young, I had a long life before me; it could not be but that this great sorrow would pass away. At least I would not nourish it. I would do what I could to help myself. Help *myself!* For the first time in my life I put up an earnest prayer for help out of myself. The words, coming as such words come but few times in life, out from the very depths of the heart, brought with them their softening influence. The tears sprung forth, those tears which I thought I should never shed again, and I burst into a passionate fit of crying, the passionate crying of a child. It shook me from head to foot with its hysterical convulsions, but it left me at last calmer, soothed into

B B

stillness, with only now and then those choking after-sobs which I, child-like, sent forth there on the bosom of the only mother I had ever known, — our kindly mother Earth.

The sun was going down when I rose up, soothed and comforted, and strengthened, too, for a time. I would do what I could. I would live down this grief: how I knew not, but the way would come to me. And gathering up my hair, which had fallen around me, I stopped, on my way home, by a running stream, and bathed my eyes and forehead until I was fit to appear before my step-mother. She did not question me: she was too used to my unexplained absences since I had grown out of her control. Sufficient for her that my tasks were always performed; sufficient for her, that, that very evening, I threw myself with an apparently untiring energy into the household work, — that I never rested a moment till she herself closed the house and insisted that I should go to bed. I slept that night, — after such fatigue, it was impossible but that I should, — and woke in the morning with a renewed determination to struggle against my sorrow.

Alas! alas! I thought I had only to resolve. I thought the struggle would be but once. How little I knew of the daily, almost hourly, changes of feeling, — of the despondency, the despair, that would come, I knew not why, directly upon my most earnest resolves, my hardest struggles, — of the weakness that would make me at times give up all struggling as useless, — of the mad hope that would sometimes arise that something, some outward change, I did not dare to say what, would bring me some relief!

I had at least the courage to keep away from the sight of all that was so miserable to me. I did not see George Hammond for weeks, and he, — ah! there was the bitterness, — he did not miss me.

And so the weary days went on. It is wonderful what endurance there is in a young heart, — for how long a time it can beat off suffering all day by unceasing labor, and lie awake all night with that same suffering for a bedfellow, and still make no sign that a careless eye can see. I look at that time now with wonder. How did I bear that constant occupation by day, alternated only with those sleepless nights, without breaking down entirely? The crisis came at last, — a sort of stupor, a cessation of suffering indeed, but a cessation, too, of all feeling. I was frightened at myself. Alas! I had no one to be frightened for me. Could it be that I was going to lose my senses? But no, I passed through that too, and then came a more natural state of mind than any I had known since the blow fell.

My suffering self seemed like something apart from me, which I could pity and help, could counsel and act for, and this one thing came clear to me. Some change of scene was necessary to me. I could never go on so; it was idle to attempt it. I could not live any longer face to face with my grief. There was the whole world before me. Was it not possible to go out into it? I had health, strength, ability, I was sure of it. How often before had I dreamed over the seeking my fortune in that world which looked to me then so full of excitement? Nothing had held me back then but the clinging to home-pleasures, to home-enjoyments, to home-comforts, poor as they were, — nothing but the sense of safety, of protection. What were these to me now? I cared nothing for them. I only asked to be away from all that reminded me of my suffering, to be so forced to struggle with external difficulties as to have no thought for myself. I did not want to love anybody; I would rather have nobody care for me. I would go. The only question was how.

A few days and nights of thought solved the problem for me, and, once roused to action, I took my steps rapidly and well. The first thing necessary was money, money enough to take me away, and to support me until I could find employment; and the means of attaining it were within my reach. I owned a watch that had been my mother's, a pretty trinket, though somewhat old-fashioned, and which had often excited the envy of the young wife of one of the head miners. I knew that her husband was flush of money just then, for he had drawn his wages only the week before, —and I knew, too, that he would give me a good price for my watch, were it only to gratify the bride to whom he had as yet denied nothing. .

The sale was made at once. I do not know if I got anything like the value of the watch, but the next day saw me with fifty dollars in my pocket, a small bundle, made up from the most available part of my wardrobe, under my arm, prepared to walk to Louisa, avowedly to buy supplies, but with the secret determination to meet there the coal-boats which were bound for the mouth, ask a passage on them as far as Catlettsburg, and there take the first steamer that passed, and let it carry me whither it would.

There was no pause of regret, no delay for parting looks or words ; from the moment that I had made up my mind to go, I felt nothing but a desperate eagerness to be away, to be in action. The few words necessary to prepare my step-mother for my ostensible errand were soon said, the good-morning calmly spoken, and I passed into the forest-path leading to the town. A pang smote me as I remembered her conscientious discharge of duty toward me for so many years ; but it was duty, not love, that had urged her, and while I said that to myself, I said, too, that time would bring to me the opportunity of repaying her.

Toward the settlement on the opposite shore I turned no look. I would not trust myself; I knew my own weakness too well ; this desperate energy which was carrying me on now would fail, if I allowed my heart one moment's indul-gence. Steadily I walked on through the woods, my own woods, which, perhaps, I should never see again, till wearied out by the exertion, which had precluded thought, I saw the houses of Louisa rise before me.

The boats lay at the fork above the town. I had informed myself of their movements, and knew they were to start at noon. A few inquiries for groceries and so forth, where I knew they could not be gotten, gave me an excuse for the proposition to the captain of the boats to give me a passage to Catlettsburg. It was readily granted, and the crew, most of them Sandy men, put up a rough awning, and, spreading under it some blankets, did their kind uttermost to make me comfortable.

I remember now, as one looks back into a dream, the afternoon and night that passed before we reached Catlettsburg. I lay perfectly quiet, watching the shadowy trees as we glided past them, noting their varied reflections in the water, marking every peculiarity of shore and stream, hearing the jests and laughter, the words of command and the oaths, that went round among the boatmen; but all passed as something with which I had nothing to do. To me there was the burning desire to put a great distance between myself and my home, — but with it, too, the consciousness, that, as I could do nothing to expedite our slow progress, so neither could I afford to waste upon it in impatient restlessness the strength which would be so much needed afterwards. The men brought me a cup of coffee from their supper, which gave me strength for the night. The biscuit I could not taste.

But how long was that night! how tedious the summer dawn! and how slowly went the hours till we brought up our boats at the landing at Catlettsburg!

I had formed my plans; so, telling the captain that I might perhaps want to go back with him, I hurried into the town. A steamboat lay by the wharf-boat. " The Bostona, for Cincinnati," said the board displayed over her upper railing. She was to leave at eight o'clock. I walked about the town till half-past seven; then, returning to the coal-boats, gave to the man left in charge a letter I had prepared in which I told my step-mother, in as few words as possible, that I wanted to see something of the world, and had determined to go for a time either to Cincinnati or to Pittsburg, — that I begged her not to be uneasy about me, I had sold my watch, and had money enough for the present; she should hear from me in due time. The man took the letter, with some remark on my not returning with them, and, with a quiet good-day, I left him and walked rapidly toward the steamer. The plank was laid from the wharf-boat, and, without daring to hesitate, I walked over it.

It was done. I was fairly separated from everything I had ever known before; everything now was new to me; I was ignorant of all around me; each step might be a mistake. I felt this, when a porter, stepping forward and taking my bundle, asked me if I would have a state-room. What was a state-room? I did not know, but saying "Yes," with a desperate feeling that it might as well be "yes" as "no," I was led back to the ladies' cabin, a key was turned in one of an infinite number of little doors, and I was ushered into what looked to me like a closet, with shelves made to take the place of beds. Here at least I was alone, and here I could be alone till dinner-time; till then there was no call for action on my part.

And how precious seemed to me every hour of rest! Singularly enough, my great sorrow did not come back to me in those pauses of action. I seemed then to be entirely absorbed in gathering strength for the next occasion; my grief was put away for the future, when there would come to me the time to indulge it.

So I lay quiet during that morning, looking sometimes through my little window at the passing shore, listening sometimes to the loud talking in the cabin, sometimes to the noises on the boat, wondering if all those strange creakings and shakings could be right, but finding a sense of security in my very ignorance. Dinner came, and in the course of it I found courage to ask the captain, at whose right hand I was placed, what time we should reach Cincinnati. "Not till after breakfast," was his welcome answer; for I had been haunted by a dread of being set adrift in a great city in the middle of the night, when I might perhaps fall into some den of thieves. I had read of such things in my books. This gave me still the afternoon before it would be necessary to think, some hours more in which to rest mind and body.

The night came at last, and I must decide what step to take next, that, my mind made up, I might perhaps get some sleep. I turned restlessly in my narrow bed, got up and stood at the window, tried first the upper shelf, and then the lower, but no possible plan presented itself. I still saw before me that terrible city where I should be ten times lonelier than in the midst of our forests, where I should make mistakes at every turn, where I should not know one face out of the many thousands that crowded upon my nervous fancy. I seemed to be afraid of nothing but human beings, and, at the thought of encountering them, my woman's heart gave way. In vain I reasoned with myself, "I shall not see all Cincinnati at once, — not more at one time, perhaps, than I saw to-day at dinner." Still came up those endless streets, all filled with strange faces ; still I saw myself pushed, jostled, by a succession of men and women who cared nothing for me. Suddenly came the thought, "Tom Salyers is in Cincinnati. There is one person there that I know. If I could only find him, he would take care of me till I knew how to take care of myself."

There came no remembrance of our last conversation to check my eager joy. Indeed, it had never made much impression upon me, followed as it had been by so much of nearer interest. I set myself to reflect on the means of finding him. He had gone down in the employ of the coal company. The captain could tell me where to look for him, and, satisfied with that, I laid my weary head on my pillow.

The next morning at breakfast I gained the needed information. "Did I want to find one of the men in Mr. Hammond's employment? I must go to the coal-yard"; and the direction was written out for me.

And now we neared the city. I stood on the guards and looked, wondering at the steamboats that lined the river-bank, at the long rows of houses that stretched before me, the tall chimneys vomiting smoke which obscured the surrounding hills, at the crowd of men and drays on the landing through which I was to make my way ; but my courage rose with the occasion, and, stepping resolutely from the plank, I walked up the hill and stood among the warehouses. I had been told to "turn to the right and take the first street, I could not miss my way"; but somehow I did miss my way again and again, and wandered weary and bewildered, not daring at first to ask for directions, till, gathering strength from my very weariness, I at last saw before me the welcome sign. It was something like home to see it; the familiar names cheered me while they moved me. I entered the office trembling with a wild dread lest I should meet Mr. Hammond there, but the sight of a stranger's face at the desk gave me courage to ask for Tom Salyers.

"He is in the yard now. Here, Jim, tell Salyers there 's a person " — he hesitated — "a lady wants to see him."

I sat down in a chair which was luckily near me, for my knees trembled so that I could not stand, and as the door opened and Tom's familiar face was before me, my whole composure gave way and I burst into a violent fit of crying.

"Janet! is it you? For Heaven's sake, what is the matter?"

But I could only sob in answer.

"Has anything happened up Sandy? Did you come for me?"

The poor fellow leaned over me, his face pale with surprise and agitation.

"Take me out of here!" was all I could muster composure enough to say.

He opened the door, and I escaped into the open air. We walked side by side through the streets, he silently respecting my agitation with a delicacy for which I had not given him credit, and I struggling to grow calm. At last he opened a little side-gate.

"Come in here, Janet; we shall be quiet here."

And I entered a sort of garden; the grounds belonging to the city water-works I have since known them to be. We sat down on a bench that overlooked the Kentucky hills. I love the seat now. I think the sight of the familiar fields and trees calmed me, and I was able at last to-answer Tom's anxious questions.

"It is nothing ; indeed, it is nothing. I am a foolish coward, and I was frightened walking through the city, and then the sight of a home-face upset me."

"But, Janet, why are you here ? Is anything wrong about the works, the men ? Did Mr. Hammond send you down ? "

"No, indeed, no ! it was only a fancy of mine to see the world. I am tired of that lonely life, and you know I am not needed there. My mother can get along without me, and I am only a burden to my father."

"Not needed ? Why, Janet, what will the Sandy country be without you ? "

My eyes filled up with tears again.

"Don't ask me any more questions, dear Tom ; only help me for a little while, till I can help myself. I want to earn my living somehow, but I have money enough to live upon till I can find something to do. Only find me a place to stay quietly in while I am looking for work. You are the only person I know in this great city ; and who will help me, if you do not ? "

"You know I will help you with my whole heart and soul, Janet," he said, his voice faltering.

I looked up, and in one moment rushed back upon me the remembrance of his words that day in the boat, and I stood aghast at the new trouble that seemed to rise before me. My voice must have changed as I said, —

" I only want you to find me a place to live in ; I can take care of myself"; for his countenance fell, and he sat silent for some moments.

At last he spoke : —

" I know I cannot do much, Janet, but what I can, I will. And, first, I will take you to the house of a widow-woman who has a room to let; one of our men wanted me to take it, but it was too far from my work. I went to see the place, though, and it is quiet and respectable ; the woman looks kind, too. Would you walk slowly down the street, while I go to the office and get my coat ? " — he was in his working-dress, — "and then I 'll join you."

I got up, feeling that I had chilled him in some way, and reproaching myself for it. When he rejoined me, we walked silently on, till, after many a turning, we found ourselves in a narrow, quiet street, before a small house, with a tiny yard in front. I do not know how the matter was arranged ; he did it all for me. There was the introducing me to a moth-erly-looking person, as a friend of his from the country ; the going up a narrow staircase to look at a small room of which all that could be said was that it was neat and clean ; the bargaining for my board, in which I was obliged to an-swer " Yes " and " No " as I could best follow his lead ; and then Tom left me with a shake of the hand, and the ad-vice that I should lie down and rest after my tedious jour-ney ; he would see me again in the evening.

The quiet dinner with my landlady, the afternoon rest, the fresh toilet, the sort of home-feeling that my room al-ready gave me, all did their part towards bringing back my usual composure before Tom came in the evening ; and then, sitting by the window in the little parlor, I could talk rationally of my plans for the future.

I had money enough for twelve weeks' board, even if I reserved ten dollars for other expenses. Surely, in that time I could find something to do. And as to what I should do, I had thought that all over before I left home. I might find some sewing, or tend in a store, or, perhaps, — did he think I could ? — I might keep school.

Tom would not hear of my sewing. He knew poor girls that worked their lives out at that. I might tend in a store, if I pleased, but still he did not believe I would like to be tied to one place for twelve hours in the day. Why should n't I keep school ? he was sure I knew enough, I was so smart, and had read so many books.

I shook my head. I did not believe the books I had read were the kind that school-mistresses studied. Still, I could learn, and certainly I might begin by teaching little children. But where was I to begin?

"If only we knew some gentleman, Janet, some city-man, who knew what to do about such things."

Suddenly a thought struck me.

"Tom, do you remember those gentlemen who came up to look at the coal mines when they were first opened? One of them stayed at our house two nights, and saw my books, and talked to me about them. Mr. Kendall was his name."

"That 's the very man; and a kind-hearted gentleman he seemed, not stuck up or proud. I 'll find him out for you, Janet, to-morrow; but there 's, no need of your hurrying yourself about going to work. You must see the city and the sights."

And Tom grew enthusiastic in describing to me all that was to be seen in this wonderful place.

Tom had altered, had improved in appearance and manners, since he had known something of city-life. I could not tell wherein the change lay, but I felt it. He told me of himself, — of his rising to be head-man, a sort of overseer, in the coal-yard, — of his good wages, — of some investments that he had made which had brought him in good returns.

"So you see, Janet, that, even if you were not so rich yourself, I have plenty of money at your service."

I thanked him most heartily, and roused myself to show some interest in all that concerned him.

So passed the rest of the week, — quiet days with my landlady, or in my room, where I busied myself in putting my wardrobe into better shape under the direction of Mrs. Barnum, and quiet walks and talks in the evening with Tom Salyers. It was evident that he was not satisfied with my alleged motives for leaving home, but I so steadily avoided all conversation on this point that he learned to respect my silence. On Sunday he told me he had found out who Mr. Kendall was.

"One of the stockholders of the Company, and a good man, they say. I 'll go to him to-morrow, if you say so, Janet, and ask him anything you want to know."

"No, Tom, I shall go myself. It is my business, and I must not let you do so much for me. If you will go with me, though," — I added.

And so the next morning saw us at Mr. Kendall's counting-room. It was before business-hours : we had cared for that. We found Mr. Kendall sitting leisurely over his papers, his feet up and his spectacles pushed back. I had been nervous enough during the walk, but a glance at his face reassured me. It was a good, a fatherly face, full of *bonhommie*, but showing, withal, a spice of business-shrewdness. I left Tom standing at the counting-room door, and, taking my fate in my own hands, walked forward and made myself known.

"O yes ! the little girl that Hammond thought so much of, that he talks about so often when he is down here. He thinks a school or two would bring the Sandy people out and holds you up as an example ; but, for my part, I think you are an exception. There are not many of them that one could do much with."

I turned quickly.

"This is Tom Salyers, sir, head-workman, overseer, at your coal-yard, and he is a Sandy man."

Mr. Kendall laughed.

"I see I must not say anything against the Sandy country ; nor need I just now. Walk in, Mr. Salyers. So, Miss Janet, you have come down to seek your fortune, earn your living, you say. I suppose Hammond sent you to me. Did you bring me a letter from him ? "

I hesitated.

"No, sir. Mr. Hammond was so much occupied when I came away that I had not seen him for a day or two. He has friends staying with him."

"True enough. Mr. Worthington has gone up there with his pretty daughter to see whether he can allow her to bury herself in the country. You saw Miss Worthington? Will she be popular among your people when she is Mrs. Hammond?"

I caught a glimpse of Tom's face, and felt myself turning pale as I answered, with a composure that did not seem to come from my own strength, —

"Miss Worthington is a very pleasant-spoken young lady. The people will like her, because she seems to care for them, just as Mr. Hammond does. But do you think, sir, that you could put me in the way of teaching school? Could I learn how to do it?"

"Well, I am just the right person to come to, Miss Janet, for the people have put me on the School Board, and — yes, we shall want some teachers next month in two of the primary departments. Could you wait a month? You might be studying up for your examination; it's not much, but it 'll not hurt you to go over their arithmetics and grammars. And I must write to Hammond to-day about some business of the Company. I 'll ask him about your qualifications, and what he thinks of it, and we 'll see what can be done. I should not wonder if I could get you a place."

Mr. Kendall shook hands with us both; and, bidding him good-morning, with many thanks for his kindness, we went out. We walked a square silently. Suddenly Tom turned to me: —

"You did not tell me, Janet, of this young lady."

"No."

"And is Mr. Hammond going to marry her?"

The blood rushed to my face till it was crimson to the very hair, while I stammered, —

"I do not know, — you heard Mr. Kendall."

Tom's voice was as gentle as a mother's in answer, but his words had little to do with the subject, they were almost as incoherent as mine, — something about his hoping I would like living in Cincinnati, that teaching would not be too tiresome for me. But from that moment George Hammond's name was never mentioned between us.

I wrote that day to my step-mother, telling her of my plans and prospects, and that evening Tom brought me the needed school-books. He had found them by asking some of the men at the yard whose children went to the public schools, and to the study of them I sat down with a determination that no slight difficulty could subdue. The next week brought a long, kind letter from Mr. Hammond, scolding me for going as I did, and declaring that he missed me every day.

"But more than all shall I miss you, Janet, when I bring Miss Worthington back as my wife; I had depended so upon you as a companion for her. But still it is a good thing for you to see something of the world, and you are bright enough to do anything you set out to do. I have written to Mr. Kendall to do all he can for you, and with Tom to take care of you I am sure you will get along. I begin to suspect that your going away was a thing contrived between Tom and yourself. Who knows how soon he may bring you back among us to show the Sandy farmers' wives how to live more comfortably than some of them do? Tom has a very pretty place below the mouth of Blackberry, if you would only show him how to take care of it."

There was comfort in this letter, in spite of the tears it caused me. My secret was safe. Miss Hammond had not been so cruel, so traitorous to her sex, as to betray it. If she had not told it now, she never would tell it, and Tom, if he suspected it, was too good, too noble, to whisper it even to himself. So I laid away my letter, and with a lighter heart turned again to my tasks.

And now three months have passed, for two of which I have been teaching. There are difficulties, yes, and there is hard work; but I can manage the children. I have the tact, the character, the gift, that nameless something which gives one person control over others; and for the studies, they are as yet a pleasure to me. I see how they will lead me on to other knowledge, how I may bring into form and make available my desultory reading, and there is a great pleasure in the very study itself. And for the rest, if my great grief is never out of mind, if it is always present to me, at least I can put it back, behind my daily occupations and interests. I begin, too, to see dimly that there are other things in life for a woman to whom the light of life is denied. My heart will always be lonely; but how much there is to live for in my mind, my tastes, my love for the beautiful! My little room has taken another aspect. I have so few wants that I can readily devote part of my earnings to gratifying myself with books, pictures. Such lovely prints as I find in the print-shops! and the flowers,—Tom Salyers, who is as kind as a brother, brings me them from the market. And then everything is so new to me; there is so much in life to see, to know. No, I will not be unhappy; happy I suppose I can never be, but I have strength and courage, and a will to rise above this sorrow which once crushed me to the ground. When I wrote the bitter words with which this record begins, I wronged the kind hearts that are around me, I lacked faith in that world wherein I have found help and comfort.

THE MAN WITHOUT A COUNTRY.

 SUPPOSE that very few casual readers of the New York Herald of August 13th observed, in an obscure corner, among the "Deaths," the announcement, —

"NOLAN. Died, on board U. S. Corvette Levant, Lat. 2° 11 S., Long. 131° W., on the 11th of May, PHILIP NOLAN."

I happened to observe it, because I was stranded at the old Mission-House in Mackinaw, waiting for a Lake-Superior steamer which did not choose to come, and I was devouring to the very stubble all the current literature I could get hold of, even down to the deaths and marriages in the Herald. My memory for names and people is good, and the reader will see, as he goes on, that I had reason enough to remember Philip Nolan. There are hundreds of readers who would have paused at that announcement, if the officer of the Levant who reported it had chosen to make it thus: —"Died, May 11th, THE MAN WITHOUT A COUNTRY." For it was as "The Man without a Country" that poor Philip Nolan had generally been known by the officers who had him in charge during some fifty years, as, indeed, by all the men who sailed under them. I dare say there is many a man who has taken wine with him once a fortnight, in a three years' cruise, who never knew that his name was "Nolan," or whether the poor wretch had any name at all.

There can now be no possible harm in telling this poor creature's story. Reason enough there has been till now, ever since Madison's Administration went out in 1817, for very strict secrecy, the secrecy of honor itself, among the gentlemen of the navy who have had Nolan in successive charge.   And certainly it speaks well for the *esprit de corps* of the profession and the personal honor of its members, that to the press this man's story has been wholly unknown, —and, I think, to the country at large also.   I have reason to think, from some investigations I made in the Naval Archives when I was attached to the Bureau of Construction, that every official report relating to him was burned when Ross burned the public buildings at Washington. One of the Tuckers, or possibly one of the Watsons, had Nolan in charge at the end of the war; and when, on returning from his cruise, he reported at Washington to one of the Crowninshields, — who was in the Navy Department when he came home, — he found that the Department ignored the whole business.   Whether they really knew nothing about it, or whether it was a " *Non mi ricordo*," determined on as a piece of policy, I do not know.   But this I do know, that since 1817, and possibly before, no naval officer has mentioned Nolan in his report of a cruise.

But, as I say, there is no need for secrecy any longer. And now the poor creature is dead, it seems to me worth while to tell a little of his story, by way of showing young Americans of to-day what it is to be

A MAN WITHOUT A COUNTRY.

Philip Nolan was as fine a young officer as there was in the "Legion of the West," as the Western division of our army was then called.   When Aaron Burr made his first dashing expedition down to New Orleans in 1805, at Fort Massac, or somewhere above on the river, he met, as the Devil would have it, this gay, dashing, bright young fellow, at some dinner-party, I think.   Burr marked him, talked to him, walked with him, took him a day or two's voyage in his flat-boat, and, in short, fascinated him.   For the next year, barrack-life was very tame to poor Nolan. He occasionally availed of the permission the great man had given him to write to him.   Long, high-worded, stilted letters the poor boy wrote and rewrote and copied.   But never a line did he have in reply from the gay deceiver. The other boys in the garrison sneered at him, because he sacrificed in this unrequited affection for a politician the time which they devoted to Monongahela, sledge, and high-low-jack.   Bourbon, euchre, and poker were still unknown. But one day Nolan had his revenge.   This time Burr came down the river, not as an attorney seeking a place for his office, but as a disguised conqueror.   He had defeated I know not how many district-attorneys; he had dined at I know not how many public dinners; he had been heralded in I know not how many Weekly Arguses, and it was ru-mored that he had an army behind him and an empire before him.   It was a great day — his arrival — to poor Nolan.   Burr had not been at the fort an hour before he sent for him.   That evening he asked Nolan to take him out in his skiff, to show him a canebrake or a cotton-wood tree, as he said, — really to seduce him; and by the time the sail was over, Nolan was enlisted body and soul.   From that time, though he did not yet know it, he lived as A MAN WITHOUT A COUNTRY.

What Burr meant to do I know no more than you, dear reader.   It is none of our business just now.   Only, when the grand catastrophe came, and Jefferson and the House of Virginia of that day undertook to break on the wheel all the possible Clarences of the then House of York, by the great treason-trial at Richmond, some of the lesser fry in that distant Mississippi Valley, which was farther from us than Puget's Sound is to-day, introduced the like novelty on their provincial stage, and, to while away the monotony of the summer at Fort Adams, got up, for *spectacles*, a string of court-martials on the officers there.   One and another of the colonels and majors were tried, and, to fill out the list,

little Nolan, against whom, Heaven knows, there was evidence enough, — that he was sick of the service, had been
willing to be false to it, and would have obeyed any order
to march any-whither with any one who would follow him,
had the order only been signed, "By command of His Exc.
A. Burr." The courts dragged on. The big flies escaped,
— rightly for all I know. Nolan was proved guilty enough,
as I say ; yet you and I would never have heard of him,
reader, but that, when the president of the court asked him
at the close, whether he wished to say anything to show that
he had always been faithful to the United States, he cried
out, in a fit of frenzy, —

"D—n the United States ! I wish I may never hear of
the United States again ! "

I suppose he did not know how the words shocked old
Colonel Morgan, who was holding the court. Half the officers who sat in it had served through the Revolution, and
their lives, not to say their necks, had been risked for the
very idea which he so cavalierly cursed in his madness.
He, on his part, had grown up in the West of those days, in
the midst of "Spanish plot," "Orleans plot," and all the
rest. He had been educated on a plantation where the
finest company was a Spanish officer or a French merchant
from Orleans. His education, such as it was, had been perfected in commercial expeditions to Vera Cruz, and I think
he told me his father once hired an Englishman to be a private tutor for a winter on the plantation. He had spent
half his youth with an older brother, hunting horses in Texas ; and, in a word, to him "United States" was scarcely
a reality. Yet he had been fed by "United States" for all
the years since he had been in the army. He had sworn on
his faith as a Christian to be true to "United States." It
was "United States" which gave him the uniform he wore,
and the sword by his side. Nay, my poor Nolan, it was
only because "United States" had picked you out first as
one of her own confidential men of honor that "A. Burr"
cared for you a straw more than for the flat-boat men who

sailed his ark for him. I do not excuse Nolan; I only explain to the reader why he damned his country, and wished
he might never hear her name again.

He never did hear her name but once again. From that
moment, September 23, 1807, till the day he died, May 11,
1863, he never heard her name again. For that half-century
and more he was a man without a country.

Old Morgan, as I said, was terribly shocked. If Nolan
had compared George Washington to Benedict Arnold, or
had cried, "God save King George," Morgan would not have
felt worse. He called the court into his private room, and
returned in fifteen minutes, with a face like a sheet, to
say, —

"Prisoner, hear the sentence of the Court! The Court
decides, subject to the approval of the President, that you
never hear the name of the United States again."

Nolan laughed. But nobody else laughed. Old Morgan
was too solemn, and the whole room was hushed dead as
night for a minute. Even Nolan lost his swagger in a moment. Then Morgan added, —

"Mr. Marshal, take the prisoner to Orleans in an armed
boat, and deliver him to the naval commander there."

The Marshal gave his orders and the prisoner was taken
out of court.

"Mr. Marshal," continued old Morgan, "see that no one
mentions the United States to the prisoner. Mr. Marshal,
make my respects to Lieutenant Mitchell at Orleans, and
request him to order that no one shall mention the United
States to the prisoner while he is on board ship. You will
receive your written orders from the officer on duty here this
evening. The court is adjourned without day."

I have always supposed that Colonel Morgan himself took
the proceedings of the court to Washington City, and explained them to Mr. Jefferson. Certain it is that the President approved them, — certain, that is, if I may believe the
men who say they have seen his signature. Before the
Nautilus got round from New Orleans to the Northern At-

lantic coast with the prisoner on board, the sentence had been approved, and he was a man without a country.

The plan then adopted was substantially the same which was necessarily followed ever after. Perhaps it was suggested by the necessity of sending him by water from Fort Adams and Orleans. The Secretary of the Navy — it must have been the first Crowninshield, though he is a man I do not remember — was requested to put Nolan on board a Government vessel bound on a long cruise, and to direct that he should be only so far confined there as to make it certain that he never saw or heard of the country. We had few long cruises then, and the navy was very much out of favor; and as almost all of this story is traditional, as I have explained, I do not know certainly what his first cruise was. But the commander to whom he was intrusted, — perhaps it was Tingey or Shaw, though I think it was one of the younger men, — we are all old enough now,— regulated the etiquette and the precautions of the affair, and according to his scheme they were carried out, I suppose, till Nolan died.

When I was second officer of the Intrepid, some thirty years after, I saw the original paper of instructions. I have been sorry ever since that I did not copy the whole of it. It ran, however, much in this way : —

"*Washington*," (with the date, which must have been late in 1807.)

"SIR, — You will receive from Lieutenant Neale the person of Philip Nolan, late a Lieutenant in the United States Army.

"This person on his trial by court-martial expressed with an oath the wish that he might 'never hear of the United States again.'

"The Court sentenced him to have his wish fulfilled.

"For the present the execution of the order is intrusted by the President to this department.

"You will take the prisoner on board your ship, and keep him there with such precautions as shall prevent his escape.

"You will provide him with such quarters, rations, and clothing as would be proper for an officer of his late rank, if he were a passenger on your vessel on the business of his Government.

"The gentlemen on board will make any arrangements agreeable to themselves regarding his society. He is to be exposed to no indignity of any kind, nor is he ever unnecessarily to be reminded that he is a prisoner.

"But under no circumstances is he ever to hear of his country or to see any information regarding it ; and you will specially caution all the officers under your command to take care, that, in the various indulgences which may be granted, this rule, in which his punishment is involved, shall not be broken.

"It is the intention of the Government that he shall never again see the country which he has disowned. ' Before the end of your cruise you will receive orders which will give effect to this intention. .

"Respectfully yours,

"W. SOUTHARD, for the
Secretary of the Navy."

If I had only preserved the whole of this paper, there would be no break in the beginning of my sketch of this story. For Captain Shaw, if it was he, handed it to his successor in the charge, and he to his, and I suppose the commander of the Levant has it to-day as his authority for keeping this man in this mild custody.

The rule adopted on board the ships on which I have met "the man without a country" was, I think, transmitted from the beginning. No mess liked to have him permanently, because his presence cut off all talk of home or of the prospect of return, of politics or letters, of peace or of war, — cut off more than half the talk men like to have at sea. But it was always thought too hard that he should never meet the rest of us, except to touch hats, and we finally sank into one system. He was not permitted to talk with the men, unless an officer was by. With officers he had unrestrained intercourse, as far as they and he chose. But he grew shy, though he had favorites: I was one. Then the captain always asked him to dinner on Monday. Every mess in succession took up the invitation in its turn. According to the size of the ship, you had him at your mess more or less often at dinner. His breakfast he ate in his own state-room, — he always had a state-room, — which was where a sentinel, or somebody on the watch, could see the door. And whatever else he ate or drank he ate or drank alone. Sometimes, when the marines or sailors had any special jollification, they were permitted to invite " Plain-Buttons," as they called him. Then Nolan was sent with some officer, and the men were forbidden to speak of home while he was there. I believe the theory was that the sight of his punishment did them good. They called him " Plain-Buttons," because, while he always chose to wear a regulation army-uniform, he was not permitted to wear the army-button, for the reason that it bore either the initials or the insignia of the country he had disowned.

I remember, soon after I joined the navy, I was on shore with some of the older officers from our ship and from the Brandywine, which we had met at Alexandria. We had leave to make a party and go up to Cairo and the Pyramids. As we jogged along, (you went on donkeys then,) some of the gentlemen (we boys called them " Dons," but the phrase was long since changed) fell to talking about Nolan, and some one told the system which was adopted from the first about his books and other reading. As he was almost never permitted to go on shore, even though the vessel lay in port for months, his time, at the best, hung heavy; and everybody was permitted to lend him books, if they were not published in America and made no allusion to it. These were common enough in the old days, when people in the other hemisphere talked of the United States as little as we do of Paraguay. He had almost all the foreign papers that came into the ship, sooner or later; only somebody must go over them first, and cut out any advertisement or stray paragraph that alluded to America. This was a little cruel sometimes, when the back of what was cut out might be as innocent as Hesiod. Right in the midst of one of Napoleon's battles, or one of Canning's speeches, poor Nolan would find a great hole, because on the back of the page of that paper there had been an advertisement of a packet for New York, or a scrap from the President's message. I say this was the first time I ever heard of this plan, which afterwards I had enough, and more than enough, to do with. I remember it, because poor Phillips, who was of the party, as soon as the allusion to reading was made, told a story of something which happened at the Cape of Good Hope on Nolan's first voyage; and it is the only thing I ever knew of that voyage. They had touched at the Cape, and had done the civil thing with the English Admiral and the fleet, and then, leaving for a long cruise up the Indian Ocean, Phillips had borrowed a lot of English books from an officer, which, in those days, as indeed in these, was quite a windfall. Among them, as the Devil would order, was the "Lay of the Last Minstrel," which they had all of them heard of, but which most of them had never seen. I think it could not have been published long. Well, nobody thought there could be any risk of anything national in that, though Phillips swore old Shaw had cut out the "Tempest" from Shakespeare before he let Nolan have it, because he said "the Bermudas ought to be ours, and, by Jove, should be one day." So Nolan was permitted to join the circle one afternoon when a lot of them sat on deck smoking and reading aloud. People do not do such things so often now; but when I was young we got rid of a great deal of time so. Well, so it happened that in his turn Nolan took the book and read to the others; and he read very well, as I know. Nobody in the circle knew a line of the poem, only it was all magic and Border chivalry, and was ten thousand years ago. Poor Nolan read steadily through the fifth canto, stopped a minute and drank something, and then began, without a thought of what was coming, —

"Breathes there the man, with soul so dead,
  Who never to himself hath said,"—

It seems impossible to us that anybody ever heard this for the first time ; but all these fellows did then, and poor Nolan himself went on, still unconsciously or mechanically, —

"This is my own, my native land !"

Then they all saw something was to pay ; but he expected to get through, I suppose, turned a little pale, but plunged on, —

" Whose heart hath ne'er within him burned,
  As home his footsteps he hath turned
  From wandering on a foreign strand ?—
  If such there breathe, go, mark him well."

By this time the men were all beside themselves, wishing there was any way to make him turn over two pages ; but he had not quite presence of mind for that ; he gagged a little, colored crimson, and staggered on, —

" For him no minstrel raptures swell ;
  High though his titles, proud his name,
  Boundless his wealth as wish can claim,
  Despite these titles, power, and pelf,
  The wretch, concentred all in self," —

and here the poor fellow choked, could not go on, but started up, swung the book into the sea, vanished into his state-room, "and by Jove," said Phillips, "we did not see him for two months again. And I had to make up some beggarly story to that English surgeon why I did not return his Walter Scott to him."

That story shows about the time when Nolan's braggadocio must have broken down. At first, they said, he took a very high tone, considered his imprisonment a mere farce, affected to enjoy the voyage, and all that ; but Phillips said that after he came out of his state-room he never was the same man again. He never read aloud again, unless it was the Bible or Shakespeare, or something else he was sure of. But it was not that merely. He never entered in with the

20

other young men exactly as a companion again. He was always shy afterwards, when I knew him, — very seldom spoke, unless he was spoken to, except to a very few friends. He lighted up occasionally, — I remember late in his life hearing him fairly eloquent on something which had been suggested to him by one of Fléchier's sermons, — but generally he had the nervous, tired look of a heart-wounded man.

When Captain Shaw was coming home, — if, as I say, it was Shaw, — rather to the surprise of everybody they made one of the Windward Islands, and lay off and on for nearly a week. The boys said the officers were sick of salt-junk, and meant to have turtle-soup before they came home. But after several days the Warren came to the same rendezvous; they exchanged signals; she sent to Phillips and these homeward-bound men letters and papers, and told them she was outward-bound, perhaps to the Mediterranean, and took poor Nolan and his traps on the boat back to try his second cruise. He looked very blank when he was told to get ready to join her. He had known enough of the signs of the sky to know that till that moment he was going "home." But this was a distinct evidence of something he had not thought of, perhaps, — that there was no going home for him, even to a prison. And this was the first of some twenty such transfers, which brought him sooner or later into half our best vessels, but which kept him all his life at least some hundred miles from the country he had hoped he might never hear of again.

It may have been on that second cruise, — it was once when he was up the Mediterranean, — that Mrs. Graff, the celebrated Southern beauty of those days, danced with him. They had been lying a long time in the Bay of Naples, and the officers were very intimate in the English fleet, and there had been great festivities, and our men thought they must give a great ball on board the ship. How they ever did it on board the Warren I am sure I do not know. Perhaps it was not the Warren, or perhaps ladies did not take

up so much room as they do now. They wanted to use
Nolan's state-room for something, and they hated to do it
without asking him to the ball; so the captain said they
might ask him, if they would be responsible that he did not
talk with the wrong people, "who would give him intelligence." So the dance went on, the finest party that had
ever been known, I dare say; for I never heard of a man-
of-war ball that was not. For ladies they had the family of
the American consul, one or two travellers who had adven-
tured so far, and a nice bevy of English girls and matrons,
perhaps Lady Hamilton herself.

Well, different officers relieved each other in standing and
talking with Nolan in a friendly way, so as to be sure that
nobody else spoke to him. The dancing went on with spirit,
and after a while even the fellows who took this honorary
guard of Nolan ceased to fear any *contre-temps*. Only when
some English lady — Lady Hamilton, as I said, perhaps —
called for a set of " American dances," an odd thing happened. Everybody then danced contra-dances. The black
band, nothing loath, conferred as to what "American
dances " were, and started off with " Virginia Reel," which
they followed with " Money-Musk," which, in its turn in
those days, should have been followed by " The Old Thirteen." But just as Dick, the leader, tapped for his fiddles
to begin, and bent forward, about to say, in true negro
state, "'The Old Thirteen,' gentlemen and ladies !" as he
had said "' Virginny Reel,' if you please !" and "' Money-
Musk,' if you please !" the captain's boy tapped him on the
shoulder, whispered to him, and he did not announce the
name of the dance ; he merely bowed, began on the air, and
they all fell to, — the officers teaching the English girls the
figure, but not telling them why it had no name.

But that is not the story I started to tell. — As the dancing went on, Nolan and our fellows all got at ease, as I said,
— so much so, that it seemed quite natural for him to bow to
that splendid Mrs. Graff, and say, —

"I hope you have not forgotten me, Miss Rutledge.
Shall I have the honor of dancing ? "

He did it so quickly, that Fellows, who was by him, could not hinder him. She laughed, and said, —

"I am not Miss Rutledge any longer, Mr. Nolan; but I will dance all the same," just nodded to Fellows, as if to say he must leave Mr. Nolan to her, and led him off to the place where the dance was forming.

Nolan thought he had got his chance. He had known her at Philadelphia, and at other places had met her, and this was a Godsend. You could not talk in contra-dances, as you do in cotillons, or even in the pauses of waltzing; but there were chances for tongues and sounds, as well as for eyes and blushes. He began with her travels, and Europe, and Vesuvius, and the French; and then, when they had worked down, and had that long talking-time at the bottom of the set, he said, boldly, — a little pale, she said, as she told me the story, years after, —

"And what do you hear from home, Mrs. Graff?"

And that splendid creature looked through him. Jove! how she must have looked through him!

"Home!! Mr. Nolan!!! I thought you were the man who never wanted to hear of home again!" — and she walked directly up the deck to her husband, and left poor Nolan alone, as he always was. — He did not dance again.

I cannot give any history of him in order; nobody can now: and, indeed, I am not trying to. These are the traditions, which I sort out, as I believe them, from the myths which have been told about this man for forty years. The lies that have been told about him are legion. The fellows used to say he was the "Iron Mask"; and poor George Pons went to his grave in the belief that this was the author of "Junius," who was being punished for his celebrated libel on Thomas Jefferson. Pons was not very strong in the historical line. A happier story than either of these I have told is of the War. That came along soon after. I have heard this affair told in three or four ways, — and, indeed, it may have happened more than once. But which ship it was on I cannot tell. However, in one, at least, of the great frigate-duels with the English, in which the navy was really baptized, it happened that a round-shot from the enemy entered one of our ports square, and took right down the officer of the gun himself, and almost every man of the gun's crew. Now you may say what you choose about courage, but that is not a nice thing to see. But, as the men who were not killed picked themselves up, and as they and the surgeon's people were carrying off the bodies, there appeared Nolan, in his shirt-sleeves, with the rammer in his hand, and, just as if he had been the officer, told them off with authority, — who should go to the cockpit with the wounded men, who should stay with him, — perfectly cheery, and with that way which makes men feel sure all is right and is going to be right. And he finished loading the gun with his own hands, aimed it, and bade the men fire. And there he stayed, captain of that gun, keeping those fellows in spirits, till the enemy struck, — sitting on the carriage while the gun was cooling, though he was exposed all the time, — showing them easier ways to handle heavy shot, — making the raw hands laugh at their own blunders, — and when the gun cooled again, getting it loaded and fired twice as often as any other gun on the ship. The captain walked forward by way of encouraging the men, and Nolan touched his hat and said, —

"I am showing them how we do this in the artillery, sir."

And this is the part of the story where all the legends agree; that the Commodore said, —

"I see you do, and I thank you, sir; and I shall never forget this day, sir, and you never shall, sir."

And after the whole thing was over, and he had the Englishman's sword, in the midst of the state and ceremony of the quarter-deck, he said, —

"Where is Mr. Nolan? Ask Mr. Nolan to come here."

And when Nolan came, the captain said, —

"Mr. Nolan, we are all very grateful to you to-day; you are one of us to-day; you will be named in the despatches.

And then the old man took off his own sword of ceremony, and gave it to Nolan, and made him put it on. The man told me this who saw it. Nolan cried like a baby, and well he might. He had not worn a sword since that infernal day at Fort Adams. But always afterwards, on occasions of ceremony, he wore that 'quaint old French sword of the Commodore's.

The captain did mention him in the despatches. It was always said he asked that he might be pardoned. He wrote a special letter to the Secretary of War. But nothing ever came of it. As I said, that was about the time when they began to ignore the whole transaction at Washington, and when Nolan's imprisonment began to carry itself on because there was nobody to stop it without any new orders from home.

I have heard it said that he was with Porter when he took possession of the Nukahiwa Islands. Not this Porter, you know, but old Porter, his father, Essex Porter, — that is, the old Essex Porter, not this Essex. As an artillery officer, who had seen service in the West, Nolan knew more about fortifications, embrasures, ravelins, stockades, and all that, than any of them did; and he worked with a right good-will in fixing that battery all right. I have always thought it was a pity Porter did not leave him in command there with Gamble. That would have settled all the question about his punishment. We should have kept the islands, and at this moment we should have one station in the Pacific Ocean. Our French friends, too, when they wanted this little watering-place, would have found it was preoccupied. But Madison and the Virginians, of course, flung all that away.

All that was near fifty years ago. If Nolan was thirty then, he must have been near eighty when he died. He looked sixty when he was forty. But he never seemed to me to change a hair afterwards. As I imagine his life, from what I have seen and heard of it, he must have been in every sea, and yet almost never on land. He must have known, in a formal way, more officers in our service than any man living knows. He told me once, with a grave smile, that no man in the world lived so methodical a life as he. " You know the boys say I am the Iron Mask, and you know how busy he was." He said it did not do for any one to try to read all the time, more than to do anything else all the time ; but that he read just five hours a day. "Then," he said, " I keep up my note-books, writing in them at such and such hours from what I have been reading; and I include in these my scrap-books." These were very curious indeed. He had six or eight, of different subjects. There was one of History, one of Natural Science, one which he called " Odds and Ends." But they were not merely books of extracts from newspapers. They had bits of plants and ribbons, shells tied on, and carved scraps of bone and wood, which he had taught the men to cut for him, and they were beautifully illustrated. He drew admirably. He had some of the funniest drawings there, and some of the most pathetic, that I have ever seen in my life. I wonder who will have Nolan's scrap-books.

Well, he said his reading and his notes were his profession, and that they took five hours and two hours respectively of each day. "Then," said he, "every man should have a diversion as well as a profession. My Natural History is my diversion." That took two hours a day more. The men used to bring him birds and fish, but on a long cruise he had to satisfy himself with centipedes and cockroaches and such small game. He was the only naturalist I ever met who knew anything about the habits of the house-fly and the mosquito. All those people can tell you whether they are *Lepidoptera* or *Steptopotera;* but as for telling how you can get rid of them, or how they get away from you when you strike them, — why, Linnæus knew as little of that as John Foy the idiot did. These nine hours made Nolan's regular daily "occupation." The rest of the time he talked or walked. Till he grew very old, he went aloft a great deal. He always kept up his exercise ; and I never heard that he was ill. If any other man was ill, he was the kindest nurse in the world; and he knew more than half the surgeons do. Then if anybody was sick or died, or if the captain wanted him to on any other occasion, he was always ready to read prayers. I have said that he read beautifully.

My own acquaintance with Philip Nolan began six or eight years after the War, on my first voyage after I was appointed a midshipman. It was in the first days after our Slave-Trade treaty, while the Reigning House, which was still the House of Virginia, had still a sort of sentimentalism about the suppression of the horrors of the Middle Passage, and something was sometimes done that way. We were in the South Atlantic on that business. From the time I joined, I believe I thought Nolan was a sort of lay chaplain,—a chaplain with a blue coat. I never asked about him. Everything in the ship was strange to me. I knew it was green to ask questions, and I suppose I thought there was a "Plain-Buttons" on every ship. We had him to dine in our mess once a week, and the caution was given that on that day nothing was to be said about home. But if they had told us not to say anything about the planet Mars or the Book of Deuteronomy, I should not have asked why; there were a great many things which seemed to me to have as little reason. I first came to understand anything about "the man without a country" one day when we overhauled a dirty little schooner which had slaves on board. An officer was sent to take charge of her, and, after a few minutes, he sent back his boat to ask that some one might be sent him who could speak Portuguese. We were all looking over the rail when the message came, and we all wished we could interpret, when the captain asked who spoke Portuguese. But none of the officers did; and just as the captain was sending forward to ask if any of the people could, Nolan stepped out and said he should be glad to interpret, if the captain wished, as he understood the language. The captain thanked him, fitted out another boat with him, and in this boat it was my luck to go.

When we got there, it was such a scene as you seldom see, and never want to. Nastiness beyond account, and chaos run loose in the midst of the nastiness. There were not a great many of the negroes; but by way of making what there were understand that they were free, Vaughan had had their hand-cuffs and ankle-cuffs knocked off, and, for convenience' sake was putting them upon the rascals of the schooner's crew. The negroes were, most of them, out of the hold, and swarming all round the dirty deck, with a central throng surrounding Vaughan and addressing him in every dialect and *patois* of a dialect, from the Zulu click up to the Parisian of Beledeljereed.

As we came on deck, Vaughan looked down from a hogs-head, on which he had mounted in desperation, and said, —

"For God's love, is there anybody who can make these wretches understand something? The men gave them rum, and that did not quiet them. I knocked that big fellow down twice, and that did not soothe him. And then I talked Choctaw to all of them together; and I 'll be hanged if they understood that as well as they understood the English."

·Nolan said he could speak Portuguese, and one or two fine-looking Kroomen were dragged out, who, as it had been found already, had worked for the Portuguese on the coast at Fernando Po.

"Tell them they are free," said Vaughan; "and tell them that these rascals are. to be hanged as soon as we can get rope enough."

Nolan "put that into Spanish," — that is, he explained it in such Portuguese as the Kroomen could understand, and they in turn to such of the negroes as could understand them. Then there was such a yell of delight, clinching of fists, leaping and dancing, kissing of Nolan's feet, and a general rush made to the hogshead by way of spontaneous worship of Vaughan, as the *deus ex machina* of the occasion.

"Tell them," said Vaughan, well pleased, "that I will take them all to Cape Palmas."

This did not answer so well. Cape Palmas was practically as far from the homes of most of them as New Orleans or Rio Janeiro was ; that is, they would be eternally separated from home there. And their interpreters, as we could understand, instantly said, "*Ah, non Palmas,*" and began to propose infinite other expedients in most voluble language. Vaughan was rather disappointed at this result of his liberality, and asked Nolan eagerly what they said. The drops stood on poor Nolan's white forehead, as he hushed the men down, and said, —

"He says, 'Not Palmas.' He says, 'Take us home, take us to our own country, take us to our own house, take us to our own pickaninnies and our own women.' He says he has an old father and mother who will die if they do not see him. And this one says he left his people all sick, and paddled down to Fernando to beg the white doctor to come and help them, and that these devils caught him in the bay just in sight of home, and that he has never seen anybody from home since then. And this one says," choked out Nolan, "that he has not heard a word from his home in six months, while he has been locked up in an infernal barracoon."

Vaughan always said he grew gray himself while Nolan struggled through this interpretation. I, who did not understand anything of the passion involved in it, saw that the very elements were melting with fervent heat, and that something was to pay somewhere. Even the negroes themselves stopped howling, as they saw Nolan's agony, and Vaughan's almost equal agony of sympathy. As quick as he could get words, he said, —

"Tell them yes, yes, yes ; tell them they shall go to the Mountains of the Moon, if they will. If I sail the schooner through the Great White Desert, they shall go \ome ! "

And after some fashion Nolan said so. And then they all fell to kissing him again, and wanted to rub his nose with theirs.

But he could not stand it long; and getting Vaughan to say he might go back, he beckoned me down into our boat. As we lay back in the stern-sheets and the men gave way, he said to me, — "Youngster, let that show you what it is to be without a family, without a home, and without a country. And if you are ever tempted to say a word or to do a thing that shall put a bar between you and your family, your home, and your country, pray God in His mercy to take you that instant home to His own heaven. Stick by your family, boy; forget you have a self, while you do everything for them. Think of your home, boy; write and send, and talk about it. Let it be nearer and nearer to your thought, the farther you have to travel from it ; and rush back to it, when you are free, as that poor black slave is doing now. And for your country, boy," and the words rattled in his throat, "and for that flag," and he pointed to the ship, "never dream a dream but of serving her as she bids you, though the service carry you through a thousand hells. No matter what happens to you, no matter who flatters you or who abuses you, never look at another flag, never let a night pass but you pray God to bless that flag. Remember, boy, that behind all these men you have to do with, behind officers, and government, and people even, there is the Country Herself, your Country, and that you belong to Her as you belong to your own mother. Stand by Her, boy, as you would stand by your mother, if those devils there had got hold of her to-day ! "

I was frightened to death by his calm, hard passion ; but I blundered out, that I would, by all that was holy, and that I had never thought of doing anything else. He hardly seemed to hear me ; but he did, almost in a whisper, say, — "Oh, if anybody had said so to me when I was of your age ! "

I think it was this half-confidence of his, which I never

abused, for I never told this story till now, which afterward
made us great friends. He was very kind to me. Often he
sat up, or even got up, at night to walk the deck with me,
when it was my watch. He explained to me a great deal
of my mathematics, and I owe to him my taste for mathematics. He lent me books, and helped me about my reading. He never alluded so directly to his story again ; but
from one and another officer I have learned, in thirty years,
what I am telling. When we parted from him in St.
Thomas harbor, at the end of our cruise, I was more sorry
than I can tell. I was very glad to meet him again in 1830 ;
and later in life, when I thought I had some influence in
Washington, I moved heaven and earth to have him discharged. But it was like getting a ghost out of prison.
They pretended there was no such man, and never was
such a man. They will say so at the Department now !
Perhaps they do not know. It will not be the first thing in
the service of which the Department appears to know
nothing !

There is a story that Nolan met Burr once on one of
our vessels, when a party of Americans came on board in
the Mediterranean. But this I believe to be a lie ; or,
rather, it is a myth, *ben trovato*, involving a tremendous
blowing-up with which he sunk Burr, — asking him how he
liked to be "without a country." But it is clear, from
Burr's life, that nothing of the sort could have happened ;
and I mention this only as an illustration of the stories
which get a-going where there is the least mystery at
bottom.

So poor Philip Nolan had his wish fulfilled. I know but
one fate more dreadful : it is the fate reserved for those
men who shall have one day to exile themselves from their
country because they have attempted her ruin, and shall
have at the same time to see the prosperity and honor to
which she rises when she has rid herself of them and their
iniquities. The wish of poor Nolan, as we all learned to
call him, not because his punishment was too great, but be-

cause his repentance was so clear, was precisely the wish of every Bragg and Beauregard who broke a soldier's oath two years ago, and of every Maury and Barron who broke a sailor's. I do not know how often they have repented. I do know that they have done all that in them lay that they might have no country, — that all the honors, associations, memories, and hopes which belong to "country" might be broken up into little shreds and distributed to the winds. I know, too, that their punishment, as they vegetate through what is left of life to them in wretched Boulognes and Leicester Squares, where they are destined to upbraid each other till they die, will have all the agony of Nolan's, with the added pang that every one who sees them will see them to despise and to execrate them. They will have their wish, like him.

For him, poor fellow, he repented of his folly, and then, like a man, submitted to the fate he had asked for. He never intentionally added to the difficulty or delicacy of the charge of those who had him in hold. Accidents would happen; but they never happened from his fault. Lieutenant Truxton told me, that, when Texas was annexed, there was a careful discussion among the officers, whether they should get hold of Nolan's handsome set of maps, and cut Texas out of it, — from the map of the world and the map of Mexico. The United States had been cut out when the atlas was bought for him. But it was voted, rightly enough, that to do this would be virtually to reveal to him what had happened, or, as Harry Cole said, to make him think Old Burr had succeeded. So it was from no fault of Nolan's that a great botch happened at my own table, when, for a short time, I was in command of the George Washington corvette, on the South-American station. We were lying in the La Plata, and some of the officers, who had been on shore, and had just joined again, were entertaining us with accounts of their misadventures in riding the half-wild horses of Buenos Ayres. Nolan was at table, and was in an unusually bright and talkative mood. Some story of a

tumble reminded him of an adventure of his own, when he
was catching wild horses in Texas with his brother Stephen,
at a time when he must have been quite a boy. He told the
story with a good deal of spirit, — so much so, that the
silence which often follows a good story hung over the table
for an instant, to be broken by Nolan himself. For he
asked, perfectly unconsciously, —

 " Pray, what has become of Texas ? After the Mexicans
got their independence, I thought that province of Texas
would come forward very fast. It is really one of the finest
regions on earth ; it is the Italy of this continent. But I
have not seen or heard a word of Texas for near twenty
years."

There were two Texan officers at the table. The reason
he had never heard of Texas was that Texas and her affairs
had been painfully cut out of his newspapers since Austin
began his settlements ; so that, while he read of Honduras
and Tamaulipas, and till, quite lately, of California, — this
virgin province, in which his brother had travelled so far,
and, I believe, had died, had ceased to be to him. Waters
and Williams, the two Texas men, looked grimly at each
other, and tried not to laugh. Edward Morris had his
attention attracted by the third link in the chain of the captain's chandelier. Watrous was seized with a convulsion
of sneezing. Nolan himself saw that something was to pay,
he did not know what. And I, as master of the feast, had
to say, —

 "Texas is out of the map, Mr. Nolan. Have you seen
Captain Back's curious account of Sir Thomas Roe's Welcome ? "

After that cruise I never saw Nolan again. I wrote to
him at least twice a year, for in that voyage we became even
confidentially intimate ; but he never wrote to me. The
other men tell me that in those fifteen years he *aged* very
fast, as well he might indeed, but that he was still the same
gentle, uncomplaining, silent sufferer that he ever was, bearing as best he could his self-appointed punishment, —

rather less social, perhaps, with new men whom he did not know, but more anxious, apparently, than ever to serve and befriend and teach the boys, some of whom fairly seemed to worship him. And now it seems the dear old fellow is dead. He has found a home at last, and a country.

Since writing this, and while considering whether or no I would print it, as a warning to the young Nolans and Vallandighams and Tatnals of to-day of what it is to throw away a country, I have received from Danforth, who is on board the Levant, a letter which gives an account of Nolan's last hours. It removes all my doubts about telling this story.

To understand the first words of the letter, the non-professional reader should remember that after 1817, the position of every officer who had Nolan in charge was one of the greatest delicacy. The government had failed to renew the order of 1807 regarding him. What was a man to do? Should he let him go? What, then, if he were called to account by the Department for violating the order of 1807? Should he keep him? What, then, if Nolan should be liberated some day, and should bring an action for false imprisonment or kidnapping against every man who had had him in charge? I urged and pressed this upon Southard, and I have reason to think that other officers did the same thing. But the Secretary always said, as they so often do at Washington, that there were no special orders to give, and that we must act on our own judgment. That means, "If you succeed, you will be sustained; if you fail, you will be disavowed." Well, as Danforth says, all that is over now, though I do not know but I expose myself to a criminal prosecution on the evidence of the very revelation I am making.

Here is the letter : —

LEVANT, 2° 2′ S. @ 131° W.

"DEAR FRED, — I try to find heart and life to tell you that it is all over with dear old Nolan. I have been with him on this voyage more than I ever was, and I can understand wholly now the way in which you used to speak of the dear old fellow. I could see that he was not strong, but I had no idea the end was so near. The doctor has been watching him very carefully, and yesterday morning came to me and told me that Nolan was not so well, and had not left his state-room, — a thing I never remember before. He had let the doctor come and see him as he lay there, — the first time the doctor had been in the state-room, — and he said he should like to see me. O dear! do you remember the mysteries we boys used to invent about his room, in the old Intrepid days? Well, I went in, and there, to be sure, the poor fellow lay in his berth, smiling pleasantly as he gave me his hand, but looking very frail. I could not help a glance round, which showed me what a little shrine he had made of the box he was lying in. The stars and stripes were triced up above and around a picture of Washington, and he had painted a majestic eagle, with lightnings blazing from his beak and his foot just clasping the whole globe, which his wings overshadowed. The dear old boy saw my glance, and said, with a sad smile, ' Here, you see, I have a country!' And then he pointed to the foot of his bed, where I had not seen before a great map of the United States, as he had drawn it from memory, and which he had there to look upon as he lay. Quaint, queer old names were on it, in large letters : ' Indiana Territory,' ' Mississippi Territory,' and ' Louisiana Territory,' as I suppose our fathers learned such things : but the old fellow had patched in Texas, too ; he had carried his western boundary all the way to the Pacific, but on that shore he had defined nothing.

"' O Danforth,' he said, ' I know I am dying. I cannot get home. Surely you will tell me something now ? — Stop! stop ! Do not speak till I say what I am sure you know, that there is not in this ship, that there is not in America, — God bless her! — a more loyal man than I. There cannot be a man who loves the old flag as I do, or prays for it as I do, or hopes for it as I do. There are thirty-four stars in it now, Danforth. I thank God for that, though I do not know what their names are. There has never been one taken away : I thank God for that. I know by that, that there has never been any successful Burr. O Danforth, Danforth,' he sighed out, 'how like a wretched night's dream a boy's idea of personal fame or of separate sovereignty seems, when one looks back on it after such a life as mine? But tell me, — tell me something, — tell me everything, Danforth, before I die!'

" Ingham, I swear to you that I felt like a monster that I had not told him everything before. Danger or no danger, delicacy or no delicacy, who was I, that I should have been acting the tyrant all this time over this dear, sainted old man, who had years ago expiated, in his whole manhood's life, the madness of a boy's treason? 'Mr. Nolan,' said I, 'I will tell you everything you ask about. Only, where shall I begin?'

"O the blessed smile that crept over his white face! and he pressed my hand and said, 'God bless you!' 'Tell me their names,' he said, and he pointed to the stars on the flag. 'The last I know is Ohio. My father lived in Kentucky. But I have guessed Michigan and Indiana and Mississippi, — that was where Fort Adams is, — they make twenty. But where are your other fourteen? You have not cut up any of the old ones, I hope?'

"Well, that was not a bad text, and I told him the names in as good order as I could, and he bade me take down his beautiful map and draw them in as I best could with my pencil. He was wild with delight about Texas, told me how his brother died there : he had marked a gold cross where he supposed his brother's grave was ; and he had guessed at Texas. Then he was delighted as he saw California and Oregon; — that, he said, he had suspected partly, because he had never been permitted to land on that shore, though the ships were there so much. ' And the men,' said he, laughing, ' brought off a good deal besides furs.' Then he went back — heavens, how far ! — to ask about the Chesapeake, and what was done to Barron for surrendering her to the Leopard, and whether Burr ever tried again, — and he ground his teeth with the only passion he showed. But in a moment that was over, and he said, ' God forgive me, for I am sure I forgive him.' Then he asked about the old war, — told me the true story of his serving the gun the day we took the Java, — asked about dear old David Porter, as he called him. Then he settled down more quietly, and very happily, to hear me tell in an hour the history of fifty years.

"How I wished it had been somebody who knew something ! But I did as well as I could. I told him of the English war. I told him about Fulton and the steamboat beginning. I told him about old Scott, and Jackson ; told him all I could think about the Mississippi, and New Orleans, and Texas, and his own old Kentucky. And do you think he asked who was in command of the ' Legion of the West.' I told him it was a very gallant officer named Grant, and that, by our last news, he was about to establish his head-quarters at Vicksburg. Then, ' Where was Vicksburg ?' I worked that out on the map ; it was about a hundred miles, more or less, above his old Fort Adams ; and I thought Fort Adams must be a ruin now. ' It must be at old Vick's plantation,' said he ; ' well, that is a change ! '

"I tell you, Ingham, it was a hard thing to condense the history of half a century into that talk with a sick man. And I do not now know what I told him, — of emigration, and the means of it, — of steamboats, and railroads, and telegraphs, — of inventions, and books, and literature, — of the colleges, and West Point, and the Naval School, — but with the queerest interruptions that ever you heard. You see it was Robinson Crusoe asking all the accumulated questions of fifty-six years !

"I remember he asked, all of a sudden, who was President now; and when I told him, he asked if old Abe was General Benjamin Lincoln's son. He said he met old General Lincoln, when he was quite a boy himself, at some Indian treaty. I said no, that old Abe was a Kentuckian like himself, but I could not tell him of what family; he had worked up from the ranks. 'Good for him!' cried Nolan; 'I am glad of that. As I have brooded and wondered, I have thought our danger was in keeping up those regular successions in the first families.' Then I got talking about my visit to Washington. I told him of meeting the Oregon Congressman, Harding; I told him about the Smithsonian, and the Exploring Expedition; I told him about the Capitol, and the statues for the pediment, and Crawford's Liberty, and Greenough's Washington: Ingham, I told him everything I could think of that would show the grandeur of his country and its prosperity; but I could not make up my mouth to tell him a word about this infernal Rebellion!

"And he drank it in, and enjoyed it as I cannot tell you. He grew more and more silent, yet I never thought he was tired or faint. I gave him a glass of water, but he just wet his lips, and told me not to go away. Then he asked me to bring the Presbyterian 'Book of Public Prayer,' which lay there, and said, with a smile, that it would open at the right place, — and so it did. There was his double red mark down the page; and I knelt down and read, and he repeated with me, 'For ourselves and our country, O gracious God, we thank Thee, that, notwithstanding our manifold transgressions of Thy holy laws, Thou hast continued to us Thy marvellous kindness,' — and so to the end of that thanksgiving. Then he turned to the end of the same book, and I read the words more familiar to me, — 'Most heartily we beseech Thee with Thy favor to behold and bless Thy servant, the President of the United States, and all others in authority,' — and the rest of the Episcopal collect. 'Danforth,' said he, 'I have repeated those prayers night and morning, it is now fifty-five years.' And then he said he would go to sleep. He bent me down over him and kissed me ; and he said, 'Look in my Bible, Danforth, when I am gone.' And I went away.

"But I had no thought it was the end. I thought he was tired and would sleep. I knew he was happy and I wanted him to be alone.

"But in an hour, when the doctor went in gently, he found Nolan had breathed his life away with a smile. He had something pressed close to his lips. It was his father's badge of the Order of Cincinnati.

"We looked in his Bible, and there was a slip of paper, at the place where he had marked the text, —

"'They desire a country, even a heavenly : wherefore God is not ashamed to be called their God : for he hath prepared for them a city.'

"On this slip of paper he had written, —

"'Bury me in the sea; it has been my home, and I love it. But will not some one set up a stone for my memory at Fort Adams or at Orleans, that my disgrace may not be more than I ought to bear ? Say on it, —

"'*In Memory of*

"'PHILIP NOLAN,

"'*Lieutenant in the Army of the United States.*

"'He loved his country as no other man has loved her ; but no man deserved less at her hands.'"

NOTE BY THE AUTHOR.

THIS story was written in the summer of 1863, as a contribution, however humble, towards the formation of a just and true national sentiment, or sentiment of love to the nation. It was at the time when Mr. Vallandigham had been sent across the border. It was my wish, indeed, that the story might be printed before the autumn elections of that year, — as my "testimony" regarding the principles involved in them, — but circumstances delayed its publication till the December number of the Atlantic appeared.

It is wholly a fiction, "founded on fact." The facts on which it is founded are these, — that Aaron Burr sailed down the Mississippi River in 1805, again in 1806, and was tried for treason in 1807. The rest, with one exception to be noticed, is all fictitious.

It was my intention that the story should have been published with no author's name, other than that of Captain Frederic Ingham, U. S. N. Whether writing under his name or my own, I have taken no liberties with history other than such as every writer of fiction is privileged to take, — indeed, must take, if fiction is to be written at all.

The story having been once published, it passed out of my hands. From that moment it has gradually acquired different accessories, for which I am not responsible. Thus I have heard it said, that at one bureau of the Navy Department they say that Nolan was pardoned, in fact, and returned home to die. At another bureau, I am told, the answer to questions is, that, though it is true that an officer was kept abroad all his life, his name was not Nolan. A venerable friend of mine in Boston, who discredits all tradition, still recollects this "Nolan court-martial." One of the most accurate of my younger friends had noticed Nolan's death in the newspaper, but recollected "that it was in September, and not in August." A lady in Baltimore writes me, I believe in good faith, that Nolan has two widowed sisters residing in that neighborhood. A correspondent of the Philadelphia Despatch believed "the article untrue, as the United States corvette Levant was lost at sea nearly three years since, between San Francisco and San Juan." I may remark that this uncertainty as to the place of her loss rather adds to the probability of her turning up after three years in Lat. 2° 11′ S., Long. 131° W. A writer in the New Orleans Picayune, in a careful historical paper, explained at length that I had been mistaken all through ; that Philip Nolan never went to sea, but to Texas ; that there he was shot in battle, March 21, 1801, and by orders from Spain every fifth man of his party was to be shot, had they not died in prison. Fortunately, however, he left his papers and maps, which fell into the hands of a friend of the Picayune's correspondent. This friend proposes to publish them, — and the public will then have, it is to be hoped, the true history of Philip Nolan, the man without a country.

With all these continuations, however, I have nothing to do. I can only repeat that my Philip Nolan is pure fiction. I cannot send his scrap-book to my friend who asks for it, because I have it not to send.

I remembered when I was collecting material for my story, that in General Wilkinson's galimatias, which he calls his "Memoirs," is frequent reference to a Jorkins-like partner of his, of the name of Nolan, who, at some time near the beginning of this century, was killed in Texas. Whenever Wilkinson found himself in rather a deeper bog than usual, he used to justify himself by saying that he could not explain such or such a charge because "the papers referring to it were lost when *Mr. Nolan* was imprisoned in Texas." Finding this mythical character in the mythical legends of a mythical time, I took the liberty to give him a brother, rather more mythical, whose adventures should be on the seas. I had the impression that Wilkinson's friend was named Stephen, — and as such he is spoken of in this story at page 470. As this book goes to press, I find that the New Orleans paper is right in saying that the Texan hero was named Philip. I am very sorry that I changed him inadvertently to Stephen. It is too late for me to change him back again. I remember to have heard a distinguished divine preach on St. Philip's day, by accident, a discourse on the life of the Evangelist Stephen. If such a mistake can happen in the best regulated of pulpits, I must be pardoned for mistaking Philip for Stephen Nolan. The reader will observe that he was dead some years before the action of this story begins. In the same connection I must add that Mr. P. Nolan, teamster in Boston, whose horse and cart I venture to recommend to an indulgent public, is no relation of the hero of this tale.

If any reader considers the invention of a brother too great a liberty to take in fiction, I venture to remind him that "'T is sixty years since"; and that I should have the highest authority in literature even for much greater liberties taken with annals so far removed from our time.

A Boston paper, in noticing the story of "My Double," contained in another part of this collection, said it was highly *improbable.* I have always agreed with that critic. I confess I have the same opinion of the story of Philip Nolan. It passes on ships which had no existence, is vouched for by officers who never lived. Its hero is in two or three places at the same time, under a process wholly impossible under any conceivable administration of affairs. In reply, therefore, to a kind adviser in Connecticut, who told me that the story must be apologized for, because it was doing great injury to the national cause by asserting such continued cruelty of the Federal Government through a half-century, I must be permitted to say that the public, like the Supreme Court of the United States, may be supposed "to know something."

Cambridge : Stereotyped and Printed by Welch, Bigelow, & Co.

www.ingramcontent.com/pod-product-compliance
Lightning Source LLC
Chambersburg PA
CBHW052330110726
47901CB00005B/1187